A Courtesan's Scandal

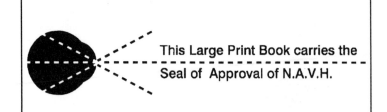

This Large Print Book carries the
Seal of Approval of N.A.V.H.

A COURTESAN'S SCANDAL

JULIA LONDON

THORNDIKE PRESS

A part of Gale, Cengage Learning

GALE
CENGAGE Learning™

Detroit • New York • San Francisco • New Haven, Conn • Waterville, Maine • London

GALE
CENGAGE Learning™

LIBRARY OF CONGRESS CATALOGING-IN-PUBLICATION DATA

London, Julia.
    A courtesan's scandal / by Julia London.
      p. cm. -- (The scandalous series ; no.3) (Thorndike Press large print core)
      ISBN-13: 978-1-4104-2401-3 (alk. paper)
      ISBN-10: 1-4104-2401-4 (alk. paper)
      1. Nobility--England--Fiction. 2. Man-woman relationships--Fiction. 3. Large type books. I. Title.
    PS3562.O78745C68 2010
    813'.54--dc22
                          2009045844

Published in 2010 in arrangement with Pocket Books, a division of Simon & Schuster, Inc.

Printed in the United States of America
1 2 3 4 5 6 7 14 13 12 11 10

*In memory of my beloved sister Karen,
the funniest woman I ever knew.
She is gone too suddenly and too soon
and I will miss her more than I ever
let her know.*

CHAPTER ONE

London, England
Christmas, 1806

On a snowy Christmas Eve, as the most elite ranks of the *haut ton* gathered at Darlington House in London's Mayfair district to usher in the twelve days of Christmas, an annoyed Duke of Darlington was across town, striding purposefully down King Street through a light dusting of snow, studying the light fans above town-house doors in search of the intertwined letters *G* and *K*.

He passed a group of revelers who called out *"Happy Christmas!"* That annoyed the duke, as they blocked the walkway and forced him to tip his hat and step around them before he continued his examination of every fan above every door in the line of tidy, respectable town homes.

He found the *G* and *K* on the last town house, a large red brick building. Quite nice, actually; the duke could not help but wonder what salacious little act the resident had performed to earn a house of this quality.

He stepped up to the door, lifted the brass knocker, rapped three times, and waited impatiently. He was in a very cross mood to be sure. He'd never been so exploited, so ill-used —

The door swung open and a gentleman of average height with a flat nose, a shock of ginger hair, and wearing a rumpled suit of clothing stood before him. He looked the duke directly in the eye and offered no greeting.

"The Duke of Darlington," the duke announced gruffly as he reached into his coat pocket and withdrew a calling card. "I have come to call on Miss Bergeron. She is expecting me."

The man held out a silver tray. Darlington tossed his card onto it. "I'll tell her," the man said, and moved to shut the door.

But Darlington had been vexed beyond all civility; he quickly threw up a hand and blocked the door. "I'll wait inside, if you please."

The man's impassive expression didn't change. He shoved the door shut, leaving Darlington standing on the stoop.

"Bloody outrageous," Darlington muttered, and glanced up the street. In spite of the snow, people had set out to various holiday gatherings. He himself was expected a half hour ago on the other side of Green Park to preside over the annual soiree held for one hundred and fifty of his family's closest friends.

The door abruptly opened, startling Darlington. The man said, "Come."

Darlington swept inside and removed his beaver hat, which he thrust at the man. "What is your name?" he demanded.

"Butler."

"I do not mean your occupation," he said shortly, "but your name."

"Butler," the man responded just as shortly. "This way," he added, and carelessly tossed the duke's hat onto a console. The hat slid off the edge of the table and landed on its crown on the floor, but Butler walked on, lifting a candelabrum high to light the way.

He led Darlington up a flight of stairs, then down a corridor that was lined with paintings and expensive china vases stuffed full of hothouse flowers. The floor covering, Darlington noted, was a fine Belgian carpet.

Miss Bergeron had done very well for herself.

Butler paused before a pair of red pocket doors and knocked. A muffled woman's voice bid him enter. He looked at Darlington. "Wait," he said before entering the room, and left the doors slightly ajar.

Darlington sighed impatiently and glanced at his pocket watch again.

"Here now, darling," he heard a feminine voice say. "Tell me, how do you like this?"

"Mmm," a male voice answered.

Darlington jerked his gaze to the pair of doors and stared in disbelief.

"And *this?*" she asked with a bit of a chuckle. "Do you like it?"

The response, from what the duke could gather, was a sigh of pleasure.

"Ah, but wait, for you've not lived until you've —"

"Caller," Butler said.

"Not *now,* Kate," the male voice objected. "Please! You leave me with such a hunger for more!"

"Digby! Keep your hands away!" There was a slight pause, and then the woman said, "Oh. It's *him.* Please show him in, Aldous."

Darlington started when Butler pulled the doors wide open. He quickly glanced down, his sense of propriety making him avert his gaze from whatever lewd act he was sure he was interrupting.

"Your Grace?"

Darlington looked up. Whatever he might have expected, it was not the sight that

10

greeted him. Yes, the room looked a bit like a French boudoir, with peach-colored walls, silken draperies, and overstuffed furnishings upholstered in floral chintz. There were gazettes, hats, and a cloak carelessly draped over a chair. But the woman inside was not lying on a daybed with a man on top of her as he'd suspected.

He was surprised to see her standing at a table piled high with pastries and sweetmeats. Moreover, there were Christmas boughs and hollies adorning the walls and the mantel, a dozen candles lit the room, and a fire was blazing in the hearth.

Her male companion, a portly fellow with thinning hair who easily weighed thirteen or fourteen stone, held nothing more lurid than a teacup. The sugary remnants of a pastry dusted his upper lip.

Darlington was stunned, first and foremost because he had supposed something entirely different was occurring in this room. But perhaps even more so because the woman, Miss Katharine Bergeron, was breathtaking.

Darlington had known this woman was unusually beautiful. He'd heard it from more than one quarter and he'd seen it with his own eyes not two nights past at the King's Opera House, when he'd attended the first London performance of Mozart's *La Clem-*

enza di Tito at the behest of his friend George, the Prince of Wales. He'd sat with George in the royal box, and it was George who had pointed out Katharine Bergeron. Seated two boxes away, she was in the company of Mr. Cousineau, a Frenchman who had made a respectable fortune selling luxurious fabrics to wealthy London society. Miss Bergeron was infamously his model and his mistress.

As Darlington observed her that evening, she'd leaned slightly forward in her seat, enraptured by the music. She'd worn a white silk gown trimmed in pink velvet that seemed to shimmer in the low light of the opera house. Pearls had dripped from her ears, her wrists, and more notably, her throat. Her hair, pale blond, was bound up with yet another string of pearls. She did not wear a plume, as so many ladies seemed to prefer, but instead allowed wisps of curls to drape the nape of her long, slender neck.

She'd turned her head slightly and discovered him observing her. She did not glance away shyly, but calmly returned his gaze a long moment before turning her attention to the stage once more.

Darlington had found her boldness mildly interesting. Nevertheless, he had not anticipated seeing her again . . . until George had summoned him. Now, he was standing in her private salon.

But she looked nothing like she had the night at the opera. She was beautiful, astonishingly so, but now, free of cosmetic, her beauty was simpler and natural. She wore a rather plain blue gown, an apron, and a shawl wrapped demurely around her shoulders. Her hair was not dressed, but hung long and full down her back.

"Your Grace," she said again, smiling warmly. She picked up a plate of muffins. "May I entice you with a Christmas treat? I just made them," she added proudly.

"They are divine, Your Grace," the portly man said, coming to his feet and bowing his head.

"No," Darlington said incredulously. Did they think he'd come for tea? "A word, madam?"

"Of course," she said, and handed the plate of muffins to her companion. "Please do go with Aldous, Digby, and mind you don't eat them all."

"I shall endeavor to be good," he said jovially, "but you know how wretched I can be." He patted his large belly, gave the duke another curt bow, and followed Butler out.

When they had left the room, Darlington frowned. "I regret that we've not had the courtesy of a proper introduction, but it would seem the situation does not lend itself to that."

"Yes," she said, eyeing the rest of the food on the table, "I had not expected you so soon."

"Your patron was rather insistent."

She gave him a wry look and gestured to a chair near the table. "Please do be seated. Are you certain I cannot tempt you to taste a muffin? I confess, I am learning the art of baking and I am not certain of the quality."

"No. You cannot."

"Please," she said again, gesturing to the chair. "I hope you will be at ease here."

"Miss Bergeron, I do not find the circumstances the least bit easy."

"Oh, I *see,*" she said, lifting a fine brow.

He rather doubted she did. She was a courtesan, hardly accustomed to the pressures of propriety that he faced every day. "I have come as the prince has demanded to make your acquaintance and to mutually agree on a public appearance or two that will serve his . . . purpose," he said with distaste.

"Very well." She smiled then, and Darlington knew in that moment how she had captivated the prince.

But if she thought that he could be so easily seduced, she was very much mistaken. And pray tell, what was that just above the dimple on her cheek? A bit of flour? "There is the Carlton House Twelfth Night Ball," he said, a bit distracted by the flour.

"That would do. Shall I meet you there?"

"I will come for you."

Her smile seemed to grow even more enticing.

"There is an opera scheduled shortly thereafter. Will that suit?"

"I adore opera," she said smoothly.

"Very well," Darlington said. "That should suffice for the time being. Furthermore, may I remind you that in the course of this *ruse,*" he said with an angry flick of his wrist, "I expect you to defer to me as one would defer to a peer. We are merely to be seen in public together and rely on the usual wagging tongues to do the rest. Therefore, I see no reason to touch or otherwise engage in any behavior that might be remarked upon by my esteemed family or close acquaintances. When these public events have concluded, I will ensure that you are escorted safely home, but I see no point in prolonging our contact any more than is required. Are we agreed?"

She smiled curiously. "Are you always so officis?"

"Officis? *Officious?*"

"Yes! Officious," she said, apparently

pleased with the word.

Officious! If only she knew what sacrifice he was making at the prince's behest. "Do not mistake me, Miss Bergeron. I have been coerced into this . . . charade," he bit out. "I take no pleasure in it. I would not give you the slightest cause for false hope of any sort. Now then — if we are agreed, I shall take my leave," he said again, and turned toward the door.

"If by false hope you mean that you will not taste my muffin and pronounce it delicious, you must not fret, Your Grace," she said, drawing his attention back to her. "I had no hope of it, I was merely being civil." She picked up a delicacy and walked toward him, her gaze unabashedly taking him in. "There is just one small matter," she said, pausing to bite into the delicacy. Her brows rose, and she smiled. "*Mmm.* Very good, if I do say so myself," she said, tilting her head back to look up at him, her pale green eyes softened by the length of her dark lashes.

Darlington had an insane urge to wipe the flour from her cheek. She was delicate, her height slightly below average. She had a softly regal bearing, an elegance that set her apart from most women. And her hair . . . her hair looked like spun silk.

"I should not like to give you cause for

false hope, either. Therefore, I must make it perfectly clear that this arrangement is not *my* preference any more than, apparently, it is yours. I am not yours to use — you may not touch me or otherwise take liberty with my person."

Darlington cocked one dark brow above the other and focused on her mouth, her lush lips. He knew what pleasure a man would find in kissing that mouth. "You may rest assured, Miss Bergeron, that is neither my desire nor my intent. I find the suggestion quite distasteful."

Something flickered in her eyes, and she smiled. "*Really?* No man has ever said that to me." She popped the last little bit of the delicacy into her mouth.

Did this chit not know who he was? What power he wielded in the House of Lords? In *London?* He shifted slightly so that he was towering over her. She did not seem the least bit cowed.

"*I* am saying it, Miss Bergeron. I am not the prince. I am not bowled over by your beauty or your apparent bedroom charms."

"Splendid! We should get on quite nicely, then, for I am not a debutante yearning for your attention or a match."

For once, Darlington was speechless. "Is there anything else?" he asked curtly as she calmly . . . and provocatively . . . used the tip of her finger to wipe the corner of her mouth.

"Yes. You may call me Kate," she said. "What may I call you?"

"Your Grace," he snapped, and strode out of the room.

CHAPTER TWO

Invitations to the annual Darlington celebration marking the start of the twelve days of Christmas were highly coveted. The event was eagerly anticipated for weeks. One could always depend on something terribly scandalous happening when the wassail and whiskey began to flow. One year, the Prince of Wales was caught in compromising circumstances with Lady Hertford, which caused her husband to whisk her away to Ireland shortly thereafter to keep her from the prince's ardent clutches.

Darlington House was a Charles Street mansion on extensive grounds in the heart of London. It was festooned for the occasion: Wassail flowed in abundance from three separate fountains built precisely for the party. Lush boughs of holly draped the family portraits and window sashes, and mistletoe hung over every doorway. Yule logs blazed in two dozen hearths, and those logs that had been presented to the Duke of Darlington as a customary gift were stacked on the marble floor of the grand entry for easy access when it was time to replenish the hearths.

The wassail, which had been liberally spiced with Scotch whiskey, made the festive mood that much happier, and more than one young lady dressed in expensive velvet and satin was so thoroughly scandalized under the mistletoe that her plumage was all askew. The gentlemen, who had donned their finest white waistcoats and black tails, were eager to scandalize. Most of them were bachelors, and the event was regarded as the best preview of the upcoming crop of debutantes.

But the most eligible of all bachelors, Grayson Christopher, the young and handsome Duke of Darlington, was not beneath the mistletoe. He was famously close-guarded, as protective of his reputation and conduct as any man in London. Furthermore, he was not near any mistletoe, but striding purposefully down a servant's corridor one floor above the festivities.

When Darlington, still clad in his greatcoat, reached the end of the corridor, he turned sharply right and heard something that sounded like a small gasp. He paused, held his candle up high, and saw Lady Eustis standing in the dim light, propped up against the stone wall.

Ah, Lady Eustis . . . a handsome woman by any man's measure. Tonight she was wearing a deep green velvet gown against which her inky black hair shone. She seemed startled by his sudden appearance and quickly pushed away from the wall, clasping her hands nervously at her waist.

"What are you doing here?" Grayson demanded softly.

"I . . . I needed a moment away from the gathering," she said, and put a hand to her nape. The small gesture caused her to sway a bit. "It's close in the ballroom and the gentlemen have drunk too much."

"I beg your pardon?" Grayson asked, walking closer, peering at her. "Has someone offended you? Tell me, and I shall see that he is removed from the premises at once."

She dropped her hand and slowly leaned back against the wall. "Yes, Your Grace, someone has offended me."

He took another step forward and held up the candle. She smiled a little lopsidedly at him. "You do not look yourself, Lady Eustis," he said as his gaze boldly wandered the length of her.

"Indeed? Perhaps that is because I have drunk a bit too much of your wassail."

"Ah." A wolfish smile curved his lips. He

21

shifted closer. "Tell me, which scoundrel has offended you?"

She put her hand up, pushing against his chest. "*You,* Your Grace. My husband has warned me about men like you."

"Has he, indeed?" Grayson murmured as his gaze lingered on her lovely décolletage. "And what, precisely, has Lord Eustis told you?"

"That certain gentlemen will attempt to take advantage of my innocence."

"He is a smart man, your husband," Grayson said, and brazenly tucked a wisp of a curl behind her ear. Lady Eustis turned her head slightly, away from his hand. "Did Lord Eustis advise what you were to do when such a wretched thing is attempted?" Grayson's finger grazed her ear and lingered beneath her earring, toying with it.

"That I should absent myself from the scoundrel's company at once and notify my husband straightaway."

"I have heard that your husband is in Shropshire."

"He is, indeed, Your Grace."

"Then it shall be quite difficult for you to notify him straightaway, particularly if the scoundrel is loath to allow you to escape."

She glanced at him from the corner of her eye, a soft smile on her lips. "Are you loath to allow me to escape?"

"Always," he murmured, and kissed her neck as he grabbed her up with one arm around her waist. Lady Eustis quickly put her hands between them, but Grayson ignored her and held her tight as he put the candle aside on a small console. "I wonder what Lord Eustis would advise if the scoundrel does not ask, but *insists,*" he said, nipping at her lips, "that you lift your skirts so that he might ravish you properly?"

"He would certainly disapprove," she said, bending her neck to give him access to it.

Grayson reached blindly for the door nearby, opening it. "Smart man," he said again and pulled her into the room, pausing only briefly to grab up the candle. Once inside the room, Grayson kicked the door shut, put the candle down, and put his hands on Lady Eustis's breasts as he pushed her up against the wall.

"What took you so long?" she asked breathlessly.

"The prince," he muttered. He didn't want to think of the prince now. He'd have to tell her in a moment what had transpired, but just this moment, he wanted . . . he *needed* —

"The prince! What would he want?" she asked breathlessly as Grayson groped at her skirts.

If there was one thing Diana could not resist, it was gossip. Grayson stilled. In the dim light of that single candle, he looked at the rosy skin of Diana's cheeks, the smooth column of her neck, the rise of her bosom. How did he tell her what he must? "You are lovely, Diana," he said huskily, and pulled her tightly to him at the same time he put his lips to hers.

She did not resist him; her hands slid up his chest, her arms went around his neck, and she pulled his head down to her. She wore the scent of roses, and it filled him with a familiar lust. His hand tightened at her waist; he kissed her madly, his tongue in her mouth, his teeth on her lips, his hand drifting to the swell of her bottom, grasping it and holding her against him. His cock grew hard, and he pressed it against her, growling softly when she slid her body against it.

But when he moved to her neck, she grasped his head between her hands and asked again, "What did the prince want?"

"Later, darling —"

"Later! Later I shall be forced to pretend I've scarcely made your acquaintance," she said as he grabbed a fistful of her gown, pulling it up, pushing it up past her waist.

"Do you think of the prince now?" he

asked as his hand slipped between her legs, stroking her.

Diana sucked in a breath and closed her eyes for a moment. "No . . . *Grayson!*" She gasped as he slid two fingers inside her and moved seductively.

The prince momentarily forgotten, Grayson watched Diana's lips part and the tip of her tongue slide across her bottom lip as he moved his fingers inside her. Her hands slid down his chest, to his erection.

Grayson fumbled with his trousers, freeing himself, then hiking up the velvet of her gown.

"Make haste," Diana whispered, and wrapped her leg around his waist. Grayson obliged her, guiding himself into her body with a sigh of longing. He held her up with an arm around her waist, a hand under her leg. Diana bit his ear lobe as Grayson began to move in her, holding her up against the wall. The more Diana moaned with pleasure, the faster he moved. When she clutched his shoulders and began to move against him, meeting his thrusts, he knew she was close to finding fulfillment, and allowed himself a few moments of pure ecstasy after Diana's body shuddered and her head fell to his shoulder.

He withdrew at the moment of climax.

The two of them clung to each other,

panting for breath until she pushed lightly against him. Grayson fished a handkerchief from his pocket and handed it to her. Diana cleaned herself and shook out her skirts. "Oh dear," she said, looking down. The skirt was crumpled. She worked her hand over it, smoothing it out as Grayson rearranged his clothing.

"I can't stay long, darling, for I will be missed," she said, returning the handkerchief to him. "Do tell me why the prince summoned you," she added, pausing to adjust his waistcoat.

"It was not the best of news," Grayson admitted.

"What do you mean?"

Grayson ran his fingers through his hair, apparently mussing it, because Diana reached out to smooth it down.

"What has happened?" she asked.

Her lovely face was softened by candlelight. Grayson did love her, he believed, and he would never do anything to hurt her. Unfortunately, George, the Prince of Wales, was embroiled in a very public scandal with his estranged wife, Princess Caroline. His desire to divorce her consumed him. He'd made his allegations of treason and adultery against Caroline, and the allegations had been thoroughly investigated by a commission of lords. In the course of the so-called Delicate Investigation, they did indeed find the princess's behavior to be egregious, but they did not find it to be treasonable.

In retaliation, Princess Caroline fought to keep the king's favor by threatening to make public all the prince's transgressions — and there were many. In fact, it was George's proclivity for adultery that had prompted him to send for Grayson. He'd been smitten by the courtesan Katharine Bergeron, and had recently arranged to make her his mistress. Rumor had it that George had essentially bought her from Mr. Cousineau by threatening to shut down the Frenchman's business in London if he did not reach some accord with the prince. Mr. Cousineau, being a tradesman first and foremost, had agreed to the prince's terms and had given her up.

George had set up Miss Bergeron in the house on King Street, but, given his very public troubles, he did not want Miss Bergeron exposed or otherwise pulled into the scandal. Nor did he want her to be used against him in a public trial should the king see his way to granting permission for George to seek a parliamentary divorce.

Therefore, George had made Grayson a proposition: that Grayson publicly put it out into society that Katharine Bergeron was his mistress, and make it seem real. That would give Katharine sufficient protection from gossip linking her to the prince, as well as keep other men of the *ton* from seeking her favors, while George dealt with the scandal.

"Christie, what is it?" Diana asked lightly, using the sobriquet that only Grayson's closest friends used.

"The divorce scandal is coming to a head," he said.

Like everyone in London, Diana was well aware of the details. "I should hope it does," she said primly. "It has cast a pall over society for far too long."

"In the meantime, the prince has taken a new mistress — or will, as soon as he is able."

Diana rolled her eyes.

"She is a courtesan, Diana. And George fears that if he openly takes her as a mistress now, it might damage his case against the princess. Therefore, he has determined he shall keep her hidden until he is able to bring her into society."

"*Well,*" she said, smoothing her gown once more. She did not like to talk of adultery, particularly as she'd been engaged in the torrid, adulterous affair with Grayson for a year now. But Diana reasoned that her

28

behavior was justified because her husband was older and interested only in producing an heir. What was a poor countess to do?

Grayson had never imagined he would be an adulterer. He'd always been conscious of his place in society, of his reputation . . . not to mention he'd long found the idea of cuckolding another man repugnant. But Diana had pursued him, and he was a man, and somehow, he had reasoned himself into giving in to his physical desires. Now, after a year of stolen hours, he'd developed a plethora of excuses to assist him in justifying his behavior, but mostly, Grayson didn't allow himself to think of it.

But tonight, he couldn't avoid thinking of it. "Diana," he said solemnly, "George has asked me to publicly present the courtesan as *my* mistress, and in a manner so convincing that no aspersions may be cast on Miss Bergeron, or the prince."

"What? Pardon?" Diana sputtered.

"He has made this request in a most . . . unyielding manner."

"And you refused!" she said adamantly.

"I did not," he said quietly.

Diana gasped. Grayson caught her hands. "Diana, hear me. I did not refuse because he threatened to expose *our* affair if I did not agree to it."

Diana's jaw went slack. "He *knows?*" she whispered.

"Quite obviously, he does."

"But how?"

"I do not know, darling, but he has men who are very loyal to him. And people are lured by gossip."

"Oh dear God," she whispered, her eyes going wide with fright.

Oh dear God, indeed. Grayson didn't want any part of the prince's deceptions. After all, Grayson was the head of a powerful family. He had his rank, his position to think of. He had younger siblings and cousins, and aunts and uncles who depended upon him and his good name for their livelihood. And he had his reputation, of which he was proud. He'd said all of that and more to George, but George was often driven by his desires, and he made it quite clear to Grayson that if he did not carry out this subterfuge, he would damage Grayson's reputation by exposing his scandalous affair with Lady Eustis.

"It's really not so bad," George had said cavalierly. "Katharine Bergeron is a very comely woman. You will enjoy her company and certainly no man who lays eyes on her will fault you in the least."

There were plenty of good men who would find fault, Grayson thought, but at least it would be Grayson's name being bandied about, and not Diana's.

"You cannot do it. Tell me you won't," Diana said plaintively.

"I don't see that I have a choice. I won't allow any harm to come to you."

"But I cannot bear to see you with another woman!"

"I will not be *with* her —"

"I have *seen* her, Grayson. She is quite beautiful. She is an Eve and will entice you to fall in love with her."

Grayson chuckled and extended his hand to her. "I will not fall in love with a merchant's whore, you may trust me," he said. "I am the Duke of Darlington — I would never be brought so low. Come, then, my love — you must go down and rejoin the party."

But Diana looked at him with imploring blue eyes. "I am begging you, Grayson. Please don't do it."

This conversation was growing tiresome. "I've told you, madam, that I have no choice in the matter. Don't fret overmuch. It will be over and done in a month's time." He opened the door. One quick look in the darkened corridor, and he sent her out, ignoring the way she looked at him as she passed.

He gave her a few minutes to rejoin the celebration downstairs before making his appearance. When he believed enough time had passed that no one would notice, he picked up his candle and went out, taking a different path to the party below, his mind on his duties as host, the merchant's whore already forgotten.

CHAPTER THREE

The Christmas Eve snow was no more than a dusting, so the streets of London were navigable the next morning. That was welcome news at Charles Street, where the last of the revelers at Darlington House stumbled out into the gray day with the help of their liveried footmen, and were foisted into coaches with emblazoned crests and withered plumes.

Across town at King Street, Reginald Digby called for Kate promptly at ten o'clock in his very plain carriage driven by a hired driver, for Digby was too large to maneuver himself into the driver's seat. Kate Bergeron, in the company of Aldous Butler — which was not his true surname, but one he now embraced — emerged from the fine little town house in a very plain cloak and gown, her hair covered by the cloak's hood.

Digby was the first friend Kate had ever had whom she could trust entirely and depend on. She'd known him longer than anyone in her acquaintance, and she could say without equivocation that he was the one man in her life who'd never expected anything from her other than friendship. Digby had introduced himself to her about eight years ago, when she was working in the cloth halls, winding cloth around bolts. He was Benoit Cousineau's man, and Kate had an instant feeling that Digby was a good soul. She'd not been wrong — their friendship had only deepened through the years.

Digby still worked for Benoit, but as a London agent, for Benoit had returned to France. Digby was always looking for new trade opportunities. He wanted to be a rich merchant one day, a true gentleman of quality, and was slowly but surely working his way toward that dream.

Which was why he disapproved of today's destination. At every opportunity, he voiced his dislike of St. Katharine's, a mean, poverty-ridden quarter along the Thames named for a medieval hospital and church. But he was far too fond of Kate to allow her to travel there on her own.

The door swung open and Digby leaned forward to peer out. "Happy Christmas, one and all!"

"Happy Christmas, Digby!" Kate returned.

Aldous carried the basket of pastries, but he was not wearing a greatcoat. Wordlessly, he put the pastry basket on the seat next to Digby.

"What? You're not coming, Aldous?"

"No," he said, and held out his hand to help Kate into the carriage.

"He's being very mysterious," Kate said to Digby, pausing to give him a peck on the cheek before settling onto her bench. "Claims to have an engagement today."

"Family, do you think?" Digby asked.

"I can't imagine it! He must be five and thirty if he's a day, and one would think a family would have presented itself ere now, wouldn't one?" Kate asked, smiling. Aldous, a man of very little humor, frowned at her as he shut the carriage door. Kate laughed. "He won't tell me a bloody thing!" she exclaimed. "But I think it must be a bird."

"A Bird of Paradise, you mean." Digby snorted.

"*Digby,*" Kate said. "Poor Aldous is entitled to a bit of happiness. He's had a wretched life."

"Haven't we all?" Digby mused, and glanced at the basket. "Speaking of which, it would be my fondest dream if you would

35

leave *your* wretched life quite behind. There's naught for you in St. Katharine's, and in going there you only put yourself in danger."

"Danger!" Kate scoffed.

"Kate," Digby said patiently. "You are an extraordinarily beautiful woman. Any number of ne'er-do-wells might do you harm."

"No one will do me harm, Digby. I am not one of the ladies from the Benefit Society —"

"Beneficent —"

"Bene*fi*cent Society. I was born and reared there — for heaven's sake, I was named for St. Katharine's church!" That was a bit of family lore that Kate had never told anyone but Digby. Kate's father, who had never warmed to an honest day's work, was without employment when her mother carried Kate. He was fortunate enough — or hounded into — finding employment at the St. Katharine quay just before Kate was born, and her mother had named her Katharine in gratitude.

Mamma might have lacked imagination, but she'd meant well. She'd named Kate's brother Jude, for a Catholic priest who had given her alms when Father had lost yet another position.

"That may very well be, but you are not

36

of them, Katharine. Not any longer," Digby said sternly. "Your kindness toward those who have sought to use you ill since you were a girl is nothing short of insanity."

Kate smiled at Digby. He believed every single person in and around the St. Katharine quays had tried to exploit her when she'd been cast out of her home at the tender age of fourteen. Or was it thirteen? Kate could no longer remember precisely. "Digby — I met *you* down at the docks."

He sniffed at that, and cast his gaze out the window.

The area of St. Katharine's might be a bit unsavory, but it was nonetheless home for Kate. Growing up, she and Jude had lived among people who worked quayside or in the cramped warehouses. They'd never had enough to eat, but in Kate's memory, her mother had been charmingly unruffled by it. She could make a single potato feed four.

Unfortunately, Kate's mother contracted consumption when Kate was ten or so — she was gone by the time Kate was twelve. Nevertheless, Kate remembered her with much love. She'd had blonde hair like Kate, and vivid green eyes. She would lie on a pallet before the hearth with Kate and Jude and they would dream of a better world. "We won't always be like this," her mother would promise them. "Not when the faeries come, we won't."

"Tell us about the faeries, Mummy," Kate had asked, never tiring of hearing about them.

"One night, they will come for us, and they will wrap us in their wings and whisk us off to a cottage in the forest."

"What's a forest?" Jude had asked.

"Oh, you've never seen anything quite so beautiful," her mother said. "There are trees and birds — not the sort of dirty birds you see on the quays, but pretty birds, blue and green and red. And there are flowers that grow wild there, and tiny little rivers and sunshine, always sunshine . . ."

The dream of being whisked away had ended when Kate's mother died. Kate's troubles started when her father remarried. His new wife, Nellie Hopkins, had two children of her own and didn't care for the responsibility of feeding two children she hadn't birthed.

"I'd not mind the place so much if your efforts were properly appreciated," Digby said, drawing Kate's attention once more as he eyed the basket she carried.

"They are appreciated," Kate said. "Would you like a muffin?"

"No," he said, folding his hands over his

large belly. "I have in mind a pie and mash from Mrs. Anderson's shop."

Kate couldn't help but laugh — for all of Digby's indignation on her behalf, he'd found something he liked in the shops and market stalls along Butcher's Row and Mary Street.

When they arrived at St. Katharine's, Kate was not the least surprised to see that the daily activity had not slowed because of a little dusting of snow or a religious holiday. The street was teeming; the denizens of the docklands did not consider Christmas a holiday. When survival was a day-to-day proposition, luxuries such as Christmas feasts and merrymaking were frivolous extravagances.

Kate and Digby departed the carriage on Butcher's Row, a long, narrow strip of cobbled lane crowded by low buildings and shop fronts. With the basket in one hand, and a firm grip of Kate's elbow in the other, Digby propelled her into a diverse throng.

If there was one thing Kate had appreciated growing up quayside, it was the different people here. There was always something new to see — people with skin as black as coal wearing brightly striped pants and black coats; Indians with turbans on their heads; Spanish sailors, whose tankards of ale sloshed over their worn peacoats. There were ladybirds sitting in their windows wrapped in wool, calling down to the men who carried cargo on their shoulders and sailors who had fallen into their cups. There were travelers newly arrived to London, wandering down the street with their portmanteaus, looking around in awe. There were shopkeepers and match girls and lads who'd been trained to pick pockets darting through the crowds.

In the storefronts, meats hung from underside of the eaves. One could only guess how fresh it might be. At least today there was no sound of braying cattle in the alleys behind the storefronts, where the butchers did their work — Kate supposed the poor beasts had been given a Christmas reprieve. As it was winter and quite cold, the smell of rotting meat and cattle dung did not permeate the air quite as heavily as it did in summer. The most notable smells this morning were those of smoke and fish.

"Eh, love, come 'ere, then," a man called out to her.

"Have a care, sir!" Digby rumbled, moving protectively in front of Kate. "Jug-bitten free-traders, the lot of them," he muttered irritably.

Kate adjusted the hood she wore over her head, pulling it lower. She'd always drawn attention, and not always the sort she wanted — one of her earliest memories was of a leering shoemaker fondling her feet under the pretense of measuring them.

Kate understood she was considered a beauty by most — after all, it was her looks that had lifted her out of this wretched place. Yet while Kate could see that she was comely enough, she did not think herself more comely than many other women. When she looked in the mirror, she saw a nose that was not quite straight and green eyes set too far apart. Her hair was an unusually pale blonde, but she did not understand why that should appeal so greatly to men . . . with the glaring exception of the Duke of Darlington, obviously, who had looked at her with such judgmental disdain that she had scarcely managed to keep a civil tongue.

Darlington reminded Kate of the difference between men of the *ton* and the men of St. Katharine's. Lords and gentlemen who fancied themselves a cut above the rest because of their education and breeding were so very quick to judge her, yet many of them still desired to use her. The men on Butcher Street made no judgments about the choices Kate had made in her life — they just wanted to use her.

Digby guided her onto Mary Street, where

cloth and wool houses rose up on either side of the street, blocking the day's light. Kate and Digby hurried past the warehouse where Kate had found work after Nellie Hopkins had determined that there wasn't enough money to feed all four children, and that either Kate or Jude must go. Jude was only ten or eleven years old — so Kate had gone, and her father had not stopped her. Then again, he'd been too foxed to stop her; he'd spent most days drunk as a wheelbarrow.

"One cannot breathe even a bit of air that is not foul," Digby groused. "I will never understand how you lived in these streets. Thank the good Lord you've escaped them."

Perhaps she'd escaped, but Kate never felt very far removed from these streets. Her situation was precarious — one false move, one slight to the wrong man, and she could lose her position and end up on these streets again. She was preparing herself the best she knew how in the event that should happen. She'd put away as much of her pin money as she could through the years, and was teaching herself how to bake under the tutelage of her daily cook, Cecelia. If the prince tired of her, or the next man after that, or the one after that, Kate planned to establish a bakery. Perhaps not in this particular part of London, but someplace where she might live quite at ease and without worry and certainly without . . . without being *kept*. She had to watch her figure now, but when she had her bakery, she would eat as many treats as she liked. She would be fat and happy and blissfully unencumbered of men. Kate despised being kept . . . but it was a far sight better than the alternative.

They reached a passage between the streets that was not worthy of a name; there Digby paused and looked sternly at Kate. "One half hour, madam. You are not to quit the building until I have come to fetch you. Am I perfectly clear?"

"Perfectly," she said cheerily. She took the basket from Digby, gave him a little wave of her gloved fingers, and set off down the passageway to a door with peeling paint. She knocked; a moment later, the door swung open and a woman dressed in a chemise and a corset, her red hair down around her shoulders, stood behind it.

"Miss Bergeron!" the woman cried, and threw her arms around Kate at the same moment she drew her inside a pair of rooms.

"Happy Christmas, Holly!" Kate said.

Four of the five women who resided in this dreadful pair of rooms were lounging on dingy mattresses. Kate rented the rooms for them. They worked in the warehouses, earning a paltry wage for backbreaking work. These rooms kept them from living on the streets, or worse. Kate had a fantasy that one day, when she had unlimited funds, she would find a lovely house for them all. They deserved lovely houses — none of them had ever lived in much better than this.

The pair of rooms had once been a windowless office or storerooms of some sort. They were perhaps ten feet by ten feet each. In addition to the mattresses, the women had a pair of buckets, one for washing and one for waste, and a small brazier for cooking and heat. On one wall, they had attached several hooks, on which they hung their work dresses. Digby had supplied the work dresses — he maintained his contacts in the cloth warehouses and had bought the fabrics for pennies on the pound.

The rooms were quite warm in spite of the cold. "Look here," Holly Bivens said, pointing to the brazier. "The factory give us coal for Christmas."

"Lovely!" Kate exclaimed. She removed her cloak and draped it across the back of one of two chairs. Her gown was a plain, dull blue, her hair wrapped tightly at her nape. She wore no cosmetics.

"Wha' ye got there?" Lucy Raney asked,

propping herself up on her elbow as she eyed Kate's basket.

"Glad Christmas tidings," Kate said, and opened the top of the basket, tipping it down a bit so they could see the muffins and sweetmeats she had packed inside. The women all cried out with delight, and Kate handed the basket to Holly, who began to pass the sweetmeats around.

"Very kind of ye to come with it," Esmeralda proclaimed. She was perhaps the oldest of the five women. "I'll never understand what makes a fancy lady like ye come round here and treat the likes of us so kindly."

"I'm not a fancy lady," Kate said.

"Ye are indeed!" Lucy said. "Ye talk like the queen, ye do."

Kate spoke like the queen only because Digby had taught her to speak and read the Queen's English eight years ago, when he'd taken her under his wing. He'd been instructed to do so by Benoit Cousineau, a wealthy French cloth merchant. Benoit had happened to see Kate working in the warehouse, and as Digby related it, the Frenchman had instantly fallen in love with her. He wanted Kate, but he would not lower himself to bed a warehouse girl. Therefore, he had charged Digby with the task of making her presentable to a man such as himself.

Kate had wanted only a fair wage for her labor — not Benoit's attention. She hadn't wanted any man's attention. She hadn't liked men, not since another gentleman — a ship's captain, to be precise — had likewise wanted Kate as his own. When she'd refused, he had taken his pleasure from her by force, and left her bleeding and bruised in an alley.

Kate wasn't sure how old she'd been, but she didn't think she'd been more than sixteen.

A year or so later, when Digby approached her on behalf of Benoit, Kate flatly refused him. But, as Digby kindly explained to her, if she did not do as Benoit asked, Benoit would have the warehouse foreman remove her from his sight. "Frenchmen are unusually proud, love," he'd said to her. "He'll not bring his cloth to this warehouse and risk seeing the lowly guttersnipe who refused him."

Young and already weary of such matters, Kate understood that Mr. Digby was telling her she would lose her employment — a position she had fought hard to obtain — if she did not become Benoit's mistress.

Still, Kate resisted.

Fannie Breen had convinced her to do it.

Kate let a room from Fannie, a palm reader who lived in a four-room house. She hired out girls to sailors, and might have done the same with Kate, but she had pitied her because of her experience with the sea captain. She allowed Kate to let a room that was no bigger than a closet, but told Kate on several occasions, "You could make me a rich woman, lass, you could indeed."

Nevertheless, Fannie had a soft spot in her heart, and Kate often confided in her. Fannie liked to read Kate's palms, too. "You'll be rich one day," she'd said. "A handsome stranger will fall in love with you." Whether or not palms truly could be read, Kate didn't know, but she liked the things Fannie told her. They fit her mother's dreams of faeries spiriting her away to a warm cottage with a full larder and a milk cow and two pigs. Kate used to delight in imagining a handsome gentleman *and* two pigs!

But Fannie's vision of her future crumbled at once when Kate told her of Benoit's demand.

Fannie had snorted at Kate's hesitance. "Are ye daft, then? If ye remain here, ye'll die in the streets at the hand of a man or bearing his brat. And such a pretty thing ye are! If I were a ruthless woman, I'd have ye working for me, aye? Go on then, go to the Frenchman and take whatever he might give ye! Ye've no choice, stupid girl! If not the Frenchman, it will be another gent — at least let him be rich!"

So on a cold winter morning, Kate left with Digby to prepare for her role as mistress. Benoit Cousineau was three and forty. She was seventeen or eighteen.

A few months ago, Kate had tried to find Fannie Breen, but the woman had disappeared into the streets of St. Katharine's.

Just as these women would disappear if Kate didn't help them.

"Me mum is coming round today," said Adele North, the youngest of the five women. "She's to bring what's left of the Christmas goose from the lord's kitchens."

"What's left!" Holly complained. "What's that then, the bones?"

"Oh no, indeed," Adele said proudly. "The fancy ladies, they eat like sparrows."

Holly and Lucy laughed at that.

"Where's Meg?" Kate asked, looking around.

Esmeralda snorted. "As foxed as a fish in brine when I last seen her, hanging onto a rake."

Kate worried about Meg. She was pretty and young and liked her ale a wee bit too much. She was always dangling after one gent or another.

"Not to fret," Esmeralda said. "She'll crawl back here when she finds herself on the rocks and finds her pockets empty, eh? What's that I smell, apple?"

"Apple and peach," Kate said proudly.

"Peach!" Lucy cried. "I *adore* peaches! How'd ye find peaches this time of year? Lucky is the day ye found Holly, aye?"

"For all of us," Holly said, and handed Lucy a muffin.

Kate had met Holly a little over a year ago. She and Digby had been searching for Kate's brother Jude — a search that was now at least seven years old. Kate had stumbled upon Holly crouched, crying, and shivering in a doorway. It had taken some doing, but Holly had finally confessed that she'd lost her job as a daily that afternoon for stealing, and she had no money for lodging or food. She was frantic.

Kate was frantic for her — she'd been Holly once.

Kate had taken Holly to Fannie Breen, and had paid Fannie an exorbitant fee to keep Holly in the room Kate had once occupied until she could find her better lodging. Kate didn't have a lot of money of her own, just the money she'd managed to save over the years. It had taken some hunting and bargaining with the very disagreeable landlord Mr. Fleming to obtain this pair of rooms for Holly.

In the year that followed, when Kate came round to see Holly, she'd find other women sleeping within. They were Holly's friends, and they had no one but each other to rely on.

They believed Kate was one of the charity ladies from St. Katharine's church, and Kate allowed them to believe it. Digby had warned her against revealing that she was the mistress of a wealthy merchant. "They'll use you ill if they discover it and you'll end up losing everything you've worked for."

Digby was right — it would take only one ruthless person to bring her house of cards tumbling down.

A knock at the door sent Lucy skipping to it; Digby stood outside and was holding a large wooden box. "Happy Christmas," he said, and handed the box to Lucy.

Lucy opened the box. "It's pasties! It *is* Christmas!"

Kate smiled at Digby — for all his complaining, he had a generous heart. Kate stood to go as the women descended on the box of meat pies.

"Merry Christmas to you all," Kate said.

"Happy Christmas!" the women responded in turn.

"Lud, Esme, won't ye tell her about her brother, then?" Adele asked, nudging Esmeralda with her foot.

Kate's heart skipped a beat and her eyes flew to Esmeralda.

"Ach, I all but forgot it," the young woman said, and paused to lick her fingers. "Meg says she saw a chap that was the spittin' image of ye. She said he might have been yer twin, what with the blond hair and green eyes, were he not so poor."

Jude. "Where? *Here?* Here in St. Katharine's? Did she say where she saw him?" Dear God, she hadn't seen Jude in ten years. She'd been searching so long she'd despaired he was even alive.

"Go' blind me, he is yer twin, eh? She was at the Rooster and the Crown, she was." She paused, frowning. "I think."

Meg! Why must she be absent on Christmas Day! "Do you know where Meg might be?" Kate asked.

"Kate," Digby said in protest.

But Kate ignored him. She would follow any clue to her brother's whereabouts, no matter how far-fetched.

CHAPTER FOUR

A bitterly cold wind blew across London later that week, and Kate received the gift of a mink-lined cloak from His Royal Highness, along with a handwritten note that she should wrap herself warmly in it that evening, as she was to attend a recital at Whitehall in the company of Lord and Lady Wellesley.

She had no idea who they were.

Digby maintained that if there was anything favorable to be said for the Prince of Wales, it was that he was a true and generous patron of the arts. "At least there is that," he said.

Digby also insisted Kate wear a jade gown with pale cream trim. Her daily ladies' maid, Amy, helped Kate dress in the silk and put up her hair.

"Oh, it goes *very* well with your eyes," Digby said proudly once Kate was dressed. "You will *stun* all the nobility."

"Doubt it," Aldous said from his place near the door, where he stood with his arms crossed over his chest, his weight on one hip. "They fancy only themselves."

"They'll fancy Kate," Digby said. "She is too beautiful to be ignored. They will be drawn to her the way plants are drawn to light. Trust me, for I am a student of the aristocracy. When one cannot *be* an aristocrat, one watches everything they do with a keen and envious eye."

Kate laughed; Aldous frowned. But Digby was right, that much Kate knew from having been Benoit's mistress. Benoit had seen to it that she was properly trained for her role by sending her to France to learn from Madame Albert, who, by the lady's own admission, was a renowned courtesan. Madame Albert had subscribed to the same theory as Digby: Do as the aristocracy does. Talk like them, drink like them, eat like them, play like them — but above all, entice them in a way they've never been enticed. And Madame Albert had spent quite a lot of time teaching Kate how to entice men, a skill she had practiced frequently in Benoit's drawing room, where he hosted evenings of gambling, to which some of the wealthiest men in London came.

A footman in an unmarked carriage called for Kate an hour later, and Aldous saw her out. He told the fellow driving that he'd better have a care with her, and she was ferried, like a princess, to Whitehall. Lord Wellesley met her on the steps. He introduced himself and hurried her inside, where Lady Wellesley joined them. She said, "Good evening," looked enviously at Kate's cloak, and never looked at her again. Kate was hardly offended — society ladies had long shunned her.

The seating was arranged in two crescent-shaped rows. Lord Wellesley escorted Kate and his wife to the front row, a little left of center, and sat between the two women. They were early; there was scarcely anyone else in the room.

In an effort to fill the uncomfortable silence, Kate said, "I very much enjoy a musical evening. Do you?"

Wellesley seemed mortified by the question. "Yes," he said.

Small talk, it seemed, was pointless. Fortunately, Kate had no tender feelings left after her years of being a courtesan. She remembered the first time Benoit had taken her to a fine Mayfair London mansion to have her model some of the silk fabrics he was importing from the Orient. Kate had felt quite elegant in the gown Benoit had commissioned for her to wear. The lady of that great mansion, whose business Benoit sought, was equally enamored of the gown. But she was not enamored of Kate. She had viewed the gown with a keen eye, asked Benoit into her private sitting room, and then instructed a footman to stand by while Kate waited in the foyer. "Keep an eye open, Jones. I'll not have anything go missing," she'd said.

"You are entirely too sensitive." Benoit had sighed when Kate complained of the slight. "What can you expect? You are *ordures* to them."

When Kate had asked Digby what that meant, her jolly good friend had paled a bit. "It means . . . rubbish," he'd said tightly.

At the time, Kate's feelings had been hurt. But through the years, she'd been dismissed, ignored, and cut directly so many times that it rarely bothered her any longer. That was the way of the *ton.* The men admired her figure and face and clamored to meet her, while the women disdained her for the attention men paid her.

Kate had learned to take pleasure however she could, and one way was in hearing music played well. That was something her life afforded her now, and she relished each performance, this one notwithstanding.

The musicians filed in and began to ready their instruments. Kate eagerly watched them until she was startled by a loud *bang* at the back of the room. She jumped and turned to see a herald, banging his staff to the floor to announce the Prince of Wales. The prince entered the room with a few companions. Everyone rose to their feet; the prince and his companions walked to seats on Kate's left. When they were seated, the audience resumed their seats.

Kate looked at Lord Wellesley, but his gaze was averted from hers. Kate wasn't entirely certain what to do; this was her first public encounter with the prince. She'd been instructed that no one was to perceive any connection between her and the prince, but she was seated one person away from him. Should she not greet him? It seemed rather odd not to at least say good evening. So with her hands folded in her lap, Kate turned a smile to the gentleman beside her. "Good evening."

He glanced at her. "Good evening, madam," he said. Across him, Kate could see the prince looking at her from the corner of his eye, the hint of a smile on his lips. Aha, so this was a childish game, was it?

"It's awfully cold out, is it not?" she asked the gentleman, and noticed the prince was trying to keep from smiling.

"Quite."

"A bit of brandy would be in order, I should think. Nothing warms the blood quite like it."

"Indeed," the gentleman said.

Kate smiled pertly at the prince, turned her attention to the musicians now that the little game was over, and waited impatiently for the performance to begin.

At last, a young man walked out and put some sheet music on a pianoforte. He moved forward, bowed before the prince, and appeared about to speak, but paused at the sound of a determined stride echoing down the central aisle. Kate naturally turned to see who was arriving so late and saw the Duke of Darlington sweeping up the aisle like a bloody peacock in full plume.

He was taller than she recalled, two or three inches over six feet she guessed. His hair was a rich brown, and his eyes a deep shade of blue. He was not a *very* handsome man, but there was nevertheless something about him that made him quite attractive. He was robust and confident and exuded power and authority. He was the sort, Kate guessed, to be dazzled by his own brilliance.

Darlington settled into a seat almost directly across from Kate in the crescent row of seating. He did not notice her right away; he said something to the two women and the man who had saved him the seat.

But then the gentleman at the pianoforte announced the recital was about to begin, and the duke looked forward, and his gaze inadvertently landed on Kate.

He froze. He blinked. He frowned.

Kate smiled and nodded her head, well aware that everyone in the room saw the exchange. She did not bother to note the duke's reaction, but turned her attention to the pianist.

He thanked the Prince of Wales for his fervent patronage and gave a brief history of the Beethoven cello concerto the small chamber orchestra would perform this evening. From the corner of her eye, Kate noticed the duke glancing at his pocket watch. He had a pressing engagement, did he? Perhaps his mistress needed him. Kate hoped he'd leave soon — she had no desire to speak to him.

The pianist took his place at the pianoforte. He held up a delicate hand to the other musicians, made a downward sweeping motion, and the music began.

Kate lost all interest in the Duke of Darlington at that moment, as she was transported with the first note. The music was magically beautiful; she marveled at the skill required to seduce such notes from an instrument. The dulcet tones washed over her, filling her mind with impossible dreams of love in springtime, of contentment in winter, of faeries and maidens and princely heroes, and cottages in dense forests with a milk cow and two pigs. She lost all track of time until the last note was played.

Kate was so moved by the music that she burst into enthusiastic applause, smiling at those around her, expecting to see everyone so enraptured. What she saw was polite restraint in the applause. She instantly lowered her hands, but she could not repress her smile, and she unthinkingly glanced across the room to where Darlington was sitting . . . had been sitting.

His chair was empty. *Good.* If luck was with her, the peacock would have quit the performance and Whitehall altogether.

The audience remained seated until the prince stood and made his way to the antechamber, at which point, Lord Wellesley said, "Miss Bergeron."

Kate glanced at him — or rather, up at him, as he was standing.

"It is the prince's practice to indulge in a glass of champagne after a performance. Tonight's offering is champagne that was found in an officer's cabin aboard a captured French naval vessel and given to the prince as a gift. He is keen to share it with the assembly this evening and assured me it is of the finest quality."

"Yes, thank you," she said, and slipped her hand into his, allowing him to help her up. Lady Wellesley, she noticed, had disappeared. Perhaps she had a lover, too. Didn't they all?

Wellesley's body was radiating tension, as if he found the touch of Kate's hand on his arm painful. He walked stiffly to the refreshment area, pausing as a footman approached with a tray of champagne flutes held high in the air. Wellesley nodded; the footman lowered the tray and allowed him to take two flutes from it. He handed one to Kate. "Champagne," he said needlessly. "If you are not accustomed to it, you might find that it tickles your nose."

Did Wellesley honestly believe the prince had found her lying in the gutter and brought her in? "Thank you," Kate said. She lifted her flute in a mock toast to him and sipped.

It was excellent champagne. Benoit would have been quite impressed, and he'd not been an easy man to please. In more ways than one.

Kate stood beside a silent Wellesley, sipping the champagne, looking about the room and wishing she were home beneath a lap rug with a book. She finished off the champagne and put the empty flute aside.

"Wellesley, you must introduce us to your lovely companion!" the prince's voice boomed behind her.

Expecting to play another silly game, Kate turned, but her eyes landed on Darlington. *Darlington!* He stood so close now that she was reminded of how blue his eyes were. She quickly shifted her gaze from the duke's broad shoulders and impeccably cut coat to the prince, who looked rather old and fat next to the duke. She instantly sank into a curtsy. "Your Highness."

"May I introduce Miss Katharine Bergeron," Wellesley said tightly.

"Miss Bergeron," the prince said, and offered his hand to help her up. Kate slipped her hand into his; he squeezed her fingers. His gaze lingered on Kate's bosom; behind him, Darlington stood stoically, his hands clasped behind him, his gaze on something in the distance.

"Did you enjoy the evening's musical offering?" the prince asked.

"Very much, Your Highness."

"Then you must come again, Miss Bergeron. Allow me to introduce to you the Duke of Darlington. He is also a lover of musical evenings."

Darlington gave her a curt nod. "Miss Bergeron, it is my pleasure," he said, sounding about as pleased as he might be with a hanging. His indigo eyes locked on hers, and Kate felt a shiver run through her.

"Your Grace," she said, sinking into another curtsy. "The pleasure is surely all mine." She smiled at him, challenging him. Kate was beginning to deduce the purpose of this evening. It was indeed a game. The prince would introduce her and Darlington in a public venue so that everyone in attendance would take note. Thereafter, no one would be entirely surprised to see the duke in the company of the courtesan again. And judging by the grim look on Darlington's face, Kate guessed he'd worked out the same.

"Miss Bergeron is a patron of the arts," Wellesley offered awkwardly, as if that were the reason for making the introductions, as if that would bamboozle even one bloody soul in this small concert hall.

"The arts?" Darlington said, cocking a brow, as if that notion were inconceivable, if not entirely unbelievable. In fact, his eyes were suddenly shining with amusement.

Kate's smile broadened and she offered him her hand. "I beg your pardon, but you look incredulous, Your Grace."

The prince laughed. "Christie, I dare say you do!"

"I apologize, Miss Bergeron, if I gave that impression," he said smoothly, and touched his fine lips to the satin of her gloves.

"You should be incredulous," she said pleasantly as he raised his head. "My patronage lies solely in my great appreciation of hearing instruments played so beautifully. I wish it could be otherwise, but my patronage does not extend beyond that."

Darlington's gaze swept over her. "That is a far more valuable form of patronage than money."

Well, well . . . perhaps this peacock had a bit of civility in him after all.

"You are quite right about that, Christie," the prince said. "Wellesley, shall we sample the champagne? Miss Bergeron, you must have a taste of this excellent champagne. Darlington, you must fetch it for her," the prince said, and with a sly smile for Kate, he put his arm congenially around Wellesley's shoulders and pulled him away, leaving Kate and Darlington standing together awkwardly in the middle of the room while others watched.

They stood so close that Kate was keenly aware of this man. He was an alluring figure, she'd admit that much. But now that they had done what Kate assumed they were supposed to do, she saw no reason to prolong their association. "You need not remain at my side, Your Grace. I am perfectly capable of fetching my own drink."

"I have no doubt that you are, but that is clearly beside the point," he said, gesturing to a footman who approached them. Darlington nodded at Kate, and the footman bowed low as he presented the tray to her.

She took a flute from the tray. "Thank you. I have my champagne. You may go to your friends, as you obviously wish to do."

"I wish to be gone from here altogether, but I shall keep you company, Miss Bergeron."

"It's not necessary."

"It is," he said stubbornly.

Kate chuckled. "I give you my word that I shall not pocket any of the silver," she whispered, and turned away from him.

"I beg your pardon," Darlington said, drawing her attention to him once more. "Are you always so decidedly intrepid and reckless with your words?"

Kate didn't know precisely what intrepid meant, but she knew from his tone it was not a compliment. "Does it disturb you, Your Grace? Would you rather I attempt to win your approval? I think we both know I shall never have it," she said laughingly. "Therefore, I have nothing to lose by speaking my mind." She smiled again and lifted her flute. "The champagne is quite good. It reminds me of the champagne that is served in the fine salons of Paris. Did you try it?"

"I did," he said, his eyes intent on her, studying her.

"I thought the performance was magical. Did you?"

"Not particularly." Now he looked impatiently about, clearly not wanting to converse.

"Well then! Now that we've had our say, I believe I will sample the delicacies," Kate said, gesturing to a table nearby groaning with platters of food. "Good evening, Your Grace."

She walked away and examined the various plates on the table, selecting a few pastries to sample. She bit into one pastry and tasted a bit of cinnamon and something else . . . mint, perhaps?

Darlington suddenly appeared beside her, his expression impatient. Kate held up her plate, offering him a sweetmeat. "Do try one of these and tell me what you think of it."

"Thank you, but no."

"They're quite good," she said, and sampled another one. She frowned slightly. "This one does not sit on the palate as it ought," she said.

65

"Miss Bergeron, I am taking my leave," Darlington said.

"Very well," she responded as she examined the other selections on the table. "We've done what is required of us."

He glanced uncomfortably around them. "I don't know what you mean."

She gave him a look that suggested he knew precisely what she meant. "Do not take me for a fool, Your Grace," she said quietly. "I don't believe the prince summoned me here to cultivate my appreciation of music. He intended to introduce us publicly."

But Darlington's gaze narrowed. "Did the two of you plan this?"

"No! I surmised it. Didn't you?"

"Of course I did," he snapped. "Miss Bergeron, I will not be taken for granted in this . . . *arrangement,*" he said tightly.

"Then you best speak to the prince," Kate responded shortly. She didn't care for the way he looked at her, as if he were suspicious of her, as if *she* had planned this evening's events. She stepped away from the table. "I shan't keep you, Your Grace. Good night," she said, and walked away once more from his unsettling blue eyes.

CHAPTER FIVE

Grayson watched Miss Bergeron walk away, his gaze drawn to the subtle swing of her hips. He was not the only one watching her, he noticed. More than one gentleman stole a glance at her with an eager gleam in his eye, undoubtedly imagining the soft skin beneath her gown as Grayson was.

Yet Grayson's conversation with Miss Bergeron had left him feeling even more cross and restless than when he'd arrived, and it didn't help matters in the least that her green eyes sparkled with irreverence, or her lips, Christ Almighty, those lips were so full and lush.

He was vexed that he was here at all. He had not wanted to attend, but his cousin Victoria had begged him. Victoria had a friend she had hoped to introduce to him, and George had personally sent her the invitation to the night's program. The friend — whose name Grayson had already forgotten — was a young woman who was coming out in the upcoming Season. She was hardly the sort who would attract him.

In addition, the seating had been uncomfortable, leaving Grayson to wonder why, with the hundreds of thousands of pounds George had squandered in his life, he had not at least seen to comfortable seating for events he forced his friends to attend. Then Grayson had seen Katharine Bergeron sitting prettily across from him, and his ire had soared.

Grayson supposed he shouldn't have been surprised at George's obvious manipulations, but he was. Once George had seen his favorable reply to the night's invitation, he'd no doubt arranged the public meeting between him and Kate. He imagined it had been hastily arranged, too, because Grayson knew Wellesley and his wife would not, under normal circumstances, be seen with a courtesan.

But Grayson was mostly unsettled by the image of a smiling young woman wearing an apron and with flour on her cheek. The woman sitting across from him this evening had the elegance of a queen and the beauty of legends. This was the woman he had seen at the opera, the woman he'd all but forgotten after calling on her at King Street.

The jade color of Miss Bergeron's gown had shimmered in the low candlelight. Wisps of pale blond hair fell about her face, the rest of her hair gathered in a velvet green ribbon wrapped around her head. Her arms were covered in white satin gloves and jewels dangled from her ears and her slender throat.

He'd watched her during the performance. Grayson was hopelessly tone-deaf, and music did not fall on his ears in the same soothing way it seemed to fall on other people's ears. So he'd passed the time by surreptitiously observing the courtesan.

She'd sat almost casually, with one hand placed on top of the other in her lap, her feet tucked to one side beneath her seat. But it was the expression on her face that had captivated him — her gaze was riveted on the musicians, her expression full of rapture, and it seemed that she was bound to each note, swaying slightly with each crescendo. For once in his life, Grayson could almost feel the music just by watching her. It had been strangely and disturbingly moving.

He knew George must have been smitten upon first meeting her. Miss Bergeron was quite lovely, that was indisputable, the loveliest of any courtesan Grayson had ever met, and he'd met a few. She had a seductive air about her that drew a man's earnest attention. Yet the most remarkable thing about her was her smile — it seemed to illuminate everything around her.

The woman could say the most outrageous, irreverent things, and they seemed very nice when delivered with that smile.

"Your Grace?"

Lord Eagleton, a viscount with political ambitions that clashed with those of Grayson's family, had sidled over to him. An important parliamentary vote on abolishing the slave trade on British vessels would be taken soon. Grayson's brother Merrick was a staunch supporter of abolition and had aligned himself with the Quakers and William Wilberforce, who were leading the movement. Like Merrick, Grayson did not believe in the concept of slavery and could not condone it. He certainly could not condone the transport of slaves by British vessels. Thanks to Merrick, Grayson had seen the conditions under which the poor souls were made to travel and they were as inhumane as anything he'd ever imagined. Merrick, an earl in his own right, was working hard to bring Parliament around to abolition. But there were powerful lords who benefited from the trade and were bucking his efforts.

Eagleton was one of them. "How fortuitous to encounter you this evening," the man said, his voice smooth enough to charm a snake. "I sent round an inquiry to your secretary that perhaps you might receive me, Your Grace. I should very much like to discuss the abolitionist movement."

Grayson appreciated the warning — he would instruct his secretary, Mr. Palmer, to decline any entreaty. To Eagleton, he said, "I think you should be speaking with my brother, Lord Merrick Christopher."

"With all due respect, Your Grace, I hoped to speak with you. Britain's trade has been built in part on the transport of slaves. Our nation's wealth could very well depend on the continuation of it. I am not certain your brother understands the import of it."

Grayson wondered which rich slave trader was lining Eagleton's pockets. "I think he understands it clearly."

Eagleton moved closer to him. "If we do not trade slaves, how soon is it before we do not trade in tobacco? Slaves harvest tobacco. Or sugar?"

Grayson turned to face Eagleton. "You underestimate us, sir. The slave trade is morally reprehensible and there is nothing you can say that will dissuade the Christophers from that."

Eagleton's smile faded. "Then you best

hope your eager younger brother has your moral fortitude, my lord. There is a movement afoot to cast Mr. Wilberforce and his supporters aside and do what is best for Britain — not what is best for the conscience of a few religious fanatics." With that, he walked away.

Grayson determined this most wretched evening deserved to end. He said good-bye to his cousin Victoria, who pouted when he took his leave. He summoned a footman and requested his cloak. He walked to the entry hall and sent a boy to tell his driver to have the carriage brought round.

He was thinking about Eagleton and the split of votes for and against abolition as he walked outside. He stood on the walk beneath the light of the public lanterns, slapping his gloves against his greatcoat, waiting for his carriage to be brought round.

A soft *ahem* startled him; Grayson glanced to his right.

Bloody hell. He could not seem to escape the beautiful courtesan this evening.

She moved closer; the hood of her cloak framed her face and made her eyes seem even greener. "You're leaving? The second movement hasn't even begun!" she said. "Perhaps you might find it more to your liking than the first."

"I rather doubt it."

She said nothing for a moment. Then added, "I adore music. It's so uplifting."

Her eyes, he noticed, were sparkling even brighter in the crisp night air.

She cocked her head, a bemused frown on her lips. "If I may, Your Grace, there is no need to be anxious around me. I do not intend to embarrass you."

He almost rolled his eyes. "You cannot embarrass me, madam. I find the mere presumption offensive."

Miss Bergeron's lovely eyes widened. "I beg your pardon. I merely meant —"

"I know precisely what you meant, Miss Bergeron. You expect me to welcome this intrusion into my life, and if I do not, you attempt to disparage me."

"No! I . . . my apologies if you thought so. I meant only to . . . to —"

"To what?" he demanded.

"To make a proper acquaintance," she said, her voice small.

"Allow me to disabuse you of that desire, Miss Bergeron. You and I will not be friends."

Something glinted in her pale green eyes. "No, I suppose we will not, for I don't believe I could ever befriend a man as unkind and ungentlemanly as you."

That certainly took him aback. *"Pardon?"*

"I explained to you the first time I met you that I did not ask for this, either, Your Grace, but I do not have the power to remove myself from the situation. I have tried to be kind and you . . . *you* have let your disdain for me be known at every opportunity!"

Grayson bristled. She was too bold by half. "You obviously do not know who you are speaking to in such a manner —"

"Oh, I am well aware," she said, her eyes glittering now. "I am aware that, by all accounts, you are quite warm and charming to your acquaintances, but to someone such as me, who is well below your station in life, you hold yourself up as a preening peacock who has had his feathers set up!"

He gaped at her. No one had ever spoken to him in this manner. "You are unconscionably brazen, Miss Bergeron!"

Her expression suddenly changed; she looked almost sad. "Perhaps I am. I will endeavor to be less brazen. But I am not diseased, Your Grace. I have only done what I must to survive."

Grayson stared at her. He was angry — one did not address a duke so boldly — but he also felt a glimmer of shame. And now that he'd been so chastised, he was uncertain *what* to say to her.

A coach was approaching on the street, and he assumed it was his. Miss Bergeron looked to the carriage. So did Grayson. It was not his, but it was, apparently, hers. As it rolled to a stop, a coachman leapt off the back runner to open the door. Without a word, Miss Bergeron walked forward and stepped gracefully into the coach without looking back.

Chapter Six

At one o'clock in the morning, Diana paced before an elaborately carved hearth in her suite of rooms. The fire had long since been reduced to coals, and Diana had been dressed in her woolen dressing gown and fur-lined slippers for over an hour. She was almost unaware of the drafts in the stately old mansion; her thoughts were racing uncontrollably, her imagination conjuring a number of horrible images.

Grayson had been expected hours ago after a recital at Whitehall, but he'd not come. Millie, Diana's personal servant, would have let him in the back door and brought him up the servant's entrance to her suite. *What could have kept him?* Diana tried to tell herself there was any number of reasonable explanations — unexpected visitors, a horse with a thrown shoe, a carriage with a broken axle.

But wouldn't Grayson have sent a messenger? Of course he would have, which meant something else, something worse had befallen him. Thieves came to mind. They were bloodthirsty and ruthless, and Diana heard they came up from the docks at night and preyed on innocent people. The very thought propelled her to pick up a single candle and leave her rooms in search of answers.

The Eustis house was dark and silent at this hour; dawn came early and the servants retired early. Diana moved silently through the wide halls, past the paintings of her husband's ancestors, past the statuary and porcelain objets d'art. She moved down the grand, curving staircase, ran across the large entry and into another corridor. At the end of that hallway was another, narrower staircase that led up to the servants' wing. These were the rooms reserved for the highest-ranking household staff — Hatt the butler, the cook, and the housekeeper — as well as two footmen and two maids. The other servants slept below stairs, two to a room. Lord Eustis did not believe in dailies; he preferred his servants to be on hand at all times.

At the third door on the right, Millie's room, Diana rapped lightly, then glanced furtively around, afraid someone might hear her and open their door. Unfortunately, no one seemed to hear her — not even Millie.

Diana rapped again, a bit louder.

After what seemed an eternity, the door swung open and Millie blinked as if the candlelight hurt her eyes. She was wearing a woolen nightgown and a cap on her head. A long, red braid hung over her shoulder. *"Mu'um?"* she whispered, clearly surprised.

Diana pushed past Millie and stepped into the room. It was small, perhaps no larger than ten feet long, and had a single dormer window. It smelled of ash and lye soap and the coals in the brazier were cold. It was wintry in that small room. "Millie . . . has no one come?" Diana demanded in a loud whisper. "Surely at least a messenger has come."

"No, mu'um," Millie said, shaking her head.

"When did you retire?" Diana asked, her tone accusing, but she couldn't help herself.

"Half past eleven," Millie said uncertainly.

"Half past eleven! What if a messenger had come? You *must* endeavor to remain below until midnight!"

"I'm sorry, mu'um, but I must be up with dawn's first light —"

"Yes, I understand, but you see my point, do you not?" Diana insisted.

"Yes, mu'um," Millie said quietly.

Heavens, it wasn't the girl's fault, Diana understood that, but she was filled with anxiety. Grayson never failed her, and on those rare occasions when something did indeed crop up, he sent word.

Millie frowned and folded her arms around her, shivering from the cold.

Diana had entrusted Millie with her secret. With her life, really — for if Millie were ever to turn on her, she could ruin Diana. Lord Eustis would never forgive her for having an affair, especially as she had not provided him the heir he so desperately wanted. That Millie had the power to ruin everything was something Diana could not forget, and even now, as frustrated as she was with Grayson's absence, with Millie's failure to stay near the door when she was most needed, Diana checked herself.

"I beg your pardon, Millie," she said. "I do not mean to be so sharp, but I've an awful headache."

"You should take a bit of laudanum for it, mu'um," Millie said frostily.

Diana looked at the girl; the uncertainty had gone from her eyes, and in its place was something much harder. "Yes," Diana said carefully. "Perhaps I should."

Something had shifted in that room. Millie sensed her power over Diana. "I would have gone to you straightaway if a messenger had come . . . just as I always do."

"Yes," Diana said. Coming here suddenly felt like a very big mistake. "Well then," she said, forcing a smile. "I shan't keep you longer. As you say, dawn comes early." She moved past Millie. As she reached for the door, Millie put her hand on the knob.

"There's just one thing, if I may, mu'um," Millie said smoothly.

Diana looked at the door. She forced herself to smile. "Yes, Millie?"

"I need more coal for the brazier."

The servants were allotted so much coal per week, and Millie had used her allotment. Yet her gaze was openly defiant, for she knew that Diana could not possibly refuse her; the price of her silence was coal.

"Very well," Diana said. "I shall ask Mr. Hatt to bring some coal to you tomorrow."

"And a blanket," Millie said.

Diana bristled. She looked away from Millie to the door. "A blanket, of course," she said. "Did I not make that perfectly clear? Coal and a blanket. Will you open the door now?"

Millie slowly pulled it open, then leaned against it, watching Diana as she walked out of the room, striding swiftly down the corridor before the chit could ask for more.

CHAPTER SEVEN

Grayson's secretary, Mr. Palmer, sat across the polished cherrywood desk from him making meticulous notes, just as he did every morning. His head was down, the bald pate of his head shining back at Grayson. The man's spectacles defied gravity and remained perched on the very end of his nose, but Mr. Palmer never seemed to notice, so intent was he on his duties. He asked questions only when absolutely necessary, and rarely made suggestions.

This morning, however, Mr. Palmer had asked Grayson three questions thus far: Did His Grace intend to decline the invitation to the Sumner supper party, as he had previously instructed the opposite? Did His Grace wish to invite his younger sister to luncheon on Sunday, as he had included all his siblings currently in town, save Mary? Did His Grace mean to authorize the payment of four geese when five geese had been purchased?

Grayson's mind was someplace other than his affairs; he quickly corrected himself. He was ready for this interview to end, but there was that thing, that little thing that kept knocking around in his head, making him cross and inefficient. Katharine Bergeron was right. He had judged her harshly because of her occupation. "There is one last thing, Palmer," Grayson said. "I should like you to purchase a trinket. A necklace, perhaps, something a lady would like."

"And deliver it to Lady Eustis?" Palmer said, his pen scratching against the vellum.

Diana, Diana, he could not forget Diana. His failure to appear last night undoubtedly had her at sixes and sevens. "Quite right — please deliver one to Lady Eustis. And one to Miss Katharine Bergeron on King Street."

Palmer's pen stopped moving on the vellum.

"I shall give you direction to Miss Bergeron along with a note to be delivered with the necklace," Grayson added.

The pen moved on the paper.

"That's all."

Mr. Palmer gathered the papers in his lap, and the case beside him, and stood. "I shall wait in the anteroom for the morning's correspondence, Your Grace."

"Good day, Mr. Palmer," Grayson mut-

82

tered, and withdrew a piece of vellum. He dipped a pen in ink, and wrote: *Miss Bergeron, please accept my sincere apology for having offended you. I assure you that was not my desire. Darlington.*

Quite short, but in his experience the ruffled feathers of a woman were better soothed with a bit of pretty jewelry than with words.

Kate would allow Digby's discerning palate to be the final judge of her latest batch of petits fours, but she thought she'd put a little too much salt in them. Nevertheless, she was putting the finishing touches on them when Aldous hurried into the kitchen. That alone was enough to startle her; Aldous never hurried.

"Come at once," Aldous said anxiously. "It is Digby." He left the kitchen just as quickly as he'd entered it.

Kate dropped her knife with a clatter, and wiping her hands on her apron, she rushed after Aldous.

She found the two men in the drawing room. Aldous was pouring whiskey and Digby was sprawled on the settee. His clothes were torn and dirty, his lip cut, and one eye swollen shut. *"Digby!"* she cried, rushing forward. "What in God's name has happened?" She fell to her knees beside him as Aldous put the whiskey into Digby's hand.

Digby did not answer straightaway, but drank the whiskey as if it was water. He grimaced at the taste of it, then handed the empty glass to Aldous. "More, please."

"Digby!"

"Is my face as mangled as it feels?" he asked tightly, touching his fingertips to his cheekbone.

"Quite," Aldous said without hesitation.

"What happened to you?" Kate cried.

"A bit of foolishness," Digby said as he gingerly probed his lip. "I was down at the quays to see a couple of gents about the perfume trade and who should I chance to see but Meg. I asked the lass about the man she'd seen who so closely resembled you. She confirmed she'd seen him at the Rooster and Crown, and I bravely ventured into that decidedly squalid public house on the quay at St. Katharine's."

"Oh *no* —"

"I foolishly believed that a pair of gold sovereigns might jog a memory or two."

"Jogged more than a memory by the look of it," Aldous quipped.

"Digby, why ever would you do such a thing? You don't have enough in your purse to be handing sovereigns about!"

"Yes, well, in spite of my mangled appearance, the sovereigns served their purpose," he said with a hint of indignation in his voice. He closed his eyes and rested his head. "I now know that one Jude Berger is a seaman on *The Princess* merchant ship, and that *The Princess* is quite adept at sailing around naval blockades and actively pursues the slave trade."

"Berger? The slave trade!" Kate exclaimed, sinking back on her heels. "What are you implying? Jude is involved in the slave trade? *My* Jude?"

Digby opened one eye. "I am fairly certain it is your Jude, the surname notwithstanding. He is not easily forgotten, it would seem, for he is rather quarrelsome when he's full of drink and when he's not, he's rather popular with the ladybirds. The description of him — provided by one such ladybird — sounded quite like you, Kate. Blond hair, green eyes, and uncommon beauty."

"Dear God," she murmured.

Digby touched his eye and winced painfully.

"Aldous, there is some beefsteak in the kitchen. Will you fetch it?" she asked.

"I smell something that stirs my appetite, and it is not beefsteak," Digby said.

"And the pastries, Aldous," Kate called after him. To Digby, she asked hopefully,

"Did you learn how to find him?"

"Unfortunately, *The Princess* set sail earlier this week. No one I spoke with knows when she will return."

Kate's soaring hopes quickly plummeted. "*Lud,* what happened to you, Digby?" she asked softly as she brushed a lock of hair from his forehead.

He flicked his wrist. "I suppose I was a bit too cavalier with my purse," he said with a grimace. "I was set upon by a pair of thugs as soon as I departed the tavern. Not only did they divest me of my purse, but my gun as well."

"Your gun!"

"I may be foolish, but I am not entirely a fool. I, too, spent more years by the quays than I care to remember and was prepared for such tomfoolery. I was *not,* however, prepared for the speed of their blows. I was quite overwhelmed."

"Oh, Digby," Kate said sorrowfully.

A sharp rap at the front door startled them both; Kate exchanged a look with Digby. "Wait here." She stood and removed her apron as she walked across the room and tossed it aside. She reached the door at the same moment Aldous did on his way back from the kitchen. He thrust the plate of petit fours at her, which Kate quickly put down, and hurried after him.

When Aldous opened the front door, still carrying the beefsteak, Kate saw a footman in livery standing outside. She assumed he was a royal footman, but on closer inspection, she realized the colors were wrong. A gust of cold wind swept into the house, lifting the hem of Kate's gown as the footman removed his hat.

"Yes?" Aldous asked coolly.

"A message, sir, for Miss Katharine Bergeron, from the Duke of Darlington." He held out something to Aldous.

Aldous, who harbored a resentment of the Quality in any shape or fashion, shut the door in the footman's face. "A package," he said to Kate. "Small."

She couldn't imagine what Darlington would be sending her, and frankly, she didn't care. He was an odious man, a mean, unkind, rotten man. "No, thank you."

Aldous opened the door. "She don't want it," he said.

"Don't want it?" the footman said, seeming confused. He looked at the package. "But I'm to deliver it."

"She don't *want* it. Take it back."

"Take it back?" the poor man repeated, as if he couldn't fathom such a thing.

"All right, all right," Kate said, hurrying

forward. She put out her hand for the package.

"Thank you, mu'um," the footman said, obviously relieved.

Kate did not reply; there was no opportunity to do so. Aldous had shut the door again. She looked at him askance, to which Aldous shrugged. "He's a footman."

The package was a small, plainly wrapped box with a sealed note tied to it. Kate returned to the drawing room with Aldous on her heels, and while he handed the beefsteak to Digby, and commanded him to press it to his eye — to which Digby protested, as he was rather fastidious about such things — Kate opened the note.

She read it. Digby had taught her to read, but she still found it laborious. When she'd managed to read it all she thought the note sounded much like Darlington — curt and cold. She then opened the box and removed a pearl necklace. It was exquisite and outlandishly extravagant for a man who was not her lover.

Kate had been the recipient of such gifts before, and they usually meant the same thing — a desire to bed her. Wasn't that what they all wanted in the end, these fancy lords with their bottomless wells of money?

"Too salty, love," Digby said.

"Pardon?" Kate asked, looking up.

Digby licked his fingers. "The petits fours are too salty. I'd recommend a dash instead of a pinch."

"I thought there was something a bit off about them," she agreed, and handed the necklace and box to Aldous. "Send it back."

"What is that?" Digby asked, eyeing the box.

"A necklace."

Aldous opened the box and withdrew the necklace, holding it up to Digby. "You don't mean to return this," Aldous said. "Sell it. It would bring a small fortune."

"It would indeed," Digby said, perusing the necklace with a critical eye.

But Kate shook her head. "The price is too high to *me*. Send it back, Aldous. Please."

Aldous sighed. Digby looked pained. Kate stubbornly swept up her apron and put it on. "Too salty, really?" she said.

Chapter Eight

Grayson's mother and father, the third Duke of Darlington, had produced four boys and three girls in their many years of matrimony. All but Randolf, who had succumbed to a fever at the age of twelve, survived into adulthood.

Grayson's father, who had been gone some six years now, had been a jolly man, as comfortable with a house full of children as a man could be. Grayson's mother never missed an occasion to remind Grayson that his opportunity to sire a big, happy family was passing with each day he remained a bachelor.

In addition to their own large family, both of Grayson's parents had come from large families. Two of his mother's sisters still lived, as did a sister and a brother of his father. That made Grayson, at the age of thirty years, the head of a very large brood. *Too* large. There were times Grayson felt stifled by his responsibilities to them all. His name was their name. His reputation bolstered theirs. His business dealings influenced their livelihoods. That sort of responsibility felt large and unwieldy, and at times, very frustrating.

But most of the time, Grayson adored his large family. On any given day, particularly leading up to the Season, which would commence in a few weeks' time, one or two of the Christopher clan was in the sprawling Darlington House on Charles Street, where Grayson resided. On this rainy afternoon, his sisters Prudence and Mary, otherwise known as the ladies Beaumont and Wallace, respectively, and Grayson's brother Merrick, Lord Christopher, had come calling with Grayson's mother, the dowager duchess. Prudence and Mary lived in their husbands' homes. The duchess was in town for the Season, and opted to stay with Prudence to be closer to her grandchildren.

Merrick had no house of his own in London. Darlington House was certainly big enough for all of them, but Merrick preferred taking private apartments in a gentleman's club near Hyde Park to being at Darlington House under the watchful eye of his brother.

Cold rain and dark gray skies had driven

the denizens of Mayfair into their salons and Grayson's siblings were restless, Merrick particularly so. He roamed from window to window, looking past the rain sluicing down the panes to the private park behind the house.

There was another caller that long afternoon: Diana. She was a close friend of Prudence, which was how Grayson had made her acquaintance. He'd been attracted to her dark beauty. She'd recognized it and had encouraged him. Diana filled an emotional and physical need in Grayson, for he found it difficult to keep the company of the fairer sex. If he paid the slightest heed to an unmarried woman, rumors instantly abounded that he intended to offer for her. There were courtesans whose company he might have kept, but his mother and his sisters would disapprove so vociferously he would never be able to rest. Diana had proved to be the best solution for him.

Since the time they had come together, Diana and Grayson had been extremely careful not to give any hint of their association, and Diana was practiced in maintaining her cool distance from him in social situations.

But today she wore the pearl necklace he'd sent her as an apology for having missed their appointed liaison.

And last, but hardly least, were Prudence's two young sons, Master Frederick and his little brother, Radcliff, six and five years respectively, both of whom had small wooden swords and were making good use of them. Grayson had a sword, too, and would circle casually, lunging when they least expected it and sending them into fits of giggles.

As Radcliff used his sword to dig at the carpet, Mary asked petulantly, "Is the rain *ever* going to end?" At nineteen years, she was really scarcely more than a child, yet she'd been married to Wallace, who was scarcely older than she, for a year. She was slouching in a chair, one arm draped across her middle, staring at the windows. "It's rained for days and days! The streets are so muddied one can hardly pass through them, and I despise going about in it."

"It is that time of year, Mary," Merrick said. "Be thankful it is not snow."

"Is it going to snow?" Frederick asked his Uncle Merrick hopefully, but Merrick didn't hear him. The boy looked at Grayson. He winked and whispered, *"Perhaps."*

"It's all the same to me," Mary replied to Merrick. "It's cold and wet and dreary. And Lord Wallace is very particular about heat. Did I tell you, Grayson? He says it is far too expensive to have all the hearths lit, and leaves me to suffer in the brutal cold. You should speak to him on my behalf."

Grayson smiled indulgently at his sister. "I best leave the delicate issue of how many hearths are to be lit in your very lovely house to you and your husband."

"But that is the very thing that will spark a disagreement!" Mary complained. "Oh, I don't know why I should expect any sympathy from you! Bachelors and dukes are never forced to compromise."

Grayson shot a furtive glance at Diana. "You may trust that I compromise on many things," he said patiently, and grabbed Radcliff, sweeping him up high overhead to the little boy's delight.

"Really, Darlington, your behavior is most unbecoming for a duke. Furthermore, it will excite the boys into illness," his mother said from her seat at a writing table.

"Who are you writing to, Mamma?" Mary asked idly as Grayson continued to play with Radcliff.

"Lady Blue. I understand her daughter will be coming out this Season and I should like to invite her to tea."

"Very soon *many* young ladies will be in town, Christie," Prudence said slyly. "Everyone agrees it is high time you made a match."

"Everyone, eh?" he asked with a grin for Radcliff. "Tell me, Rad, do you think it high time I made a match?"

"Put me in the sky again!" Radcliff cried.

"Darling, do have a care with my son," Prudence said as he tossed Radcliff up in the air.

"Throw *me!*" Frederick cried.

"Well *I* am most concerned, Your Grace," his mother said above the boys' shrieks of laughter. "You are well past the age of marrying. You must think of heirs! But I know very well you will not think of it at all, so I am determined to host a tea and invite all the debutantes and have a look at them myself."

"It is a waste of time, Mamma." Mary giggled. "Grayson won't find a single one of them suitable. He never does. They are all too silly, or too young, or too disagreeable."

"If you had been introduced to as many eligible young ladies as I have been, Mary, you would say the same."

"Really, Christie, don't you want to marry?" Prudence asked.

"Of course I do. Eventually. I have a duty to marry," he added absently.

"Then you mustn't be so particular!"

Perhaps. But he could not imagine sitting

every day for the rest of his life across the table from a woman he did not love.

"I pray he never finds a suitable match, for then you will set your matchmaking sights on *me*," Merrick said. *"Ouch,"* he said when Frederick, in a fit of laughter, crashed into his leg.

Prudence scoffed as Merrick righted the boy and sent him back to Grayson, who was now on the floor on all fours, pretending to be a beast. "We have Harry, as well, Merrick," Prudence said, speaking of Grayson's other brother. "On my word, I don't know what it is about my brothers that makes them all so averse to marriage."

"Perhaps the stifling finality of it," Merrick suggested. That drew a laugh from Grayson, and as he was momentarily distracted, Radcliff was able to deliver a playful blow that knocked him over.

"Darlington, *really*," his mother said impatiently.

Grayson grinned at the boys and poked them both in the belly. "Duty calls, lads," he said, and gained his feet, straightened his clothing, and clasped his hands behind his back. He lifted one brow and looked pointedly at his mother.

She tried to remain aloof, but he detected the barest hint of a smile.

"Do you know who I think would make an excellent match for you, Christie?" Prudence continued a moment later when Frederick and Radcliff retreated to the far end of the room to throw bits of paper into the fire. "Lady Augusta Fellows, the daughter of the Earl of Brooking. She's been out a year, and by all accounts, she is lovely. What do you think, Diana? You've had the pleasure of her company, have you not?"

"I've scarcely met her at all," Diana said. "I was introduced to her at an assembly. Poor thing was pressed to play the pianoforte." She glanced at Prudence. "And she played it very ill, indeed."

Prudence laughed. "Nevertheless, I should think her charm would make up for her lack of musical ability. What do you think, Your Grace?" Prudence said teasingly. "Charm? Or musical ability?"

"Charm, naturally, as he cannot hear the pianoforte," Diana said gaily.

Startled, Prudence looked at Diana, as did the dowager duchess. Diana's smile faded. "I beg your pardon, Your Grace," she said. "I merely remembered that you once remarked —"

"I did, indeed, Lady Eustis," he said. "It is hardly a secret that I am deaf to music."

"It's a pity, really," Mary said. "Music is so

very lovely, particularly on tedious days such as today." She suddenly sat up. "I believe I shall play the pianoforte!"

"A capital idea," Merrick said. "I'll come along. I can't bear another moment of all this talk of matchmaking."

"Frederick, Radcliff, would you like to play the pianoforte?" Mary asked, holding out her hands to them.

"Yes!" Frederick cried, and galloped across the room to his aunt, Radcliff running on his heels. The four of them went out the door, and a moment later Grayson's butler, Roarke, glided into the room.

"Beyond her lack of ability on the pianoforte, what else do you know of Augusta Fellows?" Prudence asked Diana.

Roarke whispered softly, "The footman has returned, Your Grace. The package was refused." He reached into his coat pocket and withdrew the small box and the note that had been appended to it. The seal was broken.

Grayson frowned with confusion. "Thank you," he said.

"I hardly know anything of her at all," Diana said. "I can't imagine why you'd be so keen on her. She seems rather like all the others to me."

"I suppose she might to *you*, Diana, but

you don't have all these bachelor brothers who are in desperate need of your assistance," Prudence said blithely as Roarke went out.

Grayson opened the note he'd written, expecting to find something written in reply. Astonishingly, there was nothing. Grayson could not imagine a woman — *any* woman, and certainly not *that* woman — refusing a gift from him.

"I think Lady Augusta is very comely and has a pleasant disposition," Prudence continued. "What do you think, Mamma?"

"I've heard that about the entire lot of them," the duchess said. "Which is precisely why we should have a tea, Pru. It is the only way we might see for ourselves if this Augusta Fellows is right for our duke, hmm? Have you met her, Darlington?"

Grayson glanced up. Diana was looking at him strangely; it occurred to Grayson that she must have recognized the box. "I have not," he said to his mother.

"Perhaps she will attend the prince's Twelfth Night Ball. You must make her acquaintance. If you've made a proper acquaintance, I may invite her to my tea," his mother said. "Will you?" she asked as she perused the letter she had been writing.

Grayson's hand closed around the small

box that had been returned to him. "Of course, Mother, if you wish it," he said, and signaled for the footman to pour him a whiskey as the sound of pianoforte keys being banged with something — perhaps a wooden sword — reached them through the open door.

CHAPTER NINE

Having recovered from the altercation at St. Katharine's dock, Digby lounged with Kate's latest batch of petits fours on her daybed, in her suite of private rooms, passing judgment on her gowns. With Amy's help, Kate donned each one behind a screen, then stepped out and twirled about, waiting for Digby's verdict.

Only three days ago, a woman named Mrs. Olive had appeared at Kate's doorstep with two seamstresses and four footmen, bearing boxes and boxes of gowns. Kate had recognized the name instantly because the woman was the most sought-after modiste in all of London. The prince had sent her to Kate, Mrs. Olive said, for as she put it, "he very much desired her to be the most elegantly outfitted woman at the Twelfth Night Ball."

If there was one thing Kate had become quite attached to in her years as a courtesan, it was fine ladies' clothing, and she'd welcomed Mrs. Olive with open arms.

In the end, Mrs. Olive had left her with three gowns and accoutrements. Now that the evening of the ball was upon them, Kate couldn't decide which one to wear and was leaving the decision to Digby. Fortunately for her, if there was a man who knew the drape and cut of a gown, it was Digby.

In truth, Kate was nervous. When Benoit had told her the Prince of Wales had bought her — *bought* her, he'd said, as if she were a bolt of cloth — she'd grown quite ill with worry. Not that she had any particular attachment to Benoit, or that she was even surprised. She was very much aware of her place in the world and how women like her made their way in it. Nevertheless, she loathed that she was a courtesan for many reasons, and one of them was that she was out of practice in the private arts of being a courtesan.

Benoit had seen to it that she learned those arts. He wanted her as his kept lover, but as Kate didn't know how to be that, he'd sent her to Madame Albert in Paris. Madame taught her certain skills, which she'd practiced on Benoit, and he'd been an eager participant in the beginning. But he'd become increasingly enchanted with laudanum, and in the last three or so years of their association, Kate had been summoned only occasionally to his bed. Benoit came to prefer laudanum to coupling. Most nights, he put himself to sleep with the drug.

His growing inability to couple was something for which Kate was privately thankful. She did not, and had never, possessed any amorous feelings for the man. The kindest thing she could say for him was that he was a benevolent master, but she never mistook the true nature of their liaison — he was her master and she his slave. The times they had come together had been physically uncomfortable for her and lacking in any sort of affection. The plays she'd seen, the operas she'd heard, and the poetry Digby had read to her had taught her what she knew of passion and love. There was none of it between her and Benoit.

Besides the sea captain who had robbed Kate of her virtue, there had been only Benoit.

Nevertheless, the arrangement with Benoit had tangible benefits for Kate — namely a roof over her head and food in her belly — and she had been as content with it as a woman in her position could be.

But then Benoit had privately presented Kate to the prince after the opera one evening. She'd responded politely to his inquiry of how she found the opera and had commented on the particularly wet weather. That was the sum of their meeting, but soon thereafter, Benoit informed Kate that the prince wanted her.

The Prince of Wales wanted *her*.

The very notion had sent Kate into a panic. He wanted her for all the obvious reasons. What if she couldn't please him? What would happen to her then? Would he toss her back to the streets? Would he hand her off to one of his friends? What sorts of lewd acts might he expect of her? What if he got her with child? Would she lose her appeal then? Would he provide for the child?

Her worries had kept her up more than one night, but then, as suddenly as the news of the prince's interest in her had come, she'd been given a reprieve. On the night Benoit had had her trunks moved to her new town house and had said his fare-thee-wells (which, Kate noted, was not unlike a farewell he might have given any one of his many servants), he had told her about the prince's unique situation.

"Make good use of these days, for he'll not come to you," Benoit had said cryptically.

"Pardon?"

"He'll not take a mistress at present, given

the possibility of a parliamentary trial of divorce. He won't have the likes of you dragged before Parliament to embarrass him. But as soon as his scandal is resolved, he will make you his mistress in more than name." Benoit had chuckled at that.

Kate had swallowed down a lump of fear. "His scandal?"

"*Mon dieu,* do you not read the morning papers?" Benoit had asked irritably. "Be thankful he has provided for your needs, Kate. Most gentlemen would not be so generous with water if the tree has never born fruit."

Kate didn't know what he meant, precisely, for how could a tree bear fruit without water? Digby had explained it to her later. He'd also explained that her new home was part of the contract between the prince and Benoit. Although Benoit treated Kate indifferently, he'd seen to it that the prince would provide properly for her. Kate had even been given a sum of money — nothing that would keep her if the arrangement were to end — but enough to purchase food and sundries while she resided in the prince's house. She was to live quietly, to do as the prince bid her, when he bid her. She would be allowed to keep her friends — Aldous, rescued from an impressment gang on the docks, and Digby, who would remain in Benoit's employ, even though Benoit planned to return to France.

Kate's fear of failing to be the sort of courtesan the prince desired had fueled her determination to become a proficient baker, so that she might have an occupation on which to depend when her looks faded or her situation changed irrevocably.

There was only one other stipulation in the agreement between Benoit and the prince: Kate was to pretend to be the mistress of the Duke of Darlington while she waited for the prince to become disentangled from his royal marriage.

"I don't understand why I must!" Kate had complained to Digby. "I should be just as happy to hide away in this lovely house while the prince does whatever it is he must do," she'd said one afternoon. "That is what courtesans *do* — they are tucked away and kept."

"But, my love, if you hid yourself away, the prince would not *see* you. He may not have you just yet, but he may certainly feast his eyes on you."

"He might come here and feast his eyes on me," Kate had said dismissively.

"Come *here?*" Digby laughed. "Darling, if he came *here,* the whole of London would know it! He is the Prince of Wales, and his movements about town are noted by everyone! Particularly now, when everyone is looking for the slightest bit of scandal to fuel the fires."

She hadn't quite thought of it that way.

"It's really not so very bad," Digby had tried to assure her. "The duke is by all accounts a gentleman. And you are required to accompany him to only one or two engagements. Think of it as a diversion."

A diversion, indeed.

She thought of that as Amy helped her into the last gown, an ice blue silk with white fur trim.

"Perfect," Digby proclaimed when she presented herself. "You look like a winter princess."

Kate stepped back and looked at herself in the full-length mirror, at her coiffed hair and the jewels the prince had sent that glittered at her throat and ears.

"Aye, there's a beauty," Aldous said, nodding approvingly as he handed Digby a tot of whiskey. Aldous held one for himself, and took a seat in a chair near the hearth.

"*Lud,* I feel . . . anxious," Kate said as Amy straightened the train of her gown.

"Anxious?" Digby came to his feet, put aside his tot, and stood behind her, his hands on her shoulders, looking at Kate's reflection in the mirror. "There is no reason for that. Never forget — by virtue of this face," he said, gently touching her chin with his finger, "you possess the power. You shine down everyone and men cannot resist you. Am I right, Aldous?"

Aldous's gaze flicked over Kate. "Aye," he said.

Digby stepped back, picked up his tot of whiskey. "You must go and enjoy yourself. Imagine — Kate Bergeron at a Carlton House ball!"

Kate could not imagine it. Nor did she have time to try and imagine it, as the duke called for her a few minutes later.

And he called with a very insistent knock at her door.

Kate crouched down at the top of the stairs to steal a glimpse of him through the balustrade when Aldous went down to open the door. He'd hardly pulled the door open before the duke stepped into the foyer and instantly swept the hat from his head. "I have come for —"

"I'll fetch her," Aldous interrupted, and turned away. Darlington frowned at Aldous's back, but he remained standing, his hat in hand, his legs braced apart. He was wearing a greatcoat, but it was open, and beneath it, Kate could see his suit of clothing. His white silk neck cloth was perfectly tied, and a jeweled pin glittered at his throat. The collar of his shirt rose just beneath his chin, and the ruffled cuffs peaked out from the sleeves of his coat. He wore a white silk waistcoat beneath his formal coat of black tails, which hugged a trim waist.

Kate's heart started to beat a little faster. The duke cut a very fine figure. Indeed, she'd never seen quite so fine a male figure.

When Aldous reached the top of the stairs, he looked at her curiously, crouched there as she was, and Kate quickly put a finger to her lips. She stood up, smoothed her skirts, then silently turned around in a full circle and looked questioningly at Aldous. He nodded in response to her silent question and gallantly offered his arm.

All right, then, she thought. Here she was, Kate Bergeron, off to a Carlton House Ball. If only her mother could see her — she would think the faeries had really come.

Chapter Ten

Grayson was mindful not to crush his hat in his hand as was his inclination given his irritation with the impossibly rude butler Miss Bergeron saw fit to employ. He meant to say something to the man, and looked up at the sound of footfall on the stairs . . . and promptly forgot the butler.

Miss Bergeron was indescribably bewitching as she floated down those stairs on the arm of the butler. With diamonds twinkling at her throat and hanging from her ears, and wearing a blue brushed silk gown trimmed in white fur, she reminded Grayson of a figure sculpted from ice. In her pale blond hair, she wore a single white plume.

She was stunning. She belonged in a picture book, in a frame, in a grand house of her own. He couldn't help but wonder how a woman as beautiful as she was had come to be in such a position. He would think any number of gentlemen would have eagerly sought her hand.

She smiled as they reached the bottom step and let go the butler's arm as she glided forward. "Good evening, Your Grace," she said, falling into a graceful curtsy.

"Good evening, Miss Bergeron," he said as she rose up and clasped her hands before her. "How do you fare this evening?"

"Very well indeed, thank you," she said as her gaze skimmed over him. "You are . . . you are quite well put together, aren't you?"

It was an odd thing to say — Grayson was not accustomed to ladies remarking on his appearance. "I . . . thank you," he said. "And may I remark that you . . ." Lord help him, but there were no words to describe her. "Your gown is lovely, Miss Bergeron."

A slow smile curved her perfect lips. "Thank you," she said with a gracious incline of her head. "Please, sir, do call me Kate."

He didn't intend to call her anything, really, and Grayson gestured to the door. "Shall we?"

The butler appeared behind Miss Bergeron with a cloak that matched her gown — ice blue on the outside, colorfully embroidered on the inside. She fastened the cloak, then donned a pair of long gloves the butler handed her. When Miss Bergeron was properly encased in wool, she smiled at Grayson.

"Well, then! Here I am, as tightly wrapped and tucked away as a sovereign in a beggar's coat."

She had a curious way of speaking. "Allow me," he said, and opened the door. Miss Bergeron walked forward and would have walked on without him, Grayson thought, but he caught her elbow with his hand. He glanced at the butler — scowled at him, really — and escorted her out of the house.

His carriage was waiting directly in front of the house, emblazoned with his seal, plumed for the occasion. The prince's Twelfth Night Ball was legendary among the *ton*. It happened that the social Season usually commenced a month to six weeks after Twelfth Night, and all of the pillars of society were in attendance at the ball. In years past, the event had attracted upward of eight hundred people.

A footman bundled in heavy wool and a scarf opened the carriage door and put down a step. Grayson quickly handed Miss Bergeron inside before the cold could penetrate her cloak.

When he stepped in behind her, he discovered in an awkward moment that she'd seated herself on the bench facing backward. Ladies usually rode facing forward. "Would you not be more comfortable over here?" Grayson asked, half in, half out of the coach.

"No, thank you." She smiled.

Grayson slowly entered the carriage and settled onto the bench across from her.

She was studying the interior. The walls were covered in green silk, the squabs in paler green velvet. A warming pan full of hot coals provided heat. It was a very comfortable, very expensive carriage.

"This is very large, isn't it?" Miss Bergeron said. "I've not had the pleasure of traveling in a carriage as roomy as this one."

"I suspect you will soon enough," Grayson remarked as he rapped on the ceiling to signal the driver. "The prince will undoubtedly hope to impress you with the grandest of conveyances."

She glanced at him as the carriage lurched forward. "Then it will not impress me, for now I have already seen a grand one." She settled back onto her bench with a pert smile and diamonds twinkling at her throat.

"Perhaps you have already seen a grand necklace, as well, and were not impressed with my gift," he suggested.

Miss Bergeron blinked. And then she laughed.

Grayson did not laugh. He braced one hand against his thigh and leaned forward.

"Pray tell, Miss Bergeron, why did you return the necklace I sent you?"

"I did not mean to injure your feelings, Your Grace," she said with a smile.

"You did not *injure* my feelings," he said. That was preposterous. That would imply he *cared*. "But you seem to enjoy fine jewelry," he said, indicating the necklace she wore. "Why did you not keep it?"

"Because it was too lavish."

"Too lavish," he repeated, to make certain he'd heard her correctly.

"Mmm," she said, nodding, as if that were a perfectly reasonable explanation.

"Too *lavish?*" he repeated incredulously. "Madam, I can rightly say that never, in my thirty years on this earth, have I ever heard a woman complain that a piece of jewelry offered to her was too *lavish.*"

"Then they must have been your lovers. But as I am *not* your lover, I thought it too lavish."

The word *lover* whispered across his consciousness, teasing him. "That's ridiculous," he blustered. "I am a duke. I am not in the habit of giving cheap trinkets as gifts. I was merely attempting to apologize for having been rude."

"I understood your intent quite clearly," she assured him. "But the necklace seemed far too lavish for such a trifling thing, and I did not care to be beholden to you in any way."

"You would not have been beholden to me, and furthermore, you did not seem to think it was a trifling thing at the time," he reminded her.

She shrugged a little. "Perhaps not," she admitted airily. "But I am accustomed to slights and make it a point of never allowing one to undermine my happy disposition for long. It was forgotten the moment I left Whitehall." She smiled, obviously pleased with herself.

There was something in those words that gave Grayson pause. He imagined who would treat Miss Bergeron rudely — in addition to himself, obviously — and often enough that she would become accustomed to it. The *ton,* he guessed, many of whom believed themselves far superior to mere mortals by virtue of their birth and particularly to mortals such as courtesans and tradesmen and servants. Perhaps Grayson could count himself in that group, a thought that did nothing to improve *his* happy disposition.

Still, Grayson watched her closely, trying to detect any hint of feminine pique, as it seemed impossible to him that she'd returned the necklace because it was too lavish. Between three sisters and a few lovers through the years, he'd learned to make gifts of apology larger and more expensive than gifts of affection. "You did not indicate, Miss Bergeron, if you have accepted my apology."

"*Kate*. Yes, of course I accept your apology," she said. "I thought it hardly mattered if I did, other than to appease your conscience. It's not as if we shall ever be friends."

Grayson did not like his own words being tossed back at him. "On my word, my apology was honestly offered. Thank you, Miss Bergeron."

"You are most welcome, Your Grace. Now will you please call me Kate? I am anxious enough as it is without feeling as if we are utter strangers. I mean to say that we *are* strangers, as I would never presume to know you, really, but I suppose I am better acquainted with you than with anyone else I will encounter this evening."

"You are anxious?" Grayson repeated, entirely taken aback by her admission.

Her sheepish smile was surprisingly charming. "Utterly and completely."

Was she mad? She was an extraordinarily beautiful woman. She would be the most noticed, the most remarked upon, the most envied woman at the ball. "I think you have naught to fear," he said. "You seem to be quite . . . sanguine."

"Sanguine?"

"Confident," he amended.

Her pale green eyes sparkled and a small, wry smile tipped up one corner of her mouth. Grayson felt something hot sluice through his veins. "You flatter me. But it has been some time since I have been in society." Her hand fluttered a little when she said it. "You must promise that if I misstep, you will tell me straightaway. Will you promise?"

"There will hardly be need —"

"I promise not to be the least offended, if that concerns you."

He couldn't imagine her misstepping. He thought every healthy male in Carlton House would forgive her most anything. "Very well, Miss Bergeron," he said tightly.

"*Kate,* please. We are supposed to be lovers, Your Grace. A lover would not call me Miss Bergeron."

Lovers. He could feel the notion trickling warmly through him.

"May I ask, why do they call you Christie?"

He glanced at her. "My surname is Christopher. When I was quite young, before I was duke, my friends made a name of it." Grayson toyed with the idea of inviting her to use that name, but he could not bring himself to such familiarity. Kate Bergeron seemed to sense his dilemma, for she smiled knowingly at him.

That smile held him.

The carriage stopped, and Kate leaned forward to look out the window. "We've arrived."

CHAPTER ELEVEN

Kate had seen Carlton House only from a distance. Up close, she was astounded by its grandeur. She could not possibly have imagined anything like it, had she not seen it with her own eyes.

The massive columns, as tall as church steeples, framed the entrance. Benoit had once told her that the columns were modeled on the ancient architecture of Rome. As Kate had no idea what that meant, he'd tried to explain. "It is modeled to look like the Pantheon."

"Oh," she'd responded. "What is a pantheon?"

"*Mon dieu!* What an ignorant chit you are!" Benoit had snapped, then had instructed Digby to find a drawing of the Pantheon. That had taken him a bit of doing, combing through bookshops until he found one.

But it wasn't just the building or the massive columns, or the enormous chandelier she could see hanging inside, lighting the entrance with its dozens of candles. It was the people. They spilled out of fine carriages, wearing the sort of clothing over which Digby would certainly weep. They were clearly full of juice, as Aldous would say, meaning quite rich, all hurrying inside to escape the cold, hurrying past footmen who were undoubtedly freezing as they held doors open for them.

All those fine people were crowding into the receiving hall.

Kate did not feel cold when the door of the coach swung open and a footman put the step down; she felt nothing but raw nerves rising up in her belly.

Darlington put his hand on her elbow and guided her down. On the ground, he put his arm under her hand. She was aware of him, of his body so close to hers, of the strength in him. She felt oddly safe as he escorted her up the steps and across the brick entry to the main hall. Kate tried not to gawk as they stepped inside, but it was nearly impossible — she was in a palace. A *palace.*

The entrance hall alone was as large as her little house. Fireplaces graced each end and a domed ceiling, soaring two stories overhead, was crested with glass. There were columns in this room, too, on top of which were recesses built into the walls to display statuary.

A long, red carpet had been laid over the marble floor, leading into an anteroom. Two dozen or more footmen in royal livery lined both sides of the carpet, taking cloaks. Kate handed her cloak to a waiting footman; he bowed deeply before turning around and walking briskly away. Another footman instantly took his place.

"There must be five hundred souls gathered here," Kate remarked as she looked around at the crush.

"I would guess it to be closer to eight hundred," Darlington responded. "The season-ending ball is usually twice as large."

Kate must have looked as surprised as she felt — *sixteen hundred people at one ball?* — for Darlington smiled down at her. For the first time since they'd met, he actually smiled, and the warmth in it startled her. It spread all the way up to his eyes, crinkling them at the corners, making them shine. It transformed his face; he didn't seem quite so stern and distant when he smiled. He looked almost kind.

Kate was not allowed to admire his lovely smile, however, for she felt a tap on her shoulder and turned to see Lord Perryton. Kate knew the gentleman from Benoit's card games, which Perryton had often attended in the company of his mistress, Mrs. Franklin.

He was seemingly alone tonight and smiled hungrily at Kate. "Miss Bergeron, what a pleasure to see you here. Where is Monsieur Cousineau? I've so rarely seen him without you — or you without him."

"Monsieur Cousineau is in France, my lord."

"For very long?" Perryton asked, his gaze drifting down her body.

"Perryton, how do you do," Darlington interjected, moving to stand slightly before Kate.

Perryton looked at Darlington with some surprise. "Your Grace. I had no —"

"Pardon us," Darlington said abruptly, and with his hand on the small of Kate's back, he moved her away from Perryton, into the stream of people moving into the ballroom. "He was rather too eager," he said bluntly.

Kate snorted at that. "He is an eager man in more ways than one."

"Pardon?" Darlington asked.

She smiled wryly. "He has unusual tastes," she said. Mrs. Franklin had told her of Perryton's predilection for being spanked in the course of their relations. At Darlington's blank look, Kate said, "He is an eager student when his headmistress demands it, if

122

you take my meaning."

Darlington blinked. His gaze slipped to her mouth for a moment. He looked as if he meant to speak, but they were once again interrupted by a gentleman who knew Darlington, but couldn't take his eyes off Kate. As Darlington made no move to introduce her, Kate turned away from the two men and took in the crowd. Several men looked in her direction, she noticed. So did several women.

She started at the feel of Darlington's hand on her back again. "The prince," he said. Kate followed his gaze and saw the Prince of Wales standing inside the anteroom.

If she'd not previously made his acquaintance she would believe he was the king himself, so adorned was he. He wore a red sash diagonally across his chest, anchored by a large embroidered crest of some sort at his waist. More jeweled emblems crowded his chest. His light brown hair was coiffed and curled, and his neck cloth — black, which stood in stark contrast to the white every other man wore — was wrapped around his neck, resting just beneath his chin. He was impeccably dressed, but his coat strained across his rotund abdomen. He was a heavy man, but at the age of five and forty, as Digby swore he was, he was nonetheless a handsome man.

He was very well aware of it, too, Kate thought as they inched toward him. His demeanor was superior to every guest who walked through the anteroom to the ballroom. The greeting entailed the prince putting out his hand as if it were a gift, and the guest kissing his ring.

But when Kate and Darlington reached him, the prince's demeanor changed; he smiled broadly at Kate and never looked at the duke.

"Your Highness, may I present Miss Katharine Bergeron," Darlington said.

Kate sank to the floor in a curtsy, her head bowed.

"What a treasure you have brought tonight, Christie," the prince said, and put out his hand, palm up. Kate slipped her hand into it. The prince drew her up and her hand to his lips, his eyes on hers as he kissed her gloved knuckles, lingering there a moment. "It is my great pleasure to make your acquaintance again, Miss Bergeron."

"Thank you, Your Highness," Kate said.

"Christie, you must not keep her to yourself all night," the prince said jovially. "I should like to put my name on her dance card if you'll allow it."

"Of course. You must have the dance of your choosing, sir."

Neither gentleman appeared to think Kate had much of a say in the matter. She glanced down at her hand, which the prince still held. She was aware that everyone who could see them had noticed his attention to her. The prince must have realized it, too, for he squeezed her fingers tightly, and gave her a meaningful look as he released her hand.

"You'll stand up with an old man, will you, Miss Bergeron?" he asked lightly.

"If you wish, Your Highness, but I had hoped to stand up with you," she said.

The prince laughed and looked around at his entourage, who quickly joined in the laughter. "It will be my pleasure, madam. You'll find me, won't you, Christie?"

Darlington assured him he would and led Kate onward, through the throng. "There, then, that should make you happy," he said as they entered the ballroom. "Your assignation is all but arranged."

Kate shot him a look, but the duke seemed not to notice.

The ballroom was breathtaking. A mural covered the ceiling from which no less than six chandeliers hung, all of them holding what seemed like dozens of candles. On one side of the room were three roaring hearths. Across from the hearths were arched windows that rose two stories tall. Between them, mirrors that were almost as large reflected the light, making the ballroom seem even larger and brighter than it actually was.

It had been decorated in a winter theme. There were extravagant papier-mâché sculptures in the corners of the room, carved into the shapes of winter landscapes. In addition to the chandeliers, dozens and dozens of crystal icicles were suspended from the ceiling, and the footmen were dressed all in white. There was a time when Kate thought Benoit had more money than the king, but this went far beyond anything she could ever imagine.

"Champagne?" Darlington asked, taking a pair of crystal flutes from a passing footman and handing one to her. Their fingers brushed; Kate felt a strange tingle. *Stop, Kate,* she silently chastised herself. He was a handsome man, but she really suspected that was all that could be said for him.

She sipped the champagne — it was of excellent quality. She sipped again and noticed Darlington looking at her. He'd hardly sipped from his —

"Christie!"

Darlington winced before he turned to greet a tall, comely man. "Lindsey, what are you doing here?" Darlington asked, extending his hand. "I thought you were at East-church Abbey."

"I was — I *am.* I've only come to town for the week to hire a proper carpenter," he said, his gaze sliding to Kate.

"A carpenter?"

The gentleman smiled broadly. "We are in the rather long and laborious process of re-designing the nursery." He turned that smile to Kate. "I beg your pardon, madam."

"Ah," Darlington said uneasily. "Miss Bergeron, may I present the Earl of Lindsey, Nathan Grey. Lindsey, Miss Katharine Bergeron."

"My lord," Kate said, bobbing a quick curtsy.

The earl said nothing for a moment. He glanced curiously at Darlington. When Darlington offered nothing more, he looked again at Kate and smiled. "The pleasure is mine, Miss Bergeron," he said, bowing his head. "Most certainly mine."

Kate smiled with amusement. "Thank you, my lord." She was aware of heads turning toward them, of ladies looking curiously over the tops of their fans at her, of gentlemen eyeing her appreciatively.

Darlington was aware of Lindsey's curiosity, it seemed. "When do you return to East-church?" he asked Lindsey, stepping ever so slightly away from Kate and drawing Lindsey's gaze from her. Kate felt herself color now; she realized he was ashamed of being seen with her.

"After the master carpenter has extracted a promise of a princely sum from me," Lindsey said happily. "Evie is at the abbey, and I can't bear to be away from her just now."

"No, of course not," Darlington said. An awkward moment passed. "Any word from Lambourne?" Darlington asked.

Lindsey laughed and looked at Kate again, his eyes darting the length of her. "The lad is safely tucked away in Scotland for the foreseeable future. What of Donnelly?"

Darlington shook his head. "He remains in Ireland. I've not had a proper word from him in a month."

Lindsey nodded and smiled at Kate. "I beg your pardon, Miss Bergeron, but you seem rather familiar to me."

"Do I?" she asked smoothly, and wondered if his wife had purchased cloth from Benoit. "I can't imagine where we might have met, my lord."

"Let us think on it, and perhaps we shall recall that splendid occasion," Lindsey said, shifting closer to her.

"Ah, I see the musicians are entering the stage. The first dance will begin shortly," Darlington said.

Lindsey gave him a quick, impatient look. "You wouldn't be attempting to keep a rose from me in the midst of so many thorns, would you, old friend?" he asked and turned his attention to Kate again. "Is it possible I had the pleasure of meeting Miss Bergeron at Darlington House?"

Kate couldn't help but laugh at that impossibility. "No, my lord. I've not had the pleasure of dining at Darlington House."

Darlington clasped his hands behind his back and looked at the dance floor.

"No?" Lindsey asked, seeming surprised by that. "I am certain His Grace will remedy that straightaway. Where, then, did you meet our sullen friend?" Lindsey asked, smiling at Darlington.

"We met at a musical recital," Kate offered, and smiled at Darlington.

"A *recital?*" Lindsey repeated disbelievingly.

"Mmm. A musical performance. It was the work of Beethoven," she continued blithely. "A very moving piece, really, would you not agree, Your Grace?"

His gaze narrowed a bit. "It was adequately played."

"Adequately! Sir, the music was beautifully played — it brought to mind courtly love." She smiled sweetly at him.

Darlington frowned, but Lindsey smiled broadly. "Do tell, Miss Bergeron."

"Music always makes me think of love," Kate said. "Especially opera. What do *you* think of when you hear music, Your Grace?"

"I think of how much longer I shall be forced to endure it," he said bluntly. "The prince should open the dance shortly, I should think."

"Well then," Lindsey said, clapping his hand on Darlington's shoulder. "Far be it from me to keep you two from the pleasure of the first dance."

Darlington glared at Lindsey, but the earl ignored him and grinned at Kate. "Again, it has been my extraordinary pleasure, Miss Bergeron. I do hope you enjoy the ball."

"Thank you," Kate said.

"Now, if you will pardon me, I see my cousin and must speak to him."

Kate nodded. She held her champagne flute between her fingers and let it swing loosely as she watched Lindsey stroll away. When he'd gone, she thrust the empty flute at Darlington.

He attempted to take it, but Kate would not let it go. "I realize you are ashamed of me, but must you appear so wretchedly un-happy?"

"That's absurd," he said and dislodged

the flute from her grip. He handed it off instantly to a passing footman, along with his glass, still half full. "I have done nothing for which I should be ashamed," he said, putting his hand on her elbow and directing her to one side.

"Please! You were clearly ashamed when your friend understood you had accompanied me here."

He looked at her incredulously. "Did you expect that I would rejoice in our association and boast of it to my friends?" he quietly demanded. "I treated you cordially."

"*Cordially?* You were appalled!"

"*Appalled?*" His dark blue gaze ran down her body, then up again, lingering on her bosom, then on her mouth. "I am not appalled by you, Kate. Frankly, I think you are one of the most beautiful women I have ever had the good grace to see."

She could scarcely refrain from rolling her eyes at that. If there was one man who was immune to her looks, it was *this* one.

"But I am appalled by this ghastly situation."

"Well then," she said impatiently. "I am quite clear now."

"Good," he said, and his gaze, that dark blue, ocean deep gaze, slowly slid from her eyes to her lips once more.

"Good," she snapped. Perhaps Kate was the one who was doing the looking, for she was suddenly very aware of him, of his height, of the intricate knot of his neck cloth, the fine fit of his coat across his shoulders. His thick brown hair. His jaw, clean-shaven and square. Something warm began to flow in Kate as they stood there glaring at one another, something so warm that, ironically, it made her shiver.

Their gazes remained locked on each other for a moment or two, but then someone jostled Kate, and she inadvertently looked to her right — and was instantly captivated by the procession of the prince onto the dance floor. On his arm was a girl about ten years of age in a glittering gold gown. They stood in the middle of the cleared dance floor, facing each other.

"Who is she?" Kate asked.

"The Princess Charlotte," Darlington said. "His daughter."

Trumpets sounded, and children — very small children, all dressed in winter costumes trimmed in white fur — ran from a corner of the room onto the dance floor, and lined up on either side of the prince and his daughter. The music began, and as the prince and his daughter began to dance, the children who joined them began to dance as well with snow falling from above.

Kate gasped with delight — it was magnificent! The children danced perfectly in the imitation snow, mirroring the sure-footed prince and the budding grace of the princess. It was quite a show, and when the music ended, the children scampered off the dance floor, the snow stopped falling, and the guests began to crowd onto the floor for the next set.

Kate stood there beside Darlington, expecting him to ask her to dance, and feeling a bit awkward when he did not. People were looking at them.

"Kate?"

Startled, Kate looked away from the dance floor to the man who had spoken to her. She smiled when she saw Mr. Sampson, another of Benoit's gaming partners. She'd always liked him; he was quiet and kind. Even now, he glanced at Darlington and said softly, "I'd heard you'd left Cousineau. The poor man must be despondent."

"Oh, he's quite all right," Kate said laughingly.

"Mr. Sampson! Do you intend to dance with your wife?" a dark-headed woman suddenly demanded. She looped her arm through Mr. Sampson's.

"Of course, darling," he said, and smiled

apologetically at Kate. "Good evening, Miss Bergeron."

"Mr. Sampson," she said, and watched his wife pull him away from her.

"An acquaintance of yours?" Darlington drawled.

She looked at him sidelong. "Not precisely."

"Aha."

"Don't smile so smugly, sir — he was a friend of my former benefactor. Not a lover."

Darlington looked skeptical, but yet another of his acquaintances had approached them.

"Good evening, Christie!"

Darlington sighed. "Good evening, Thomas." He glanced at Kate. "May I introduce Mr. Thomas Black," he said. "Mr. Black, Miss Bergeron."

He bowed his head. "It is a great pleasure, madam. Have you a space on your dance card, Miss —"

"She does not," Darlington said, and suddenly took her hand. "If you will excuse us," he said, and suddenly pulled Kate to the dance floor.

"Well! After such a kind invitation, I am delighted to stand up with you," Kate said.

"Had I known I would be required to parade about a dance floor, I would have never agreed to this ridiculous ruse." He put her hand on his arm. "But Mr. Black was practically salivating on your décolletage as it was."

"Your flattery is overwhelming me." Kate smiled serenely at him.

Darlington covered her hand with his and squeezed it lightly. "You may think that smile will charm me, madam, but you are quite mistaken."

"Please endeavor not to be *quite* so gallant, sir, for I may swoon."

A soft smile of amusement lit his face. "I beg of you, Kate, please do not swoon, for if I am forced to revive you, that will derail all my attempts to deny our acquaintance."

Kate blinked with surprise. "I beg your pardon, but was that a flash of humor, Your Grace?" she asked gaily. "I scarcely recognized it coming from you." With a laugh, she turned to join the dance queue.

CHAPTER TWELVE

If there was one thing Grayson despised more than opera, it was dancing. It was almost impossible for him, what with his inability to hear music properly. He so rarely danced, in fact, that he had to endure several looks of stark astonishment from acquaintances as he led Kate onto the dance floor and took his place in the dancer's queue across from her.

He could just imagine the titillation that would spread like a scourge in salons across Mayfair on the morrow. The Duke of Darlington, so famously close-guarded, so famously opposed to dancing, had not only come to the Twelfth Night Ball in the company of a renowned courtesan, he had bloody well kicked up his heels and danced with the grace of a milk cow. He wasn't even certain why he was *doing* it; he could very well have passed her off to someone other than Black. But there was something provocative in Kate's bright smile, something from which he could not back down.

Bloody hell, he hoped he remembered the figures; it had been so long since he'd attempted to dance.

As the music started and the ladies curtsied and the men bowed, Grayson could at least be thankful that Diana was not here to see this. Lord Eustis had come to town unexpectedly, and Eustis did not suffer fools lightly — which meant he did not care for George's tendency to excess. He had refused the invitation to the ball on behalf of him and Diana both.

Diana had been distraught, of course, but Grayson had been relieved. Seeing Kate tonight — as she took her steps toward Grayson to curtsy, then skip back again — would have sparked quite a lot of trouble with Diana.

The men went next, including Grayson, who felt stiff and foolish, his feet confused by the tinny music that fell on his ears. He moved forward, he bowed; he somehow made it back to his place.

Whatever he had done, Kate looked surprised. She stepped forward and up on her toes, twirling around his back, then going down on her heels as she walked back to her place. When Grayson took his turn around her, Kate's expression turned from surprise to amusement.

They next met in the middle to lock arms and turn together — in the direction Kate tugged him, actually, as Grayson started off on the wrong foot. They turned twice, returned to their places, and joined hands above their heads as a couple danced down the two rows of dancers. Then they proceeded to repeat the steps.

As Kate danced around him, her smile lighting the entire dance floor, she said, "You might have mentioned you are a horrible dancer." With a laugh, she skipped back to her place.

"How kind," he said as he took his turn around her.

"Did you think I would rejoice in your two left feet?" Kate teased him as they met in the middle and twirled one way, then the other. "I would *never* have agreed to this arrangement had I known!" They stepped back and joined hands above their heads.

"Perhaps I should have mentioned that my lack of dancing skill is the unfortunate result of being quite tone-deaf," he said before letting her go and stepping into place.

Across from him, Kate blinked. She skipped forward. "Tone-deaf," she repeated. "What is that?" She skipped back.

Grayson moved forward. "It means one cannot hear music."

Her smile faded. She looked at him differently now, and Grayson suddenly felt very annoyed and vulnerable. It was obvious that this courtesan felt pity for him. For *him.*

She didn't say anything else until the dance was over, but continued to smile and dance lightly on her feet. She was an excellent dancer, in truth. Grayson envied her ability to move as elegantly as she did. But he was eternally thankful when the music ended, and quickly bowed, then held out his hand for her.

Kate slipped her hand into his and as he guided her off the dance floor, she asked bluntly, "Why can't you hear music?"

"I don't know," he admitted. "I only know that I can't hear music as you can, nor can I follow but the simplest steps, obviously," he said with an apologetic smile. "Music sounds like a lot of noise with no rhyme or reason to me."

"I've never known anyone who can't hear music," she said, looking at him curiously with vivid green eyes. "It must be rather unsettling to see people enjoying music and not be able to hear what they are hearing."

He thought that rather astute of her. "Yes, indeed it is." Friends and family who knew of his affliction were convinced that he *could* hear music if only he would listen properly. But there was nothing Grayson could do to make sense of it. As a lad, he'd gone through one music instructor after another until his father had given up in frustration.

Kate suddenly smiled. "Honestly, I don't know if I am more surprised to learn of such an unusual affliction, or that you actually have a slight imperfection."

He lifted a brow.

"Slight," she emphasized, "but an imperfection nonetheless."

She was teasing him. "Then you have discovered my secret," he said. "In spite of all appearances to the contrary, I am merely a man."

A slow, sensual smile curved her lips. "And a very interesting man at that," she said. She gave his hand a slight tug. Grayson realized he was still holding hers. Her smile seemed to deepen, and Grayson detected a bit of supposition in it, as if she expected him to hold her hand. As if she expected him to fall victim to her charms.

Granted, her considerable charms would be difficult for most men to deny. But he was not most men and he dropped her hand. "Perhaps we should repair to the —"

"Your Grace, there you are!"

He swallowed down the niggle of annoyance George's voice caused in him. He turned slightly; a path had cleared behind him, guests curtsying and bowing as the prince and his entourage made their way to him and Kate. Grayson dutifully stood back and bowed, too.

"Are you enjoying the ball, Miss Bergeron?" George asked, his gaze roaming her.

"It is divine, Your Highness."

"I don't suppose I might entice you away from Darlington for a dance?"

She gave the prince a brilliant, heart-warming smile. Perhaps she esteemed him, Grayson thought. She wouldn't be the first woman to do so. "I could not possibly be more delighted, Your Highness."

"You won't mind, will you, Christie?" George asked, his arm already extended to Kate.

"Of course not." Grayson watched Kate put her hand on George's arm, watched George cover it with his thick hand and lead Kate to the dance floor.

As they lined up for the next dance, Grayson watched the prince's ravenous gaze boldly take Kate in as if she were a turkey leg.

Kate smiled and said something to make the prince laugh.

141

"Your Grace!"

God grant him patience; Grayson was certainly going to need it now. That voice belonged to one of his mother's closest friends, the dowager Lady Babington, and she was presently eyeing Grayson through her lorgnette. She was wearing a purple gown, which, given her generous bosom, made her look a bit like a giant plum. She was in the company of Miss Francesca Boudine, who Grayson knew was hoping for a match with Lady Babington's son, if Prudence could be believed.

"Lady Babington," he said, inclining his head. "Miss Boudine. How do you do?"

Miss Boudine curtsied; Lady Babington did not. "I am doing quite well, thank you!" Lady Babington boomed, and lifted her lorgnette, peering closely at him. "How do *you* fare, Your Grace?"

"Very well. Thank you."

Lady Babington fancied herself the reigning matriarch of the *ton* and never missed an event. Though she was rich as Croesus, she never managed to *host* a society event, but she was always available to attend. Somehow, she thought it was her duty to keep her many, *many* acquaintances abreast of everything she saw and heard. Prudence swore Lady Babington was the source of many of the *on dits* in the society pages of *The Times*.

"You will make me a very happy woman indeed if you tell me that you've escorted your dear mother to the ball," she said, lowering her lorgnette, apparently satisfied with Grayson's appearance.

"Regrettably, I have not. She doesn't care for the late hours of balls."

"Yes, they do go very late. You will give her my regards —"

"I'd be delighted to do so. Miss Boudine," Grayson said, trying to make a clean escape, but Lady Babington was too quick for him.

"Then have you come alone, Your Grace, or have you brought along your darling sisters?" she asked loudly.

"Alone." He nodded again, tried to turn away again.

"But did I not see you dancing, Your Grace?" Lady Babington asked in an incredulous voice.

The woman was a worthy adversary.

"I saw you dancing," she continued before he could answer. "I remarked it immediately, for I said to Miss Boudine, 'I cannot recall the last time I saw Darlington stand up,' to which she said, 'He rarely stands up with any lady,' which I thought passing strange for surely I've seen you dance, have I not? But upon further reflection Miss Boudine and I agree — you so *rarely* dance!"

Miss Boudine's pale white face was suddenly flushed; she looked down at her feet.

"I danced this evening, yes," Grayson said shortly.

"Who was she?" Lady Babington asked.

Her effrontery astonished Grayson. "Who?"

"The lady you stood up with!"

"She was . . . a lady." Grayson made the mistake of looking back to the dance floor. He spotted Kate instantly — the ice blue of her gown stood out, as did her pale blonde hair. She appeared to be enjoying herself.

Lady Babington raised her lorgnette and followed his gaze to the dance floor. The woman was unconscionably bold, and Grayson couldn't help but wonder if he had even a prayer of keeping this from Diana. But as he was a betting man, he would have to bet not.

"If your curiosity about my dancing has been gratified, ladies, please excuse me. I am wanted in the gaming room." He moved this time, unwilling to let Lady Babington detain him further.

It was quite a bit of work making his way across the room. The throng was very thick, and many of his acquaintances stopped him to express their good wishes for a new year.

When he'd put enough distance between himself and the troublesome Lady Babington, he risked a look at the dance floor.

Kate was nowhere to be seen. Neither was the prince. Grayson guessed that he'd whisked her away for a private tête-à-tête. That was, after all, the reason they were here, wasn't it?

Grayson walked on to the gaming room.

CHAPTER THIRTEEN

The prince was an excellent dancer, and as long as Kate politely looked the other way whilst he looked at her bosom, she was very happy to dance with him.

When the dance concluded, however, her enjoyment of him diminished dramatically when he escorted her from the dance floor to an area to the side of the musicians. "I find it unbearable to be so close to you as this and not touch you, *ma petite,*" he said softly. "Do you see that door there?"

Kate looked in the direction he indicated. It was a rather dark corner, really, which seemed odd to her, given how well lit the ballroom was.

"Behind the footman," he said impatiently.

She saw it then — it was almost hidden, a door that was made to look like part of the wall. She nodded.

"Go there and wait. I'll join you in a few

minutes." He turned on his heel and walked away from her.

Kate looked suspiciously at the door and slowly walked to it. The footman didn't look at her, but kept his gaze straight ahead. With a quick look behind her, Kate pushed the door open and walked into a small room where linens were neatly folded and stacked on shelves almost to the ceiling. Another open door led into a hallway, which provided a bit of light. Kate could hear laughter and voices drifting down the corridor and peeked out — a few doors down, she saw a man and a woman emerge from a room; another gentleman passed them and went in. The gaming room, she guessed.

She looked around the linen closet impatiently. How long would she be made to wait? It was dark and close. After what seemed an eternity, she determined she did not like waiting in this room like a whore and in a moment of disgust stepped out, just as the prince was striding down the corridor toward her.

He smiled and pointed at the linen closet. "Inside, inside — be quick!" he whispered, and ushered her back inside. "Kate," he said, his hands going to her shoulders, caressing her arms as his gaze greedily roamed over her. "Have you any idea how beautiful you are?" he whispered as he pulled her into his embrace.

He kissed her neck, her décolletage. "Are you as eager as I am for this accursed situation with the princess Caroline to be at an end?"

"More," she whispered, and ran her fingers lightly down his spine.

The prince drew an uneven breath and ran his hands over her breasts. Kate arched her back and pressed herself against him as she kissed his brow. His grip on her breasts tightened. She hoped he did not intend to couple with her here, where she would undoubtedly be pushed up against the wall, as if they were standing in an alley.

"I cannot bear the wait," he said breathlessly, and kissed her on the mouth. She returned his kiss with a show of ardor. It would not do to risk his displeasure in any way, no matter if she were forced to engage in relations in this linen closet.

The prince moved to the flesh above her bodice; Kate looked heavenward and stroked his head as his mouth moved on her skin. But then he straightened and, grinning, cupped her face. "Christie is the perfect accomplice, is he not?" he asked. "He's a stiff collar, that one, far too concerned about propriety and decorum to be brought low by you."

Kate suppressed a small gasp of indignation and turned her head from the prince's seeking mouth. "Do you not fear I shall bring *you* low, Your Highness?" she asked sweetly.

He chuckled lustily. "You will bring me low enough," he said, and shifted her about, so that she was pressed up against the shelves. Linens fell, knocking the door open a little farther. He groped for the hem of her gown and pushed it up, over her knee. Kate obliged him by wrapping a leg around his waist.

"Ah, Kate," he said. "What a treasure you are." She smiled and caressed his shoulders. He began to stroke the skin of her thigh, and Kate was not unmoved by it. She could feel her body warming, and she was resigned to what would come. Leaning her head back, she closed her eyes as his fingers sought her warmth.

"Your Highness."

Darlington's voice startled Kate badly, and the prince, too. "Your intrusion is not appreciated, Christie," he snapped.

Kate looked at Darlington, and he met her gaze. Even in the dim light, she could see the way he looked at her and the prince's hand buried beneath her skirts. "I beg your pardon, Your Highness, but more than one of your guests has seen you enter this closet and has remarked on it. Have a care."

Kate held his gaze, wondering what he thought.

"You wouldn't want to be discovered here," Darlington added softly. "One never knows who is looking."

The prince sighed and lifted his head. "He's right," he said apologetically to Kate, as if she had instigated this assignation. "That bitch has spies everywhere. She'd have it all over London by the morrow." He stroked Kate's cheek, then leaned down and kissed her aggressively.

When he lifted his head, he ran this thumb along her bottom lip. "Ah, Kate, beautiful Kate . . . this situation cannot go on for long, you have my word. I have sent a letter to the king and I believe that even as we stand here, he is determining what course we shall seek to end this scandal once and for all. I expect a tolerable resolution is forthcoming, so I ask for your patience a little longer."

Kate smiled softly; the prince groaned and kissed her once more.

"Be very good, *ma petite,* and you and I shall be together soon." He stepped back and looked at Darlington. "I leave her to you, Christie," he said, and yanked on the ends of his waistcoat.

He walked out, leaving Kate standing in

the closet, Darlington outside. He didn't look at her, but watched the prince. A moment later, he said, "He's gone."

Kate smoothed her skirt and adjusted her bodice. "I should like a retiring room. Will you show me where I can find one?"

Darlington turned his head to look at her, his gaze flicking quickly over her body. His eyes were full of . . . of what, concern? Pity? She expected to see disdain, but there was none in his expression.

"Kate —"

"The retiring room?" she asked again. "Please," she added softly.

"This way," he said, and put his hand to her elbow to draw her out of the closet.

In the retiring room, Kate took her time regaining her composure. When she felt sufficiently calmed, she splashed water on her face, and looked at herself in the mirror. "All right, then," she muttered. What was done was done. It was no secret who she was, particularly not to Darlington. So when she was certain she looked presentable, she walked out.

She'd assumed that Darlington would be waiting for her, but she didn't see him. If he was there, she missed him as she got caught up in a stream of ladies coming and going from the retiring room, and was swept along a corridor.

The crowd had become quite lively, with all of the champagne being proffered by footmen and whiskey that seemed to flow from the sap taps of snow-flocked spruce trees set up in every corner. Kate still saw no sign of Darlington, but then again, it was not unlike trying to find someone on the quays — the sea of humanity made it impossible.

She found herself in the ballroom once more. Some of the men eyed her lewdly, particularly a group of young bucks who were well on their way to falling into their cups. Kate saw other men she'd met over the years. Perhaps it was her imagination, but it seemed to Kate as if everyone in that crowded ballroom knew the sort of woman she was. Madame Albert had told her that would happen, reminded her more than once, "No one will mistake the woman all men desire and all women envy."

"Pardon." The man who put himself in Kate's path was Mr. Black.

Kate curtsied. "I beg your pardon, sir —"

"Madam," he said, "if your dance card is not yet full, I should like to request the pleasure of a dance."

"Ah . . ." Kate glanced around. People were watching. *Where was Darlington?* She might not be of this aristocratic, but she wasn't exactly a sheltered debutante, either. "I should find my escort —"

"His Grace is in the gaming room," Mr. Black said.

Kate looked at him, her eyes narrowing slightly.

"Miss Bergeron, I deserve the look of suspicion you are directing at me, but I have been an admirer of yours for very long, and while I cannot hope to entice you to share your lovely affections with me, I would be delighted to dance the next set with you, if you would be so kind."

Kate did like to dance. And she appreciated the man's honesty. She smiled at Mr. Black. "Thank you, my lord. It would be my pleasure," she said, and took the hand he offered.

Grayson had waited outside the retiring rooms as long as he thought proper — considering that he had no notion of what was proper in this circumstance.

What *was* this circumstance, for God's sake? He was not in the habit of interrupting lovers, but he didn't know what to make of this arrangement, really. George had forced Grayson to give his word that he'd not allow rumors of Kate's association with the prince to abound, yet then the prince himself had stepped into that linen closet with her in full view of his guests.

Grayson hadn't known quite what to do. He hadn't wanted to interrupt, but when two gentlemen began to jest about the prince relieving himself, he'd felt compelled to do it.

Now, the image of Kate's shapely leg, the flush of her skin, and the prince's hands on her were burned in his mind's eye. That, and the detached way she'd looked at him. What had he expected, to find them holding hands?

He could not erase that image. He wanted to see her again, to look into those green eyes once more. To see what, he didn't know.

But when he thought he'd stood outside the retiring room so long that it was starting to seem odd, he returned to the gaming rooms.

He had no luck there and finally made his way to the ballroom once more. He spotted Kate dancing with Black and sighed irritably. George despised Thomas Black, as did Grayson. Grayson noticed a group of young lords watching her, as well. They were scarcely of age, eager to prove themselves men in the usual ways: drinking, fighting, and whoring.

Grayson found that thought vaguely disquieting.

He helped himself to champagne and chatted with Lady Wilkinson.

When the dance concluded, Kate accepted the invitation of a gentleman he did not know. As she continued to dance, her smile never faltered and her energy seemed boundless.

Grayson didn't see all of her dances, for he had many acquaintances in attendance, and he lost sight of her from time to time when he was engrossed in conversation. But when the supper hour approached, and drunken guests began to make their way to the dining hall, Grayson spotted Kate once more. This time, she was sitting alone on a blue chair. The seats on either side of her were empty. He made his way across the room to her.

She looked up as he approached her. A warm smile lit her face, and Grayson felt it trickle all the way through him.

"May I?" he asked, gesturing to a chair.

"I'll be quite cross if you don't," she said.

He smiled and flipped his tails, sitting beside her. The two of them stared at the crowd around them for a moment. "How have you found the evening?" he asked.

"Oh, but I am exhausted!" she said lightly. "I've danced all night and I am typically in bed by now."

He glanced at her. "So early?"

"Early! It is very late, sir! I must be up

every morning with the sun's light, as I have very many things to do."

An elderly couple standing across the way was looking at them. The lady said something to her husband and then turned her back. The gentleman's gaze lingered on Kate, but then he, too, turned away.

Kate had seen them, too; she smiled ruefully at Grayson. "Would you be terribly disappointed if we retired from the ball?" she asked. "My feet are aching!"

She had to be the first young woman in London to want to quit a royal ball early, but Grayson was glad of it. "Would you like to dine before we take our leave?"

"Oh." She put a hand to an earring and played with it. Grayson had the sense she was trying to think her way out of supper. "I am so weary I could scarcely eat a bite . . . but perhaps we might have a pastry or two."

"Of course. What is a meeting between us without a pastry or two?" he asked, and smiled.

A sparkle flashed in her lovely eyes. "Laugh if you will, but I happen to enjoy them, and I am suspicious of a man who is so determined to avoid them."

"That is not at all true," he said as her rose up and offered his hand to her. "I do enjoy a sweetmeat on occasion."

She slipped her hand into his. "Then perhaps you were in a foul mood when you had the opportunity to sample mine."

"And you were decidedly flippant," he said as he put her hand on his arm. "I should have complained to the prince straightaway."

"And what might your complaint have been? Your Highness, Miss Bergeron must be drawn by a team of four into this ridiculous arrangement of yours, whereas *I* am *most* determined to be as difficult as I can be?" Kate laughed at her own joke. "You really should have tried one of my muffins, Your Grace. I believe you would have found your disposition remarkably improved."

"Mmm," he said skeptically, looking down at her.

"*Mmm,* indeed," she retorted, smiling smartly up at him.

Neither of them looked away. Her green eyes seemed to dance with amusement and Grayson was, imprudently, captivated. Aroused. Intrigued.

"How are you, sir? I hope the evening hasn't been too terribly vexing for you."

He smiled down at her. "Not too terribly."

"Well you must endure my company only once or twice more." She gave him a coquettish smile. "Do you think you will survive it?" she whispered.

"It will be a trial, but I think I might."

She laughed. "I promise to be gentle," she assured him.

He really rather hoped she wouldn't be.

CHAPTER FOURTEEN

Two days after the ball, Lord and Lady Eustis were breaking their fast at their very fashionable town home on Upper Grosvenor Street.

They were served poached eggs, dry toast, and tea, as was the case every morning Charles was in residence. When he was away, Diana had an orange and coffee, which was her preference, a fact her husband generally ignored. He thought eggs were vital to a person's constitution.

Diana thought making love with Grayson was vital to her constitution. She missed him terribly.

As Charles ate his eggs, Diana read the morning *Times*. She was riveted to the society page and the *on dits* there.

A large crowd attended the Twelfth Night Ball, celebrating the end of the Christmas Season at Carlton House.

"Diana, Hatt tells me that you have doubled the coal allotment for your girl."

"Pardon?" Diana asked, looking up from the paper.

"The coal allotment for your personal maid," Charles repeated, frowning lightly. "Hatt said you doubled it."

"Yes?"

"What have you to say for yourself?"

The man had a fortune of fifty thousand pounds, and he worried about an extra bit of coal? "She . . . she was cold, dearest."

"I suspect all the servants are a bit cold; after all, it is the heart of winter. I have instructed Hatt to return the girl's coal rations to the proper level for her position."

Diana swallowed. "Charles, please," she said. "It is such a trifling thing and it has been unusually cold this winter."

"I suppose it is a trifling thing to those who do not pay for it," he sniffed, and picked up his morning paper.

So quick to tighten the purse strings! "Perhaps . . . perhaps you might take it out of my allowance," Diana suggested uncertainly.

That brought Charles's balding head up. He peered closely at her over the tops of his spectacles. "To purchase coal for your maid?" he asked incredulously.

Diana nodded.

He studied her a moment, then shrugged. "As you wish," he said, and resumed his morning reading.

With a silent sigh of relief, so did Diana.

The supper consisted of twelve courses, including pheasant in a cranberry sauce . . .

"Have you corresponded with my sister recently?" Charles asked, drawing Diana's attention away from the review of the prince's ball.

"Elizabeth?"

Charles rolled his eyes. "Have I any other sister?"

Damn him, but he had a way of making her feel so . . . *small.* "No . . . but I had a letter from her just before Christmas."

"Yes. And she complained that she had no response from you. She kindly offered that as you are in London, you must be preoccupied with social events."

"I shall write her straightaway," Diana said.

"Please see that you do."

Diana glanced again at the paper, skimming past the ball's menu and the review of the fashionable gowns.

The dancing was commenced with HRH

the Prince of Wales taking his place with HRH the Princess Charlotte, who performed the Cotillion admirably well under a light dusting of "snow." All dances were pleasingly done. It was noted by more than one observer that Lady B——took her place across from Lord F——on three sets. Yet perhaps nothing was quite as surprising as seeing the duke of D——stand up on the second set and partner with a diamond of the first water, who is perhaps known in many salons as one who is devoted to fine fabrics and clothing. Of late, it would seem that her devotions have spread beyond fabrics. The lady partnered with other notables, such as HRH and Lord B——.

Diana did not read the rest of it. She stared blindly at the words, trying to picture it: Grayson dancing! With a *diamond of the first water.* But Grayson did not dance. He *could* not dance, not with his hearing so peculiarly affected by music.

"I think I should like to ride down to Bath and partake of the waters," Charles said as a serving girl picked up his empty plate. "My knees ache in damp weather."

Because he was an ancient specimen, Diana thought. He was fifteen years her senior, but sometimes seemed much older than that. "I am very sorry to hear it," she said.

"I should like you to accompany me," Charles added.

Diana blanched. "To Bath? Now?"

"Yes, now," he said. "There is time before the Season begins, and the weather in Bath is more pleasant than it is in London."

"Yes, darling, but there are many things that must be done before the Season begins."

"Such as?"

"Such as proper clothing and invitations —"

"My secretary can see to all that."

As if his secretary, who was even older than Charles, could see to her clothing! "How . . . how long did you have in mind?"

He cocked his head to one side and considered her. "Perhaps a week. Perhaps longer. Why do you ask? Have you something more important than fittings planned?"

"There is the Ladies' Beneficent Society tea next week. My charity work is very important to me."

Charles smiled indulgently as he reached across the table and covered her hand with his. "I think they can manage to be charitable without you, sweetheart."

How Diana managed to keep her expression calm was nothing short of a miracle.

"Do you mean to leave soon?" she asked, trying to keep the panic from her voice.

"In a few days. Your eggs are untouched, dear. Do please eat them — it would not do to waste them."

"Charles —"

"Diana, please do not argue," Charles said curtly. "It is not as if I am asking you to up and sail to France, is it? I should like to take the waters at Bath, and I should like to have my wife with me. It's all quite simple and not open to debate. Do I make myself clear?"

"Yes, darling." She had to think of something. She could not leave Grayson here now with that woman, the *diamond of the first water,* while she attended bloody Charles in bloody Bath.

Grayson's sisters were entirely too titillated by the idea that he'd danced at a ball. Mary sent him a note, apparently before the ink had dried on her copy of the *Times,* demanding he come around and give her all the details of his dance. Prudence pounced on him the moment he entered her drawing room later that afternoon to see his mother. "You *danced!*" she cried, throwing her arms wide.

"I danced," Grayson said, kissing his sister. "I have danced before. It is not as shocking as that."

"Who was she?" Prudence demanded. "I must know the identity of the mysterious lady who beguiled my brother into dancing, for *I* do not know her, of that I am sure. And the only woman I know who is devoted to her clothing is Ginny, and as she is not in London, it was obviously someone else."

"Prudence! Stop interrogating your brother!" his mother said from her seat at a small round table where she was taking tea. "It is neither here nor there who His Grace stood up with, it is nothing but gossip. Will you please go and see about your beautiful boys so that I might have a word with my son?"

Prudence sighed heavily. "Very well, Mamma." She looked at Grayson, her eyes narrowing. "But I'm not through with you, dear brother," she warned as she flounced out.

"Mother, you look very well," Grayson said.

"Of course I do! I am as fit as that young man there," the duchess said irritably as she gestured vaguely to the pair of footmen who stood against the wall. "Never mind that — will you please explain to your poor mother *why,* with all the comely, suitable young ladies in attendance at the prince's ball, you were *possessed* to stand up with a . . . a *cloth merchant's* woman and draw such attention to yourself? Do you realize what speculation is spinning around London just now? The whole of the *ton* believes you have taken that woman as your mistress!"

She had indeed heard an earful from Lady Babington, just as Grayson expected she would. "I asked her to dance, because . . ." He paused to kiss his mother's cheek. "She is very comely."

"Oh Darlington, really!" his mother said, her voice softer. "You know very well my meaning! You are a duke with a reputation to protect. And as you dance so rarely, you really must have a care *who* you stand up with. Your father never danced with anyone but family after we were married, and he was the model of decorum and restraint before we were wed. Now, everyone is talking about your dancing."

"My dancing?" Grayson smiled. "I realize my steps were deplorably bad, but I would hope there was little more than that to be said of it."

His mother smiled wryly. "Not your *dancing,* my love. The *lady* . . . if she may indeed be called a lady." She gestured to one of the footmen. "Stevens, do come and pour the duke some tea."

"No, thank you," Grayson said. "I cannot stay, Mother. I wanted only to see that you are well." He took her hand in his and lifted it up, kissing her knuckles. "And by the bye, Your Grace, it was merely a dance. It was not a compromising situation. I did not offer for her hand. It was a single dance. You are unduly aggravated."

"I will be the judge of whether I am unduly aggravated," the duchess said primly. "What will your brothers think? I have a devil of a time keeping them in check as it is."

"They will think that I danced with a beautiful woman," he said, and tried to let go of her hand.

But his mother held on to his and whispered loudly, "Lady Babington informs me that the lady in question is a *courtesan*."

She spoke as if she had just uttered an unthinkable curse word, and to a woman of fine breeding and impeccable morals, he supposed it was. Grayson hesitated to answer — Kate *was* a courtesan, but oddly, that fact did not seem as objectionable to him as it had when he'd first made her acquaintance.

"Well?"

"She is. What of it?"

His mother sighed. She let go of his hand and picked up her spoon. "I would remind you that the Prince of Wales has lost the support of the people because *he* sees nothing wrong with keeping the company of the demimonde." She slowly stirred her tea.

Lord help him. He was a duke in his own right, a grown man, and he was still subjected to the occasional maternal scolding. "You must not worry and you must not allow Lady Babington to put such thoughts into your head."

"Lady Babington put no thoughts in *my* head. They all leapt there of their own accord when I heard the news," she said, wiggling her fingers at her head. She sighed heavenward. "I have too many children. That is yet another thought that leaps to mind — too many of you to look after properly."

Grayson chuckled. "I am happy to see you well and in fine spirits, Mother. If you will excuse me, I've only a moment to see my nephews, and then I must be off."

"For heaven's sake, do stay off the floor. Oh, and please, if you would be so good as to call on your brother?" she added as Grayson started to the door. "Merrick seemed rather discouraged about rounding up enough votes for the abolition."

"I will see him today," Grayson promised.

CHAPTER FIFTEEN

Two days after the ball, Kate begged Aldous to accompany her to St. Katharine's. Aldous did not care for the quays. He'd almost cocked up his toes there two years ago, fighting off an illegal press gang. He'd been a bluecoat serving in the Royal Navy, and he'd come in from a month at sea. He was quite happily foxed when the slave traders fell upon him. Aldous had heard of it happening from time to time — the merchants needed sailors, just like the Navy, and if they couldn't assemble a crew for the voyage, they'd forcibly take however many men they needed.

He'd fought hard when he realized what was happening, but he'd been one man against three. He'd begun to lose consciousness when he understood someone had come to his rescue. That was all he remembered; the next thing he recalled was waking up in Digby's rooms.

169

Later, Digby told him what had happened. Returning from the cloth halls in Cousineau's company, Kate had seen the slave traders fall on Aldous. She'd begged Cousineau to send his men in to rescue Aldous. They'd had quite a row, apparently, but in the end, when Kate attempted to remove one of the men from Aldous herself, Cousineau had relented and sent his two henchmen in after her.

How or why they had brought him to Digby, Aldous had never learned; but on one point, he was very clear: If Kate had not intervened, he would be lying on the bottom of the ocean or would be enslaved in a foreign land, on a foreign ship. Having been spared that fate, Aldous owed his undying gratitude to Kate.

He'd not been able to resume his duties with the Navy, for he'd been badly injured during the attack. Digby and the angel Kate had nursed him through the worst of it.

Aldous had been rather madly in love with her then. He'd amused himself during his long hours of recuperation with the fantasy of bedding her. When that had become too painful . . . and apparent . . . Aldous had imagined marrying Kate. But as he'd grown stronger, he'd realized she would never be his. Not in a thousand years would a woman of her beauty and kindness settle for a life with a sailor.

It had been nigh on two years since Kate had rescued him, and standing here now, on the St. Katharine's quay, he caught the scent of the sea, felt the lure of it in his bones.

He wondered how long he might remain in London to keep an eye on Kate. He didn't trust the Prince of Wales or his intentions, and he felt a strong need now, more than ever, to protect her to the extent that he could.

Aldous waited outside the rooms Kate let for the girls, leaning against the wall and watching people come and go. He wished she'd be quick about it — it was damn cold. Aldous glanced to his right and happened to spot the chap who let the rooms to Kate — it was hard to miss his hook nose — striding down the alley toward him. Aldous straightened up.

Before the man reached him, however, Kate came out of the building. "Meg has gone missing again," she said frantically. "I don't know —"

"Miss Bergeron!" the owner called out.

Startled, Kate whirled around. "Mr. Fleming!"

He tipped his hat to her and eyed Aldous. "This is a good omen, meeting you like this, as I have wanted to speak with you. I am increasing the cost of the rooms."

"What?" Kate cried. "Why? It's hardly a set of rooms at all, Mr. Fleming, and I pay you a pound a month!"

Aldous almost choked at the exorbitant price. Twelve pounds a year for that sty? *Bloody scoundrel.*

"The new cost is fourteen pounds per annum, Miss Bergeron. But I suspect you can afford it, given the company you keep."

Kate gaped at him.

"Have a care, sir," Aldous said.

"I beg your pardon?" Fleming said almost jovially. "Did you think you'd not be recognized in the *Times*?"

Kate looked questioningly at Aldous, but he shook his head. "I have no idea what you mean," she said, turning back to the scoundrel. "You are trifling with me."

"Did you not see the morning *Times*, then?" he asked gleefully. "It was printed just yesterday."

Kate blinked.

"On my word, did you think your acquaintances who can read would not see you in those words? And with a duke, no less!"

Aldous could see the blood drain from Kate's face. "The *Times*?" she repeated.

Fleming laughed jovially. "Read it for yourself — you *can* read, can you not?"

"Of course she can read," Aldous snapped, although neither he nor Kate was particularly adept at it.

Fleming smirked and stepped forward to rap on the door. "By the bye, are you still a chum of the fat fellow?"

"I beg your pardon!" Kate exclaimed angrily.

"Tell your Mr. Digby that he ought to have a care whose perfume trade he attempts to pilfer," he said sharply.

The door swung open just then; Holly groaned when she saw him.

"I shall expect a pound and a few shillings on the first day of the month, Miss Bergeron," Fleming said, then looked at Holly. "Move aside," he ordered her and stepped past her, into the room. Behind his back, Holly rolled her eyes, waved at Kate, then shut the door.

Aldous could only imagine what business Fleming had here —

"A newspaper!" Kate cried, latching on to his arm. "We must find yesterday's newspaper!"

"Calm yourself," Aldous said, and took her elbow, urging her to walk. "That rat likes to kick up a lark, but he's a fool. I'll find a newspaper for you, and you'll discover there is naught to alarm you, lass."

As it turned out, Fleming was a leech, but he'd not been untruthful about the *Times*. Aldous found a copy at the fishmonger's later that evening that required an airing before Kate would allow it in the house. The following morning, Kate and Aldous pored over it, but the nuances of the *on dit* confused them. It wasn't until the following evening, four days after the Twelfth Night Ball, that Digby arrived to read it and interpret it for them. In the same edition of the newspaper, Digby read aloud an interesting bit about Lord Merrick Christopher's work to abolish the slave trade. It was the first Kate had heard of the movement. "They say the duke has been instrumental in bringing votes to his brother's side," Digby said.

That night, as Amy dressed Kate for the opera behind a screen, Digby read the *on dits* again.

"Here we are," he said, and cleared his throat like an orator. *"'Yet perhaps nothing was quite as surprising as seeing the duke of D—— stand up on the second set and partner with a diamond of the first water, who is perhaps known in many salons as the one who is devoted to fine fabrics and clothing. Of late, it would seem that her devotions have spread beyond fabrics. The lady partnered with other notables, such as HRH and Lord B——.'"*

"Devoted to clothing!" Kate scoffed behind the screen. "There was not a single woman at Carlton House who was not devoted to her clothing!"

"Who is Lord Bee?" Aldous asked.

"Not *Bee*," Digby said. "Some gobblecock whose surname begins with the letter B, to protect his identity."

"What for?" Aldous demanded. "Ain't he man enough to say he danced if he did?"

"It has nothing to do with that." Digby sighed with vexation as Kate stepped around the screen. "Honestly, Mr. Butler, it is *impossible* to make you understand the ways of the Quality — Lord help us!" he said as Kate moved into his view. He beamed at her. "A diamond of the first water, indeed!" he exclaimed gleefully as he admired her pink silk gown with the embroidered champagne overlay. "There, you see? I *knew* you'd be the most celebrated of all the ladies at the ball. Now you must tell your good friends, Kate — what of our man Darlington? A very graceful dancer, I would suspect. They train those high in the instep to dance almost the moment they learn to walk, you know."

Kate hesitated. She never kept anything from Aldous or Digby, but it didn't seem her place to share Darlington's affliction. He was a powerful man, a confident man. A *handsome* man. She kept thinking of the way his eyes had looked when he'd agreed with her that their association wasn't so terribly awful. And the way his hand had felt on the small of her back. And his smile. "Fine," she said, turning her attention to the jewelry the prince had sent her. "But he does not care for dancing, I think."

"He likely prefers the gaming room to dancing," Digby said with an air of authority. "Most men would, I should think. However, *I* prefer dancing." He stood up and began to move around the room, mimicking the steps of a cotillion.

The young maid giggled. Aldous rolled his eyes.

A knock at the front door below filtered up to them, bringing the dance to a halt. As Aldous went to open the door, Digby fussed with Kate's hair. "They shall all be agog when they see you tonight, Kate. Tomorrow morning *The Times* will report that bodies littered the opera house, all of them overcome by your beauty," he said, and tucked a strand of her hair up under the pearls Amy had wrapped around her head to hold her locks in place.

"You are given to exaggeration, Digby."

"Perhaps I am, but not on this occasion. Now then, enjoy yourself! Lord knows you deserve to."

Kate didn't know if she deserved to, but she was incautiously enlivened by the idea of another evening spent in the duke's company.

CHAPTER SIXTEEN

Something crystallized for Grayson when he saw Kate come down the stairs with that soft, sultry smile. He realized he'd thought of her quite a lot in the last few days. And when she looked pleased to see him, he felt something flutter strangely in his chest.

He understood, in a rare moment of self-awareness, that he was pleased to see her, too.

The prince was a lucky man in more ways than one, he thought, looking at Kate now. She was wearing an exquisite gown scalloped along the hem. The overlying tunic split down her lap to reveal elaborate embroidery on the underskirt. It was a masterpiece of construction, a gown that even he recognized every woman in London would covet. She was desirable in a way that could drive a man to his knees in certain, intimate circumstances.

He drew a steadying breath at that thought.

He was feeling the effects of abstinence, he reasoned. With Eustis in London, Grayson had seen Diana only once in the last fortnight, and that had been in a public forum where he couldn't touch her or speak to her more than in passing.

"Good evening, Your Grace," Kate said, curtseying so low that the large pearl pendant she wore danced about her décolletage.

"Miss Bergeron. I hope the evening finds you well," he greeted her.

"Exceedingly!" she said brightly. "I have very much looked forward to this evening, for I adore the opera." The butler held up a pelisse that matched her gown; she put her arms into it, then fastened the buttons. "I hope you won't find it too tiresome."

The evening's opera was *The Dragon of Wantley* by John Frederick Lampe. Grayson hoped it would be short and painless, but was resigned to the likelihood that it would be neither of those things. "I think I shall find it much more tolerable with such pleasant company."

"Oh *my*," Kate said, her brows rising with surprise. "It would seem that we have become partners in this ruse after all."

"My goodness, Miss Bergeron, did you ever doubt it?" he asked.

Kate grinned. "I *did* think you rather boorish at the beginning, Your Grace . . . but I never thought you beyond redemption."

Grayson smiled and offered his arm to her. "How kind of you to believe that I can be a redeemed boor." He opened the door.

Kate smiled as they stepped out, and called over her shoulder, "Good night, Aldous!"

"Good night, Kate," he said after her.

Startled by the butler's use of her given name, Grayson looked back at the servant, but he had, as was his bothersome habit, shut the door the very moment they'd stepped over the threshold. There were many things Grayson desired to know about Kate, and now he added another item to the list: Why did she allow the butler to call her by her given name?

In his carriage — Kate sitting backward again — Grayson signaled the driver to proceed. As the carriage rolled on, Kate asked, "How have you fared since the ball, Your Grace?"

"Very well, thank you. And you?"

"Oh, very well," she said, smiling a little. "But I've not been burdened with the counting of votes for abolition."

He could not have been more surprised. "You know of the abolition bill?"

"It would seem everyone in London knows

of it, sir. Shockingly, even me."

"I didn't mean —"

"Do you have the votes?" she politely interjected.

"I'm not certain."

"What will you do if you can't manage enough votes?"

"It is hard to say," he admitted, and told her about the abolition movement and particularly Merrick's role in it. She listened attentively, nodding at the things he said, but quite honestly, there were times Grayson felt as if he was speaking in a foreign tongue so captivated was he by her pale green eyes. They glittered as he talked, illuminating her face in the very dim light of the coach.

When he finished talking, she proclaimed, "I think what you and your brother are doing is wonderful. No one should be master of another."

It was, Grayson thought, an ironic thing for her to say, given that she was a woman whose livelihood depended on having a master. He couldn't help his mind wandering a little with that thought. If she were his to command . . .

"Is something wrong?" she asked.

"Wrong?"

"You are looking at me curiously." Her voice was smooth, her eyes shining. She was well aware of her ability to enchant men.

"I was admiring your necklace," he said casually.

"Thank you." She touched her fingers to the pearl, toying with it, then lightly touched the hollow of her throat.

"It is lavish," Grayson said. "It must be a gift from a lover."

"One does not reveal such intimate secrets," she said with a wry smile. "Only to lovers."

The coach hit a rut; the force of it bounced Kate off her seat. Grayson caught her by the arms, and for one highly charged moment he looked at her mouth. He imagined those lips on him — *all* of him.

Kate swallowed — even in the soft light he could see it and he wondered, did he frighten her? "I know that look in your eye," she said softly.

"Do you object?"

Her gaze slipped to his mouth. Her lips parted and she drew a shallow breath. "I don't know," she said, sounding the slightest bit bewildered.

God help him, but Grayson had never wanted to kiss a woman as ardently as he wanted to kiss her, to feel her mouth beneath his, to feel her bare skin, warm and fragrant, against his, to feel her body hot and wet around his. *"Kate . . ."*

"I think we're here," she whispered.

He didn't quite understand her.

"Here," she said again. "The Royal Opera House."

Grayson made the mistake of looking; Kate faded back and away from him.

The moment was lost and he felt the bitter disappointment in the hard beat of his heart. "Yes," he said.

There was hardly anyone about when they stepped out of the carriage; they'd arrived late. They walked quickly inside and up to the Darlington family box, where they tossed their coats to the footman who hurried up behind them. They could hear the musicians tuning their instruments — the curtain would rise in a matter of minutes.

Another footman stood just outside the door of Grayson's box and bowed as he opened it for them. Much to Grayson's surprise and chagrin, his sister Prudence and her husband, Robert Carlisle, the Earl of Beaumont, were already seated. For a moment, Grayson was at a loss for words; his blood was still racing from being so close to Kate. He hadn't known his sister would attend, hadn't even thought to ask his secretary who might be at the opera this evening.

Beaumont saved the moment by greeting

Grayson first. Prudence was much slower to find her feet, as her wide eyes were riveted on Kate. But Kate smiled at Prudence as if they were old friends as Grayson ushered her into the box.

"It is our good fortune you have come, Your Grace . . . is that not right, Pru, darling?" Beaumont asked, giving Prudence a pointed look.

"Yes! Of course!" Prudence said, and remembered herself. She stepped forward to kiss Grayson's cheek. But when she stepped back again, she was gaping at Kate.

Kate glanced at Grayson. He could see a twinkle in her eye, as if she knew he found the situation disconcerting, and was amused by it. His gaze narrowed slightly in warning. "Prudence, Robert," he said, his eyes on Kate, "may I present Miss Katharine Bergeron. Miss Bergeron, I am pleased to introduce Lord and Lady Beaumont. Lady Beaumont is my sister."

"A pleasure to make your acquaintance," Kate said with a curtsy.

Prudence was only a year younger than Grayson, and he knew her perhaps better than his other siblings. And what he knew about his sister at that moment was that she was aghast. He could scarcely blame her — he rarely attended the opera, and when he did, it was in the company of family or close friends. He was very careful with his public persona and reputation and did nothing to give rise to the slightest bit of gossip. Looking at his sister's face now, Grayson realized he was unduly agitated.

"Miss Bergeron, it is our pleasure," Prudence said, slyly taking in Kate's gown. "How did you become acquainted with my brother, if I may ask?"

"The Prince of Wales introduced us," Kate said easily.

"The Prince of Wales?"

"Mmm," Kate said, and looked across the opera house to the prince's box. "There he is." She smiled and lifted her hand in greeting.

Prudence, Robert, and Grayson looked across the house. The prince acknowledged them with a nod of his head.

Prudence looked at Kate again, her eyes even wider. "I think you look rather familiar to me. Is it possible we've met?"

"I am sure we've not," Kate said politely.

"Then are you new to London?"

"Not at all. I've lived in London all my life."

"In *Mayfair?*" Prudence asked disbelievingly.

Kate laughed. "No. Not Mayfair." She said

185

it as if Prudence had asked if she lived on the sun.

Fortunately, Beaumont caught Prudence's elbow. "You will have to keep your questions for a more opportune time, darling. The performance is about to begin."

"Please, be seated," Grayson urged them, and escorted Kate to the two front seats of the box, directly in front of the Beaumonts, where Grayson could feel Prudence's gaze burning a hole through his collar.

He straightened his waistcoat, smiled at Kate. The footmen were dousing the lights in preparation for the performance; the house was beginning to settle. Kate leaned forward, peering down into the musicians' stalls. Grayson inadvertently glanced toward the prince again. George was speaking with his brother, the Duke of Clarence, who was an ardent supporter of the slave trade and stood in direct opposition to Merrick. Grayson absently looked to the left of the prince — and his heart stilled.

Lord and Lady Eustis were also present this evening, and Diana was staring at him. Her blue eyes were round and even from this distance, he could see her mouth was set in a rigid line.

Bloody hell. He'd been so preoccupied with business and political matters and carrying out this ruse for the prince that he had not thought clearly about who might be in attendance this evening, who might see him. And as he'd not seen Diana in a fortnight, he'd had no opportunity to inform her.

He was spared any more awkwardness when the curtain rose a moment later. Kate turned a beaming smile to him, and settled in for the performance. As the music began and several singers walked onstage to set the tale, Kate leaned closer to Grayson and touched his sleeve. "The music is rather plain just now," she whispered.

Surprised, Grayson looked at her, but she'd returned her attention to the stage, had removed her hand.

The tale was rather simple. A dragon — who represented the crown's taxation — lived in a cave and menaced the children and the livestock of a village. A knight was dispatched to battle him to the death and emerged victorious, thereby defeating taxation. The parody also made light of opera, with exaggerated dancing and singing.

Throughout the performance, Kate continued to interpret the music to Grayson, lightly laying her hand on his arm, or touching his knee. "The music is very boastful, to match the knight," she whispered, "much like the ship horns that blast on the Thames. Have

187

you heard them? They are *dreadfully* loud."
When she leaned away from him again, she
left the tantalizing scent of her perfume behind.

When a young woman entered the stage
and began to sing, she touched his knee and
said, "The song is very sweet. She's quite
taken with the knight." She leaned so close
he felt a bit of her hair brush his cheek, and
whispered, "Do you see how she pressed her
hands to his chest?"

Grayson glanced at Kate. She smiled coyly.
"She's flirting with him."

When the knight went off to slay the
dragon, Kate suddenly grasped his wrist as if
she were frightened. "The music is very low
and foreboding, like the fog when it rolls in
and swallows up the town." An unexpectedly
loud crash of cymbals caused her to flinch
into him. Grayson caught that lovely, indel-
ible scent of her perfume again. But Kate
pressed her hand to her heart and slowly
leaned back in her seat with an apologetic
smile. "The music is very dark," she said
simply.

It was the first time in Grayson's memory
that anyone had attempted to interpret the
sound of music to him. It didn't help him
distinguish the notes any better than he usually did, but he did understand what she

meant when she explained it to him, and for once in his life, the music — albeit tinny and strange to his ears — seemed to make sense.

When the last scene began, she wrinkled her nose and looked at him. "Now it sounds a bit like a gaggle of geese," she whispered.

"It *looks* like a gaggle of geese," Grayson whispered, given the way the dancers were hopping about in some strange dance and singing over one another. "Tell me, is anyone singing of love?" he asked, harking back to her comments at the ball, that music reminded her of courtly love.

Kate giggled. "Not as yet," she whispered. "They always save that for the end. Best to end with ecstasy . . . wouldn't you agree?"

He looked at Kate, and the sparkle of amusement in her eyes. Oh, but he wholeheartedly agreed.

When the curtain at long last came down, Grayson was the first to applaud the end of such an appalling production. The actors had scarcely cleared the stage after taking their bows before Prudence was upon them. "How did you find the opera, Miss Bergeron?" she asked, eagerly linking her arm with Kate's and walking out of the box with her before Grayson could intervene.

"Honestly, I thought it overwrought."

"*Did* you," Prudence repeated thoughtfully,

studying her closely.

Grayson couldn't hear the rest of their conversation; in the lobby, the swirl of people around them made it impossible to hear anything. Nevertheless, Grayson found himself introducing Kate over and over again. It seemed as if every one of his acquaintances had attended the opera this evening, and all were anxious to meet his guest.

He was anxious to be gone. They were to attend a private gathering at St. James's Palace, hosted by Clarence, the prince's brother. Grayson worked to extract Kate from the throng, and thought he'd managed it, was waiting for their cloaks when Lord Eustis put himself directly in Grayson's path.

God help him. Grayson forced a smile. "My lord Eustis, how good to see you. I'd heard you were in Shropshire for the winter."

"I've come to town to see after my young wife."

As if on cue, Diana slid into place beside him, her gaze fixed on Grayson's. "Your Grace," she murmured, her gaze sliding to Kate.

"And how is your mother, Your Grace?" Eustis asked, ignoring Kate completely.

"She is very well, thank you. Please allow me to introduce Miss Katharine Bergeron,"

Grayson said, glancing at Diana. "Miss Bergeron, Lord and Lady Eustis."

Kate curtsied gracefully.

"Good evening, madam," Eustis said indifferently as he fit his hands into gloves. A footman appeared on Kate's left, holding her pelisse.

"There you are!" Prudence suddenly appeared in their midst and gave Diana a kiss on the cheek. "My lord!" she said with surprise to Lord Eustis. "I had not heard you've come to town. You must come to dine."

"I'd like that very much, Lady Beaumont, but we are to Bath shortly. We'll have you for tea, but for now, we must bid you adieu — our carriage is in queue."

"Good night," Prudence said.

Diana fixed Grayson with a look as she followed her husband out.

When they'd disappeared into the crowd, Prudence whirled about to Grayson. "We must take our leave as well, Christie. I can't bear to be parted from my children another moment. Miss Bergeron, it was a pleasure making your acquaintance. You must come and join the duchess and myself for tea. I know she'd be very happy to make your acquaintance. Will you?"

"I'd be delighted," Kate said charmingly, but Grayson's gut sank a little. A courtesan in a salon with his mother? It was more likely that hell would freeze.

Prudence smiled and waved as she turned around and sailed back to Beaumont, who was deep in conversation with a pair of gentlemen.

"Shall we?" Grayson said, taking the pelisse from the footman and helping Kate into it.

"You seem anxious," Kate said as he escorted her out to the queue of waiting carriages. "But you mustn't fret. Your sister will not issue an invitation to tea. She was being polite."

Grayson snorted. "You underestimate Prudence."

"She won't. She'll make some gentle inquiries, and once she's determined who I am, she will politely forget the conversation."

A footman opened the door to the coach; Grayson handed Kate up. When he climbed in behind her and took his seat, she said, "Your mistress is lovely."

Startled, Grayson stared at Kate.

"Lady Eustis *is* your mistress, is she not?"

He found himself quite unable to speak. He nodded.

Kate smiled as she adjusted her pelisse about her. "She is quite lovely. I can see why you are in love with her."

"In *love?*"

Kate looked up. "Aren't you? I rather thought love was the point of a having a mistress —"

"I'd rather not speak of Lady Eustis," he said abruptly.

"Oh . . . of course not." Smiling faintly, Kate looked out the window.

Grayson sighed. He hadn't meant to be so short, but hearing Kate mention Diana's name made him strangely cross. He really wasn't feeling quite himself. "I beg your pardon for that," he said, gesturing toward the opera house. "I might have warned you had I known the whole of London would be on hand."

With a very subtle flick of her wrist, Kate said, "It is a trifling thing. Have you many brothers and sisters?"

"Two brothers and three sisters."

"So many!" she exclaimed. "You must have been very happy in your childhood with so many playmates."

He'd indeed been blessed with a very happy, idyllic childhood. "I was."

"And are they here in London?" Kate asked idly as she glanced out the window at the moonlit night sky.

He had to think for a moment before answering. "My youngest brother, Harry, is in France presently. My sister Ginny is in the country. She is not yet out and is still being tutored. Yet my other siblings are in London, in preparation for the social Season." Which, in essence, amounted to finding a match for their brother Grayson. "What of you? Have you any siblings?"

"A brother."

"Has this brother a name?"

"Yes." She smiled a little. "Jude."

"And where is Jude?" he asked, imagining him in some Southwark gaming hell.

"He . . . honestly, I'm not entirely sure," she admitted sheepishly. "I lost him several years ago."

"*Lost* him?"

"He, ah . . . he changed his residence and I do not know where he resides now."

Grayson looked at her expectantly, but Kate shrugged. "I've been looking for him for quite a long time. I heard recently that he's on a ship."

"What of your parents? Has he not kept in contact with them?"

"My mother died when I was twelve, and if I had to hazard a guess, I would say that my father has long been gone from this world. He was never in particularly good health that I can recall."

"Do you mean to say that you don't know if your father lives?" he asked incredulously.

She smiled wryly. "It's a rather long and sordid tale, sir," she said softly. "Please do not trouble yourself with the details, for I assure you, you will not find them agreeable."

Grayson tried to imagine not knowing if his father lived or died. But the coach jerked to a halt in front of St James's Palace, and his thoughts immediately turned to the prince, and how anxiously he would be waiting to see Kate.

CHAPTER SEVENTEEN

In the entrance hall to the Duke of Clarence's private apartments in St. James's Palace there stood a marble statue of a woman dressed in ancient robes. She held a bowl above her head, in which someone had placed rose petals. *Rose petals.* In the dead of winter.

Kate ran her fingers over the statue, feeling the cold, smooth marble.

How did one ever grow accustomed to such opulence?

"Miss Bergeron, will you allow me to acquaint you with some friends of mine?"

Kate looked up; Mrs. Jordan, Clarence's mistress, smiled at her. When she'd entered with Darlington, Clarence had instantly swept him away, leaving her with Mrs. Jordan. Kate knew of her — every courtesan knew of her — she'd been a famous actress before becoming the duke's mistress and borne him several children. She was now past the age of forty, but she was still quite handsome, with a trim figure and fine features. Her situation was widely accepted among the *ton* — as long as it remained behind closed doors. Years ago, Madame Albert had told Kate that as a courtesan she might very well be accepted into society, but never into the *ton*'s private salons.

Mrs. Jordan was quite charming and kindly took Kate in hand to introduce her around.

The private gathering didn't seem at all private to Kate — there were at least one hundred people within. There was gambling at one end of the salon and musicians played at the other end. A few hearty souls were attempting to dance without benefit of a proper dance floor. In between, people milled about with libations in hand.

Kate felt as if she'd been introduced to everyone in attendance when the prince made an unsteady entrance in the company of two much younger men who appeared to be as foxed as he was. Mrs. Jordan fell into a deep curtsey, yanking Kate's hand and pulling her down as well. "Your Highness," Mrs. Jordan said.

"Mrs. Jordan, we are here," the prince said.

"You are most welcome, Your Highness."

"Miss Bergeron, how do you do?"

"Very well, Your Highness, thank you."

"Where is Clarence?"

"At the tables, sir," Mrs. Jordan said.

The prince shifted his gaze to Kate. "Miss Bergeron, where is your escort?" he demanded, swaying a bit.

"He is at the tables as well," Mrs. Jordan said.

"Thank you, Mrs. Jordan," the prince said. "Perhaps you might inform him I have arrived. I'd like a word."

"At once, Your Highness," Mrs. Jordan said, and walked away.

The prince caught Kate's elbow, gripped it tightly, and propelled her forward. "You may join me for some refreshment and tell me how you found the opera," he said tightly.

Kate could smell the whiskey on his breath. She glanced over her shoulder; the two young men who had come with him were following behind, engrossed in their own conversation.

"*Kate.* You must have a care to remain at Darlington's side," he said low. He stumbled slightly. "People will suspect that you are quite unattached, particularly if you keep the company of Mrs. Jordan. And if they think you are unattached, they might link you to *me.* I cannot risk it, do you hear me? Bloody Caroline has spies everywhere," he said, glancing around them.

Kate glanced around, too. She thought people might more readily assume an attachment between them when he marched her across the room as he was doing now than through her association with Mrs. Jordan.

"Kate, Kate," the prince said suddenly, "I've thought of little else but you since our last meeting. Did you receive the necklace I sent you?"

Kate indicated the pearl at her throat. "Thank you, Your Highness."

"Exquisite." He sighed — in reference to the pearl or her décolletage, she wasn't certain. "God in heaven, I must see you in private!" he said anxiously. "It pains me to be so close, yet so far from you!"

Kate felt entirely conspicuous and was certain the entire room had heard what he'd said and knew that he lusted after her. She had the terrifying thought that perhaps Princess Caroline did have spies all around them. "Your patience will be rewarded," she said softly.

He groaned and leaned closer, causing her to inadvertently rear back. "Let me tell you something," he murmured. His mouth was only inches from hers; one misstep and he could pitch headlong into her. As it was, he drew a breath, licked his lips. "The ladies' retiring room is down the main corridor to your left," he said quietly. "Just beyond that door is another that leads —"

"Your Highness."

"What?" George snapped at the intruder, jerking partially around.

Darlington steadied the prince, but the prince seemed not to notice.

Relieved, Kate quickly put out her hand to Darlington. "Here is my escort now, Your Highness." Thankfully, Darlington seemed to sense her distress and took her hand, pulling her away from what she was certain would have been another meeting in another linen closet.

The prince looked at her hand in Darlington's and scowled. "Now that I've arrived you play your part very well," he snapped. "Have a care you keep her close, Christie. I'll not have the scoundrels here lusting after what is mine. I want this one as untainted as I might reasonably expect."

Kate somehow managed to suppress her gasp of indignation. She was *not* a whore. And she'd not come to this gathering ape-drunk as *he* had! She had learned as a young girl to push her feelings into a hard little box she imagined was lodged beside her heart, to turn a deaf ear to the things that were said about her or her body. That box had turned to stone over the years, cold hard stone, and she felt herself turning cold and hard now. It was the only way she could do what she must, the only way she could bear to receive the insults and attentions of a man who disgusted her, and by God, at this moment, the Prince of Wales disgusted her.

Yes, she was living in the prince's house and was, for all intents and purposes, his property. And were she not his property, she'd be living somewhere little better than the rooms she let from Mr. Fleming. But Kate's desire to be free, to be her own person with control over her own body, her own life, was growing stronger by the day. Dangerously strong. It would rise up one day and jeopardize her livelihood, for she'd not be able to swallow her spleen and keep from speaking her bloody mind.

"Are you agreeable?"

"Pardon?" she asked, looking at Darlington.

"I was saying that I'd hoped you would play a round of cards. We have need of a fourth." Darlington's voice was smooth and strong and soothed her instantly.

"Yes. By all means," she said, and looked at the prince. His gaze was on another woman who slowly walked by.

"Thank you, Your Highness," Darlington

said, and tightened, his grip on Kate's hand. "Come then, Miss Bergeron, before our seats are taken."

The prince, drunk as he was, didn't seem to notice that she'd left. Kate followed Darlington to a table occupied by two gentlemen, who rose from their seats when Darlington introduced her. She knew Lord Green; his wife had bought bolts and bolts of China silk and he'd been a frequent guest at Benoit's gaming table. He smiled broadly and hurried to hold out a chair for her.

Once Kate had taken her seat, the gentlemen took theirs. The other man, Lord Dunning, nodded. "The game is Speculation, Miss Bergeron. Are you familiar with it?"

"Yes," she said, and blushed. "But I . . . I beg your pardon, gentlemen, I . . . I have no purse —"

"Ah, but you do," Darlington said, nodding at a few coins at her elbow. "They were left by my uncle, Lord Richland, who was called away. He willed them to the next player rather than break up the game."

Kate looked again at the coins, which she guessed amounted to ten pounds. Ten pounds would come very close to paying the lease on the rooms at St. Katharine's for a full year. She looked at Darlington skeptically. He gave her a very subtle wink, and

Kate could not help but smile. "How very kind," she said. "You must introduce me to him, Your Grace, so that I might thank him."

"If His Grace does not, it would certainly be my pleasure to make the introductions," Green said.

"Thank you, my lord, but I would be happy to introduce Miss Bergeron to Lord Richland," Darlington said, his gaze still on her. He picked up the deck of cards.

"How did you find the opera this evening, Miss Bergeron?" Lord Green asked as Darlington shuffled.

"Not very well, in all honesty. But I did enjoy the dancing."

"Perhaps you found it not to your liking as it was a parody," Dunning suggested in a superior tone as Darlington dealt. "It was not intended to be a realistic story."

Darlington frowned sternly at the man — not that Dunning seemed to notice — but Kate laughed lightly. "I will admit to often misunderstanding the stories in opera, but on this occasion, I was aware."

"Gentlemen. Miss Bergeron. The play is to Green," Darlington said.

Green laid his card, followed by Darlington and Dunning. With delight, Kate trumped and triumphantly raked the few coins in the center toward her. They played four more rounds, with Kate taking two. She laughed gaily each time she won and tried to assure her partners that she wasn't typically so lucky in cards.

"The words of an expert gambler," Green said jovially. "I've had the delightful pleasure of sitting at a table with Miss Bergeron, and I will warn you, sirs, that her skill is masked by her charming smile."

"You give me far too much credit, my lord," Kate said cheerfully.

A footman appeared at her side and at Darlington's very subtle signal, he put a glass of wine beside her. Kate picked it up and inclined her head in gratitude. "Thank you. I have developed a bit of a thirst."

"I should think so, having worked so hard to divest three poor gentlemen of their funds."

They played several more rounds, Kate winning a fair number of times. Several times during the evening, she would glance up and find Darlington watching her. There was something in his deep blue gaze, something mysterious that trickled down her spine and made her feel very warm and sparkly inside.

Or perhaps that was the wine.

The only person who did not seem to be winning was Lord Dunning, and he grew more sullen with each hand. He didn't seem the sort of man who liked to lose — and particularly not to a woman. But Kate couldn't help his luck. As for herself, she was silently counting the coins at her elbow and thanking the heavens for them. With what she'd accumulated, she could not only pay the increased fee to Fleming, she would also have some money to put aside.

Kate won another hand and Green remarked he'd been robbed of all his luck. "I seem to have found mine for once," she remarked cheerfully.

"You have, indeed," Dunning said. "Tell me, Miss Bergeron . . . do they teach games such as Speculation in the cloth halls?"

Stunned, Kate slowly picked up the cards Green had just dealt her. "No, my lord," she said carefully. "A friend taught it to me."

"A *friend*," Dunning scoffed. "Perhaps he taught you some special tricks as well," he muttered, and glanced at the number of coins at her elbow.

His implication could not have been clearer — he'd just accused her of cheating, and Kate was horrified. Darlington suddenly clamped his hand down on Dunning's arm. "I never thought you to be a poor sport, my lord. Perhaps the evening has fatigued you. You should apologize to the lady."

205

"Lady?" Dunning sneered.

Darlington stood so suddenly that Kate had to grab the table to keep it from toppling. "Apologize to the lady," he repeated tightly.

It seemed as if everything and everyone around them suddenly quieted, their gazes riveted on Darlington. Dunning glared at the duke, then glanced at Kate. "My apologies, madam," he said coldly.

"I beg your pardon, Miss Bergeron," Darlington snapped. "I did not realize we were in such poor company." He strode around to her chair. "Have I shown you the view from the private gardens?" he asked, helping her to her feet.

Kate's face was flaming. Of the many things she'd been called in her life, *cheater* had never been among them. She looked uncertainly at the coins on the table. She didn't want to leave them, but was too ashamed to sweep them into her reticule.

Darlington politely solved the problem for her by picking up the coins and putting them in his pocket. "Miss Bergeron?"

She would have kissed him if it wouldn't have inflamed the situation. "Thank you, Your Grace."

"Good night, Miss Bergeron," Lord Green said, coming to his feet. "It has been a pleasure, as always."

Dunning did not look at her as they quit the table.

Grayson was appalled. He did not linger for polite farewells; he moved Kate through the boisterous crowd, past women who looked at him longingly, past men who eyed him jealously and Kate lustfully. He saw the prince across the room; he looked even more foxed than he'd been earlier, and was talking to the bosom of a voluptuous woman while the two young men who had accompanied him hovered about. He wondered if Kate noticed the prince.

Grayson did not take Kate to the private terraces as he'd suggested, but to the main foyer, where he sent a footman for their coats. He was far too angry to remain here and held his jaw clenched shut, afraid of what he might say if he allowed himself to speak.

The footman returned with the coats. A light snow had begun to fall, but Grayson scarcely noticed; he marched Kate to his carriage. His footman was there before them, lowering the steps. Grayson quickly handed her up and swept in behind her, sitting across from her, his expression quite cold as he stared out the open door, waiting for the footman to raise the step.

When the footman had shut the door, Kate said, "I did *not* cheat, if that is what you think."

Surprised, he looked at her.

"I may be a courtesan, sir, but I am *not* a cheat! I'd rather never lay another card on a table than have anyone believe that I cheat, but especially *you,* for I have been utterly forthright in all our dealings!"

"Kate —"

"Have I given you any reason to suspect that I am less than perfectly honest? Have I done anything to suggest that I am as low as a thief? You may think me low, sir, but I —"

Grayson suddenly reached across the coach and put his hand on hers. "I do not think you cheated," he said evenly. "I sat across from you all evening. I *know* you didn't cheat."

That silenced her. She frowned with confusion. "But . . . but you seem so angry."

"I am *quite* angry," he agreed. "I am angry because you did not deserve that."

Something flickered in Kate's eyes. He could see her surprise, the rush of color to her face, and the smile of gratitude. "Thank you for that. Yet I don't understand Lord Dunning — how could he think it of me?"

Grayson squeezed her hand. "Because he is an ass."

Kate gasped. And then she smiled. "You

championed me," she said, sounding a little breathless, a little incredulous. "In front of your friends and acquaintances!"

"Is that so odd?"

"I suppose it depends on one's perspective, but yes, in my experience a duke would not take the word of a courtesan over the word of a lord. You really are quite kind, sir."

Grayson tried to frown, but when she was smiling so beatifically at him, he couldn't muster much of one. "I am not kind," he cautioned her. "Never accuse me of it."

Kate smiled and shook her head, settling back against the squabs. "Well . . . you *did* say you would show me the view from the private terrace, and yet you did not. That wasn't very kind."

"Did I say that?" he asked, stretching one arm across the back of the squabs as his gaze wandered over her. "Forgive my oversight and allow me to describe it to you. There are quite a lot of trees and bushes and a frozen pond on which the royal family — the princesses, really — sometimes skate."

"*Skate?*" Kate asked, her eyes lighting with delight. "Now I am very cross you did not show me! I have long desired to try to skate."

"Miss Bergeron, do you mean to tell me you have never skated on ice?"

She laughed. *"Never!"*

"That is a tragedy."

The carriage turned to the right; it was very dark to the left of the coach, and Grayson guessed they were passing Green Park. She'd be home soon. But when he turned his head to look at Kate again, he silently caught his breath. She was gazing at him in a manner that made his pulse leap. It was the sort of look that men all over the world hoped to see in a woman's eyes — the soft glow of desire. He didn't speak, but boldly allowed his gaze to wander over her, lingering here and there, sliding down to her embroidered slippers, and up again, to her neck, to her mouth and eyes.

The carriage rolled to a stop. Grayson surmised they were at her house and knocked three times on the ceiling, indicating he was to be left alone. "We've arrived at your home," he said simply.

She nodded. But she was looking at his mouth.

He leaned forward. "Kate . . . I beg your pardon for what happened this evening."

She sighed softly. "Please don't feel the need to apologize. I am well aware of where I stand."

"Not everyone among the *ton* is as boorish as some of the people you have met this evening."

She smiled dubiously. "I would not expect *you* to think so. No one would dare treat you ill."

He supposed she had a point — he was a wealthy duke, too powerful and influential to be toyed with. It was precisely the reason the prince had chosen him to escort Kate. No one would attempt to steal his mistress. As to that, however, he had a mistress, and one that had been neglected of late. "We have come to the end of our arranged outings," he said, and was, amazingly, disappointed by his own announcement.

Kate glanced out the window. "I suppose we caused a bit of commotion after all, did we not?"

"We did, indeed." He watched her, trying to read her. But whatever Kate thought, she was not revealing her feelings. She smiled that lovely, captivating smile that came to her so easily. Perhaps she was quite at ease with ending their public association; he could scarcely blame her. "I shall speak with George on our behalf and inquire if he is sat- isfied with . . . this," he said, gesturing lamely to the two of them.

"Yes," she said. "I imagine you are anxious to return to your life. I want you to know that I am very grateful for the kindness you

211

showed me this evening."

Kindness. He hadn't been particularly kind to her at all.

There seemed nothing left to say. Kate smiled and shifted forward, and Grayson lifted his hand and rapped once on the ceiling to indicate that the door should be opened.

"There is just one thing, if I may be so bold?" Kate asked as the coach dipped to one side as a footman came down.

"Yes?"

She looked in the area of his waist. "It's rather awkward, really, but I was wondering if I might have my winnings," she said, and lifted her green eyes to him.

That was not what Grayson was hoping she would say. He was hoping she'd say she wasn't ready for their association to end, because he wasn't ready. But he'd completely forgotten the few coins she'd won and instantly reached into his pocket.

"Those coins will help some friends of mine," she said apologetically.

He really didn't know what she meant by that, and he didn't care. He silently withdrew the coins. Kate opened her reticule; he dropped the coins into it, and as she drew it closed, Grayson caught her hand.

At the same moment, the door swung open

and the footman reached inside to lower the steps. Grayson felt uncharacteristically uncertain and awkward. He gave the footman a look, and the man instantly closed the door. "Kate," he said low, settling his gaze on her again, "I should like to say that it has been my extraordinary pleasure to have escorted you . . . in spite of my initial misgivings."

She laughed softly. "It has been my great pleasure to have been escorted, in spite of *my* initial misgivings," she agreed, and leaned closer still. "You aren't like the others, Christie," she whispered. "But I shall keep your secret."

His pet name on her breath sent a faint shiver through Grayson, and he smiled wryly. "I'm afraid that I am like them, but perhaps a little less so now."

Kate's smile deepened. She tried to remove her hand, but Grayson wasn't ready to let go. She gave him a skeptical look. "Your poor footman is out there freezing unto death."

Grayson couldn't think of the man now. He could think of nothing but Kate, lured in by the faint scent of her perfume, the glittering green eyes. He leaned in so close that he was almost touching her. "You don't have to take your leave," he murmured. "The night is young yet."

She turned her head, so that her mouth

was now only a fraction of an inch from his. Her lips parted slightly; she wanted him to kiss her, he could sense it. Grayson removed his glove and touched his knuckles to her cheek. Her skin was smooth and warm in spite of the cold, her green eyes were shining and locked on his. Grayson slid his hand to the hollow of her throat, spreading his fingers against the column of her neck, and slowly down, inside her coat. Kate flinched slightly, but she did not move. Her breath was warm on his mouth as he skimmed his hand over the pearl necklace to the bare skin of her décolletage, resting against her heart.

He could feel it beating as strong as his. He moved his hand down, to the swell of her breast, and Kate slowly drew a breath. Her skin began to heat under his hand, and she shifted closer to him.

Grayson's blood began to roil; when Kate's eyes fluttered shut, he could not help himself, and touched his lips to hers. The moment he kissed her, his heart lurched; he drew her lip in between his teeth then probed deeply, his tongue swirling around hers while he filled his hand with her breast.

Kate made a soft sound of pleasure that was Grayson's undoing. He pushed her back against the squabs, moving with her. He pressed his hardness against her leg, let her feel what she was doing to him, and Lord Grayson was completely enchanted by her kiss, by the sweet sensation of her mouth and tongue against his, by the pressure of her body as she pressed against his hand.

His body was swelling and simmering with passion, on the verge of exploding with the need to know her intimately. It was insanity, it was dangerous, and it could cost him dearly with the prince. Yet it was wildly erotic. He slipped his hand into her bodice. Her breast was taut, her skin warm and fragrant. The passion unfurling in Grayson's body erased all reasoned thought. Her hands tangled in his hair, fell to the muscles in his shoulders and arms. She dragged her hands down his back and to his hips as Grayson bent his head and skimmed his lips over her neck.

With one hand to the small of her waist, he drew her to him. He was thinking of escorting her inside — quickly — when Kate suddenly put her hand between them and pushed. Grayson lifted his head; Kate gasped for air.

"I'll come inside," he said breathlessly.

"No," she said, and shook her head, her eyes piercing his. "I cannot. I *will* not."

"Kate —"

"No," she said again, and pushed with both hands. "I have made a contract with the prince. I have given my word."

Of all the courtesans in London, Grayson had to experience unfathomable desire for the one who had a bloody conscience. He anxiously caught her hand and kissed her knuckles. "Let me come in, Kate. We will discuss it —"

She surprised him by pulling her hand free of her glove. She pushed past him and opened the door, startling the footman who waited patiently outside.

On the ground, she looked back over her shoulder at Grayson. He was still holding her glove. Gripping it. "Good night, Your Grace," she said, and hurried to her door. She fumbled with the lock; a moment later, the door swung open, and the butler glared at the carriage as Kate darted inside. The door quickly swung shut behind her, and not a moment later, the carriage door swung shut and the conveyence was rolling down King Street.

Grayson brought Kate's glove to his nose. He was well aware that he'd just crossed some threshold of madness, but at the moment, with his body still pulsing, the feel of her warm flesh still fresh on his mind, he didn't bloody well care.

CHAPTER EIGHTEEN

Kate pressed her back to the closed door. Her breathing was still ragged, her skin still flushed.

Aldous looked at her askance as he took her pelisse and frowned before moving to put it away. With Aldous's back to her, Kate touched her fingers to her lips. She never wanted to forget the sensation or the power of that kiss. Never.

Aldous turned round and put his hands on his hips as he studied her. "Where is your glove?"

"Ah . . ." She looked at her bare hand. "Ruined," she said sheepishly. "I spilled wine."

"Wine, is it? What, then, love — the good gent is going to launder it?"

Kate could feel herself color. She lifted her chin and looked Aldous in the eye. "I hardly think so."

But she didn't fool Aldous in the least. He suddenly grinned and sauntered toward her.

He put his arm around her shoulders and pulled her away from the door. "You needn't worry about what thoughts go round *my* head, lass," he said. "You best be fretting what thoughts circle round beneath Digby's bald pate."

Kate groaned.

Aldous was not wrong. When Digby called the next afternoon, he was beside himself with anticipation of Kate's news. He found Kate in her private rooms, *en dishabille.* She was on the chaise, idly studying the latest fashion gazette, but her mind was in another place entirely. A plate of fresh-baked scones was at her side, but Kate had no appetite.

Digby swept into the room behind Aldous, tossing his cloak on the settee as he strode across the room. He dipped elegantly in spite of his girth to kiss Kate's cheek. "Miss Bergeron, you look as ravishing as always, yet you appear as if you entertained well into the morning hours."

"I did not," she said, playfully tapping his arm. "I was home at the very reasonable hour of two o'clock."

"Two o'clock!" Digby cried, his brows rising high with curiosity. "Therefore your outing did not end with the opera!"

She coyly shook her head.

Beaming with delight, Digby patted her

legs, indicating she should move them over, and sat beside her. "Tell me *all,* darling," he said as he helped himself to a scone, "and don't omit a single detail."

Kate did not hesitate to tell him all — she'd been dying to talk of the evening, to hear the words from her own lips. She told him about the opera, the magnificence of the Duke of Darlington's box, of meeting the duke's sister and, of course, his lover. She told him about St. James's Palace — for which Aldous had reentered the room and hovered about, listening closely to her description.

When Aldous took his leave once more, Kate told Digby about the prince, and the game of Speculation, and her winning an astounding twenty-four pounds.

"Twenty-four pounds?" Digby cried. "Where is it?"

"Safely put away — half for the ladies down at the docks, half for my future endeavors."

"What else, what else?" Digby insisted, helping himself to a second scone and Kate's tea.

She told him about the accusation of cheating, which angered Digby terribly and prompted him to curse. But when he'd calmed himself, he gestured for her to continue. So Kate told him how the duke had stood up for her.

Kate leaned forward. "He removed me from the room instantly," she whispered. "He was very angry with Lord Dunning and assured me I'd done nothing to deserve such treatment."

"Of course you hadn't!"

"But when we arrived here, he . . . he *kissed* me, Digby." Or perhaps she had kissed him. She wasn't really certain.

Digby froze mid-bite for a moment, then swallowed and put the rest of the scone aside. He removed a kerchief from his pocket and carefully wiped his hands, and returned it to his pocket before speaking. When he did, he looked Kate directly in the eye. "You must use this opportunity to extract something of value from him."

"Pardon?"

"Kate, listen to me," Digby said firmly. "The duke has fallen under your spell. Most men do, eventually — one needed only to glance around Cousineau's tables to see how besotted they all were with you. But *this* is a golden opportunity to ask for money or goods. Whatever you might need."

"No," she said with a shake of her head.

Digby caught her hand and held it tightly. "*Yes,*" he said vehemently. "You cannot waste an opportunity such as this!"

"I will not use him!" Kate cried, appalled,

and tried to pull away from Digby's hand.

"And why should you not? He would use you! Darling, how many years do you think you might have before your looks fade and these lords begin to look elsewhere?"

"Digby!"

"Now, don't be missish," he chastised her. "*I* shall always find you incomparably beautiful, but these gentlemen will look to a younger, beautiful face as you grow older. You are a flower, yes, but the bloom will eventually fade and wither in the shadow of new flowers."

"*Ack!*" Kate cried, jerking her hand free. "It wasn't like that," she insisted. "It felt entirely different from lust!"

Digby blinked. And then his eyes widened with surprise. "My poor darling!" he cried laughingly. "Oh dear, my love, you mustn't allow yourself to fancy that his kiss was anything *but* lust!"

"*No,* Digby," she said angrily, scrambling up off the chaise longue. She wasn't going to allow him to ruin that kiss for her. It *had* been different. For once in her bloody life, it had been different! "It was . . . respectful," she said, folding her arms across her body, rubbing her hands on her arms. "He meant to please me and not merely take his pleasure."

"Bloody hell, Kate," Digby said. "I tell you this for your own good. You must heed me — do not romanticize —"

"I am not!" Kate protested, whirling away from him.

"You certainly are! There *will* come a day when you will meet a gentleman who will love you utterly and completely, but the Duke of Darlington is not he. He is one of *them,* and he'll not change his stripes, not even for a beauty like you! You cannot allow yourself to believe that he will!"

"What did I say of love?" Kate snapped. "You make too much of it, Reginald Digby! I merely said it was different. Respectful! I think I would know the difference!"

She could tell by Digby's pinched expression that he did not believe her, but Kate didn't care. Inside, she was seething. Was she nothing more than a face and a comely body? Was it so absurd to think that perhaps a man, even the Duke of Darlington, might see something in her besides a means to slake his lust?

"Kate —"

"Honestly, I rather wonder what sort of fool you think I am," she said curtly, and sat hard on the chaise. "Let us please discuss more important things. What did you think of the scones?"

Digby eyed her closely; Kate leaned across him, picked up the plate, and thrust it under his nose. "Perhaps you might try another and give me your expert opinion?"

Digby sighed at her shallow attempt to change the subject, but the poor man could not refuse. Everyone had a deepest desire — Digby's happened to be food.

One day passed after the night of the opera, and then two, and still Grayson did not call on the prince as he'd said he would. He made excuses to himself — he had too many pressing issues; it was too bitterly cold to make social calls; Merrick needed him to help round up the necessary votes to pass the abolition bill. But the truth, which Grayson acknowledged at last, was that he didn't want George to agree he'd done all the prince had needed him to do as far as Kate Bergeron was concerned. No, Grayson needed an excuse to see Kate again — not stay away.

A third day passed, during which the bitter cold improved to merely cold, and Grayson went round to see his mother.

The duchess was seated next to a roaring hearth at Beaumont House, embroidering. His nephews, Frederick and Radcliff, were playing with toy wooden horses and soldiers on the floor nearby, and were chastised every few minutes by their grandmamma, who had little tolerance for what she called "rambunctious nonsense" in the house.

Prudence greeted her older brother distractedly. She was dressed as if she intended to go out.

"Did I come round at an inconvenient time?" Grayson asked after greeting his mother and tousling the boys' hair.

"Your call could never be inconvenient, Christie. I am waiting for the carriage so that I may pay a call to Lady Eustis. She has taken ill."

Grayson felt a pang of guilt — the fortnight of having been away from her was rapidly stretching into the three weeks. "Nothing serious, I hope?"

"An ague," Prudence said. "From her note I guess it is the same sort of illness that has the boys' governess in bed. Unfortunately, Diana's illness will keep her at home while Eustis travels on to Bath without her."

So he would have his opportunity to see her after all. It was strange, he thought, that the news didn't rouse him in the least. Grayson smiled at the boys and nudged one of the toy horses with his boot.

Frederick sat back on his heels and announced, "I shall be a pirate one day."

"Master Frederick, you most certainly will not be a *pirate,*" the duchess said.

Frederick's face fell; Grayson winked at him. "One never knows, Mother. Freddie might very well be the most accomplished pirate of the high seas. Or perhaps an officer in the Royal Navy?"

"Don't be absurd, Darlington. That occupation is better left to men who are destined for a life of hard work, and not the gentle occupations of titled gentlemen. Please don't put such ridiculous notions in the heads of my grandchildren," his mother complained, and put down her embroidery, peering at him over the tops of her spectacles. "Speaking of ridiculous notions, I thought we'd agreed that you would not associate with the cloth merchant's woman."

Grayson glanced at Prudence, who wisely averted her gaze and fussed with her cloak. "Dearest Mamma," Grayson said, clasping his hands behind his back, "I am a grown man. I am quite capable of deciding with whom I will or will not acquaint myself."

"I'll have you know that Lady Babington was quite scandalized by your appearance at the opera," his mother continued stubbornly. "She said that everyone in attendance remarked upon it."

"Why is it that Lady Babington does not keep close to her hearth like most ladies in their dotage?" he asked with great exasperation.

"One's dotage does not necessarily mean one is confined to a hearth. And you are intentionally missing the point."

"I am not. I am disagreeing with your point."

"What do you mean?" his mother demanded, clearly appalled. "Do you intend to see her again?"

"I really couldn't say," Grayson said with a shrug. "I find Miss Bergeron to be rather pleasant company."

"On my word! You cannot think to continue this acquaintance!"

Grayson leaned over and kissed his mother's cheek. "Mother, have I ever done anything to disappoint you?"

She frowned. "Of course you haven't. You are a model of decorum."

"Then you needn't fret so," he assured her. "And Lady Babington is in dire need of a hobby."

A cry went up from Radcliff; Grayson looked around to see that Frederick had wrested a wooden horse from his younger brother's hands. Radcliff threw himself at Frederick.

"Stop that at once!" Prudence cried, and grabbed Radcliff up and set him aside. She took the horse from Frederick and returned it to a crying Radcliff. "Freddie, what is the matter with you?"

"The matter with them both is that they are lacking sunshine," the duchess said. "They've not been out of doors in an age and boys need sunshine."

"Why don't you allow me to take them this afternoon, Pru," Grayson suggested. "I shall bring them round to Eustis House when we are done soaking up the sunshine."

"Whatever will you do with them?" Prudence asked laughingly.

Grayson looked at the boys. "Oh, I don't know," he said casually. "I've had a desire to skate on ice of late," he said.

"*Skate!*" Frederick cried, leaping up and down, his dark hair bouncing with him. "Skate, skate, *skate!*"

"Skate!" Radcliff joined in.

"It's a lovely idea! You are a dear, Christie, for thinking of them. Very well, then! I'll send Porter to fetch the skates —"

"Have Porter fetch their coats and scarves. I'll find the skates. I might need to sharpen them a bit," Grayson said. "Come on then, lads," he said. "The sun might very well melt all the ice if we dawdle."

"No!" Radcliff cried, and raced for the door.

"One moment, young lads!" the duchess said sternly. "Are you forgetting something?"

The two boys raced to their grandmother's open arms and didn't squirm too awfully as she covered them with kisses.

With the skates sharpened and tucked beneath the carriage bench on which Grayson sat, and the boys properly bundled, Grayson and the two moppets set out for a frozen pond in Hyde Park.

They took a slight detour and headed around Green Park, then turned onto King Street.

When the carriage rolled to a stop, Frederick and Radcliff fought for a place at the window. "Are we there?" Frederick asked eagerly.

"Not quite yet," Grayson said, gently pulling them back from the window and then pushing them into their bench across from him. "But we shall be on our way shortly. Now sit here, lads, and be very good. Any mischief, and I shall be forced to return you to Grandmamma for discipline."

That had the desired effect — they both sat back and put their hands on their laps.

The door of the carriage swung open and Grayson stepped out. He considered the possibility that he'd lost his mind but walked to Kate's door nonetheless, lifted the door-knocker, and rapped sharply.

Then waited.

Several moments passed. Grayson glanced back at the carriage, could see Frederick and Radcliff's eager faces pressed to the window. He really had no hope they'd wait patiently.

He knocked once more. A moment later, the door swung open and Butler stood in his shirtsleeves, wiping his hands on a towel. "Yes?" he asked brusquely.

Grayson gave him a withering look. "I know this will come as quite a shock to you, Mr. Butler, but I have come to call on Miss Bergeron."

"Not here," Butler said.

That disappointed him much more than Grayson might have guessed. "Is she expected soon?" he asked.

Butler glanced at his carriage. Grayson heard a muffled cry and looked over his shoulder. The boys' faces had disappeared from the window, and the carriage was bouncing oddly. He sighed and shifted his gaze to Butler. "Miss Bergeron?" he reminded him.

"Don't know when she'll return," he said.

"She's gone down to the quays."

"The *quays?*"

Butler frowned. "I won't discuss Miss Bergeron's whereabouts, gov'na."

Another shriek made Grayson wince slightly. "Will you please tell her I called?"

Butler moved to shut the door.

"Is that a yes or no?" Grayson asked.

"Aye, aye, I'll tell her," Butler said, and shut the door.

Grayson stared at the green door for a moment, feeling incredibly disappointed. "Bloody idiot," he muttered under his breath. What was he doing, standing at the door like a spurned lover? What in God's name was he doing here at all?

He heard another muffled shout and pivoted about, striding for the carriage, determined to have a stern word with the two rowdies in his charge.

CHAPTER NINETEEN

"Is that the *duke?*" Digby asked, squinting at something ahead as he and Kate rounded the street corner.

Kate stopped mid-stride. It *was* Darlington. Her heart fluttered strangely as the footman opened the carriage door for him; she felt a warm rush of hope that she hadn't even realized she was harboring. A thousand thoughts ran through her mind, all of them swirling around a very secret fantasy that perhaps he did esteem her.

"Uncle, Freddie pulled my hair!" a boy shouted as Darlington reached the carriage door.

Kate and Digby exchanged a puzzled look.

"Freddie, on my word, I'll tan your hide," the duke said, and put his boot on the step.

He meant to go inside, to drive away. Kate acted quickly, slamming the basket up against Digby's middle at the same time calling, "Your Grace?"

Darlington whirled around at the sound of her voice and he looked, she thought, almost relieved to see her.

In spite of the fact that she was dressed in her plainest clothing and her face was without cosmetic, Kate moved toward him. She could be thankful that the hood of her cloak covered her hair, which was knotted tightly at her nape.

Darlington's gaze was riveted on her face. He took a step toward her, but was startled when a wooden horse flew out the open door and hit him square in the shoulder before clattering to the ground before him.

Kate paused and looked at the toy horse.

So did he. "Kate, please," he said, throwing up a hand, "please wait." He stuck his head in the carriage and said, quite low, "I shall hang you from the highest tree and dangle sweetmeats just beyond your reach if you don't *sit still*," he said firmly. He nodded to the footman, stepped over the wooden horse, and strode to Kate. "I beg your pardon for coming unannounced," he said. "But as you can see, I have my nephews and I promised them an afternoon of ice skating. And I . . . I recalled your desire to try skating and I thought perhaps you might like to join us."

Kate blinked. She looked at the carriage.

Darlington shifted. He seemed strangely anxious. When Kate looked at him again, he said quickly, "Naturally, I will understand if the wooden horse and the complaints of hair-pulling have put you off." Behind him, the footman picked up the wooden horse.

"Uncle Christie!" Freddie called.

Kate couldn't help but notice that Darlington's expression was slightly pained. He had come to take her skating, and this man, this powerful duke, capable of things Kate could scarcely imagine, capable of things Kate could only dream about, looked like a schoolboy asking for his first dance.

Her silence seemed to make him only more anxious. He clasped his hands at his back and said, "I beg your pardon for being so presumptuous." He obviously believed her hesitation meant she would decline his invitation. "I should never have —"

"I'd love to go skating."

Darlington blinked. And then he smiled. "Then . . . then you dare enter the carriage and acquaint yourself with Master Frederick and Master Radcliff?"

"I dare."

"I should like that very much —"

"But I haven't any skates," she hastily added.

"I brought an extra pair with the hope

you might join us."

She couldn't help but smile a little. "You are being kind again, sir, but I must warn you that I have never skated. I haven't the slightest idea how to do it."

"I am prepared to teach you."

Her smile broadened at his hopeful look. "You seem to have thought of everything. I need only a moment with Mr. Digby."

He nodded.

Kate returned to Digby while Darlington waited, and explained what Darlington had come for.

Digby nearly levitated. "If you are to ride off with the Duke of Darlington and his nephews, then you *must* make it very clear that you will expect some sort of payment in return!" he whispered excitedly.

"I most certainly will not!" Kate whispered.

"If you do not, you are a fool."

"I am *not* a fool, and neither am I immoral!"

"This has naught to do with morals!" Digby complained. "This has to do with survival!"

With a roll of her eyes, she handed her reticule to him. "Will you please tell Aldous where I've gone?" she asked, and turned away from Digby before he tried to persuade her further.

She caught Darlington glaring into the interior of the carriage. He straightened up when he saw her walking toward him and seemed to hesitate before gesturing to the carriage door.

Kate looked apprehensively into the carriage. Two young boys were seated side by side on one of the benches, regarding her curiously.

Darlington looked into the interior, too, and said, "We have a guest, lads, and I trust you will be on your best behavior."

The boys looked at Kate again.

Darlington offered his hand to her and helped her up. He took a seat beside her on the bench, his body pressed against hers. The boys stared at Kate.

Darlington smiled as he knocked on the ceiling to send the carriage on. "Miss Bergeron, may I introduce my nephews, Master Frederick," he said, indicating the older one, "and Master Radcliff."

Kate smiled and put out her hand. "How do you do, young sirs?"

The older one — Frederick — took her hand and shook it firmly.

"A pleasure to make your acquaintance, madam," Frederick said automatically, then looked at Darlington. "But who is she, Uncle

Christie?"

"She is my friend, Freddie."

"Is she Mummy's friend, too?"

"Ah . . . well, not as yet," Darlington said uncertainly.

"You can be Mummy's friend, too," Radcliff said to Kate as he swung his feet, knocking his heels against the bench. "She likes friends. She has lots of them."

"That would be delightful," Kate said. "Is that a horse, Master Radcliff?"

"It's *my* horse," he confirmed with a glare for his brother.

"Has he a name?"

"Leo."

"He's *not* Leo!" Frederick cried suddenly. "He's *Robbie*." He reached for the horse, but Radcliff quickly moved it out of his reach.

"Radcliff!" Darlington exclaimed, looking mortified, and reached across the carriage, wresting the horse from the young boy. "It would appear my nephews have quite forgotten their manners, Miss Bergeron. Here now, lads, look there and tell me what you see," he said, pointing to the window.

Both boys instantly pressed their faces to the window, and began to call out the sights — a cart full of cheese wheels. A lady beating a carpet. A dog sniffing around a lamppost as a lamplighter filled it with oil.

Darlington winked at Kate. "They are young and very foolish," he said softly. "They think nothing of disobeying adults and scuffing up floors. You must forgive them for having been raised quite poorly thus far."

Kate laughed, and Darlington's smile warmed considerably.

They were soon at Hyde Park. As they neared the ice skating pond, the boys could hardly be contained in the carriage. Once there, it took quite a lot of doing for Darlington to get them into skates, but when he had them securely fastened onto their feet, they were off, sliding around and at times colliding with other skaters.

"Pardon," Darlington said, "but I really must ensure they do not harm anyone," he said as he quickly strapped on skates. He handed the last pair to Kate. "I'll return in a moment."

He left Kate sitting on a bench. She looked down at the skates. Then at Darlington, who skated easily, the strokes of his legs strong and smooth as he glided along. And when he caught up to the boys, he twirled and grabbed their arms, pulled them close, and leaned down to have a chat with them.

As he led his nephews around the pond, Kate watched the other skaters. One man had his hands clasped behind his back and skated along in a rhythm, his face tilted toward the sun. Young couples held hands and twirled around one another as if they were on a dance floor.

When she spotted Darlington again, he was leading the boys around the pond at a much slower pace, obviously instructing them. Within a matter of minutes, the boys were skating as well as Darlington, and Frederick even attempted to twirl around on one leg. Darlington continued to mind them, catching them if they skated too close to other skaters.

When he was, at last, apparently satisfied that the boys would not crash into anyone or otherwise cause themselves harm, he skated across the pond to Kate, sliding to a stop at the edge of the pond. He looked at the skates in her lap and frowned. "You've not donned your skates, madam."

"I don't know how."

"Mmm," he said. "That sounds a bit like an excuse."

"It's not!" she protested, but when Darlington gave her a dubious look, she admitted, "Maybe a wee bit of one."

He stepped up onto the bank, knelt before her, and gestured to her foot. "May I?"

Kate lifted her skirt to reveal her boots. Darlington put his hand under her ankle and lifted her foot up. He placed the flat surface of the skate against her sole, then lowered her foot and strapped the skate into place. When he'd done the same with the second foot, he stood up and held out his hand.

Kate stood. She felt fairly steady as long as she was merely standing on firm ground, but when she tried to move her foot, she faltered and grabbed his outstretched arm to right herself. "Blast it," she uttered unthinkingly, and righted herself.

Darlington laughed. "It will be easier on the ice," he assured her. He stepped onto the ice, holding out his hand to her, but Kate stood rooted to her spot. "Just put one foot on the ice," he urged her.

"I don't think I can." She felt wobbly, and was certain if she lifted her foot, she would lose her balance.

"Put your hand in mine," Darlington said as a pair of boys rushed past them and jumped onto the ice.

Kate leaned forward as far as she dared, but couldn't quite reach his hand. "Perhaps I should just wait —"

He surprised her by stepping up and grabbing her by the waist and lifting her out onto the ice. He slid backward with the force of her weight; Kate cried out with alarm and instinctively threw her arm around his neck.

Darlington grinned and smoothly put her on her feet, his hands on her waist to steady her, his grip firm and possessive.

But Kate didn't feel the least bit steady and clung to his arms. They were facing each other, still sliding, moving farther out onto the ice. Her legs were locked; other skaters swirled around them, but she could not move. Darlington's nephews suddenly appeared on her right, almost colliding with her in their haste to reach her, and causing Kate to cry out with alarm again.

"Shall we hold her hands, Uncle?" Frederick asked as he skated in a circle around them.

"Thank you, but I've got her," he assured them, and smiled down at Kate with great amusement. "Pardon, madam, but you do not seem as light on your feet as you were at the ball."

"Would that I were at the ball at this very moment," she said breathlessly.

"You must move your feet!" Radcliff exclaimed, squatting down to have a look at her feet.

"I'll instruct her if it's all the same to you, Radcliff," Darlington said. As he moved backward, he moved his legs far apart and then together again, the motion giving him just enough momentum to move them slowly along in a straight line.

"It looks so easy!" Kate exclaimed. "On my word, my ankles will never hold me."

"They will," he assured her. "I have seen your ankles and they appeared quite sturdy."

That brought her head up. For a moment. "And when have you seen my ankles?" she demanded, looking down again.

"I've had mere glimpses," he said. "At the ball. And the opera. Moments ago when I was strapping on your skates."

Kate looked up again, but it was a mistake; one foot slipped. She made a sound of terror as she slid into Darlington's hard chest.

He steadied her with one arm around her back. It was not entirely necessary, as she was already clinging to him, her arms around his back. His strong, broad back. She could feel the strength in him, the hardness of his body, the easy way he held her.

"Perhaps you'd do better if I let go —"

"No, *no!*" she cried. Her hood slipped off, exposing her head and the severe bun at the nape of her neck.

"You're awfully slow, Uncle Christie," Frederick observed.

In her moment of panic, Kate had forgotten the boys were even there.

"Thank you, Frederick, for that helpful

comment. I have a farthing for the first one of you to reach the far side of the pond."

That was all the invitation the boys needed; Frederick pushed Radcliff in an effort to get ahead of him, which caused Radcliff to shout in anger and chase after his older brother.

"As for you, Kate, as agreeable as I find our present arrangement, it does not serve the purpose of actually teaching you to skate."

"That's quite all right. I don't want to know how to skate any longer."

"You do."

"I do *not*. You can put me back on the shore, and I should be delighted to watch you and the boys."

"I am going to hold your arms out —"

"No, no, I can't!" she cried in a panic.

"I won't let you fall," he assured her, his eyes twinkling with amusement.

Kate stared into those eyes. Trust did not come easy to her, but with him . . . it felt different. She reluctantly released her tight hold. He held out one of her arms. Then the other. She could feel the warmth of his hands even through the wool of her cloak. Still holding her, he smiled warmly.

Kate looked down.

"Look at me, not your feet," he said. "Now push with your right leg."

Kate did as he suggested.

"Wonderful. Now the other."

She did it again and gasped with delight. "I'm skating!" she cried, and looked down at her feet.

"Look at me," he reminded her. "Now then, let us have you skate of your own power."

"Christie, no!" she cried, but he'd already let go of her. Kate instantly started to whirl with her arms, but felt her balance slipping. Darlington quickly moved behind her and put his hands on her waist to help steady her. "Slow and easy," he said into her hair, his breath warm on her ear. When she'd found her balance, he let go of her completely.

Kate was suddenly gliding, her arms out for ballast, her legs wide apart. But she was skating. *She was skating!* With a laugh of joy — which momentarily unbalanced her, but from which she was able to regain her balance with a bit more frantic whirling — Kate continued on, methodically pushing with one leg, and then the other.

Unfortunately, she had not yet learned the art of turning, and realized she was headed directly for a group of women who were skating with their arms linked.

"Turn to the right, Kate," Darlington called from behind her.

"How in God's name shall I do that?" she exclaimed frantically.

"Turn to the right!" he said, a bit more urgently.

The women were unaware of Kate hurtling toward them. She would have collided with them headlong, too, had Darlington not grabbed her by the waist at the last moment and veered sharply right. But in saving the ladies from injury, if not death, Darlington's skate tangled with Kate's, and down the two of them went, Kate landing directly on top of Darlington. The fall knocked the air from Kate's lungs for a moment. She looked at Darlington wide-eyed, aware that her breasts were pressed against his chest, and her body stretched the length of his, her feet tangled with his. She suddenly felt awfully warm in her cloak.

Darlington suddenly began to laugh. He cupped her face with his hands. "Are you all right?" he asked laughingly.

"*Me?* Are you?"

"Perfectly fine," he said, and laughed again as Kate struggled to get off of him and help him up. He didn't need her help; he leapt to his feet. "You may think me a wretched dancer, madam, but *you* are the most wretched skater in all of London!" he exclaimed.

"You might have at least instructed me how to stop before hurtling me across the pond!"

"I did not hurtle you. You were listing along like a great galleon across the high seas. Here, put your arms around my neck," he said, leaning down to help her up. He finally managed to get Kate on her feet, but in doing so, he'd had to take firm hold of her, holding her to him in a loose embrace.

"A *galleon?*" she asked, a little breathlessly.

He looked down at her with clear blue eyes; a strand of hair fell over his forehead. His cheeks were rosy from the cold and his lips . . . oh, his lips, those magnificent lips that had created such fantasies in her, were only a few short inches from hers. "A galleon. Clearly, you require more instruction," he said, and his mouth seemed to drift closer to hers.

Kate felt her body go soft, felt the tingling of desire and the instinctive need to yield to the softness. "I should have warned you that I don't take instruction well," she said.

His brow arched in surprise. She felt his hands on her arms. "An unruly student, are you?" he asked softly. "I will have to discipline you accordingly, I suppose."

Kate smiled. She wished she could remove

her cloak and feel the cool air on her very warm skin. "I don't take discipline as well as I give it."

His eyes went dark and his grip of her arms tightened. "That sounds like a challenge," he murmured.

Kate's heart began to flutter; she didn't care that they were in the middle of a public place, that people were sliding by them, laughing and twirling around them. She lifted her face to his . . .

But instead of feelings his lips on hers, she felt a pair of small hands grab her around the knees. "Race with us, will you?" one of the boys shouted. "Madam, will you race?"

Darlington's hands fell away from her; Kate's eyes flew open as she thrust her arms out to balance herself. Radcliff caught one of his uncle's hands; Darlington held out the other to Kate, his dark gaze was still upon her. "We've been challenged to a race, madam. Prepare to set sail."

Kate's skating skills improved only marginally over the course of the next hour, but her ankles, legs, and hips ached from the physical exertion. She begged to be freed from the pond and was grateful when Frederick and Radcliff escorted her off.

Kate sat on the bench and removed her skates. A few moments later, she was joined by Darlington, who had skated off the pond as if he'd only just arrived. "Well then," he asked as he took a seat next to her. "What do you think of skating?"

"Exhilarating," she said and shifted to face him, but the movement caused a sharp pain in her muscles. *"Ow, ow, ow,"* she hissed.

"I forgot to warn you about that," Darlington said with a chuckle.

Kate rubbed her calf. "I must thank you for this, Christie," she said sincerely. "I have wanted to try skating since the first time I first saw people skating on the Thames when I was a girl."

"Grayson," he said.

"Pardon?" She glanced up at him as she continued to rub her calf.

"My given name is Grayson," he clarified. "Rarely used, I grant you, as my family and close acquaintances seem to prefer Christie. But I thought you should know."

Kate slowly straightened up. "Does that mean you consider me a close acquaintance?"

His eyes flitted over her face. "I believe I do."

"How far we have come since our first meeting."

"How far, indeed," he said with a slow smile. He glanced out over the pond, his gaze finding the boys. Kate noticed they'd found a stick and were trying to poke through the ice at the pond's edge. "I have not as yet called on the prince," Grayson said.

Kate kept her gaze on the boys. "Oh," she said airily, "have you not?"

"No." She looked at him then, and he smiled with charming diffidence. "I wanted — want — more time."

Warmth swelled in Kate.

"I wouldn't be the least surprised if you are on the verge of vapors," he said self-consciously. "Wondering how you might send me politely on my way."

She admired his fine profile. "Not at all," she said. But in truth, she wasn't precisely certain what she should say. Benoit had signed a contract for her services. Even though she'd been completely beguiled by the Duke of Darlington and his interest in her was far too exciting to ignore, she was painfully aware of all she risked by even thinking about him.

He looked at her questioningly, and Kate smiled. "Perhaps we might practice skating some more now that I have come so close to mastering it," she suggested, but then shifted and winced at the surprising pain in her hips.

"Oh no," he said, frowning. "Your butler may very well call me out if you look so pained when you return."

Kate laughed.

"I'll be thinking of a suitable second, but in the meantime, I think you should walk. It will help keep your limbs from stiffening."

"I can't possibly walk," she complained.

"Come now," he said, standing and offering his hand. "We can't have your newfound mastery of skating meet such an early demise."

She couldn't help but smile and put her hand in his. He closed his fingers possessively around hers and helped her up.

CHAPTER TWENTY

"His Grace, the Duke of Darlington, Master Frederick Carlisle and Master Radcliff Carlisle," the butler announced at the door of Diana's salon.

"Thank you, Hatt," Diana said and stood from her seat along with Prudence·as Grayson and the boys walked in behind Hatt.

"There you are, my darlings! And how was your skating?" Prudence asked, opening her arms wide for her sons, who ran forward to tell her all.

Diana looked at Grayson and curtsied.

"Lady Eustis, had I not heard you were under the weather, I would not suspect it, for you are the picture of health," Grayson said graciously.

"Indeed, I am suddenly feeling much improved, Your Grace."

"She is the picture of health!" Prudence exclaimed. "I was just saying to her that she might join Lord Eustis in Bath yet. There is still time and the waters would do her good. Don't you agree, Christie?"

"I don't know," Grayson said thoughtfully. "It is quite cold and the journey might do her more harm than good."

"Mummy, I skated as fast as Frederick!" Radcliff said excitedly.

"Did you!" Prudence asked, feigning astonishment. Both boys began to chatter at once, Frederick boasting that he was the far superior skater, and Radcliff complaining that he was not.

Diana smiled at the boys' excitement and their eagerness to recount their adventures of the day. She so desired a pair of boys. Or girls. Any child, as long it was her own. Unfortunately, Charles was incapable of producing an heir. That was quite obvious to Diana. It certainly wasn't from lack of trying, and as she was his third wife, and he'd yet to sire any offspring, she could not help but conclude he was incapable.

The one time she'd suggested this to Charles, he'd slapped her.

"I trust they behaved?" Prudence asked Grayson.

"Perfectly," he said. "And now that I have delivered them safely to your care, Pru, I must take my leave."

"Thank you, Grayson," she said with a

fond smile. "They so enjoy their outings with their Uncle Christie."

"It was my great pleasure." He looked at Diana. "Lady Eustis."

"Your Grace, you must stay for tea," Diana said quickly, hurrying toward him. "Hatt has just brought it up."

"I'm afraid I cannot," he said, and Diana thought he seemed a bit anxious. "I promised Merrick I'd accompany him on a call to Lord Granbury about the upcoming abolition vote."

She was wildly disappointed — she'd not been with him in almost three weeks and was desperate for his attention and affection. "Yes," she said, and put her hand in her pocket and withdrew a small folded vellum. "As to the vote . . . Lord Eustis asked that I see this delivered to you." She handed him the note. It was not from Charles, certainly not — he'd never vote for abolition. It was from her, penned late last night, and she'd been carrying it in her pocket, trying to think of a way to have it delivered to him.

Grayson looked at the sealed note.

"He asked that I have it delivered to you, but here you are," she said with a nervous laugh.

He looked directly into her eyes, but Diana noted a distance in his. "Thank you."

She tried to read something more in his expression, but she could find nothing. That shouldn't surprise her, for Grayson was always so inscrutable in public. He said it was for her sake, to protect her from the slightest bit of innuendo or hint of scandal. Usually, Diana appreciated his circumspection, for it was true that the slightest scandal would be her undoing. Charles held her responsible for their lack of an heir, and he would never forgive her for an affair before she gave him one. Never. She shuddered to think what he might do if he ever learned the truth about Grayson.

Nevertheless, Diana couldn't bear the distance that had sprung up between her and Grayson. Something felt very different, and it was alarming her.

But then Grayson gave her hope; he smiled and winked very subtly. "Very well then, Lady Eustis. Pru, and my young gentlemen, I shall leave you to enjoy your visit."

"Thank your Uncle Christie," Prudence said to her children.

Frederick did so by throwing his arms around Grayson's legs; Grayson laughed and picked the boy up, slinging him over his shoulder and bouncing him a bit before putting him down and doing the same to Radcliff.

As the boys called out a farewell to him, Diana imagined another salon, another town, another time, when the children Grayson held would be theirs. It was a fantasy, completely unattainable in any way, shape, or form. But she liked imagining it. It was the only thing that made her truly happy.

"Diana? Are you all right?" Prudence asked.

Diana turned slightly and realized she was staring at the door through which Grayson had gone. "I, ah . . . I'm feeling a bit flush, that's all," she said, and returned to her seat, sitting heavily.

"Mummy, Freddie pushed me when we were skating," Radcliff complained.

"I didn't!" Frederick insisted.

"He did, Mummy, he pushed me twice, and he pushed the lady and made *her* fall down."

"Oh dear. I hope the lady wasn't hurt," Prudence exclaimed.

"No. She and Uncle Christie laughed."

Diana's gaze darted to little Radcliff.

"I hope you apologized to her, darling," Prudence said, running her hand over Radcliff's head.

Radcliff nodded enthusiastically that he had. "Uncle Christie said she'd be black and blue because she fell so many times."

"Once, she fell like this," Frederick said, and dramatically fell backward onto the carpet. He and Radcliff laughed.

Diana's heart began to race. She sat up in her seat. "Who was the lady, Frederick?" she asked, trying to sound as nonchalant as possible.

"Uncle Christie's friend," Frederick said as he picked himself up.

"Uncle Christie's friend?" Prudence repeated, frowning with a bit of confusion. "And who might that be?"

"I don't know," Frederick said with a shrug.

"May we play with these?" Radcliff asked, squatting down to have a look at a pair of ornamental brass peacocks that were placed at the corner of the hearth.

"Yes, of course you may," Diana said absently, but her mind was whirling, her belly churning. She glanced at Prudence, who seemed completely unbothered by the boys' remarks — she was far more concerned that Radcliff not try and pick up one of the heavy brass birds.

Diana knew instinctively that Grayson's friend was Katharine Bergeron. She didn't know how she could possibly know such a thing, seeing as how she'd not witnessed it herself or heard more than the boy's utterance . . . but she'd never been more certain of anything in her life.

CHAPTER TWENTY-ONE

Later that week, Digby told Kate that he had business that would take him away from London for a few days. He explained that he was trying to break into the growing perfume trade, for he believed a good profit was to be had there.

Kate told Digby what Fleming had said that afternoon in St. Katharine's. "Why would he accuse you of pilfering?" she asked.

"Because he believes there is opportunity in the perfume trade as well, and he doesn't care for the competent competition I give him." Digby sniffed. "I've not pilfered a bloody thing from that scoundrel, but I am the agent for a French perfumerie whose products Fleming had hoped to sell in England. And now, I have it on very good word that an Italian perfume should arrive in Deptford tomorrow evening. If rumors can be believed, this perfume will be the most sought-after scent in London, and I intend to get there before Fleming. He thinks to throw a rub in *my* way," Digby scoffed. "He fancies himself far superior, but the man is no better than a gutted fish on the quay. He should have a care with me, he should. I am quite well-connected." With that, Digby had given Kate a kiss on the cheek and gone off to find his fortune in perfume.

Coincidentally, Aldous sought her out that very same day and told her he'd been invited to a private card game down at the Wapping quays.

"Really?" Kate said. "With whom?"

"Captain Smith of the *St. Marie*," he said proudly. "He holds a table for high stakes when he's in port."

"I didn't know you were acquainted with him," Kate said curiously.

"I'm not," Aldous said. "But I'm a fine gambler, I am. Word's gone round, that's all."

That likely was true — Aldous was a frequent visitor to the gaming hells.

"You'll be alone," Aldous said. "I'll send for Amy —"

"No, no, I'll be fine!" she assured him. "I want to bake tonight." In truth, Kate was so rarely alone that she relished the idea.

Kate and her daily cook, Cecelia, made a

trip to a local market — one that was decidedly more hospitable than St. Katharine's. They bought leeks for soup, beef to be roasted, as well as some winter vegetables, and of course, the necessary ingredients for the sweetmeats Kate would bake.

"Sure you won't need my help with the roast, mu'um?" Cecelia asked later that afternoon when Kate handed over her wages for the week.

"Thank you, but no."

"Very well, then," Cecelia said, and donned her cloak. "You'll remember what I said, aye?"

"I will," Kate said. It couldn't be so terribly difficult to roast beef. She wasn't a novice, after all — she was becoming quite adept at baking, and roasting didn't seem so far removed from that. "Have a lovely evening, Cecelia."

"I'd wager there's little hope of that, mu'um. Two children and a husband fond of his drink." She pulled her old hood over her hair and grinned. "But I think the evening will be a bit more bearable if I give him a shilling for a tankard or two, aye? Good night, mu'um."

"Good night, Cecelia," Kate said, and saw the cook out the back door. As Cecelia hurried down the alley, Kate glanced up at the sky. Clouds were beginning to gather and the air was damp. A storm was moving into London.

In the kitchen again, Kate set out preparing her evening meal of roast beef and vegetables, and putting the finishing touches on her marzipan creation. Every good baker had to master the artistry of marzipan, and her recent outing had inspired Kate. With Cecelia's help, Kate had made several small figures of ice skaters out of marzipan, and set them on a piece of glass. The figures weren't as lifelike as she'd hoped they'd be, but one could not mistake them — they were clearly skaters. Kate had even made marzipan trees and placed them at the edges of her frozen pond. Digby would be pleased and amused when she showed him the elaborate confection.

Kate checked on the beef roasting in a small oven. "The trick is to keep it moist, or it will look and taste like an old abandoned shoe," Cecelia had warned her with a wrinkle of her nose.

Satisfied there was enough liquid in the pan to keep it moist, Kate removed her apron and poured herself a glass of wine.

Her thoughts turned to Grayson, as they had so many times since the afternoon of skating in Hyde Park. Somewhere between the dozens of times she'd fallen and he had helped her up, Kate had realized she was feeling something rather extraordinary for him, something she'd never felt for a man before.

In the days since, she'd created quite a fantasy surrounding him, of when she might see him, of the things they'd do. She'd even convinced herself that she could see Grayson and the prince would be very pleased with her efforts to befriend the duke. After all, Darlington was doing the prince an enormous favor. Wouldn't the prince be pleased that she'd been so kind to his friend?

Kate couldn't sustain that absurd fantasy, but it amused her to think it nonetheless, and in some respects, it made her feel less . . . disobedient.

"You've not disobeyed, old girl," she muttered to herself as she tied herbs she and Cecelia had bought and hung them to dry. "It's not as if you've taken a lover." A wanton smile curved her lips.

That was another little fantasy altogether.

But it was one she'd never act on. Benoit had signed a contract with the prince that Kate had agreed to honor. She could not be enticed to break it or dishonor it, for she'd learned long ago she was nothing without her word.

And if she were tempted, she need only remember how much she stood to lose. This house, certainly. The fine clothes and jewels she wore every day. She'd be put out, forced out "on the town," so to speak, with nowhere to turn but prostitution to make her living. That was if the prince didn't do something drastic in his anger, such as send her from London and out of his sight. Or worse — Kate had heard rumors that he'd attempted to have his wife murdered! Might he be so angry he'd contemplate her murder? Perhaps he would prefer to see her publicly disgraced —

A knock at the door startled her. Kate glanced at the clock. It was a quarter to eight.

"Bloody hell," she said, and put a hand to her hair — she guessed she looked a fright. Who could it be? *The prince.* Of course! She quickly smoothed her gown and pinched her cheeks, but her hair hung loosely down her back. There was nothing to be done for it, and when a second, firmer knock sounded, Kate hurried to the door. She pulled it open with a smile to greet the prince, but words escaped her — it wasn't the prince at all, but Mr. Fleming.

Kate hesitated, and in that moment, the man had a hand on the door, was pushing it

— and her — with enough force to make her stumble backward.

"Mr. Fleming!" she cried, pushing back against the door. "What are you doing here?"

His response was to shove harder and stride into her foyer. "That's not the proper way to greet a gentleman caller, is it?" he said coolly.

"You are not welcome here!" she insisted. "Mr. Digby will be here at any moment and I —"

"Your *Digby* won't be round. I warned you he should not steal what I've worked hard to build! I've sent him chasing after ghosts. He is a fool if he believes a decent perfume would come out of Italy."

Kate gaped at him.

"And your sailor is in a pub on the quay at Wapping with a tankard or two, thanks to my generosity. I doubt he'll be rushing to your side, either."

Fear settled in Kate's belly. *The rent.* He'd come for his blasted rent! "How did you find me?" she demanded.

Fleming laughed. "Have you been gone from St. Katharine's so long that you don't suspect every young ragamuffin who follows along behind you?"

She had a vague memory of a pair of lads

Digby had shooed away with a half pence recently.

With the heel of his boot, Fleming kicked at the door and walked deeper into her foyer. He glanced around at the furnishings. "Well then, this is quite nice, eh?" he said, nodding his approval. "It pays very well to be the duke's whore."

Anger mingled with terror, but Kate said nothing as she looked about for something with which to defend herself. But when she looked at Fleming again, his gaze was raking over her unbound hair, his hunger apparent.

"If you think to intimidate me with threat of violence, you will be disappointed," she snapped. "I have nothing. Everything you see here belongs to someone else. None of it is mine."

"Miss Bergeron," he said, stepping closer to her. "Do you *really* think I came all this way for money? I have a personal message for your man," he said snidely, his gaze on her bosom.

Kate suddenly understood. "This is how you will punish Digby? By abusing me?"

He snorted. "Do you know a better way to gain a whale's attention than by dangling a prized fish before its snout?"

A knife. She needed a knife to defend herself, but realized that if she bolted for the kitchen, he would catch her. She had to somehow maneuver around to the corridor to have even a chance. "Leave my house, Mr. Fleming," she said, her voice shaking with impotent fury.

He chuckled and his gaze drifted lower. "I won't leave until I have what I want, Miss Bergeron. I've wanted it from the moment we met, and I will have it. One way or another."

Kate's fear made her feel ill. "Do you honestly think you'll get away with something so vile?" she asked as she backed away from him, toward the hallway door.

Fleming's cold smile disappeared. "No one will believe the word of a whore," he said, and suddenly lunged for her, grabbing her hair when she whirled and tried to run.

"Take your hand from me!" Kate cried.

"You seem to forget, madam, that I have the power to put your wards out on their arscs by morning." He wrapped her hair around his fist and yanked it hard. "And I can put you on yours, here and now."

Kate's blood ran cold. She tried to pull away from him, but he yanked her hair again, causing her to gasp with pain. "I shall tell the duke!" she cried.

"Tell him," Fleming snarled. "Likely he will hold *you* responsible for not having safeguarded your body for him, aye? You will lose all *this*," he said, gesturing with one hand while yanking her hair with the other.

Kate swung with her elbow, connecting with the soft part of Fleming's belly. He grunted, yanked her hair harder, and pulled her head back. He leaned over, so that she could see the harsh expression on his face. "Think of what you are doing, woman," he said hotly. "I will take my pleasure whether or not you take yours."

That sickened her; her mind swam back to another bitterly cold and dark night.

"Be a love now, and don't fight me."

CHAPTER TWENTY-TWO

Grayson didn't intend to come to Kate's when he'd stepped into his carriage that evening, but he found himself before her house nonetheless. He noticed, standing outside his carriage, that her door was ajar and imagined that a party was taking place inside, with gentlemen and courtesans.

And him, out of place, the fool who had stopped here like some lovesick lad. He was expected at Mary's for supper in an hour, but he couldn't keep away from Kate one more moment. He felt ridiculous, standing there on the street, looking at her door.

The wind was picking up; a winter storm was moving in. Grayson walked to the door. Even if there was a party within, the wind would make the house cold, and he could at least make himself useful by seeing that it was shut. But as Grayson neared the door, he heard the snarl of a male voice and the distress in a woman's cry. That alarmed him;

he didn't bother to knock, but pushed the door open and saw the man with his hand in Kate's hair.

Wild, raw anger shot through him; Grayson dove into the small foyer and grabbed the man by the shoulder. When he saw the sneer on the man's face, the wild, raw anger soared dangerously. *"Unhand her!"*

Kate cried out; Grayson grabbed the bastard by the lapels of his coat, shoved him hard against the wall, forcing him to let go of Kate's hair. He held the man against the wall, one arm across his throat, his knee in the man's groin. "I should kill you," he breathed.

"She owes me money!" the man insisted.

"You have an abusive way of asking for it," Grayson said tightly, and pushing him toward the door.

The man stumbled and righted himself; Grayson lunged again, pushing him so hard that he went tumbling out the door, almost landing on his arse. A couple passing by cried out in alarm, but the bastard was already up and running, disappearing around the corner.

Grayson stepped back in and closed the door. His hat, which had come off his head, lay on the floor. Kate was standing just where he'd left her, her eyes wide, her chest rising with each deep breath, looking appalled and frightened. Her beautiful corn silk hair was rudely messed.

"God help me — are you all right?" Grayson asked, and started toward her, but Kate gasped and took an abrupt step backward, as if she now feared *him*. Grayson hesitated, uncertain what to do. He made a move toward her again, and she suddenly ran into the drawing room, looking wildly about, as if seeking an escape.

"Kate!"

Kate ran to the window. "They aren't locked. They must be locked!"

Grayson strode forward, catching her before she could run again, putting his arms around her and pulling her back against his body. "It's all right, Kate," he said soothingly. "You're safe. I'm here now, and you are safe."

"Oh God, Christie . . ." She sagged with relief. "The windows —"

"I'll get them," he said, and reluctantly let her go to check them, finding them locked.

"I am so very sorry," Kate said.

Grayson whirled around. "Why should you apologize? Are you all right? Did he harm you?"

"No, not really —"

"What is his name? Give me his name

and I will see to it that he never bothers you again."

She made a sound of helplessness. "Your sort of power has no meaning in his world."

"His world? *What* world?"

"It's too complicated." She suddenly covered her face with her hands.

Feeling helpless, Grayson reached for her, but she dipped to her right to avoid his hand. "Where is your butler?" he demanded.

"Gone," she said. "They're all gone. He made certain of it."

His anger began to rise again. "What do you mean?" She was shaking, and he put his hands on her shoulders. Kate flinched, but at least she did not move away. "Who *is* he?" Grayson demanded.

"Fleming, his name is Fleming. But here now, I will not have you believe I owe him money!" she said suddenly, and gripped his arms. "I am *not* a debtor! I let a pair of rooms from him and he recently — *very* recently — decided to increase the rent."

"Rooms?"

"Rooms," she said, wincing. "In St. Katharine's, down by the quays."

St. Katharine's? Grayson knew the area of St. Katharine's. There were parts of it, most notably around the old hospital and church, that had once been respectable, but today the streets on the water's edge were quite mean.

Kate colored slightly at his expression of surprise and dropped her hands from him. "I lease the room for some . . . acquaintances."

Grayson instantly thought of the sort of "acquaintances" she might have that required a room.

Kate realized what he was thinking, because she gasped. "Oh no. No, no, not *that*," she said quickly. "My acquaintances are young women who have no home," she clarified. "They need a place to live, and if they didn't have the place I let — I assure you, it is hardly more than a hovel — I fear they would have to take different accommodations . . . if you take my meaning."

"I do," he said, frowning. "But it is dangerous for you to go there."

"Now you sound like Digby," she said wearily. "He will not allow me to go there unaccompanied. But as I've said to Digby on more than one occasion, I am probably better suited to St. Katharine's than he is, as I hail from there, whereas *he* hails from Southwark."

Grayson stilled a moment and looked at Kate. If she thought she'd said anything unusual, she certainly didn't show it. He didn't know what he expected, really — he supposed he thought her a merchant's daughter, come to London from some village. Some place not quite as . . . as loathsome as St. Katharine's. "You hail from St. Katharine's?" he asked carefully.

"I was named for it, actually. Not the quay, mind you, but the church."

He couldn't think of that now. "Did this Fleming come for the rent?" he asked. "Do you need some assistance —"

"No!" she exclaimed, clearly mortified by his suggestion. "No, no, his anger is with Digby. He happened to see a mention of the ball in the morning *Times,* and he believes that you are my benefactor, and . . . and well, you know, he thinks I am swimming in lard."

Grayson may not have used those words, but he knew very well what she meant — the man thought she had money. There were charlatans and users who always sought to use him and his family ill because of their money. He sighed sadly and caressed the side of her face with his palm. "I am sorry that my burden has extended to you, Kate. It is a burden that comes with privilege."

"There is a certain burden that comes from having nothing, too," she said. "He was convinced I'd never speak of this to you for fear of losing everything — Oh, but it never would have happened, for Aldous is always nearby, and I . . . I thank you, Grayson. Thank you for saving me."

Saving her. He hadn't saved her, he couldn't save her from her life. He'd just arrived at the right moment. He stroked her hair again. "Tell me you are all right."

"I'm all right," she said, and tried to smile, even though tears filled her eyes. "I have weathered worse."

"That does not ease my mind." He twisted a strand of her hair around his finger. "That does not ease it in the least, for you are an extraordinarily beautiful woman, and I, like most breathing men, cannot take my eyes from you. I cannot bear to know there are those who would take advantage of that beauty."

Kate had been told all her life she was beautiful, but when he said it, it sent a flash of warmth through her.

"But as much as I admire your beauty, I think I admire your spirit far more," he added, and caressed her cheek with his knuckles.

It was the one thing Kate desired above all else, to be admired for something other than her looks. In Grayson's blue eyes she could see her yearning mirrored back at her. She felt wholly desirable for the first time in her life and not simply like a vessel into which he could shed his lust, as she'd felt with Benoit and the prince and other men who looked at her in that way. *"Don't,"* she whispered. "Don't say those things."

One of Grayson's brows rose quizzically above the other. "Why not?"

"Because it makes me want you," she said. "I am safer if I don't want."

Grayson frowned and touched his thumb to her bottom lip. "How tedious," he said softly. "If you don't allow yourself to want . . . and to want with every fiber of your being . . . how will you know pleasure?"

"That's easy for you to say — you're a duke," she said, helplessly entwining her fingers with his. "But I would risk everything I have for pleasure."

"I risk more than you know — I have been entrusted by my prince to keep you safe for him."

"And I have given him my word. It's all I have; I cannot go back on it. Just your being here is a risk, although I am grateful for it." She peeked up at him. "But why did you come?"

He didn't answer straightaway, but slipped two fingers beneath her chin and studied her face. "I had to see you."

Kate shook her head. "You are attempting to seduce a seductress —"

"It is dangerous, it is insanity," he quickly interjected. "I told myself as much, yet I could not stay away."

She couldn't listen to this; the temptation was too great. Kate abruptly turned away from him, took several steps to put some distance between them. When he stood so close —

Grayson moved to where she stood and drew his finger down her spine. She gasped softly at the sensation. "One moment," she said raggedly. "One moment is all it would take to put me on the street."

Grayson responded by moving her hair and then kissing her nape.

Kate knew she should move away, ask him to leave, to go, to stop tempting her. But her yearning weakened her. "Just one moment," she whispered.

"I cannot help my desire," he said, and kissed her nape again. "It grows, it beats a constant drum —"

"Stop!" she cried, and whirled around to face him. "Please don't say another word."

"I am not asking you to act on it, but I must know if you feel that desire, too."

"You know I do." She felt it deep in her marrow. She felt it so deeply that she was on the verge of risking everything for love, real love, the sort of love she'd never dared dream of.

"Just . . . don't," she said again, as if those words somehow protected her. But at the same time, she leaned closer to him, so that her lips were only a breath from his.

His fingers moved lightly across her jaw, to the bottom of her ear, inflaming her skin. "I want to kiss you but my conscience fights me. If I do that, I have betrayed the prince and enticed you to do the same."

His words only weakened her further. She didn't have the power or the desire to turn away from him. She had nothing in her but need — raw, pulsing need.

His dark blue gaze fell to her lips. "And I will have betrayed someone else."

She knew precisely whom he meant, but Kate hadn't thought of his lover until this moment. That was the thing that would hold him back.

Her disappointment was sharp; she lowered her head. Honestly, she could be such a fool at times. There was nothing here for her; she was living a fantasy, still waiting like a little girl for faeries to come and carry her off. Bitter dismay had her by the throat.

"Fear of risk will often outweigh a man's desire," he muttered.

Kate looked up. "I suppose this is one of those times."

Grayson laid his palm against her cheek

and shook his head. *"No,* Kate," he said. "No, this is *not* one of those times. This is a moment unlike any other."

He kissed her.

The tension in Kate's body didn't ease with his kiss; her anticipation of more only heightened it. He put his hand on her waist and slowly slid his palm up, to her ribcage, to her breast. Her body thrilled to his touch; she gravitated closer to him.

Grayson suddenly caught her in an embrace, his hand sinking into her hair, pulling her against his body as he kissed her with the same wild need swirling in her.

Another breath, and they were on the settee. Grayson's hand was on her ankle beneath the hem of her gown, sliding up her leg, to the top of her stocking and then to her bare thigh, to the space between her legs.

Kate dug her fingers into his shoulders and gasped into his mouth when he touched her there. She was damp, and as his fingers danced in the furrow of her sex, shivers of passion began to radiate through her body. There was no going back. She had crossed the boundary of integrity for a maddening desire.

Grayson suddenly shifted about. "Your gown," he said breathlessly, "it must come off." His fingers eagerly began to fly down the buttons of her back.

Kate stopped him. She took his hands from her body and pressed them to his chest. He watched her with avid curiosity. Madame Albert had once told Kate that men are aroused by what they see, and women by what they hear. She stood up and slowly, carefully, pushed the gown off one shoulder. Grayson swallowed, his gaze on her shoulder. She pushed the gown off the other shoulder and let it slide down her body and stepped out of the gown.

Grayson's blue eyes darkened as he looked at her body. His nostrils flared with his intake of air as his gaze skimmed over her breasts that strained against the fabric of her thin chemise. "My God, you are feminine perfection," he said roughly and quickly shed his coat, waistcoat, and neck cloth.

She smiled wantonly and untied the ribbon of her chemise. It gaped open and his eyes fixed on her breasts. A moment later, Kate lifted her chemise over her head and tossed it aside. She stood before him completely bare, letting him see her. His arousal was evident; Kate stepped over his legs, straddling him, and lowered herself to his lap.

He groaned with pleasure, and put his hands to her breasts. "Beautiful Kate," he said, and bent his head, kissed one shoulder, then the other, biting her lightly, then took her breast into his mouth.

The sensation was divine; Kate's head fell back and she closed her eyes, floating along on the desire he stirred in her.

As he teased her breast with his lips and tongue, Kate moaned. "You are snatching my breath away," she whispered, and pushed her fingers through his hair.

"You are snatching my reason away." His hand moved up her leg.

"Are we mad?" Kate asked breathlessly as her hands began an exploration of their own.

"Utterly and completely." He suddenly gathered her in his arms and stood from the settee with her, then put her on her back on the rug before the hearth. His body covered hers, his lips on her lips.

Kate had never felt anything more than tolerance at the prospect of physical relations with a man, but tonight . . . tonight she felt urgency, a strong and natural flow of desire for Grayson. She sought his body, her hands beneath his shirt, raking down his chest and back. Her mouth was open beneath his, her tongue twirling around his. She pressed her breasts against him, and when he pushed her hands away to unbutton his shirt, she boldly moved her hand to the front of his trousers and slid her palm down his erection.

Grayson lifted his head as if he meant to say something, but he didn't speak at first. He could only look at her with eyes darkened by his longing. She cupped him, rubbed her hand against him.

"Kate," he said hoarsely.

Benoit had never used her name in such intimate circumstances — he'd never said a word, really, other than "move here" or "there." But when Grayson whispered her name with such raw desire, Kate was astoundingly aroused by it. The dam of yearning burst within her. It was unlike any corporeal sensation she'd ever experienced; it was pleasure beyond her wildest imagination. She felt no apprehension, no resignation. She felt nothing but a need to be with him, to feel him inside her body, his hands on her flesh.

Grayson removed his shirt. He was truly magnificent, his shoulders broad and muscled, his chest hard and sculpted to a man's most alluring form. She impulsively kissed his chest, her tongue on his nipples as her hands flitted over his body.

"God help me, I want you," he said fervently, his hand moving between her legs.

"What passion you stir in me," she whispered breathlessly.

Those words excited Grayson's blood to a raging river in his veins. His desire for her was overpowering him. Her hair lay in wild silken waves about her shoulders; her pale green eyes were like twin beacons of light. She was panting a little as her hands roamed his body; her plump lips parted slightly, her skin flushed.

He pushed the boots from his feet and unfastened the flap of his trousers. She was lying beneath him now, her breasts rising with each furious breath, as enticing as any woman could possibly be. Her gaze devoured him, her seductive smile conveyed the pleasure he was giving her.

That smile deepened when she took him in hand and began to stroke him. Grayson slipped his fingers into the wet groove of her sex and watched her eyes flutter shut as he stroked her with as much passion as she stroked him. He moved in between her legs, pushed them aside with his knees, and when her hand fell away from his engorged cock, he pressed the tip of it against her, moving in tantalizingly slow motions against her body.

Kate's breathing deepened; she grasped his hips, pulling him closer, her body pulsating against him. Grayson closed his eyes, concentrating on the exquisite pleasure, and slipped his hand between her legs to caress her again as he guided the tip of him into her sheath.

But as he slid into her and began to move, Kate's eyes suddenly opened and she looked up at him as if she were surprised. For a moment, Grayson feared he'd hurt her, but then a smile of pure pleasure lit her face. "Oh my," she said as she raked her hands down his back and lifted her knees. "Oh *my.*"

Her obvious delight made him burn to give her more. Grayson was beyond redemption; he stroked her as he moved inside her, kissed her with all the longing he felt, catching her bottom lip between his teeth, swirling his tongue inside her mouth. Her body fit him perfectly; her response to him was so instinctive that the force of emotion swirling in him astounded him.

Kate wrapped one leg around his back, her arms around his neck, and returned his kiss with abandon. With her hand, she reached between them to feel his body slide into hers.

When she began to pant, Grayson clasped her hard and tightly, lifted his hips, and thrust deep into her. With a cry of ecstasy, Kate's body spasmed around his. Grayson thrust faster until the shudder of his own release racked his body.

He dropped his forehead to her shoulder.

It was several moments before he could find the strength to lift his head. He was spent, his body wrung dry. He brushed Kate's hair from her eyes and took pleasure in her glowing smile. She pressed her hand to his face. "I have never, *never* been so moved. I had no idea such pleasure was possible." She caressed his face and kissed his mouth. "That was glorious, Grayson." She kissed his eyes.

Who was this beauty? Who was this woman who could take his breath away with a mere smile? He kissed her again, eased out of her body, and rolled onto his back. Kate rested her head on his chest and draped an arm across him.

They lay that way a few moments until Grayson smelled something odd. "What is burning?" he asked.

Kate idly kissed his chest. And then gasped loudly. "The roast!" she cried, and began groping for her clothing, finding only her chemise and his coat handy, which she donned as she dashed from the room.

Grayson remained behind at first, propped on one elbow, feeling a little unsteady. This was a profound night, one that transcended his previous experiences with women. He'd entered a realm of seductive pleasure he'd only brushed up against before. It was entirely different from anything he'd known with Diana, and as much as he didn't want to compare the two women, he could scarcely avoid it.

Naturally, it raised some very uncomfortable questions in his mind. With Diana, the act was always frenzied and quick, and he wasn't certain they could ever relax enough to simply enjoy one another as completely, as wantonly, as he and Kate had done.

Now, as he found his trousers and pulled them on, he wasn't certain he even wanted to try.

In Kate's arms, he felt wholly satisfied but strangely vulnerable, as if he was wandering aimlessly down an unmarked path, uncertain of which way to turn, of what he was doing, of how to find his way back to the man he knew himself to be. He only knew that he did not know this uncertain man. He could not *be* this man, this man who was falling in love with a courtesan.

CHAPTER TWENTY-THREE

When he'd dressed, Grayson followed the sounds to the small kitchen, carrying Kate's gown and slippers.

"It's ruined," she said, holding up a pan containing something that looked like a brick when he entered.

"I am sorry," he said uncertainly. She'd never looked more beautiful than she did now with her hair tangled about her shoulders, wearing a chemise and his very large coat.

She put the pan aside, and with hands on hips, she surveyed the room. "I'll make leek soup. Will that suit?" she asked hopefully.

Grayson hesitated. He hadn't intended to stay; he was expected at Mary's at this very hour. He should go, he had to go before he caused any more damage than he'd already done. But looking at her now, his heart still beating strongly from their lovemaking, he heard himself say, "I adore leek soup."

Kate smiled with relief. "Perhaps we should . . ." She gestured between his coat and her gown, which Grayson held.

"Perhaps we should," he said sheepishly, and took the coat she'd slipped out of and handed her the gown. When she'd donned the gown, she presented her back to him as if that were perfectly natural. Grayson buttoned her up.

As she prepared the hearth to make her soup, Grayson went out to his carriage and told his driver to come round for him at dawn. When he returned, he found Kate wearing an apron, her hair tied in a knot at her nape. She had several vegetables before her on a wooden table and looked charmingly domestic. Over her head hung a variety of pots and dried herbs and flowers.

"Let me recall . . . *leek.* Two pounds of leeks, said Squeak. With four carrots said Harriet. And six potatoes said Ignacio, but don't forget a dash of me, cried Marjoram and Rosemary."

"I beg your pardon?"

"That's the recipe," Kate said with a sheepish smile. "My mother taught me that song to remember the ingredients." She picked up a knife and began to chop leeks.

Grayson tried to imagine a small Kate helping her mother make soup. "How long did you say it had been since your mother died?"

"Oh, she's been gone quite a long time," Kate said. "Perhaps as long as fourteen or fifteen years. I know that I was twelve years old when she died of consumption, for my birthday came just before her passing."

He thought that was an odd thing to say. She was uncertain how much time had passed since her mother had died? Or if her father lived?

"It's been quite a long time, but I still miss her terribly," Kate added as she put the leeks in the kettle and started to slice another batch. "Is your mother in good health?" she asked curiously.

"Ah, the dowager duchess of Darlington is very much alive and in good health, thank you." Grayson chuckled.

"You're very fortunate, then," she said as she gathered more potatoes from a small crate.

Grayson swiped one of the pieces she'd cut. "Tell me about Mr. Digby and Mr. Butler."

"They are my friends," she said, putting potatoes in the pot. "Mr. Digby and I have been very close for many years. He has helped me immeasurably."

"How so?"

"Well, he taught me to read and to speak

properly."

"He was your tutor?" Grayson asked, confused.

Kate laughed. "I suppose one might call him that," she said. "Digby was very honest with me from the beginning. He worked for Benoit Cousineau, as did I, in the cloth halls of St. Katharine's. When Mr. Cousineau expressed a desire . . . a desire to have me," she said, averting her gaze, "I refused. But Digby made me understand that if I didn't give in to my lot, I would suffer far worse. And he was right, you know."

"How could you believe that he was right?" Grayson blurted, appalled.

Kate looked at him with surprise. "It wasn't as if I had a choice. I was not born to a life of privilege. I was on my own by the age of thirteen or fourteen. If I had not done as Mr. Cousineau wished, I would have found myself without honest employment. And had I lost gainful employment, I would have been forced to find another way to pay for my room. There are not many ways a young miss can earn a shilling, which Digby pointed out to me. He assured me I could make a far better and comfortable living as a courtesan."

Grayson gaped at her, shocked at how pragmatically she'd spoken. "Surely there was *something* you might have done."

She put down her knife. "What?" When he didn't have an answer for her, she said, "I am not a proud courtesan, but I am a practical one. When Digby came to my rescue, my virtue had already been taken from me against my will. I have found it easier to go along willingly than to fight the inevitable." She picked up the knife and began slicing potatoes.

Grayson couldn't speak for a moment. He tried very hard to imagine that the beautiful woman standing before him had risen from such base circumstances. He tried to imagine a girl — thirteen or fourteen years, by her own admission — making her way in what was clearly a cruel world. But he could only think of the enormous estate of Darlington Park and the idyllic childhood he'd known there. He couldn't imagine himself at the age of thirteen having the wits about him to survive.

"As for Aldous," Kate said, smiling again, "he'd not like to hear you call him a butler. But it was unavoidable, I'm afraid. The agreement Benoit signed with the prince allows me a butler, a daily maid, and a daily cook. So Aldous became Mr. Butler. But I assure you, he does not fancy himself one," she said with a laugh.

"That is painfully obvious," Grayson snorted. "What does he fancy himself?"

"A bluecoat," she said proudly. "He came ashore after one voyage and fell into a spot of trouble. Mr. Cousineau and I happened to witness it, and the ruffians might have killed him had we not intervened. Aldous was badly injured, however, so I had him brought to Digby. Together, we nursed him back to health." She smiled as she put the potatoes in the soup pot. "I know he feels indebted to me, although he won't own up to it. But I think he should live his own life again. He won't hear of it — he thinks that would be disloyal to me. So he stays on, insists that he is quite happy, and that I need him about."

"I daresay you do," Grayson grudgingly admitted, the night's events still on his mind.

"Do you know that he has been as far away as India?" Kate said, her eyes brightening with delight.

Grayson was fascinated by Kate. As she recounted the tales of Aldous's sea voyages, he thought of the first time he'd made her acquaintance. He'd assumed she'd chosen the path of a highly placed courtesan. As he'd come to know Kate better, he'd discovered she was warm and vibrant, and he'd thought that very pleasing in a beautiful woman. He could certainly understand why George found her so appealing.

But now he was hearing of a woman who wasn't entirely certain of her own age, of a life carved out of the crowded streets near the St. Katharine quay, of alliances with perhaps the only two men she'd ever known who didn't exploit her.

And he thought, with the smell of leek soup and the sound of her lovely laughter around him, that it was very odd the Duke of Darlington had never felt quite as comfortable with another person as he felt in this little kitchen with beautiful Kate.

He was not alone in his marveling. Kate couldn't keep from looking across the scarred wooden table to the man who'd just made passionate love to her. It seemed impossible that the Duke of Darlington, with his mussed hair, rumpled shirt, and neck cloth hanging loose down his chest, was eating a carrot in her kitchen beneath drying herbs and flowers.

She could almost believe the faeries had whisked her away to a cottage in the woods.

"What is that?" Grayson asked suddenly.

Kate followed his gaze. He was looking at the marzipan skaters. "Oh . . . just something I made," she said.

His eyes widened. "You *made* this?" He got up from the table and moved to the sideboard where the marzipan scene had been placed. "This is remarkable," he said. "I can't begin to imagine how you did it."

"Oh, it is a trifling thing." So trifling that she and Cecelia had spent hours yesterday making the little skater forms and filling them with the paste.

Grayson picked up one of the skaters to have a closer look.

"It . . . it is my fondest hope to own a bakery one day," she said. "I've been saving money where I can and learning the art of making confections."

"A baker!" he exclaimed, casting a warm smile at her. "And how did you learn to do this?"

"Trial and error," she admitted. "Digby is a great help to me, of course. He samples everything and has a very fine palate."

Grayson laughed, his eyes shimmering. He seemed nothing like the man who had strode into her house a few weeks ago and looked at her with such contempt. "Digby is not the only one with a fine palate," he said, and popped the skater he held into his mouth.

Kate cried out and dropped her knife, hurrying to the sideboard to protect the rest of her marzipan skaters.

Grayson grinned as he chewed. "Quite good." He reached for another.

"No!" she cried, and grabbed his wrist.

"No?" he challenged her, his smiled broadening. "What, then, did you mean for these to be merely admired?" he asked, turning his hand and grabbing her wrist in kind, pulling her into his arms.

"I thought you might at least admire them for a moment!"

He smiled and bent his head dangerously close to hers. "I admire *you,* Kate Bergeron." When he kissed her, Kate could feel herself melting all over again.

They never ate the soup Kate had made. They retreated to her private rooms, where Grayson built a fire, and then they discovered each other again. When they had satisfied their physical craving for each other, Grayson insisted on hearing more of her upbringing. In turn, Kate wanted to know more of his life, his family, his ducal responsibilities.

Grayson was circumspect about it. He spoke of his responsibilities overseeing a vast number of holdings on which so many of his family depended for their living. He talked of how his reputation as head of the family extended to them all, and the pressure to keep that reputation pristine for their sake. He said that to fall out of favor was to see business and social associations flutter away.

He had indeed risked much to be with her, Kate realized.

Nevertheless, it was a magical night, and one Kate never wanted to end. And as the first pink rays of light filtered into her room, Kate climbed on top of Grayson, pulling the thick counterpane up over her shoulders. He was sleeping, but when she kissed his bare chest, he smiled.

"Good morning, Your Grace."

"Miss Bergeron," he said with a yawn and a stroke of her hair, "how do you do?"

"Have you seen the British museum at Montagu House?" she asked.

He opened his eyes. "Pardon?"

"I've never seen it. Digby said they have quite a lot of baubles from the South Seas. Aldous said the South Seas are filled with savages."

Grayson grinned and kissed her forehead. "A *museum*, Miss Bergeron? You wake with thoughts of baubles and savages? Surely something far more enjoyable comes to mind?"

"That," she said, with all the confidence of a courtesan, "never *left* my mind."

She kissed his chest again and moved down his body, wanting to do the same things to him that he'd done to her the night before. As she took him into her mouth and heard his groan of pleasure, she felt pleasure begin to swell in her body, too.

Grayson left her shortly thereafter, but not before promising to meet her later. He declared he would not abide another day of her missing the South Sea exhibit.

When he'd gone, Kate fairly floated about her house; she was all smiles and warmth as she cleaned up the debris in the drawing room before Amy arrived, but she was not so quick with the spoiled meat. Cecelia clucked her tongue when she saw it. "A bit of basting might have helped it," she said as she tossed it out. "And the soup, miss! The fire's gone cold!"

Kate could only laugh.

True to his word, Grayson met her that afternoon at Montagu House, where the treasures of the South Seas awaited them. They wandered about the museum, going far afield of the South Seas exhibit, observing antiquities and making up stories about them that had each other laughing like children, whispering like thieves.

It was a brilliant afternoon, marred only slightly when Grayson happened to look up and see an acquaintance. He slyly walked away from Kate, putting several feet between them. It was quite awkward — the gentleman and his female companion clearly understood that she was with Grayson, however she was at such a distance from Grayson and the couple that Grayson was not pressed to introduce her.

She said nothing of it, naturally, for she'd been trained to smile prettily and accept what was. Frankly, had she been walking with Benoit or the prince, she'd have no desire to meet any of their acquaintances. With Grayson, everything was different. But in that chance encounter, Kate understood that in spite of the intimacy between them, she was nothing to him. She was only a trinket, an exciting affair, and she could never hope to be more than that to him.

She could dream of it, but she should not hope for it.

After their visit to the museum, they took tea in a public house. Kate laughed as she recalled how she'd stood before a large pastoral painting, pretending to be part of it.

"You looked entirely at home in the country, madam," Grayson said of her pastoral pose.

"Did I?" Kate had asked with delight. "A talent I did not know I possessed, for I have never been to the country."

Grayson stared at her.

Kate laughed at his astonishment.

"Do you mean to say that you have never

been out of London?" he asked incredulously.

"I have been out of London. I've been to Paris. But I've never been in the country, really. I know only what I have seen from the windows of a coach."

"That is something we must remedy straightaway. I cannot allow you to have lived six and twenty years —"

"Or seven and twenty —"

"— without having seen the beautiful countryside that is England. Not to mention that clean air does a body good. We are to the country, madam at this week's end. I've a small property near Hadley Green, but it is a landscape so beautiful you will believe it is a glimpse of heaven."

Kate gasped with delight. "Digby will swoon with jealousy!"

"Let him swoon, then, for I am taking you where you may be at your country leisure."

"Will we hunt?"

"That depends. Can you shoot?"

"No."

"Then yes, we will hunt," he said with a wink.

She beamed with delight. She couldn't imagine a finer outing. She couldn't, for the life of her, conjure up an image of a hunting lodge, but it sounded terribly romantic and private. It sounded too good to be true.

It *was* too good to be true, and that made Kate sober.

"What is it?" Grayson asked.

"I find it rather sad that it can only be a fantasy," she admitted sheepishly.

Grayson nodded and glanced down a moment. But when he looked up, his blue eyes were glittering with determination. "Perhaps it doesn't have to be a fantasy."

Kate smiled. He did not. "That's impossible," she said.

"Why?"

"What of your duties?" she asked incredulously.

He shrugged. "Perhaps my duties can take me to Hadley Green. I've not been in some time. It seems a review might be in order."

He was serious. Kate blinked. "But . . ." She glanced around them and leaned across the table. "What of the prince?" she whispered.

"The prince," Grayson said thoughtfully. He, too, glanced around them and shifted forward, speaking softly. "The prince might be persuaded that you have taken ill with a highly contagious ague."

"He'd send a physician."

"Not if he believed one had already seen you and declared you in need of bed rest and seclusion."

Could they possibly accomplish such a daring ruse? Part of Kate thrilled at the thought of going to the country with Grayson. Part of her felt sick. "I gave him my word," she said reluctantly.

"As did I. But we have broken our word, Kate. The betrayal has been done."

He was right. She'd broken her word and there was no reclaiming it. What did a few more days matter at this point? She'd spent a lifetime worrying about the future — could she not have this? A few days with Grayson? A trip to the *country?*

Oh, but it was a dangerous game she was playing with her heart! Kate knew very well that for the first time in her blessed life, she was falling hard and fast into love. She was leaping off the precipice with abandon and soaring into the depths of it. It was ridiculous, ill advised, and so dangerous to her livelihood — yet once again, she could not seem to stop herself. She had no strength to deny herself this. God help her, but Grayson bewitched her, enchanted her, seduced her completely and she loved — *adored* — the feeling. The indescribably happy feeling of love.

"All right," she said, her voice catching a little.

Grayson's eyes narrowed. "Are you entirely certain?"

She nodded.

He reached across the table and took her hand. They made plans. Kate would meet him at Charing Cross, at an old inn and post station there. They'd be gone only a few days, leaving at week's end.

Duty called Grayson away after their tea. He sent her home in a hired hackney, and Kate's pulse pounded with exhilaration the entire drive home.

Digby came calling shortly after Kate arrived home, irate that he'd been duped. *"Fleming!"* he spat, pacing before the hearth in the salon. "He'll not keep me from a fair living!"

Kate did not tell Digby about Fleming's attack — it would only have enraged him further, and she was too anxious to have an irate Digby about. As Digby went on about his useless journey, and the poor fare he'd been made to suffer, Kate nodded and fed him freshly baked muffins . . . but she could think of little besides Grayson.

Grayson. Her mind's eye was filled with the way he'd looked as he'd held himself above her, of the desire in his eyes. She remembered how he'd sighed with pleasure as she moved on him, riding a crest to another glorious physical climax. She thought of his low laugh, and when his dark blue eyes were trained on her, how they had the power to make her feel weightless. Angelic. Another sort of woman altogether.

Aldous returned late that evening looking quite fatigued. He asked Kate nothing and offered nothing, either. Kate smiled at him as he stalked through the foyer and up the stairs. "Good night, Aldous," she called lightly after him.

Her response was the closing of his door.

At noon the next day, when Kate heard someone at the door, her heart began to race. She hurried to the top of the stairs, still fastening her gown. She squatted down behind the banister to have a look as Aldous opened the door. It was a messenger!

When Aldous had shut the door Kate ran down the stairs, almost colliding with him in her eagerness to receive the message.

With a fatherly frown, Aldous handed her the folded vellum.

She grinned as she took it from him, but then she noticed the seal. "Oh," she said, her smile disappearing. It was from the prince.

"Mind you have a care, Kate," Aldous said as he began to walk away. "Angering the prince won't do you any good. You'll not want to be out on your arse at this time of year, aye?"

Kate made a face at his back, then opened the vellum.

My love, my dearest, the prince wrote. *I count the hours and minutes until you are mine,* et cetera, et cetera, et cetera. Kate skimmed the note, then folded it and put it in her pocket. She didn't want love letters from George. She wanted love letters from Grayson.

God help her, but she had to be very careful.

CHAPTER TWENTY-FOUR

Responsibility kept Grayson from Kate, but his thoughts were never far from her. He made several calls with Merrick in defense of the abolition bill, and was surprised by some of the resistance they were facing.

"You would put legitimate men out of their livelihood, Your Grace," Lord Bradenton insisted when they called on him one afternoon. "My wife's brother has a stake in a trading company and he assures me that they are handling the Negroes as humanely as might reasonably be expected."

"Humanely?" Merrick bristled. "I have seen these slave ships, sir, and it is not humane to force the Africans to live in a space no larger than a coffin for three months! It is the height of degradation and cruelty."

Bradenton looked extremely uncomfortable. "What would you have me tell my wife's brother, my lord?" he said hotly to Merrick. "That because *you* think it inhumane, he should lose his livelihood?"

Fortunately, Merrick and Grayson found support in other quarters, some of which surprised Grayson. Lord Townshend had long been an ardent supporter of the British slave trade, but he'd had a change of heart recently. He'd traveled back from the West Indies on a slave ship and whatever he had seen had changed him profoundly. "Please tell me how I may help," he'd said.

In addition to working with Merrick and helping other members of his large family with financial, social, and personal matters, Grayson hosted a luncheon for the Ladies Beneficent Society, which his mother and sisters had arranged with the goal of displaying several debutantes before him.

The debutantes paraded about the room in their winter finery. He could scarcely keep their names in his head. Miss Keystone, Miss Shetland, Miss Brooks. Miss Augusta Fellows, who was very friendly. It seemed to Grayson that every lady at the luncheon thought it a foregone conclusion that he would find her irresistible and offer for her this Season. But he could think of no one but Kate. The debutantes' shining faces began to blur after an hour, and before the luncheon was served, they all began to look like Diana, all looking at him as if he were the means to their end, as if he were the savior.

Not one of them looked at him the way Kate looked at him — with no expectations, with not the slightest bit of anxiety. She looked at him as if she genuinely enjoyed his company.

Not that Grayson believed Diana didn't enjoy his company, but theirs was an anxious affair. Perhaps that is what had attracted him to her in part in the beginning. Now, it felt tiresome. He pondered if this was a new feeling, one that had come on suddenly, as suddenly as his feelings for Kate had come on him, or if it had been creeping into his consciousness for a time now?

Nevertheless, when Diana sent a second note begging him to come to her, he sent back his affirmative reply out of a sense of respect and responsibility. But he did something else first — he paid a call to the Prince of Wales.

George was happy to see him. He was in a room devoted to his thousands of wooden soldiers, with which he liked to stage mock battles. He was aligning his cavalry when Grayson was shown in. "Christie!" he said happily. "It is a delight to see you!"

They chatted about the news around town. George asked if he'd heard from Lambourne, against whom he held a very firm grudge.

Grayson assured him he hadn't. They spoke of the Delicate Investigation, with George professing once again he felt certain the king would see reason and proceed with the parliamentary divorce. "Very soon this ugly business shall be done and I can follow my heart's true inclinations," he'd said.

"By the bye," Grayson said as casually as he could, "I thought you should know that our mutual friend has been brought to bed by an ague."

"What?" George said, his head coming up. "When? How serious is it?"

Grayson felt entirely ill with his lie. But his desire to be with Kate was inexplicably stronger than his desire to be the man he'd been raised to be — trustworthy, forthright, dependable. *Honest.* "It is a winter ague, nothing more," he said, glancing at the window. "The physician proclaims that she will be good as new in a matter of days, but that she should keep to her bed and rest."

"I will go to her —"

"I'd not, were I you, Your Highness," he said. "It is highly contagious."

"Oh," George said.

"Perhaps a gift of some sort might cheer her?" Grayson suggested. *What was he doing?* Who had he suddenly become? He was not only lying to the prince, he was building upon his lie, engaging in fraud.

"Yes, of course," the prince said. "Books. Bedridden people enjoy books. Do you think she reads French?"

George scarcely knew Kate at all. He knew only of her beauty, he wanted only to bed the beauty, and somehow, that helped Grayson to reason that what he was doing was not entirely evil. "No, I think not."

"Fashion plates, then," George decided. "How long must I stay away?"

"A week to be entirely safe."

George seemed to accept that and turned the conversation to another subject. Grayson left a bit later, uncomfortable with his new-found treachery and feelings of guilt.

He was resolved, therefore, to be completely honest with Diana. But when Millie opened the door onto the mews and showed him inside, he felt awkward.

Millie moved silently ahead, leading him up a familiar path to Diana's suite of rooms. She knocked three times on Diana's door and opened it. Grayson walked across the threshold; Diana was standing before the hearth wearing a chemise and a dressing gown, her dark hair hanging in a tail down her back. When Millie shut the door behind Grayson, Diana rushed to him, throwing her arms around him, kissing him ardently.

Grayson kissed her, too, but he didn't realize he was setting her back until she gasped softly and tossed her head back to look up at him. Her blue eyes were filled with hurt. "Darling, what is wrong? Have I displeased you?"

"No," he said, quickly shaking his head. "No, no I . . . I beg your pardon, Diana." He took her hand in his and kissed her knuckles.

Diana blinked. She looked down at her hand. "I don't understand," she said simply, then abruptly yanked her hand free of his. "I've not seen you alone in nearly a month, and this is how you greet me?"

"I am aware —"

"No, no, you are not aware, Grayson! If you were aware, you would have come to me! You've not been away from me as long as this since the beginning!"

"Diana!" he said sternly. "You know that things have happened beyond our control. You were not expecting Charles to return to London —"

"He's in Bath for days now, and this is the first you come to me!"

Grayson frowned at her. She was furious with him and still, Grayson could say nothing to comfort her. He didn't know what *to* say. For the second time today, he felt guilty. He could not recall another time in his life he'd felt guilt, save those first days with Diana, when he'd understood he was cuckolding Eustis. But then he'd managed to alleviate his guilt with the knowledge that among the *haut ton,* affairs were more the rule than the exception, particularly when marital unions were made for the purpose of shoring up rank and privilege as opposed to true feelings of love. Of course love happened, but often it did not, and it was quite common for one to take a lover.

Even Eustis had had his dalliances here and there, and everyone knew it.

But now Grayson was faced with a deeper guilt. He'd betrayed Diana. It was not something he would ever have thought himself capable of, yet . . . yet there was Kate. There was something different about Kate, something about her that drove him to do things he never thought he'd do.

Grayson had wronged Diana, and he knew in that moment that their liaison had come to an end. He hadn't understood or perhaps admitted it to himself until this moment, but it was very clear to him now.

He suspected Diana knew it, too, for her shoulders sagged. "Is it she?"

Grayson couldn't own to anything about which he wasn't entirely certain himself. He didn't know the depth of his feeling for Kate, precisely, but that he desired her. Madly.

"Will you at least be honest with me?"

"Diana, darling . . . perhaps some time apart has given us both a moment to reflect —"

"Don't," she said, throwing up a hand. "Don't do this, Grayson. Is what we've shared over the last year as fragile as this? Can it not endure a slight absence before it grows brittle?"

"I don't know," he answered honestly.

Diana pressed her lips together. Her eyes filled with tears. "She is a *courtesan.*"

He couldn't bear to see the pain in his lover's eyes and reached for her, but Diana drew back, just out of his reach. "Whatever has come of us, at least tell me you are not leaving me for her!"

"Calm yourself —"

"I could tell the prince, you know," Diana snapped. "I could tell him that you have taken his mistress as your own."

"You are jumping to conclusions. If you attempt something so foolish, you risk letting *your* sins be made public."

"Do you not see she is a whore?" Diana asked plaintively. "Do you honestly believe your family will stand for your association with *that* woman?"

Grayson unthinkingly clenched his fist in an effort to maintain his calm. "You are overstepping your bounds, madam."

"You cannot have her!" Diana said heedlessly. "She is a *whore!*"

His blood began to thrum in his veins. He didn't want to leave like this, but he feared what he might say. He turned away, intending to leave.

"Grayson!" Diana cried when she realized what he meant to do. "Grayson, please!"

He hesitated; she was crying now, and he was responsible for her tears. *"Diana,"* he said, turning round to her.

"Please don't do this," she begged him. "Please don't end it, Grayson! You know how unhappy I am in my marriage — you are my one happiness!"

It pained him to see her so woeful, and it distressed him that he was unable to say what she needed him to say. He'd never really thought how their affair would end; he'd not planned for it. But he'd never wanted this. He walked back to where Diana stood and laid his palm against her cheek. She closed her eyes and leaned into it, then covered his hand with hers.

"Don't be so sad, love," Grayson said. "We both knew it would end one day. How could it not?" He kissed her tenderly. When he lifted his head, Diana drew a shaky breath and moved away, putting her back to him. She stood at her hearth, holding herself tightly, staring into the flames.

Grayson went out quietly, closing the door behind him, taking the stairs two at a time.

He strode down the street through a cold rain, an inexplicable anger swelling with each step he took.

He was angry with himself first and foremost. He had crossed some invisible line with his personal morals. He had always been the one his close acquaintances counted on to be reasoned in his thinking, to be morally upright in his deeds, to be a pillar of propriety. And with the exception of his dalliance with Diana, he *was* those things.

But this fascination, this obsession he'd developed for Kate was unlike anything he'd ever experienced. He was doing things that were beyond him. Deceptions, deceits — he was compromising who he was for the sake of desire.

Or was it possible his feelings for Kate were quite real? Was it possible he had found that elusive feeling of love with the one woman in all of England who was as wrong for him as wrong could be?

Diana sobbed for a half hour before she

picked herself up and washed her face. By then, grief had given way to a soul-consuming anger. How dare Grayson cast her aside for little more than a common whore?

She tightened the belt of her dressing gown and angrily yanked on the bell pull.

A few minutes later, Millie appeared, looking fatigued. "Aye, mu'um?"

Diana motioned for her to come in. She wiped the stray tears from her cheeks and walked to her wardrobe and threw open the doors. As Millie curiously looked on, Diana fell to her knees and rummaged in the very back of the wardrobe until she found a beaded reticule. She came to her feet. "There is a woman, a courtesan," she said bitterly as she opened the reticule. "Her name is Katharine Bergeron. I want to know everything there is to know about her. *Everything.*" She removed several notes from the reticule, which she thrust at Millie. "Find out everything you can."

Millie's eyes widened with surprise. "And how am I to do this, then?" she scoffed, eyeing the notes. "What do I know of courtesans?"

"Come now, Millie," Diana said angrily as she grabbed Millie's hand and shoved the notes into her palm and curled her fingers around it. "Surely you have a brother

313

or a cousin or some such person who can find out a thing or two about Katharine Bergeron! She is an infamous courtesan! She was in the employ of Mr. Cousineau, the cloth merchant. You might start there. He is very well known about Mayfair."

Millie stared at the notes in her hand. "There must be twenty pounds here," she said.

"And there will be twenty pounds more if you can bring me information I might use, do you understand?"

Millie glanced up at Diana. A dark smile turned up one corner of her mouth. "I understand."

"Good," Diana said sharply, and gestured to the door. "Now make haste. I need information about the whore as soon as possible."

CHAPTER TWENTY-FIVE

"This is madness!" Digby blustered the morning Kate packed a portmanteau for her trip to the country. "Have you the slightest idea of the sort of trouble you are courting?"

"I have a fair idea, yes," she said evenly. She held up a brown brocade gown. Digby was no help at all when it came to proper clothing for hunting lodges — he'd never seen one. "I've never heard anything more dreadful than the words *hunting* and *lodge* put together," he'd said.

Kate picked up a dark blue woolen cloak. "Do you think it's as cold in the country as it is in town?"

"Colder," Aldous said, walking unannounced into their midst. "And you'll not have need of fancy gowns." His pronouncement drew curious looks from both Kate and Digby. Aldous frowned. "What, did you think I was born at sea, then? A little Moses drifting across the North Sea? No, I hail from Bedfordshire, which is quite full of hunting lodges and all of them little more than piles of stones. Were I you, I'd take along some fur-lined drawers."

"Pity I do not possess a pair," Kate muttered.

"Digby's right, Kate," Aldous added. "You ought not to go off with the duke, not if you want to keep your place here."

Kate sighed impatiently and twirled around to her wardrobe, turning her back on both men. "Thank you, gentlemen, you've both made it abominably clear —"

"Abundantly," Digby corrected her.

"Abundantly clear," Kate blithely continued, "that you do not approve of my friendship with the duke. I understand your concern, God knows that I do, but I . . . I can't help myself." It was the honest truth.

"You *can* help yourself!" Digby insisted. "If you are discovered, the prince will take his revenge and I assure you, my love, it will not be pleasant. Look at the lengths to which he has gone to rid himself of a wife! You will be treated like rubbish, Kate, tossed to the wolves."

"I *know*, Digby," she said. She did know it — she could hardly sleep from knowing it. "But he won't know," she added stubbornly.

"I am very discreet."

"She's made up her mind, that's obvious," Aldous said, to which Digby snorted.

No one spoke. The tension between Digby and Kate was rather stifling.

"By the bye, I've heard *The Princess* has turned back to port," Aldous said a moment later.

Kate stopped what she was doing and gaped at Aldous. "Jude's ship? What have you heard?"

"Just that. Heard it at the quays. She was dismasted in a storm and is slowly making her way to port."

"Do you know when the ship is expected?" Kate asked eagerly.

"A fortnight or so. They'll be sailing into Deptford."

Kate looked at Digby, her heart in her throat. "I can't believe it," she said. "I might very well find Jude! I might *find* him, Digby!"

"You might indeed. And then you might find yourself out on the street for all your nonsense," Digby sniffed as he gestured to her portmanteau.

Kate clucked at him and folded the brocade gown. "To think that after all this time, I may have my brother back in a mere fortnight!"

Merrick could not understand why Grayson had decided to spend a few days away. "I need you here, Grayson," he implored.

"I'll not be gone more than a few days," Grayson assured his brother. "And you hardly need me. You are very eloquent on the subject of abolition. You have Wilberforce with you."

"You are the duke," Merrick said irritably. "Your title carries quite a lot of weight with members of Parliament. Why must you go now?"

"Because I have business that I must tend to," Grayson said. It annoyed him that he needed a reason, even more that he must lie about it. Was he not allowed a few days away from all the duties and responsibilities for once in his bloody life?

Apparently not, for Merrick's frown grew darker. "I've heard the rumors," he said quietly.

"Rumors," Grayson scoffed. There were always a host of rumors about him and his family, and they were seldom true.

"I've heard that you've been in the company of the courtesan."

That prompted Grayson to look up.

"It's in all the *on dits,* Gray," Merrick said.

"Little hints about the company you keep. A certain duke in the company of a certain lady, at Montagu House, of all places."

Grayson hadn't read a paper in days and was surprised by the news. He glanced down at his desk, at the stack of correspondence Palmer had left for him to review. He'd left the newspapers and correspondence unread as he and Merrick had chased after votes. For once, he was *living* his bloody *life.* Why couldn't they all leave him alone?

"I would never presume to advise you," Merrick continued. "But we are so close to a vote, and I . . . I desperately need your support."

"You *have* my support, Merrick. Look here, I am going to be away from London for a few days! I do not intend to be gone for weeks and I'll be no more than two hours away on horseback. Is that so far? When I return I shall help you convince the last few doubters of the wisdom of the abolition bill. You will not need my help, but I shall offer it all the same. Do not doubt it."

"Well then," Merrick said with a curt bow of his head. "I suppose there is nothing left to say but God's speed." With that, he strode from the study.

Grayson sighed and glanced at correspondence on his desk and wondered what else he'd failed to realize. He picked up the stack and flipped through it. It was the usual assembly — petitions from his tenants, official documents from the solicitors for those businesses in which he held an interest, a slew of invitations for the upcoming Season.

In the middle of the stack was a vellum sealed with the crest of the Prince of Wales. Grayson frowned and broke the seal. It was an invitation to his annual fête. He hosted one every year to celebrate the opening of Parliament and the beginning of the Season. George had scribbled a note at the bottom:

I pray our jewel has recovered and shines brightly. You must have it adorn your arm at the fête.

"Damn if I will," Grayson muttered, and tossed the vellum onto the pile of correspondence. He moved to the windows and looked out at the park behind the mansion. *What was he doing?* What madness allowed him to court such dangerous consequences? He withdrew his pocket watch; it was a quarter to noon.

The coach would be waiting.

Feeling uneasy and uncertain, Grayson arrived at Charing Cross, and spotted Kate instantly when she arrived in the company of Butler. She looked small and tense as they walked down the sidewalk. When they reached the coach, a footman opened the door, and Kate smiled up at Grayson.

He felt instantly lighter, and his doubts momentarily scattered to the four corners of his mind.

She was wearing a dark blue woolen cloak and matching bonnet. Grayson signaled for the footman to take her bag. She said good-bye to Butler — who eyed Grayson warily — and then accepted the footman's hand to enter the coach. The footman moved to shut the door, but Butler suddenly surged forward and glared at Grayson. "When will you have her back?" he asked bluntly.

"Monday," Grayson promised.

"Aye, and if she's not, I'll hie myself up to that fancy house of yours and demand direction to your lodge in a manner that will have all the tongues in London wagging."

"Aldous!" Kate cried.

"Were you a jailer at some point in your illustrious career, Mr. Butler?" Grayson asked.

"Have her back on Monday or you'll have me to face," Butler snapped, and shut the door.

"Oh, for heaven's sake!" Kate cried, embarrassed. "He's not very cordial, I'll grant you, but he means well."

Grayson didn't want to think of Butler. "How are you?" he asked.

She smiled. "Good. A bit anxious, in truth. And you?"

He smiled, too. "A bit of the same, but better now that I've seen you."

Kate's smile deepened. "Do you think anyone suspects anything?" she asked quietly.

He shook his head.

"Thank goodness," she said, leaning back. "I've been at sixes and sevens all week."

"As have I," he agreed.

"The prince sent flowers and wished me a quick recovery," she said. "He also wrote that he'd be at Bagshot Park with his brother Clarence."

Thank God, Grayson thought. "Let us not think of that now," he suggested, and knocked on the ceiling of the coach to signal the driver.

"Wait!" Kate quickly exclaimed, putting her hand to his knee. "Will you humor me and allow me one short diversion before we leave London?"

When those pale green eyes shone up at him like that, Grayson imagined he would allow her the world. "What is the diversion?"

"The market. And before you say no," she added hastily before he could object, "there is a sweetmeat I should very much like to make for you while we are in the country, but I haven't all the ingredients. There is a kitchen of some sort, isn't there?"

Not only was there a kitchen, there was a cook and a scullery maid. "Yes, but —"

"I promise you will be quite pleased with this treat and wonder how you lived without it all your life. But I must have rose hips."

"Pardon?"

"Rose hips. Don't be alarmed," she said hastily. "They aren't *really* poisonous. That's a silly rumor."

Grayson didn't want to stop; he wanted to be as far from London as he could be, as quickly as possible, but her eyes, her smile . . .

He opened the vent to the coachman. "The nearest market," he instructed him.

Finding rose hips proved easier said than done. They were not, Grayson quickly realized, very easy to come by in winter. They wended their way through the market stalls, looking for them.

"Are you certain this item can be found in January?" Grayson asked, batting away woolen stockings, which hung incongruently over a row of spices.

"Yes," she said as she studied some bottles filled with dark liquids.

"And it is absolutely necessary?"

"Oh yes! They give the pastry a very distinctive flavor. And a palm reader once told me that they will ward off ague brought on by cold." She looked up at him. "I thought that was important, given that it is colder in the country than in town."

Grayson blinked. "Did the palm reader tell you that, as well?"

"No. Aldous told me. He hails from the country, can you believe it?"

Grayson wasn't certain why he shouldn't believe it as he admired the high color in Kate's cheeks.

She paused, holding a jar of something that looked very foul, and considered him a moment. "Have you never had your palm read?"

"Certainly not," he said instantly. "That's a lot of nonsense."

"It's not!" she insisted, her skin radiant in the cold sunlight. "That very same palm reader told me that I would one day live in a fine house, and now I do. How do you explain that?"

"Quite simply. She saw a beautiful woman and knew that some day, not only would a man lift that beautiful woman out of her situation and put her in a fine house, but that the beautiful woman also would be divested of her coin in the hopes of being told as much. She didn't read your palm, Kate. She read your lovely face. Are those rose hips?"

"Pig's feet." She put them down. "You're awfully skeptical about things, aren't you?"

"Skeptical?"

"Yes, skeptical," she said absently. "Oh here! Rose hips!" she cried, finding a bottle among several. "How much?" she asked the woman.

"Tuppence, mu'um."

Grayson reached for his purse, but Kate put her hand on his. "If you please, sir, this is *my* creation and I have my own money." She handed a coin to the woman behind the table. "There!" she said, and turned to Grayson, obviously pleased with her purchase. She looked as if she meant to speak, but an intolerably filthy woman suddenly appeared and put her hand on Kate's arm.

Grayson instinctively moved forward to put himself between the old woman and Kate, but Kate startled him with a cry. "Agnes Miller!" she cried. "Lud, where have you been, old girl?"

Grayson recoiled — she *knew* this hag?

"Here and there," the woman said, eyeing Grayson up and down from the corner of her eye. "I lost me place on St. Katharine's street and I had to go to the almshouse till I could find work. Filthy sties, those charities. Aye, but ye've done well for yerself, ain't ye, Katie? I knew ye would, pretty lass that ye are. Wasn't hard to know. Ye heard 'bout Fannie Breen, eh?"

"Fannie! Not a word! I looked for her a year or so ago and couldn't find her about town. How is she?"

"I'll tell ye how she is, lass — she's cocked her toes up, she has! Aye, she tried to take a baby out of her belly."

Kate gasped. Grayson was revolted by the mere mention of it.

" 'Twas the rat catcher's wife who done it. I was very surprised, I was, for she's typically quite good."

"Fannie," Kate whispered, and looked at Grayson. "Fannie helped me at a time when no one else would," she said softly.

"Here now, Katie, ye gots something for an old friend, hasn't ye?"

"Ah. Yes," Kate said, and reached once more for her reticule.

"Kate —"

She smiled thinly at Grayson as she fished a few coins from her reticule. "I haven't much," she said to the old woman. "But you may have what I've got."

"Kind of ye, Katie. But then again, I's always kind to ye, weren't I?"

Kate looked as if she might disagree with that, but placed several coins in the woman's palm.

Agnes looked at the coins in her hand, then slyly shifted her gaze to Grayson. "What 'ave ye got, gov'na?"

"You've got your coin, old woman. Off with you now."

She gave him a toothless grin and put the coins away with the practiced ease of a thief and shuffled away.

"Well . . . well, good day, Agnes!" Kate called after her, then looked at Grayson with wide green eyes. "Poor Fannie Breen."

"It is a gruesome tragedy, to be sure," he agreed, and took Kate firmly in hand and steered her in the opposite direction. "Are you in the habit of giving all your money to beggars?"

"She wasn't just any beggar, Grayson," Kate answered evenly. "Agnes and I worked alongside each other in the cloth halls, and everyone needs a helping hand now and then."

Grayson supposed some people took advantage of helping hands.

Kate had come from a very cruel world, and as they made their way out of the crowded market stalls, he realized that knowledge made him uncomfortable. Kate was a beautiful, vibrant woman, but her circumstances couldn't be any worse. She didn't belong in his world. Nor did she belong in that world.

Honestly, Grayson didn't know where, exactly, Kate belonged, and the doubt was beginning to eat at him.

CHAPTER TWENTY-SIX

Grayson was subdued on the drive to Hadley Green. He spoke politely to Kate, but he seemed distant to her.

Something felt out of sorts between them.

The tension diminished somewhat once they were outside of London and Kate began to see the countryside. The land beyond London stretched out before them in quaint little patches of farmland, dotted with cattle and sheep and thatched roof cottages and barns with smoke curling out of the chimneys. They rode over stone bridges, through narrow, cobblestone lanes in picturesque villages. Children rushed out and ran alongside the coach, calling out to them. They rode over frozen rivers and past thick stands of trees and green hedges and empty fields.

What amazed Kate most of all was the sky. Buildings, the tall masts of ships, and the ever-present haze crowded out the sky over London. This sky was so vast, the azure color of it so rich and bright that it seemed to swallow the world.

Kate kept her face glued to the window, calling out what she saw, making Grayson look and explain the things she was seeing. That was a cistern. The big thing in the field was a plow, and those animals were oxen. A whole new world was opening to Kate, and in every corner there was beauty, bathed by brilliant winter sunlight.

When they neared the village of Hadley Green, Grayson told her they would be at the lodge shortly. Minutes later, they turned through a narrow stone gate that bore a sign that Kate could not read quickly enough. "What does it say?" she asked.

"Kitridge Lodge. It once belonged to my mother's uncle, but was given to my father's family as part of her dowry," he explained as they rolled past a field where horses grazed.

When the lodge came into view, Kate was surprised to see that it was not the pile of stones Aldous had claimed it would be, but a small castle. It reminded Kate of the paintings they'd seen at Montagu House. An ivy-covered round tower stood at one of the front corners, anchoring the L-shaped building. A high stone fence swept off to one side, but through an open door, Kate could see fields beyond it.

As they pulled into the drive, the front door of the small castle opened and seven people in servant's dress hurried out and stood in a line. "This is the hunting lodge?" she asked uncertainly.

Grayson chuckled. "You were expecting something grander? I suppose most of them are."

"No, I —"

The coach door opened before she could finish her sentence. Grayson went out first. Kate stepped out self-consciously. If the servants noticed her, they gave no indication; their eyes were fixed on Grayson. The men bowed, the women sank into deep curtsies. Grayson spoke to each of the servants as he led Kate past them, thanking them for preparing for his visit on such short notice.

The small door that was apparently the entrance to the lodge opened onto a deceptively large hall. Kate gaped at her surroundings as the servants bustled in behind them, carrying their bags. There was a variety of animal heads with impressive antlers hanging high on the walls, as well as the Darlington coat of arms, painted on a very large wooden crest.

"Mr. Noakes," Grayson said to a gentleman in buckskins and a tweed coat, "allow me to introduce Miss Bergeron. Is there any particular set of rooms to which I should show her?"

"I would suggest the Queen's room, Your Grace," Mr. Noakes said, bowing his head.

The *Queen's* room! Kate was awestruck.

"Thank you," Grayson agreed. "Have someone bring up her baggage."

"Very good. May I inquire as to when you would like supper served?"

Grayson looked at Kate. "Would eight suit?"

She hadn't thought of supper being served — she had thought to serve it. "Of course," she said softly.

The room Grayson showed her to was not as large as she would imagine a queen's room to be, but it nonetheless had a lovely view of the park behind the lodge. The lawn was pristine in spite of it being winter, and the large stone fence Kate had noticed on their arrival stretched as far as she could see and disappeared over a rise. "It's beautiful," Kate said of the room. "Why do you call it the Queen's room?"

"Queen Anne was a guest, I believe," he said idly, as if queens were quite often guests in his house. He put his arm around her waist and held her against his body as she gazed out the window. Kate closed her eyes. His touch seemed to bridge the distance she'd been feeling between them.

"I had forgotten how peaceful it is here," he said.

Kate leaned her head against his shoulder, and Grayson tenderly kissed the top of her head. She turned in his arms, lifting her face to his. Grayson kissed her —

A knock at the door brought his head up; Grayson stepped away from her and called "Come!" A footman entered with Kate's portmanteau. "There," Grayson said, pointing, and moved farther away from Kate. As the footman put the portmanteau where Grayson had indicated, a maid walked into the room carrying a pitcher of fresh water and clean linens.

"I shall leave you to freshen up," Grayson said, already moving toward the door.

"Oh. I . . . yes, all right," Kate stammered, and watched him quit the room on the heels of the footman, leaving Kate with the young maid. Kate shifted her gaze to the girl, who curtsied before putting down her burden, but as she bustled about the room, Kate had the uncomfortable feeling that the girl was examining her. Judging her. Understanding who and what Kate was.

She was being ridiculous, for she was often

observed and judged. But that was in London. She had had such high hopes for something better here! She'd harbored a fantasy that she could be a woman like any other for a few days. A woman who loved a man, who cooked and cared for him, who made love to him.

But she was a courtesan, and as it seemed she'd not escape that simple fact, she could feel herself slipping into that role. The stone walls were coming up, walls she'd learned to erect many years ago to protect her heart from hurt.

She didn't want those walls to come up with Grayson. She wanted to be just Kate with him, but it was beginning to feel impossible.

When the maid left, Kate sank onto the edge of the bed and stared at the carpet. Aldous and Digby were right — she was playing a dangerous game. How had she failed to understand there would be servants here? Grayson was one of the most powerful men in England — he'd not be without his servants and Kate was a fool to have believed that he would step into her fantastical daydream. What in the bloody hell had she been thinking?

Kate stood up and walked to the window of her lovely room and looked out over the lovely park. *Bloody fool,* she told herself.

There had been times in Grayson's life when he found the quiet of the country stifling, but on this early evening, he found it comforting. He sat before a fire in the drawing room, nursing a tot of whiskey Noakes had been so good to find him. There was no sound but the ticking of the mantel clock and the occasional hiss and crackle of the fire in the hearth.

A slight knock at the door brought him to his feet, and he turned to the door as a footman opened it. Kate peeked around the edge of it. "May I come in?" she asked, and started slightly when she saw the footman standing there.

"Please," Grayson said, smiling.

Kate entered the room hesitantly and stood just over the threshold, looking at her surroundings. She was wearing a rich brown gown trimmed in shades of green that perfectly matched her eyes. She wore a plain gold cross at her neck.

Her beauty astounded Grayson every time he saw her. "Would you like some wine?" he asked, moving to the sideboard.

"Please."

He poured a glass for her, which she held up in a toast and said, "To hunting lodges in

335

the country."

"To hunting lodges," he agreed, and touched his tot to her glass. "I hope you have found the accommodations to your liking."

"They are lovely," she said. "Your hunting lodge is much larger than I imagined."

"Is it?" He'd always thought it a small lodge. "It's suitable for its purpose, I suppose."

She smiled a little and glanced at the footman.

"Are you hungry?" Grayson asked. He was ravenous — for her. He could devour her here, before the hearth. "Mr. Noakes informs me venison will be served this evening."

"Venison," she said, nodding.

The way she said the word made him wonder if she approved of it. Frankly, it seemed some of the warmth had gone out of Kate. "It's rather quiet here," he said, thinking perhaps she was cowed by the silence in the country. "If one is accustomed to the bustle in London, this might seem rather . . . tedious."

"Not at all," she assured him. "It's wonderful. I could not have imagined how wonderful. That is a beautiful painting," she said, indicating one behind the settee.

Grayson looked at it. It was another pastoral scene, complete with a barefoot shepherdess.

"Your Grace." It was Noakes, and Grayson was a bit relieved by the intrusion. "Supper is served."

"Thank you, Noakes. Kate?" He offered his arm to her.

Kate looked at his arm as if she were debating whether to take it, but then walked across the room and put her hand lightly on top of it. She looked straight ahead as he led her out.

The dining room was long and narrow and the décor similar to the rest of the lodge — lots of stag heads and the accoutrements of hunting. There was even a pair of crossed swords above the door, the significance of which Grayson had long forgotten. "My father loved this place," he said as a footman seated Kate. He waited until she was in her chair before taking his place on her left. "He was an avid hunter and we spent many weeks here when I was a child."

"Are you an avid hunter?" she asked as another footman ladled soup into her bowl.

"Ah . . . no, not really," he admitted. "I suppose if I had to hunt to put food on my table, I should like it more than I do. But as a sport, I do not care for it." There was something about the useless slaughter of animals that made him a little ill, a fact that had earned him a lot of good-natured teasing from his friends through the years.

"What is your preferred sport, if I may ask?"

"Horses."

Kate nodded and picked up her spoon. It almost seemed as if they were sitting at someone's table in London, making the obligatory polite conversation.

It was too polite. They ate their first course in silence. Two footmen stood directly behind them, waiting to serve. The only sounds were the occasional clink of a spoon to the bowl, the wineglass on the table. When the soup was removed and the main course brought out, Kate sat with her hands in her lap, staring at the dish.

The meal was exceedingly uncomfortable, and for the life of him, Grayson could not imagine why that was. All his attempts at conversation failed. He ate quickly, wishing the meal to be over as soon as possible. But Kate scarcely ate at all. Grayson finally put down his fork and looked at her. "Is the food not to your liking?"

Startled, Kate looked at him wide-eyed. "It is excellent, Your Grace."

"When did you revert to calling me Your Grace?" he asked, suddenly annoyed by it.

Kate blinked. She stole a look at the footman behind him, and picked up her fork.

Grayson sighed irritably. "What is wrong, Kate?"

She put down her fork. "Shall I speak plainly?"

"Have you ever spoken any other way?"

She frowned a little, and folded her hands in her lap. "It is this," she said. "Everything."

"What? The hunting lodge is rather rustic, I grant you —"

"No! No, it is not rustic! It is a *castle,* Grayson, not a cottage!"

"A cottage?" he repeated, confused.

"Yes! A cottage!" she exclaimed. "I had rather imagined a small cottage, and I imagined that . . ." She remembered the footmen and glanced slyly in their direction.

So did Grayson . . . for a moment. "You were saying?" he asked impatiently.

"Nothing."

"You were saying *something,*" he argued.

She gave him a withering look and then glanced at the footmen again. Grayson understood her then. He looked at the pair and said, "Thank you. You may leave us now," then drummed his fingers on the table as he waited for them to quit the room. When they were gone, he said, "You may speak."

She looked at him with surprise. He hadn't

meant to speak so abruptly, but —

Kate suddenly stood from her chair, startling him. "What are you doing?" he demanded. "Sit down!"

"I won't! I was trying to tell you that I rather imagined a *small* cottage, and that there would only be the *two* of us, not a dozen, and I thought *I* would cook for you."

It was so absurd that Grayson couldn't help but laugh. "What . . . do you want me to send them away?"

She frowned darkly at his laughter. "Is that such an absurd suggestion? So impossible for you to imagine?"

"Frankly, yes," he retorted. In all honesty, he couldn't believe what he was hearing. She had to be the only woman in all of England who did not want a host of servants tending her every need, and he found her attitude preposterous. There were times he felt stifled by all that was done for him, but he had a very complicated life and a large number of properties and holdings. It was impossible for him to do it on his own. Houses the size of Kitridge Lodge did not tend to themselves.

But Kate must have believed differently, for she was suddenly marching for the door. "For God's sake, don't be so missish," he chided her.

"Missish!" she cried, whirling around to him. "Perhaps you should not be so officious!"

That angered him. He stood up and threw his napkin aside. "What is the matter with you, Kate? You've been acting strangely all day!"

"So have you!" she insisted. "In the market, you could scarcely wait to be gone!"

"What of it?" he retorted angrily. "It was risking too much, and I cannot abide so much rabble in one place!"

"Rabble? Agnes was my *friend*."

"I find that even more disconcerting," he snapped.

She gasped. Her eyes narrowed dangerously and she folded her arms tightly across her. "You know who I am, Christie. You know I don't have fancy friends with titles to suit your lofty world."

"And you know who I am, madam. I have servants and houses larger than bloody cottages."

She gaped at him. Her green eyes flashed with her anger, but she suddenly turned about and marched from the dining room.

Grayson listened to the door slam behind her, then resumed his seat. He pushed his plate away and reached for his wine. It would seem the serenity he had believed he'd found was fool's gold. He finished his wine and reached for the decanter, pouring more.

This was a ridiculous plan. If he would only own to it, Grayson reasoned, he could salvage the situation and return to London with Kate on the morrow. There was really no other reasonable, sane thing he could possibly do. They shouldn't be here! He should never have suggested it, much less brought her here! And now, their first few hours together had convinced him that it was possibly the most wretchedly stupid thing he'd ever done.

An hour of brooding convinced Grayson he was right, and he decided there was no time like the present to tell Kate of his decision. He walked up the narrow stairwell to the bedchambers, pausing to discard his coat and neck cloth on a chair outside the master suite before continuing on to the Queen's room. He knocked on the door, opened it, and walked inside, holding a single candle aloft.

Kate was lying on her side, her back to the door. She'd let down her hair and it spilled like a river behind her. "Kate," he said softly.

She did not respond.

He moved closer. *"Kate."*

"I am here," she said quietly.

He walked to the bed and stood beside it, peering down at her. She was staring at the darkened window, her face softened by the low light of the fire and his candle. "Kate, I've been thinking —"

"When I was a girl," she interjected, "we lived in a tiny house with three rooms. Jude and I slept on pallets before the hearth. My mother used to lie with us at night and tell us stories until we went to sleep." She smiled faintly. "One of her favorite tales was that faeries would come in the night and carry us away to a cottage in the forest. In that cottage, we'd have love and laughter and all the food we could possibly eat. And a cat," she added, her smile deepening. "I always wanted a cat. We were to be very happy in our cottage in the forest." She glanced at Grayson over her shoulder; he could see she'd been crying. "I naively believed you would find that fantasy appealing, too. I didn't think how silly it must seem to someone like you. But then again, I can never seem to think much at all when you are near."

"Ah, Kate," Grayson said. He put aside the candle. He crawled into bed with her, curving himself around her, draping his arm over her middle and holding her close.

Kate twisted about to face him. She stroked his cheek with her finger. "I want to cook

343

for you. I want to clean for you. I want to do whatever it is you need in a cottage in the forest. I want to be with you, Grayson. Only you," she whispered, and kissed the corner of his mouth. "Imagine, just the two of us," she said softly as she trailed her fingers down his chest to his trousers, "free to lie about, to dine when we want, with or without our clothing —"

"Pardon?"

"To be as easy or as loud as we like in the queen's bed." She kissed the other corner of his mouth.

Grayson couldn't help but smile as her fingers found the buttons of his trousers. "I will admit the idea has some merit."

"I give you my word you won't regret it," she whispered, and slipped her hand into his trousers, taking him in hand. Grayson drew a steadying breath. "Just you and me," she continued as she toyed with him. "No markets, no fancy friends, no rabble. It will be our fantasy, and for a few short days, we can pretend to be what we both know we can never be."

It was an appealing idea.

Kate moved on top of him and kissed his throat. *"Please?"* she murmured, and kissed his lips.

Grayson had never been without servants.

Never. But Kate's hands and mouth were on him and he was her slave. "You render me powerless, Kate," he sighed. "Do you promise me we shall not starve?"

She slipped her hand beneath his shirt and pushed it up. "I promise," she said, and ran her tongue over his nipple, then licked a path to his groin. As her tongue and lips moved on him, Grayson groaned. He was lost in the pleasure she gave him, in his desire and his regard for her.

"All right," he said, and groaned again as her tongue flicked around the head of his cock.

But he would not take his pleasure without giving her hers, and gripped her arms, hauling her up to him. Kate smiled and cupped his face. "Has anyone ever told you what a comely man you are?"

"No," he said, and tangled his hand in her loose hair, searching for the clasp of her gown. The fire flared behind him as he solemnly undressed her; a flare of the fire filled the room with a bright light for a moment and reflected in her eyes. When he'd divested her of her clothing, Kate sat before him on her knees, watching him as he discarded his clothing. Kate was beautiful, too beautiful. Men could be driven to insanity by such beauty, and Grayson wasn't entirely certain he hadn't been.

When he had removed his clothes, Kate leaned forward on all fours and kissed him. Her breath was warm, her lips moist, her breasts soft and full.

Grayson wrapped his arms around her, pulled her into his body, caressing her, savoring her softness, the feel of her hair on his skin as she feathered his torso with kisses, caressed his body and cock with her hands. Everything ceased to exist; he was aware of nothing but Kate, of his hands arousing her breasts, of his mouth inflaming her with his kisses and his tongue, stroking her to a dampness that stirred the deepest parts of him.

He put her on her back and covered them against the chill in the room, then moved down her body, to her breast, which he took in his mouth. All the while, his hands were moving, caressing her, making her slick with desire, and then retreating to more untouched skin. Kate's breath was soon ragged, her body almost limp.

He straddled her body and pressed his cock into her belly, and kissed her eyes, her nose, and her mouth. He moved to the hollow of her throat, the valley between her breasts, and down farther still, his hands cradling her hips.

Kate's knees came up and apart as he sank between her thighs, she groaned with the madness of pleasure. Grayson swirled his tongue on her, circling around and dipping inside her, teasing her to greater madness. Her hips moved against him, her hands clutched at his head. When she began to pant, he closed his lips around her and sucked her in, drawing an intense climax.

Kate muffled her cry into a pillow. When she was spent, Grayson slowly eased himself up her body, sank his hand into her hair and his cock into her body with a long sigh of relief. He moved smoothly in and out, gaining strength as he felt himself nearing his release. His body moved in time to the pounding of his heart, until he erupted within her and felt the intense gratification rain down on him.

Yes, *yes,* he wanted to be alone with this woman, with only Kate, and no one else. He wanted every moment with her in these few days he could steal from his life. He wanted this glimpse of heaven, no matter how short or how painful in the end.

Grayson didn't know how much time passed before she slept, but still he held her, occasionally brushing the hair from her face, marveling at his new and deep sense of fulfillment.

CHAPTER TWENTY-SEVEN

Cold seeped into Kate's bones and woke her. She was shivering; she pulled the covers up beneath her chin and slid her hand out next to her. The linens were cool.

She opened her eyes — Grayson was gone, and she was nude and alone in bed. The fire had gone out, but in its place, the drapes had been pulled back and another gloriously sunny day was streaming in through the window.

She rubbed her eyes and sat up, pulling the counterpane up around her shoulders. She drew her knees up and used both hands to feel the mess that was her hair. *"Lud,"* she muttered . . .

But she was smiling. Last night had been spectacular, one she would never forget.

She was contemplating how best to reach her chemise — it had somehow ended up on the chaise across the room — when the door suddenly opened and Grayson strode in.

He was wearing buckskins and his shirttails hung to his thighs. He wore a blanket about his shoulders, but his feet were bare. And he was carrying a tray.

Kate laughed with surprise at the sight of him.

"Your breakfast, madam, such as it is," he said, bowing low and almost toppling the small teapot off the tray. "I confess that I do not know much about kitchens," he said, hastily righting the pot. "In fact, I had to search for the blasted room. One wonders why it is so very far away from where food is consumed. Nevertheless, I found it and Mrs. Williams was kind enough to assist me in boiling some water and in making toast points until Mr. Williams called for her. Regrettably, I burned it."

"Mrs. Williams?"

"The cook," he said, as he carefully put the tray down on the end of the bed. "She's gone on holiday, to visit her sister in Brighton."

Kate gaped at him.

He grinned proudly. "They've gone, all of them on holiday. We shall either survive by our sheer wits and cunning, or they will find us perished somewhere in the vicinity of the kitchens for want of food, for there is no one left in this dreary little castle but you and me."

"Grayson!" she cried happily. "Do you mean it? Even Mr. Noakes?"

He laughed. "Especially Mr. Noakes. He'd never leave us be." He smiled down at her. "It's not a cottage, but at least, for a few days, it is ours and ours alone."

She surged up and threw her arms around his neck.

"It's freezing," Grayson said, and pushed her back into the pillows and covered her up. "I will not allow you to catch your death at the first sign of freedom," he said, fetching her chemise and another blanket. "Now I grant you the toast looks rather bleak, but Mrs. Williams assured me that with a good butter knife and an adequate amount of jam, we might manage to swallow it down nonetheless."

Kate pulled on the dressing gown and reached for a piece and took a bite. "I think it is possibly the most delicious toast I have ever tasted," she proclaimed.

After the burned breakfast, Grayson had Kate dress very warmly in a pair of buckskins he'd found in one of the closed rooms. "I don't know who they belong to, but I think they will do."

"I don't like them," Kate said, wrinkling her nose as she twisted around to see them on her body. "What sort of game requires that I wear them?"

"It's not a game, darling," he said, and Kate realized she very much loved the way he said *darling.* "I thought I'd teach you to ride a horse."

"A horse!" she cried with delight. "I've always wanted to ride one! But . . . but can you actually dress one with a saddle and whatnot?"

Grayson laughed. "I have servants, Kate, but I am not entirely addled. I am quite capable of saddling a horse."

The news that she was to ride a horse elated Kate.

She trudged alongside Grayson to the stables wearing a pair of boys' boots Digby had insisted she bring, and the buckskins, which they'd managed to cinch up with one of his neck cloths, as well as her fur-lined cloak.

She fairly skipped inside the stables when Grayson pulled the large door open. But the horse in the first stall towered over her, and worse, he looked down at her with an enormous brown eye.

Kate had a sudden change of heart. "No!" she said adamantly.

"No?" Grayson echoed. "I will not accept a *no,* madam. You wanted this."

"Yes, indeed I said I should like to be alone with you, Christie, but I did not mean to *die* for it," she insisted.

"Die for it!" Grayson cried. "Have you no faith in yourself? Or my horses? I will have you know that I purchase only the finest horseflesh from the finest horse trader in all of Britain and Ireland! Lord Donnelly is my good friend and he would not have sold me a murderous equine!"

"Why can I not ride with you?" she pleaded.

"Come now, it's all really quite easy. Just use your knees and your hands and let the horse do the rest."

"No," she said resolutely, folding her arms. "I will not climb on that beast."

"Do you not want to know the thrill of being on the back of a horse?"

"Not at my own peril!"

In the end, Grayson relented and put her on his mount, in the saddle before him. She very much enjoyed the intimacy of that, and snuggled back against him. "Move like that once more, lass, and you will discover what peril you truly risk," he growled as they rode from the paddock.

With a laugh, Kate wiggled against him. In retaliation, Grayson sent the horse galloping into the park, laughing at her squeals of fright.

They rode down to the river, where they

dismounted. Holding hands, they walked along the banks, pausing occasionally to examine a curious rock, or for Grayson to point out the various types of trees that grew close to the banks of the river.

Then Grayson showed her the game of chase he and his siblings used to play as children. Kate was very quick on her feet in spite of her clunky boots. It seemed to surprise Grayson that she managed to stay just beyond his reach. In frustration, he lunged and grabbed her, but he lost his footing, and the two of them went down, rolling down an embankment.

Kate landed facedown, on her belly.

"Kate!" Grayson cried, and scrambled to her side. "Dear God," he said anxiously and rolled her onto her back. Kate flung her arms wide and lay there with her eyes closed.

"Kate," he said, cupping her face with his hands.

She suddenly opened her eyes and laughed up at the blue sky.

"Damn your hide," Grayson said, and smothered her laughter with kisses.

When they picked themselves up from the ground — and the leaves from her hair — Grayson announced that it was Kate's turn.

"My turn for what?" she asked breathlessly.

"To teach me a game from your childhood."

She laughed. "We didn't play many games."

"You were a child once. Children play games," he said, his hands on his hips. "Let's have one."

"All right," she said. "But I must warn you, you will not care for it. I thought it disgraceful and I must make it quite clear that *I* never played."

"I'm curious now — what is the game?"

"Very well," Kate said. She pushed him with her hands, forcing him back a step or two. "Stand there and pretend to be a gentleman."

"As opposed to the rogue that I am, I suppose," he said with a laugh.

"You are on a crowded London street," she said, walking in a circle around him, studying him. "There are people all round, bumping into you quite accidentally. But you hardly notice, because you are perusing the wares of a particular merchant — let me think, what would a duke want to purchase? Quills! That's it, you mean to purchase some quills."

"I've never purchased a quill in my life," Grayson said with a grin. "But I shall pretend it."

"Peruse, peruse," Kate said, gesturing for him to turn his head. "And remember, there are people here and there, and a lot of jostling about. Someone shouts, look there!" she cried, and whirled around.

Grayson looked behind her.

"Someone cries *thief, thief!* And you look to see where he is running!"

Grayson looked at her.

"Try and see," she urged him. He did as she asked, attempting to step around her.

"But as you move, you bump into a child you've not seen before," she said, and collided quite hard with him. She quickly stepped back, grinning with delight. Grayson looked confused. "I beg your pardon, sir," she said sweetly.

"What is the game?" he asked. "I don't understand."

With a laugh, Kate held up his pocket watch.

Stunned, Grayson looked down to the pocket of his waistcoat, from which she had snatched the watch when she collided with him. "The devil you say!"

Kate laughed again and curtsied deeply as she held it out to him. "I assure you, I have never been a cutpurse. I've never stolen a thing in my life. Unfortunately, Jude was not as careful with his moral virtue as was I and he taught me how to do it, should I ever need to know."

Something clouded Grayson's eyes for a sliver of a moment, and Kate instantly regretted showing him the game. Digby had once told her she was far too forthcoming, and she guessed this was one of those times. "I'm famished!" she said lightly in an attempt to change the subject.

They ate the cheese and nuts Grayson had brought. Afterward, the encroachment of clouds from the west brought an end to their outing and sent them back to the lodge.

Kate left Grayson in the stables to tend to the horses and walked up to the lodge, which now seemed even larger to her with no one about. She changed from the buckskins — which, frankly, weren't so bad after all — and into a suitable gown for the late afternoon. She had begun the evening meal preparation when Grayson joined her a half hour later.

He'd removed his waistcoat and neck cloth and looked like a cobbler with one arm shoved into a boot he was polishing. As Kate made the pastries for which she'd needed the rose hips, she asked him about his childhood. She imagined children in fine clothing, playing chase on a green lawn.

She and Jude had built playhouses with

rotten potatoes.

Grayson shrugged as he polished. "I was the eldest and the heir, and as such, many expectations were placed on me. My schooling had to be done in a certain manner. I had to attend royal functions. I was expected to go abroad and sow my wild oats before returning to study being a duke at my father's knee." He paused a moment. "He was an excellent duke, my father. And he was taken from us far too soon."

"I am sorry," Kate said. "Was it an illness?"

"No," Grayson said, frowning at the memory. "Quite the opposite, in fact. He'd never been sick a day in his life that I can recall, but one day, his heart suddenly stopped working. And just like that, he was gone. And just like that, I was a duke."

"But you were prepared."

"Not at all," Grayson said. "There is not enough schooling in the world to prepare one for it. I knew the sorts of things that must be done, but I was not the least bit prepared for the enormous pressure of it all. When the livelihood of dozens depends on you, or the happiness of so many whose marriages must be made on the basis of compatibility and advantage to the Christophers, or one's public persona must reflect the morals of title and family, the pressure can feel quite heavy." He put one boot down and picked up the other one. "What of you, Kate? What sort of child were you?"

"Oh, I scarcely remember, really," she said, thinking back. "In a strange way, I was like you in that there were quite a lot of expectations of me. Not the same sort, obviously, but when my mother died, and there wasn't enough money, and it was my responsibility to look after Jude, and to bring in money in any manner that I could."

Grayson looked up, his expression one of shock.

It made Kate feel strange. She put down her bowl and rubbed her hands on the apron she'd found. "Now what have I done with the rose hips?"

Grayson did not ask her any more questions about her childhood, which she supposed was just as well. She thought she'd probably said more than she ought to have said anyway. Pickpockets and match girls, as if he needed to be reminded of her ignoble beginnings!

Fortunately, he began to regale her with tales of his friends, and Kate relaxed. She was quite happy that the meal of Cornish game hens turned out as well as it did and Grayson's fear that they would starve banished. He was very pleased with her pastries, which he declared the best he'd ever eaten. Kate didn't believe it for a moment, but she was flattered all the same.

After they'd eaten their fill, they wandered into the drawing room, where Grayson built a fire in the hearth. "Do you play chess?" he asked.

"Never," Kate said.

"Come then, you must learn." He brought the game into the room — a marble board with marble figures — and explained the basics of the game.

Kate lost the first game far too easily. However, she was pleased that it took Grayson a little longer to defeat her a second time.

The third match took them into the early morning hours, but Kate won her first chess match.

"You're very clever, are you aware?" Grayson said with a fond smile at her squeal of delight when she had him at checkmate.

"I'm not very clever at all," she said with a wink as she stretched her arms high above her head. "But I do know when a gentleman allows me to win."

He did not deny it; he smiled warmly as he put out his hand to her. "Shall we retire, madam?"

"I thought you'd never ask," she sighed

happily. With their arms around one another's waist, they walked to the Queen's room, pausing every few feet to snuff the candles.

They made love slowly and easily, in a manner that might have suggested they didn't believe the morrow would come, that there was no moment but this one.

CHAPTER TWENTY-EIGHT

Grayson had just built a kitchen fire the next morning when a caller announced their presence by banging on the front door.

He glanced at his pocket watch — it was a quarter to ten. As he walked briskly to the front door, the banging came again, only louder. The caller was clearly impatient.

Grayson opened the front door to a pair of women who bore some resemblance to each other, however one was old enough to be his mother. Grayson instantly assumed the younger was unmarried and the elder was determined to gain an introduction to the duke — it wouldn't be the first time it had happened. "Yes?" he asked impatiently.

The older woman squinted up at him. "How long have you been at Kitridge?" she demanded. "I've not seen you in Hadley Green."

"I only just arrived," he said, momentarily knocked off balance by her blunt question.

"Mamma," the younger woman said. "Might you introduce yourself before you begin questioning the poor man?"

"I beg your pardon, sir I am Mrs. Edward Ogle, and this is my daughter, Mrs. Theodore Blakely. We have come to pay our respects to the duke, who we are given to understand has come to winter at Kitridge."

"*Winter* in Kitridge?" Grayson said. "Like an old bear who has wandered off to hibernate?"

"Pardon?" She frowned irritably. "Please inform the duke we have come." She held out her hand. "Here is my calling card."

Grayson almost laughed — he leaned up against the jamb and shoved his thumb in the waist of his trousers. "I'll give it to the old bear, all right."

Mrs. Ogle gestured impatiently to the door. "The common practice is to take the calling card to the lord of the house, young man."

"The duke is indisposed at present."

Mrs. Ogle did not respond; she'd shifted her gaze to a point behind him. Grayson looked over his shoulder and saw what they'd noticed — Kate had entered the hall in her dressing gown and her hair was loose about her shoulders.

"Mamma, we must go at once," Mrs. Blakely muttered, and was suddenly studying her feet. But her mother was gaping at Kate. She snapped her gaze to Grayson. "I cannot believe that a man of the duke's stature would tolerate such . . . such immoral acts in his lodge under his very nose! Where is he? And how can you be so casual with your employer's honor in the middle of the day, sir? That may be the way in London, but it is *not* the way in Hadley Green!"

"I am hardly casual with my honor, madam, but I do believe a man might do as he pleases in his own home. For your information, I *am* the duke of Darlington, and I am wondering how one woman could be so meddlesome before noon!"

"Oh dear *God,*" Mrs. Blakely muttered.

"Mamma, come away!" she pleaded, putting her hand on her mother's arm and turning toward the drive. "Please don't make this any worse than you have. *Please.*"

But Mrs. Ogle was suddenly all smiles. "I beg your pardon, Your Grace," she said, dipping into a graceful curtsy as if they'd just been properly introduced. "I confess, I've not seen you since you were a wee lad, and I did not realize . . ." She laughed lightly. "Had you not answered your own door, I would have never assumed you were a servant."

"Yes," he drawled, straightening up. "That is rather clear. And now that you have made your acquaintance known —"

"I welcome you with open arms to Hadley Green," she said, as if nothing had happened. "We've not seen your esteemed family in some time, and it is a delight for us all to welcome you into our fold."

"I do not intend to enter the fold, Mrs. Ogle," Grayson said. "We will be returning to London shortly."

"Oh!" Mrs. Ogle looked at Kate.

"Good day, Mrs. Ogle. Mrs. Blakely," Grayson said and moved to shut the door.

"I hope you will not be a stranger to Hadley Green!" Mrs. Ogle called out to him. "I think you will find it quite tranquil here. I understand it is very restorative!"

Grayson shut the door.

Kate hurried to the front receiving room and looked out the window as the two women walked back to their curricle, the younger daughter pulling her mother along. "Unbelievable!" Kate said as Grayson stepped up behind her and wrapped his arms around her. "At least we won't have to endure them at some social function." She twisted around in his arms and rose up on her toes to kiss him. "Did you burn the toast?"

"Just for you," he said with a wink.

"I must return to London on the morrow," Grayson said the following afternoon as the two of them soaked in a bath before the kitchen hearth. A light snow was falling outside; they could see the fat flakes coming down outside the small kitchen window.

"Tomorrow?" Kate repeated, unable to hide the disappointment in her voice. "So soon?"

Grayson smiled sympathetically. "We've been away four days now, and unfortunately, I have many responsibilities that will be neglected if I don't return." He teased her between her legs with his foot. "I promised Merrick I wouldn't be away long. The abolition vote will happen shortly after the parliamentary session opens, and he is still rounding up the necessary votes." He lifted his foot to her breast. "He needs me."

Kate needed him. She needed him more with each passing moment. She needed Kitridge Lodge, and this bath, and the pastries she'd made, and the riding in the park and the archery he'd attempted to teach her this afternoon before the cold drove them inside. She never wanted this holiday to end. She never wanted to face the truth of her life again. She swirled her fingers on the water's surface.

"If I don't have you back on the morrow, your Mr. Butler will bloody well break my neck, I think."

Ah, Aldous and Digby. They'd be frantic if she didn't return on the morrow. There was no escape from her life, no matter how hard she might wish it. She sighed. "I wish it could always be like this," she admitted softly.

Grayson nudged her with his foot; when she glanced up, he smiled at her and said, "So do I, darling. But we both know it can't possibly be."

But Kate *didn't* know that, not really. She felt slightly foolish for even wanting it to be different; she understood the ocean of differences between them. But couldn't oceans be crossed? Couldn't Grayson see that they could? "I should be home," she said, working to convince herself. "Digby will be sick with worry, and Jude might return to London."

"And there is George to think of," Grayson reminded her.

Kate glanced up at him. There was nothing that could have ruined everything quite like the mention of the prince. "Oh. Him," Kate said sullenly. "I have a bloody agreement with him, don't I?"

"I believe he thinks you do," Grayson said solemnly, and touched his fingers to hers. "By the bye, I have, for all intents and purposes, ended my association with Lady Eustis."

That brought Kate's head up. She was almost afraid to ask how or when, or perhaps most importantly, *why.*

He pressed his lips together. "It seemed the prudent thing to do," he said. "My heart has not been hers of late, obviously, and . . . and it was never meant to be more than a casual sort of affair."

"I'd wager Lady Eustis has a different opinion."

"Yes. But she and I both knew from the beginning that it would end eventually. It's the way of the *ton.*"

"I don't care for the ways of the *ton,*" Kate said peevishly. "Why shouldn't men and women marry whom they love? People like you and Lady Eustis, who were born to privilege, should be free to marry whoever you love. I am sure Lady Eustis loves you, Grayson. How could she not?"

Grayson looked at her so closely that Kate blushed. He sat up, put his fingers under her chin. "Do you love me, Kate?"

Kate faltered; tears began to build behind her eyes. "How could I not?"

He smiled sadly and slipped his hands under her arms, drawing her to his chest. She laid her head against his shoulder; he caressed her wet hair. "Do you love *me?*" she asked tearfully.

"How could I not?"

Kate closed her eyes. A single tear fell from the corner of one.

They remained like that until the water grew cold. Grayson was the first to get out, reaching for the towels they'd left warming by the fire. Kate admired his body, his magnificent torso, the muscular thighs. It seemed so unfair that she could know and love a man so intimately, yet not have him.

Grayson wrapped a towel around his waist and brought one to Kate. When she stood up, he wrapped her in it and dried her hair. "I hope you'll make more pastries. I am determined to eat as many of them as I can before I am returned to the rigors of Cook's diet."

She promised they would, and they spent the evening as they had the two prior evenings, cooking together, drinking wine, playing chess, and laughing. They laughed at silly things and teased each other. And as they had each night at Kitridge Lodge, they made love in the Queen's room and then lay in each other's arms. But that night they both seemed to be lost in their own private thoughts.

Kate stared into the fire for some time.

When she looked at Grayson, she discovered he was watching her. He smiled, touched her face. "What are you thinking, beauty?"

"I am wondering why you told me about Lady Eustis," she admitted.

He traced his thumb along her lips. "I thought you'd want to know."

"But what does it mean?"

"It means that my heart is with you."

"And if I am in your heart, then . . . ?"

He cupped her chin. "Then . . . we go back to London and we resume our lives, and we continue on as long as we might. That's all, Kate. You do understand that is all we can hope for, do you not?"

She understood it. But she desperately wanted him to tell her it wasn't true.

Were Digby here, he would chastise her for being silly and predictably female, then scold her for wanting more from her life than she might reasonably expect. "Your life is what it is, Kate," he'd told her when she'd first met him. "The sooner you understand it, the happier you shall be."

Digby couldn't have been more wrong, for Kate understood very clearly what her life was, and she'd never been unhappier.

Grayson left their bed before Kate woke. He didn't think he could bear to face her this morning, knowing these few idyllic days had come to an end. He left a fire in the hearth for her, dressed, and went down to the kitchen to boil water, a skill he'd mastered the last two mornings. But as he neared the kitchen, he heard pots being moved about, and the voice of Mrs. Williams calling out to Mr. Williams.

The servants had returned.

Grayson stopped. He stood a long moment before reluctantly turning about and going back the way he'd come.

Grayson and Kate departed shortly after luncheon, which Mrs. Williams insisted on serving them. They said little to each other on the drive back to London. Kate looked out the window at a world made white by a thin blanket of snow. As they drew closer to London, Grayson's spirits began to flag. He wasn't ready to return to his life as a duke. To his life without Kate.

The traffic was quite bad in London, and Grayson grew impatient. When they reached Kate's residence, he went out before her. As he turned to help Kate down, his gaze fixed on a carriage at the curb.

Kate stepped out and followed his gaze. "God in heaven," she muttered.

Neither one of them moved; they could only stand and stare at the seal of the Prince of Wales emblazoned on the side of that carriage.

Chapter Twenty-nine

An angry Prince of Wales was waiting impatiently in the drawing room in the house he'd paid for, standing with two gentlemen Kate had never seen before. There were wineglasses scattered about various tables and Kate wondered how long he'd been waiting for her. A small shiver of fear ran down her spine; she looked around for any sign of Aldous or Digby and could see nothing that indicated either of them was close by.

She'd made a horrible, horrible mistake.

"Your Highness," Grayson said.

The prince fixed his eyes on Grayson. "I see *you* are not afraid of contagion, Your Grace." His voice was hard and cold. He shifted his dark look to Kate and put out his hand, palm up. "Give me your hand, Kate," he snapped.

She did as he asked, laying her fingers across his open palm. He closed his fingers tightly around hers and pulled her to his side, and said coolly, "I expected better from you, Darlington."

"I have done as you asked," Grayson returned coldly.

"You have done far more than I asked," the prince snapped. "I no longer have need of your assistance. Leave us."

Kate could feel Grayson's eyes on her, but she knew better than to look at him, not with the prince watching her every move with eyes blazing in anger. She looked down.

"Kate . . . if you are not comfortable, you may come with me," Grayson said evenly.

"Pardon?" the prince snapped.

"Kate?" Grayson asked, ignoring the prince. "Come with me."

"No," she said. She could hardly speak, her heart was beating so fiercely. She had no idea what to expect, but she knew instinctively that if she walked out with Grayson, it would be far worse. "I am perfectly fine," she forced herself to say.

Still, Grayson hesitated. Why didn't he go, just *go!* They'd made a horrible mistake, and the longer he stood there looking at her, the worse he made it. She'd tried to tell him as much outside — "Let me go in alone!" she'd begged him — but Grayson wouldn't hear of it. He wouldn't leave her to face the prince alone.

"Leave my house, Darlington!" the prince said angrily. "All of you! Leave us!" he bellowed, his fingers curling more tightly around Kate's hand, squeezing it painfully.

Kate risked a look at Grayson. "Please go," she said, and quickly turned away.

A moment later, she could feel Grayson move away from her with the others; she heard the door shut behind her. Only then did she lift her gaze to George.

The prince dragged her across the drawing room and Kate feared the worst. He pushed her down on the settee, but instead of striking her, as Kate fully expected and braced herself for, he turned away. She could see his shoulders rise with his breath and sink again before he finally faced her. His eyes were blazing, his jaw set tightly. "Are you mad?" he asked sharply. "Do you intentionally seek my displeasure? For you have found it in abundance, madam!"

"I — No," she said. She had learned with Benoit that it was pointless to reason with a man when he was angry.

Unfortunately, her short answer seemed to make the prince angrier. He took a menacing step toward her. "Perhaps I should explain why I am so deeply perturbed," he sneered. "You are *mine,* Kate. I bargained for you fairly! I have provided for you very well indeed, and I made arrangements to keep you occupied until such time I might take advantage of our arrangement! If I did not make myself perfectly clear in the course of our agreement, then allow me to do it now. You are not to . . . to *frolic* with any man but *me!* In giving you Darlington as an escort, I meant only to give you the opportunity to be in society without drawing attention to me! And instead of showing your great gratitude for my generosity, you have betrayed me!"

"I have not," she said instantly and firmly, and put a hand to her roiling stomach.

The prince suddenly lunged at her and grabbed her arm, yanking her off the settee, looming over her. "Have you bedded him?" he demanded hotly.

"No!" she lied, and prayed that her face did not give her away. "I misunderstood you, Your Highness," she said, trying desperately not to sound panicked. "I thought you desired me to be seen with his grace at every opportunity, so that society might think he'd engaged my services. I did it to keep your name as far from me as possible."

His eyes narrowed skeptically and he pursed his lips together as he regarded her. She returned his gaze with eyes wide open, knowing that the slightest quiver, the slightest hint of uncertainty would give her away.

"I thought you were ill, brought to bed by an ague," he said, watching her closely, studying her for any deception.

Kate prayed her knees would not give way. "I was, but the weather has been foul and I thought . . . I thought a country airing would help me, and the duke kindly offered to take me."

"And just like that, the two of you carried yourselves off to the country without a word to anyone?"

"I wouldn't have dared to contact you, Your Highness, not with the delicate matters that surround you."

"You could have written me!" he roared.

"Your Highness, I've written you only when your man has waited for my response! I would never be so bold as to seek to contact you on my own!"

"Do not lie to me, Kate!" he shouted, and raised his hand, as if he meant to strike her.

She looked him in the eye. "I do not lie," she said, and her heart beat painfully with her dreadful deceit.

He said nothing for a long, tense moment. And then, "You have misunderstood me." His voice was considerably calmer, and Kate thought she might swoon with relief. The prince touched her ear lobe with his finger. "I merely meant for you to accompany him on occasion, sweetling. I did not mean for you to befriend him so completely. But allow me to be very clear: If I find you have betrayed me, not only shall I turn you out, I shall ruin you. You will spread your legs for sailors, not lords. And I will see to it that Darlington is punished as well. His affair with Lady Eustis will be exposed. His brother's vote on abolition will be imperiled." He leaned closer. "And any scandal that touches him will touch each and every member of his family."

The image of Frederick and Radcliff suddenly loomed in her mind.

"Imagine that," the prince sneered. "Scandal has never touched the Christopher family, so I should think the slightest bit would make quite a large splash."

Kate could not believe what little regard the prince had for Grayson's family, particularly after scandal had so impacted the prince's life. She forced a smile. "You have nothing to fear, Your Highness," she said breathlessly.

He let go of her arm and caressed her neck with his knuckles. "Kate, lovely Kate." He put his arm around her waist and drew her to him. "I know you are impatient. I have applied again to the king for relief in my suit. I have asked that he make a decision about a parliamentary divorce as quickly as possible.

I understand he is considering my letter very carefully and I have reason to believe he will deliver a decision very soon. That means, *jolie fleur,* that in only a matter of days, you will be my mistress in more than fantasy."

"How my heart swells to hear it," she said.

He smiled and kissed her, his lips lingering long enough to repulse her. "When I see your smile I can scarcely abide the wait." He ran his hands possessively down her body. "Sometimes I would like to throw caution to the wind and take what is mine."

"Your Highness flatters me," Kate said. "And while I could scarcely hope for more than that, I think . . . I think you chance too much."

"How so?" he muttered, kissing her temple.

"Don't you see, darling?" she whispered. "If anyone suspects you have taken a mistress and the news reaches the king, it will surely weigh in his decision as to whether he puts your marriage to a trial."

"Yes, I know. That is why I've hidden you here," he said, and cupped her breast.

"But . . . but His Majesty could be persuaded that you desire a trial to end your marriage in order to satisfy your own personal desires, and not for the good of the monarchy or your daughter, as you have stated."

The prince chuckled softly. "I *know,* Kate." He slipped his fingers into her bodice, brushed them across her nipple. "But how will the king know of one stolen afternoon? I think we are quite safe."

Her heart skipped. She couldn't bear it, not after being with Grayson. "But your carriage is waiting just outside, Your Highness. Many have surely noticed it. There is hardly anything on King Street to entice a prince and speculation will be rife . . . if it is not already."

His smile faded a bit. He glanced at the window.

"I'd wager talk has already begun."

George looked at her. "You are very clever, *ma petite* Kate. Very clever." He kissed her. He wrapped his arm around her and pulled her to him. His tongue dipped into her mouth, twirling around hers while his hand kneaded her bosom.

Kate feared he'd ignored her advice and would take her then and there, but he abruptly released her. "I find it impossible to contain my desire."

Kate smiled coyly. "You must think of your reward for doing so."

He laughed softly. "The reward will be yours, *ma petite oiseau.*" He kissed her once

379

more, and turned to leave. He paused to give her one final admonishment. "So that we are clear, you are not to see Darlington again. If you do, there will be dire consequences for you both. I would prefer you keep to your house until my situation is resolved."

"Yes sir," she said, curtsying.

"There are many things I will tolerate, but infidelity is not one of them."

If the man who had the reputation of being London's greatest adulterer saw the irony in his own words, he did not show it.

"Please forgive me for being so dreadfully foolish," Kate said sweetly.

The prince smiled — it was obviously what he'd wanted to hear her say. "You are forgiven . . . this time," he said ominously, and with a pat to her cheek, he took his leave of her.

CHAPTER THIRTY

"Don't bother, sir, I shall announce myself!"

Grayson groaned upon hearing his mother's voice through the open door of his study. He rose just as the footman dashed ahead of the duchess, bowing and quickly announcing her as she swept into his room.

"Good afternoon, Mother," he said, walking forward to greet her.

She responded by slapping the *Morning Times* into his outstretched hand. "I don't suppose I have to tell you that Lady Babington brought this to my attention," she said irritably before marching to the settee and sitting there.

Grayson glanced curiously at the paper.

"What on earth has come over you, Grayson?" she demanded. Grayson steeled himself — the duchess rarely used his given name, and only when she was very cross with him. "You have always been so very responsible and careful of our name!"

"I have not become any less so, I assure you."

"Then how do you account for *that*," she said, gesturing wildly at the newspaper. "You know very well what you've done. And at Kitridge Lodge! My grandfather built that lodge!"

Bloody hell. Grayson didn't have to read the news to know that a certain Mrs. Ogle had spread her gossip-laden wings and flown to London with her news. He sighed. "The society pages, I assume?"

"I marked it."

He unfolded the paper and scanned the page, finding her ink mark next to the society *on dit.*

Of late, a certain duke has been on the hunt for fresh country air. It was noted that he bagged a lovely bird whilst there, a species unknown to the quaint countryside of Hadley Green, but perhaps better known in town around the cloth halls where she has been known to roost.

Grayson's blood riled; he tossed the paper aside and dragged his fingers through his hair. Was there no part of his life that went without observation and comment? Was he not allowed a single weekend at an old hunting lodge for his leisure? Must he answer to all of bloody England for it?

"I will beg you to tell me that it was *not* that courtesan," his mother said stiffly.

"Beg all you like," he said roughly.

She gasped. "God in heaven, I cannot believe it!"

"For heaven's sake, Mother —"

"Do not speak to me!" she said angrily. "You have shamed me before our family and friends and all of London! There is nothing you can say that will improve it!"

"It was never my intent to shame you, madam," he said evenly. "But neither do I feel a need to improve anything."

"Grayson Robert Henry Christopher!" she exclaimed with great exasperation. "There are young women who would fall at your feet but for a single look from you! There are lovely debutantes who would make you a proud and dutiful wife, who would deliver the heirs you surely must want. Why, therefore, must you consort with . . . with an immoral woman?"

Grayson loved his mother dearly, but her elitism had pushed him to his limit. He stood abruptly from his seat, startling her. "Katharine Bergeron is not an immoral woman," he said, and threw up a hand when his mother gasped. "Furthermore, I think you might actually find her very agreeable if you could ever step off your pedestal to make her acquaintance."

"You wouldn't *dare* do such a wretched thing!"

"You cannot fault the woman for the circumstances of her birth, Mother, nor, I daresay, for the circumstances of her life. She did not choose her profession, but she did choose to survive in a world that can be quite cruel at times, and particularly to women and the disadvantaged. So I will ask you to please find a bit of compassion in your heart and stop fretting about my bloody reputation!"

"You are speaking to me in a most reprehensible manner!" she said hotly. "I would not have thought it at all possible!"

"I am speaking to you quite honestly. I did not seek Miss Bergeron's acquaintance; the Prince of Wales pressed it upon me. But I can assure you that once I could see past my own prejudices, I found a very delightful companion in her. And I will not stand for her to be derided by you or anyone else because of her unfortunate circumstance."

The duchess gaped at him. She slowly gained her feet. "I will not sit here and subject myself to this."

Grayson shrugged. "As you wish."

His mother marched from the room, almost bowling over the footman who hurried to open the door for her. When she had gone, Grayson calmly resumed his seat, but internally, he was working very hard to keep his rage in check. He loved his mother — she was no more and no less a product of her upbringing than was Kate — or himself for that matter. But he could not abide her prejudice or her complete censure of Kate. Or her presumption that she had the right to lecture him as to whom he would or would not befriend.

Grayson stood and walked to the windows overlooking the grounds. He'd been thinking of Kate ever since they'd returned to London two days ago. He was a blessed fool for taking her to Kitridge. He'd let his emotions rule him, let his fantasies consume him, and now he worried that Kate was suffering the consequences. And that, he could scarcely bear.

Yet his hands were tied. What could he do, take her and risk the damage George could do to the Christophers? George had expressed his ire quite clearly last night, when he'd summoned Grayson to Carlton House.

When Grayson arrived, he found the prince in an inebriated and irate state. "You have *astounded* me!" the prince ranted. "Did I not make clear to you that I wanted her for myself?"

Grayson chafed at being spoken to as if he were a naughty child. "You did," he said curtly.

"I cannot fathom why you, of *all* men, would attempt to make a fool of *me,*" the prince continued to rail. "My position is precarious, Darlington, you know that very well. I trusted you, but you have disappointed me like so many others. First Wilkes, then Lambourne, now *you!*"

It was all Grayson could do to keep from lashing out at him. Wilkes had hanged for his treachery. As for Lambourne . . . Grayson believed Lambourne was innocent of the accusations of adultery with George's wife, the Princess of Wales, but nevertheless he did not care to be compared to him.

"Don't go near her, Darlington," George snarled. "Do *not* go near her again, lest you desire to see her fend for herself on the street like a common whore!"

Grayson blanched. "You would exact your displeasure with me from a woman?"

"She is not so innocent!" George snapped. "Let me remind you that your brother requires a few pivotal votes to see his precious abolition bill passed!"

Grayson's eyes narrowed. "What has that to do with it?"

"Your brother can scarcely cobble the votes together as it is. One word from me — *one* word — and he and Wilberforce will lose. That word shall come if you do not keep your distance from *my* mistress."

"By God, if you were not my prince — how could you allow a practice as abominable as the slave trade to continue just so that you might make a bloody point with me?" he demanded loudly.

"Look at you now, Grayson, so high and mighty," George said mockingly. "What will it be, then? Will you have the slave trade on *your* conscience for the sake of a poke?"

Grayson had never despised a man as he did in that moment. "With all due respect, *Your Highness,*" Grayson said heatedly, "you disgust me."

"Spare me your indignation! I trusted you!" George thundered. "Leave me!"

"Gladly," Grayson said, and walked out of his privy chambers.

He fought the urge to go to her then, but the prince's threats against Merrick echoed in his brain, dogging his every step. While he would not stand to see Kate cast out of her house, at least he could do something about it. But Merrick . . . Merrick had devoted the last two years to working with Wilberforce to bring about an end to the British slave trade. It was very important to Merrick and their nation, and Grayson could not, under any circumstance, derail that effort.

Yet his worry for Kate loomed in his mind. What Grayson feared most was that George would take his pleasure from Kate, a thought so abhorrent to him that even now, he clenched his fist and swiped at the oil lamp on his desk. It crashed to the ground, spilling oil across the carpet.

A footman hurried to retrieve the lamp. Grayson stepped around him and walked out of his study. He couldn't bear the thought of George's hands or mouth on her. He'd worried so much, in fact, that he'd sent a footman to keep an eye on the house on King Street. The footman assured Grayson she was still there and the prince had not called on her.

This abominable situation was making him mad. Grayson had never felt so impotent, had never felt the mantle of his title weigh as heavily as it did now.

Grayson found himself at his sister Mary's house. Mary was young and spirited, and he enjoyed her company. If anyone could cheer him, it was Mary. He'd not seen her in more than a week, as she had been, according to Prudence, busily putting together her Season's wardrobe and making a list of suitable matches for her brothers.

When Grayson was shown into Mary's salon, however, he was rudely surprised to find Mary in the company of Prudence and Diana. *Dear God.*

"What a pleasure!" Mary cried, hurrying to place a kiss on his cheek. "You never call here at Wallace House — you are always off to Pru's."

"I am very happy to see you, Mary," he said fondly, and kissed her cheek and gave Prudence a hug. "Lady Eustis," he said, bowing.

She curtsied, her gaze cold.

"Christie, what have you gone and done?" Prudence exclaimed. "*Everyone* is speaking of it. It is one thing to be seen around London with certain ladies, but quite another to take them all the way to the lodge."

There would be no end to the opinions about his life, Grayson supposed, but for once in his blessed life, he resented the hell out of it. "And when did you become the arbiter of such matters, Pru?"

His abrupt comment took her aback; she and Mary exchanged wide-eyed looks.

"Well. If *I* had done something like that

before I was married, I would have been sent to live with some spinster aunt," Mary said.

"We don't have a spinster aunt, Mary. And as for you, my darling sister," Grayson said to Prudence, "I shall thank you to mind your own affairs. This is not your concern." He'd come here for some relief from his dilemma with the prince and the stifling rules in London, but he found the same judgmental attitudes, the same expectations of a life that was feeling less and less like his own.

"Look here, Christie, look what was just this moment delivered to me," Mary said, whirling around to a large box. She took off the lid and pulled out a beautiful ivory gown. She held it up to her body and twirled around with it, just as she used to do when she was a girl playing in their mother's wardrobe. Mary prattled on about the gowns she'd commissioned in excruciating detail.

Grayson tried to listen, but with the exception of Mary, who was blessedly unaware, it was very uncomfortable. Prudence was pouting and Grayson could sense Diana's bitterness.

He stayed as long as he could bear it. He thought of Brooks, of whiskey, of sanctuary. The moment he could gracefully make his exit, he did. He bid them all a good afternoon, insisted to Mary that she need not see him out, and strode to the foyer, anxious to be on his way. He'd donned his cloak and hat and was fitting his hands into his gloves when he saw Diana from the corner of his eye.

"Your Grace, wait, please," she said.

Grayson stifled a groan of impatience; he could hardly deny her. There was a footman attending the door, so he gestured across the foyer into a receiving room just off the entrance. "I am sorry," he said once he'd shut the door behind them. "I would that you had not seen or heard the gossip —"

"I don't care," Diana said instantly. "I don't care even that you've been with her — I miss you. I have thought long and hard about our unique situation, and I want you to know that if you have two mistresses, so be it."

Stunned, Grayson stepped back from her. "Diana! Do you realize what you are saying?"

"What possible difference can it make?" she exclaimed excitedly. "I have a husband and a lover — why shouldn't you have two lovers?"

"Diana!"

"Please!" she cried, putting her hand on his chest. "I have missed you so, Grayson. I cannot bear your absence."

Grayson took her hand and removed it from his coat. "You and I both knew from the beginning that our affair could not possibly last," he said as calmly as he might. "It has come to its inevitable end, Diana. I don't want to hurt you any more than I already have, so I will ask you to please accept that."

Diana pulled her hand free of his. "She is not what you think," she said coldly.

Grayson turned away.

"She hails from St. Katharine's and she is the daughter of a drunkard! She is as base-born as one might possibly be, and you must know that she is not anyone your family will ever accept."

"How in God's name —" Grayson stopped himself from asking how she knew. He wouldn't prolong this conversation as much as a moment. "It is no concern of yours," he said angrily.

"If you were married, no one would care," Diana desperately continued. "But you have not yet produced an heir, Grayson. Your family, and I dare say, society, would never accept a bastard child as your heir."

Something brittle snapped inside Grayson and he grabbed Diana's arm. "This is the second time you've attempted to tell me what society will or will not accept in my behavior. You were my lover, madam, not my *wife.* I suggest you go home to your husband and try to deliver the heir *he* so desperately needs."

"Bastard!" she spat.

He let go of her arm and strode from the receiving room as his impotent fury raged in his veins.

Chapter Thirty-one

The week after her return from Kitridge Lodge had been one of the worst in Kate's life, and that in and of itself was remarkable.

In addition to being effectively imprisoned by the prince and her secretly broken heart, Kate received some awful news.

After Fleming's attack on her, Kate had sent Aldous to Holly with a note, warning her not to open the door to Fleming. She worried Fleming might take his revenge on them. After several days of trying to convince Digby to accompany her into St. Katharine's to see about the women, he agreed to do so. When Kate arrived there, she found them all snugly resting in their rooms sharing a loaf of bread and some cheese.

"What did ye bring us?" Holly asked excitedly, eyeing Kate's basket.

"Petits fours," Kate said, and laughed when they all squealed with delight at once. "And some sundry things," she added, although no one was listening, as they'd begun to devour the petits fours.

"They are as delicious as always," Esmeralda said. "They were Meg's favorite." She paused. "A pity, isn't it?"

"Mmm," Lucy agreed.

"A pity?" Kate asked.

"Don't ye know, mu'um?" Holly asked, wiping the crumbs from her lips.

"Know what?" Kate asked.

Holly suddenly paled and exchanged a look with Esmeralda.

"She's gone," Esmeralda said. "Found drowned in the Thames."

Kate dropped the candles she'd just taken from her basket.

"Murdered," Lucy whispered ominously as Esmeralda stooped to pick up the candles.

"Murdered!" Kate exclaimed, choking on the word. "But why? *Who?"*

"Billy Hopkins is who, if ye ask me," Adele sniffed. "I told Meg he was a lout, but she'd not listen to me, she never did. She was too fond of her drink, that one, and Billy kept her belly full of it, didn't he?"

"It's the devil's poison," Esmeralda agreed.

A wave of nausea overcame Kate, and she put a hand to her belly. "What have they done with her?" she asked thickly.

"What they do with all paupers," Holly said matter-of-factly.

"Oh dear God." Kate closed her eyes and seemed to melt down onto her haunches, her arms folded tightly against her belly. She tried to banish the image of Meg drowning, of Meg lying cold and wet and dead on the banks of the Thames. As a child, Kate had seen a dead man who had washed up on the banks, and that memory, merging together with Meg's pretty face in Kate's mind, was her undoing — she was abruptly sick into a chamber pot.

"Miss Bergeron!" Esmeralda cried, hurrying to help her.

"I am so very sorry," Kate said shakily. "I can't bear the news of Meg."

There was nothing any of them could say to help her feel better. Kate had failed Meg. Meg had failed herself. Another life had been destroyed by the brutality and poverty of St. Katharine's.

Digby couldn't console Kate, either. "There is nothing you might have done to prevent it. You know as well as I that Meg wasn't long for this world," he said on their way home.

"That's not true! She might have lived a very long life if I had somehow removed her from this place," Kate exclaimed, gesturing at the crowded street around them.

"Perhaps, but I suspect Meg would not have gone so easily. She liked men's attentions. She liked her ale." Digby put his arm around Kate's shoulders. "There are some who are destined for this life, and others who are destined to leave it behind."

"*No* one is destined for this wretched life, Digby," Kate said irritably. 'They are unvoluntarily brought into this world and without anything or anyone to guide them, they can't leave it."

"Involuntarily," he corrected her. "Don't be so mawkish, love! I know of at least one other person who has left this world but who will be returning shortly."

Kate jerked her gaze to him. "Jude? It is Jude?"

He smiled broadly. "The ship has reached Deptford. But because of the cargo she carried — and by that I mean slaves — she was not allowed to moor. Another ship is en route to take her cargo, at which point *The Princess* will come into the West India docks for repairs."

Kate stared at him, her mind dancing with the image of a fair-haired boy who had followed her about a tiny set of rooms. "Jude is really coming home?"

"I do believe he is."

With a cry of delight, Kate grabbed Digby's forearms. *"When?"*

"No more than a fortnight, I should think. I've a man watching at the shipyards. He'll let me know as soon as she's given the authority to sail."

Kate threw her arms around Digby. "Thank you, Digby! This is the best news you possibly might have given me!"

But the happy news of Jude's potential return did not boost Kate's spirits for long. Aldous began to worry about her. Losing her lover and the girl Meg all in one week had obviously taken a toll on Kate. Aldous understood it — she was young and, in some respects, woefully inexperienced. She hadn't understood how deeply a lost love could hurt, and there had never been any question, at least to Aldous, that she would lose her love.

Aldous understood how deep that sort of pain ran — when he'd lost the sea, he'd lost his heart.

That was perhaps the thing that surprised Aldous, for all the time he'd known Kate, she'd been inordinately guarded with her heart. Even he, one of her closest friends, could sense the distance between her and men. But for reasons Aldous would never understand, of all the men who admired her, Kate had allowed the duke into her heart.

It baffled Aldous as to *why* the duke. Aldous saw nothing special about him. He seemed like all the other men of privilege — arrogant and dismissive. Nor was he particularly handsome. Or even charming, for that matter. Yet Kate had seen something in the duke, and once the prince had discovered their ill-fated affair, Kate had discovered the pain of a broken heart.

She moped about the house, unsmiling, unwilling to talk. And she was dreadfully pale, too. By the end of the week, Aldous threatened to send a note around to the prince demanding a physician be sent to her.

"No!" Kate cried. "No, no, you mustn't!"

"You are not well, Kate," Aldous said. "I fear for your health."

"I am quite all right," she said, flicking her wrist at him. "It is nothing that will not run its course in due time." She glanced at the window and swallowed. "I am as well as I could possibly hope to be."

"Kate —"

"There is nothing wrong with me, Aldous!"

Aldous hesitated. He ached for her. "This . . . this melancholy will ease with time," he said awkwardly. "It may not seem as if it will, but . . . but time will ease it."

Kate's eyes filled with tears. "There are some things, I think, Aldous, that are never made easier with time."

He'd said too much. He'd wanted to comfort her and he'd succeeded in increasing her agony. That was why, he reminded himself as he made his excuses and left her in the drawing room, that he preferred the sea to women. He didn't have to comfort the sea.

Once Lord Eustis returned from Bath, he declared it too cold to return to his country estate and determined he would stay in London for another fortnight.

Diana thought she might perish.

She could scarcely bear to be in the same room with him. She could not watch him chew his food, or hear him tap his spoon against his teacup, or smell the heavy cologne he wore. But she had no choice — when Charles and Diana were living in the same home, he wanted her to be with him. He said it was the path to marital accord.

For Diana, it was the path to her private hell.

They were seated in the red drawing room one evening, Charles quietly reading, Diana chafing at her invisible chains, when Hatt entered the room and bowed. "My lady," he said softly, which caused Charles to look up from his book.

"Yes?" Diana asked, curious. Hatt hardly looked at her when Charles was in residence.

"If you would, mu'um, Millie requests an audience."

"Who is Millie?" Charles asked, looking at Diana.

Stupid man. Millie had been in her employ for three years now. "My ladies' maid, my love," she reminded him.

Charles looked at Hatt. "What does Millie want at this time of night?" he asked irritably, as if it were well past midnight instead of eight o'clock.

"My darling, would you mind terribly if I have a word?" Diana asked, coming to her feet.

"Sit, sit," Charles said, gesturing for her to resume her seat.

"Charles —"

"Show her in, Hatt," he said, ignoring her. "Whatever Millie must say to my wife, she may say in front of me as well."

Diana's belly dipped. She slowly resumed her seat as Hatt went out.

A moment later, Hatt returned, Millie slinking in behind him. She curtsied, kept her gaze on the carpet, her hands clasped before her.

"What is so important, Millie, that it requires you to interrupt our evening?" Charles asked without even bothering to look up from his book.

"Beg your pardon, milord," Millie said. "I ah . . . Lady Eustis, the ah . . . the things you wanted shall arrive by the end of next week."

Diana's heart skipped a beat. *The brother.* Millie — or whoever Millie had paid — had learned that Miss Bergeron not only hailed from St. Katharine's, she'd been plucked out of a cloth hall to be the merchant's whore. She had a brother she seemed particularly anxious to find — she'd made inquiries up and down the quay. Millie had discovered it all — her brother's name, the fact that he was a seaman on a slave ship. Miss Bergeron wanted to find her brother, but Diana was rather desperate to find him first. Her own affair with Grayson may have come to its "inevitable end," as he put it, but her scorn for Grayson and his new lover had only begun to blossom.

"What is this?" Charles asked, now glaring at Millie. "What things? That makes no sense, girl."

Millie looked helplessly at Diana.

"My lord," Diana said soothingly. "You will ruin my surprise for you if you force her to tell you."

"My *what?*" he snapped, looking at Diana now.

"My surprise for you."

For once in his blessed life, Charles looked astounded and even pleased. "For me?" he asked, smiling as much as he could.

"Yes. For you."

His smile broadened. "Well then. A surprise for me, is it?" He glanced at Millie. "Very well, Millie. You've delivered your message. You may take your leave."

"Yes, milord," Millie said, dipping another curtsy. But she didn't leave. She hesitated, her eyes on Charles. Diana frowned darkly, trying to relay her fervent desire that Millie quit the room *now,* before she angered Charles or did something entirely foolish.

"Pardon, milady," Millie said. "I don't have enough to pay for it."

Diana thought she might be ill. She didn't dare look at Charles. She kept her eyes on Millie, the pleasant smile on her face. "I see —"

"How much?" Charles asked.

"Five pounds, milord."

"Five *pounds,*" he echoed, his brows rising with his surprise. He looked at Diana. "It must be quite a special surprise, darling. My, how you have pleased me this evening." He shifted his gaze to Millie once more. "Ask Hatt for it on the morrow. Now leave us."

"Thank you, milord," Millie said and gave Diana the slightest smirk.

As she watched Millie leave the room, Charles startled Diana by touching her hand. "Thank you, love," Charles said when Diana looked at him. "I am quite touched by your thoughtfulness."

"No, darling, I am the one who is pleased," Diana said. As Charles resumed his reading, Diana fretted about how she would ever produce a suitable surprise for Charles, much less pay for it.

CHAPTER THIRTY-TWO

Kate's situation did not improve in the course of the next few days. The prince was determined to keep a close eye on her and sent "friends" to visit her at odd hours to see if she was about. He wrote her love letters and had them delivered whenever the mood struck him, and demanded the messenger wait for written responses. Kate struggled to provide them, particularly when Digby was not present to help her. Aldous was very little help in writing love letters.

Moreover, on two occasions, Kate was given word at the last possible moment that she was to attend a social event.

The first event, an intimate supper party for forty people, including the prince, hosted by the Earl of Berkshire, was nothing but a bit of fog in her memory. She'd smiled when anyone gazed at her, and had replied when anyone spoke to her, but she hadn't felt as if she were really present. She'd known people were looking at her strangely, whispering about her behind their fans and their wine goblets, but Kate had hardly cared — she'd been so bitterly disappointed when Grayson hadn't appeared at the party that she could think of little else.

It wasn't that she hadn't heard or understood the prince's warning to her — she had, and very clearly. His warning kept her from sleeping soundly. Kate was so intimidated, in fact, that she'd returned the four letters Grayson had written her without opening them. She would not be responsible for his downfall, or that of any member of his family.

But that did not stop her from wanting to see him, to somehow nurture her memory of him.

When the prince openly challenged her to join a game of whist with him and his friends, she bantered flirtatiously, and all in all, had proven herself to be a good courtesan. Judging by the way George kept smiling at her as he drank himself into his cups, he was proud of her.

But Kate's heart and her thoughts were filled with Grayson. She wondered what he was doing, if he skated with his nephews, if he brooded about her as she did about him. She remembered him standing in the entry of Carlton House, a resplendent, masculine figure, and then how he'd looked when he'd stood in the bathing tub, naked and wet, his hard body glistening in the firelight.

She remembered those things and more at night when she was unable to sleep. In a moment of weakness, she'd even attempted to pen him a letter, asking him to come to her, telling him she loved him. But her writing skills were so rudimentary that she couldn't properly put into words what she wanted to say. She burned the letter.

Tonight, Kate had been summoned to a casino evening at Marlborough House. She assumed it would entail more torturous flirting with the prince. She did not allow herself to think about the day when the prince would come to her wanting that for which he'd paid so handsomely. The very thought of intimacy with him made her ill.

Kate felt ill now. She was dressed for the evening and seated at her vanity, her hand pressed against her forehead.

"You look beautiful, love," Digby said from her bed, where he was stretched out, a plate of freshly baked scones balanced on his belly. "You'll shine tonight."

She was wearing a jade green gown that complemented the emerald earrings George had sent her for "being good," along with a love letter, in which he declared he could not wait any longer to claim her.

"I couldn't possibly care less for a casino," she said irritably to Digby.

"You must learn to care for them, Kate. I suspect this sort of gathering might be your lot for a time until the prince grows weary of your company."

She glanced at Digby's reflection in her mirror. "You make it sound so certain."

"Have I not explained to you that the prince and gentlemen like him will always lose interest? It is their nature. The world is at their fingertips and they may have whatever they like just for the asking. But once they've had their fill, their eyes begin to wander. Oh now, don't look so glum. It isn't *you,* darling. It is what you are."

"Forgive me, but it is difficult for me to separate what I *am* from my heart."

"Well, you must. Stand now, and let me admire you."

With a weary sigh, Kate did as he asked. He smiled and nodded approvingly, but as his gaze swept over her, Digby frowned a little. "You're getting a little plump, Kate. You must have a care for your figure — the prince will not want a fat girl."

"A man who easily weighs eighteen stone if he weighs one would find fault with my figure?" she demanded sharply.

"He is a shallow man," Digby said, shaking his head sympathetically.

A fortnight had passed since Grayson had held Kate. One excruciatingly long fortnight in which he had chafed at his title, his name, everything about his life that kept him from her. When he entered the soiree at Marlborough House, he felt entirely put upon. He didn't want to be part of this society any longer. He didn't want to be part of London, or Darlington, or even England, for that matter.

He wanted to be with Kate.

Alas, that was impossible. Grayson looked at his brother Merrick, who had already engaged Lord Salisbury, a holdout in the abolition vote that would come before Parliament soon after the official opening. And he couldn't help but look across the room at Diana, who was in the company of her husband. She looked so sullen.

It pained Grayson to know that Merrick's and Diana's happiness depended so much on him. As for *his* happiness . . . that had been dashed to pieces when he'd come back from Kitridge Lodge. What a goddamn fool he'd been to think, even in a moment of madness, that he might have his way. It angered him that he couldn't, that he'd allowed himself to be manipulated — or perhaps he'd done the manipulating. He didn't know, and he didn't care. He just wanted to be free of the chains that were binding him.

His anger had grown with each passing day until now Grayson felt on the verge of bursting with it. His demeanor was not helped in the least when he turned to the door and saw Kate as she walked across the threshold. She was alone and although she looked beautiful, her eyes were so full of sadness that they pierced his bloody heart.

But her beauty took his breath away. The gown she wore was the color of the peacocks that roamed the grounds at his ducal seat. Her hair was the silk he could still feel on his fingers, her skin a smoothness he could still feel on his tongue.

Kate didn't see him; she looked straight ahead as she disappeared into the crowd. As he watched her, Grayson noticed that others had noticed her, too. More than one made a remark to a companion as she walked by. In spite of George's machinations to hide his mistress, the *ton* was too shrewd. Grayson suspected everyone knew precisely who she was and why she was here, and George had proven himself an extravagant fool once again.

"There he is," Merrick suddenly said, his arm on Grayson's. "Lord Abergine." His frustration mounting rapidly, Grayson forced himself to look away from the top of Kate's head. "He's just there," Merrick said. "He'll listen to you, Gray. He's a sycophant if nothing else."

Abergine was speaking to George. Grayson clenched his jaw and his pulse began to race — he'd not seen the prince arrive. But George had clearly seen him; he was looking directly at Grayson with a thin smile on his face, as if he were enjoying Grayson's anger.

The wine was flowing freely at Marlborough House. Food was displayed on console tables around the perimeter of the room and available for the taking whenever hunger struck. The gaming tables were full of people with fat purses. Kate wandered aimlessly through the throng, a wineglass in hand, and her mind a thousand miles away from this room.

She felt entirely conspicuous, unescorted as she was. She was painfully aware of the way people looked at her, of the whispering behind her back. At a sideboard, Kate helped herself to a pastry and stood to one side, taking small bites as she watched the people around her. She had yet to see the prince, although she was certain he would make his presence known to her when he was ready. He liked to play his little games and pretend chance meetings.

The pastry was bland and Kate tossed half of it into a waste receptacle.

That was the moment she happened to see Lord and Lady Eustis. She was really very pretty, Kate thought, and self-consciously put a hand to her earring. How witless, how imprudent she'd been, to have dreamed that Grayson might choose her over Lady Eustis. What did she possibly have to recommend her to a man like Grayson? He'd be a bloody fool if he hadn't gone back to Lady Eustis.

Disgusted with her reckless, uncontrollable desire, furious with herself for falling in love with a bloody duke, Kate turned around and examined the pastries again.

"Christie! I've not seen you in an age!" a female voice exclaimed.

Kate was suddenly rigid, paralyzed. It suddenly seemed as if some unseen force was pressing up against her. She could feel him in her heart, in her sudden struggle to breathe. Somehow, she managed to draw a breath, to turn around and look at him.

He was only a few feet away. He looked magnificent — his dark hair neatly coiffed, his blue eyes bright. He was dressed formally, and in the close-cut clothing, he looked broader, taller, and leaner than in her memory. He was handsome, so handsome. Kate was overwhelmed with the desire to touch him, to feel his arms around her, his lips on her skin.

An elderly woman had his ear, her hands moving in great animation as she spoke to him. Grayson unexpectedly looked to his right and saw Kate standing there. She expected a smile, a nod — but he politely inclined his head and shifted his gaze to the woman again.

Kate was dumbstruck. Her heart raced, her breathing grew shallow. And she was moving toward him, drawn to him like a flower to the sun.

Grayson gave no indication that he knew she was approaching. He stood very still, his head cocked slightly to one side, his hands clasped behind his back. But when Kate reached him, she saw the clench of his jaw. He said something to the woman, then looked at Kate. "Miss Bergeron," he said. "How do you do?"

How did she do? The earth was shifting under her feet. But she said, "Very well, thank you, Your Grace," and curtsied gracefully, in spite of feeling so unbalanced. "How do you do?"

Something flickered across his eyes. "I am well, thank you. May I introduce you to Lady Babington?" he said, nodding to the woman.

The woman's gaze flicked over Kate. "Good evening," she said, and turned her gaze from Kate before Kate could speak.

"A pleasure," Kate muttered, and looked at Grayson again, searching his expression for something, anything, to show her his feelings.

"And my brother, Lord Christopher."

It was only then that Kate noticed the gentleman who resembled Grayson standing beside him. "My Lord Christopher," she said, but she never heard what he said in return because she couldn't take her gaze from Grayson. His behavior was so aloof, so polite. Yet she thought she could see the same painful uncertainty in his eyes that she felt. She could, couldn't she?

He glanced impatiently at his brother and Kate felt the earth shift again. Had she misread him so completely? He made no effort to engage her.

She suddenly needed air. She gulped down a slight swell of nausea. "It is quite crowded this evening," she said, a little thickly.

"Indeed." He glanced away, over her shoulder.

Humiliation sank the bit of hope she'd been feeling. "If you will excuse me," she said, and nodded to the lady and Grayson's brother. She looked him directly in the eye. "Your Grace," she added coolly, and made herself walk away.

Perhaps Digby was right, she thought as she moved through the crowd. Perhaps his affections had changed after the prince had discovered them. She hadn't read Grayson's letters to her, but perhaps he'd written to tell her their affair was over and done instead of how much he missed her, as she'd assumed. Really, what more could he say under the circumstances? He was a proud and responsible man. He'd not risk everything for the likes of her. Honestly, Kate didn't know what disappointed her more — Grayson's showing her that he was like all the others? Or that she was surprised by it?

"Miss Bergeron."

Kate had been so lost in thought she hadn't seen the prince until he was upon her. She quickly curtsied. "Your Highness."

The prince smiled. "Well, then, I was looking for a lucky charm, wasn't I, Richard?" he said to the man beside him. "Miss Bergeron, you were so helpful to me during a game of whist recently. Would you be so kind as to join us at the roulette table? There is one last seat. That is . . . if you care to game?"

"I would be delighted," she said, and walked in the direction he indicated, her heart and mind racing.

Grayson had never felt so close to losing his composure as he did that evening at Marlborough House. He found it physically painful to be in the same room as Kate and not hold her or at least speak to her. She looked pale, he thought, and her face was slightly swollen. From tears, perhaps? Mostly what he noticed was the sadness that seemed to pervade her. It had doused the sparkle in her eyes and the brilliance of her smile.

That angered him more than anything. He felt a fury with the world at large, but mostly, with himself. *He* was the cause of her sadness, the reason those green eyes were so dull. He, Grayson Christopher, the Duke of Darlington, responsible for the happiness and well-being of so many bloody souls, had let down the one person who mattered to him above all others.

It was an impossible situation. Were he not a duke and merely a man, he could take her from here. It was an incredible irony — he was held captive by his privilege.

He looked over at Kate sitting at the roulette table where the prince was holding court. She had a pile of coins near her elbow, and very methodically placed her bets. How could he speak to her? Merrick was in this room, making his best effort to keep his votes for abolition intact. Diana kept looking at him, her expression alternating between mournful one moment and scornful the next. Grayson was keenly aware that with one whisper, George could destroy Diana's life and derail everything Merrick had worked so hard to achieve.

If Grayson had any doubt of it, George reminded him of it later when he left the roulette table to speak to someone, and managed to walk by Grayson. "Christie, you look rather unhappy," he said jovially. "What's the matter? The wine not to your liking? Or have you lost your purse at the tables?"

When Grayson did not respond — he feared if he opened his mouth, his fist might accompany it — George tipped his head back and peered up at him, assessing him. "You have surely heard, have you not, that the king has requested my presence in his privy chamber as early as Monday?"

"Frankly, Your Highness, I have better things to do than wonder about the king's calendar."

George's face darkened. "Perhaps you should wonder, Christie. I believe the king means to tell me that a public trial will be held straightaway, which in turn means that I will be free to shower my affections on whomever I please, openly and honestly." He looked pointedly at Kate as she placed a bet. "I rather hope to introduce my lovely new mistress at the fête I will host to celebrate the opening of Parliament next week."

"Public sentiment is fully on the side of the Princess of Wales," Grayson scoffed. "Do you honestly believe there will be a trial?"

George's eyes narrowed slightly. "I understand Merrick has all but convinced Lord Abergine to join him in abolishing the slave trade. I wonder what Lord Abergine might say to the Duke of Clarence, my brother, to whom Abergine is beholden, if Clarence were to ask him to vote with him and uphold the trade?"

Everyone knew that Clarence was a famous opponent of abolition.

"If Abergine has a conscience, he shall decline the invitation," Grayson said. "You will not intimidate me with such threats."

"It is not a threat, Christie. I am thinking of the good of British trade. And I am thinking of the good of Lord Eustis when I ponder whether or not his wife's adultery should be mentioned to him. After all, I'd not want a loyal subject to be fooled into accepting a child as the heir he did not sire."

"As there is no child, Your Highness, I hardly see why you'd want to destroy a loyal subject's marriage with mere innuendo."

"Don't push at the lion's gate, Darlington," George snapped, and turned away from him, ending the conversation.

The fury pounded in Grayson's veins. He wouldn't be subjected to this, not by the Prince of Wales, not by any man. And when he spotted Kate a few moments later walking out of the gaming room, he was determined to intercept her.

He encountered her in the wide corridor that ran between the gaming room and the dining room. When Kate saw him walking toward her, she tried to avoid his gaze, but Grayson would not allow it. There were several other people milling about; he had only a moment to intercept her without drawing attention, and fortunately, luck was on his side. He managed to catch her arm and pull her aside. People were passing only a few feet from them. It was audacious, but Grayson was willing to take the risk.

"What are you doing?" Kate whispered. "Let me go!"

"No," he said, and cupped her lovely face.

She slapped his hand away. "Our affair is at an end, Christie," she whispered hotly. "Let me *go*."

They were the same words Grayson had used with Diana, and they knifed through him. "Oh no," he said low, and, gripping her elbow, he abruptly propelled her down the corridor until he found an open door. He ushered her through it, uncaring who saw them.

Kate instantly lunged for the door, and Grayson quickly blocked it. "What are you doing?" she cried. "Move away from the door and let me pass, or I shall scream and bring the entire house running!" she angrily warned him, her eyes filling with tears.

"You won't," he assured her, and reached for her.

But Kate lurched away. "Do not think you can push me into a room and have your way with me. Have you forgotten our arrangement? I am not yours to use!"

"To *use?*" he repeated angrily. "Is that what you think I have done?"

"You used me until it no longer suited you! And to think I believed you were different than the others, Christie," she said, swiping at the tears that were falling down her cheeks. "But you aren't different at all. You are *just* like them!"

"For God's sake," he snapped, and caught her wrist and jerked her against his body.

Kate tried to pull away, but Grayson held her firmly with an arm anchored around her waist. "Do you think I used you when I kissed you? When I made love to you?" He caught her face and held it, and kissed her. Kate moaned against his mouth and stood rigidly in his arms, but when he deepened the kiss, she softened, sinking into him, returning his kiss with the passion he'd known from her since the beginning.

His blood began to rise with need for her. The fragrance in her hair reminded him of the intimate moments they'd shared, and he traced the curves of her body with his hand, so well known to him now. He cupped her breast, kneading it as their kiss grew more fevered. He suddenly picked her up and twirled her around, pressing her up against the wall, then moving down her body, his mouth on the skin above her bodice, his hands seeking the hem of her gown.

"Grayson," Kate said, her voice soft and full of need.

He did not, could not, answer her. He was enthralled by the moment, by the days and hours and minutes spent missing her and needing her. He found her leg, slid his hand up past her stocking, to the warm flesh of her inner thigh. But when he brushed against her sex, Kate gasped and abruptly stopped him by jerking away from him.

Grayson was not deterred; he kissed her neck.

"Stop, *stop!*" she cried, and pushed against him, stumbling out of his embrace. "It's *over,* Grayson! This is too dangerous, for both of us, and I will not be taken like some doxy!"

"Then come with me, Kate. Let us leave this place now, be done with this charade. Let us go where we might be alone —"

"Grayson!" She suddenly whirled around to him, caught his head between her hands and looked him in the eye. "Unless you are willing to bargain with the prince, we can never *be* alone!"

The words had a sobering effect on Grayson. He wanted nothing more than to take her from George, but the image of Merrick and Diana held him back. It was the dilemma that had enraged him this long fortnight.

Kate's green eyes searched his face, her hopeful expression vanishing with his hesitation. "There is my answer." Her hands fell away from him. She smoothed the lap of her skirt and walked to the door, opening it and moving into the corridor, leaving Grayson standing there, wondering just how much he would sacrifice for his family.

CHAPTER THIRTY-THREE

The next afternoon, Digby appeared at Kate's bedside with toast points and hot chocolate. She was exhausted and shattered, having arrived home at four in the morning and suffering from heartbreak so deep that she ached with it. The smell of toast made Kate instantly nauseous — she pushed past Digby and rushed to the privy.

When she emerged, Digby was frowning darkly.

"Why do you look at me like that?" she asked shakily.

"You know very well why."

Kate climbed onto the bed and curled up. "Leave me alone, please," she said, and dragged a pillow over her head.

Digby yanked the pillow from her head and loomed over her. "How long did you think you might go before I guessed the truth?"

"Digby!" Kate cried plaintively. "Please leave me be! I am not well!"

"What's this?" Aldous said, appearing at her open door.

"Lord God, must everyone come?" Kate complained and rolled onto her side, putting her back to the door.

"Our Katie has a bit of news, Aldous," Digby said with mock lightness. "Will you tell him, or shall I?"

"It is none of your concern!"

"Kate is with child," Digby said stubbornly.

"The hell you say!" Aldous blustered. "Bloody hell! What have you gone and done, Kate?"

"Leave me *alone!*" Tears were sliding down her cheeks now.

She heard Digby sigh; the mattress sagged under his weight as he sat on the edge of her bed. "Ah, love," he said, and put his hand on her shoulder. "We're a bit surprised, that's all. But you must stop crying so we might determine what is to be done."

What was to be *done?* That was precisely the problem and the reason for her tears — Kate didn't know what to do. She could scarcely face the truth of what she'd believed for a week now: She was carrying Grayson's child. Part of her was filled with joy at the prospect of having a child, *her* child, someone to love. But the practical side of her understood it was the worst news for a woman in her position. "What can be done? This will be the end of my arrangement with the prince and I don't have the money I need to start my bakery!"

"Come, now, Kate," Digby said, patting her arm. "Turn around. We must determine a course of action before it is apparent to everyone and the prince."

"You must ask for trinkets, anything that might be sold," Aldous said, pacing at the foot of her bed. "Do whatever you must to get them."

"Dear God," Kate moaned.

"He's right," Digby agreed. "Tell Darlington as well — he'll pay to keep his bastard child a secret until after the vote."

While Digby and Aldous plotted Kate's future — one that sounded so bleak, what with a child and no steady source of income — Kate lay with her back to them, tears silently falling.

She did not leave the house that day, preferring to mope about and look out at the steady rain that had begun to fall. But when the following day dawned bright and cold, Digby insisted she go for a walkabout. "It will do you a world of good."

While they were out, Digby purchased the *Morning Times.*

425

Cecelia made soup for Kate at luncheon. "Me mum made this soup for me when I was carrying Billy," she said. "It will help with the sickness."

Kate gaped at Digby. "Does *everyone* know?" she demanded of Digby.

But Digby wasn't listening. He suddenly sat up. "Damnation," he said.

"What?" she asked, looking up from her soup.

"They know," he said.

"Who knows?" Kate exclaimed, putting down her spoon. "Knows what?"

"*'A certain flower cut from the finest cloth in London is thought to be budding. One cannot say who might have watered this little plant, but it is most certainly D——or perhaps a person of a higher cloth. If this speculation proves true, one might expect to see a little blossom in summer.'*"

Kate gasped, horrified. "Oh God, Digby! How could anyone possibly know it?"

"They don't know it!" he said, angrily tossing the paper aside. "Someone guessed, or was determined to spread malicious rumors — that is all that is required in this town, Kate. One whisper, and it becomes fact! Look at the Princess of Wales, suspected of high treason all because of the ugly whispers of a few. But never mind that! You

426

may be assured that the prince has seen this and you must be prepared for his call."

"I am not with child." She hastily stood up and began to pace. "He might accuse me of it, but I will assure him that it's all nonsense. I will remind him that he has had someone watching me from the moment I returned from the country!" She looked at Digby, hoping he would agree.

"I would not mention the country, were I you. We must make provisions," Digby said, more to himself than to her. "We must have a place for you to go when the prince learns of this."

A place for her to go . . . All Kate could picture was that wretched pair of rooms in St. Katharine's. She and her baby and four other women all living like rats beneath a roof.

A knock on the door startled them both; they looked at one another, both fearing the prince had come. Kate smoothed her gown and pinched her cheeks. She strode from the dining room, walking purposefully down the corridor.

But in the foyer, she saw a woman and a young man at the door. They were standing patiently while Aldous read something they'd handed him.

"Aldous?"

He turned from the door and held out the

paper. "They've a letter from the prince."

"If I may?" the woman asked, and pushed back the hood from her head — she was older than Kate by at least ten years, but she was quite pretty. "I am Madame Renard. I have long been a friend of His Highness, the Prince of Wales."

Another courtesan.

"He has asked me a very special favor. May we speak in the drawing room?"

Kate looked at Aldous, then Digby. "Please," she said, gesturing to the drawing room.

Madame Renard indicated the young man should follow her. He doffed his hat and entered the drawing room carrying an instrument case. Madame Renard handed Aldous her cloak and followed the young man, pausing just inside the drawing room to look around at the furnishings. "Quite nice," she said, glancing over her shoulder at Kate. "You are fortunate."

"What do you want?" Kate asked.

"I have a message from His Highness."

Here it was then. Kate would be put out on the street, and this was some little game the prince had designed in order to tell her. Perhaps this woman was to take her place. Kate would be forced to sleep in Meg's empty bed —

"I am to teach you to dance," Madame Renard said.

"Pardon?"

"To *dance,*" Madame Renard said again as the young man opened his case and removed a violin.

"I don't understand. I know how to dance," Kate said.

"You know the ballroom dances, mademoiselle, but you do not know the sort of dance the prince should like to see performed at his fête."

"His feet?" Kate repeated uncertainly.

"A *fête.* A celebration. His Highness is producing a fête, and you are to dance in the pageant, Miss Bergeron."

"No!" Kate said instantly.

"Miss Bergeron is not a cabaret performer," Digby added indignantly.

"No one is suggesting that she is, Mr. . . . ?"

"Digby."

"Mr. Digby. This fête is a tradition of the Prince of Wales. He holds one every year to celebrate the opening of Parliament and the social Season. And at every fête, a pageant is performed. Miss Bergeron will not be the only performer, and her part is quite brief in comparison to the other performances that will be given that evening."

"What *is* a pageant?" Kate asked.

Madame Renard smiled. "Allow me to explain," she said, and helped herself to a seat on the settee while the young man tuned his instrument.

The ways of the Quality never failed to amaze Aldous — he could not comprehend the amount of money they spent on frivolity. All this talk of pageants and fêtes and dancing when there were so many people in need, like the women Kate was so desperate to save from their inevitable fates. Thinking about the expense of this fête at which Kate would be forced to dance like a trained monkey made him quite ill at ease.

Aldous longed to be at sea.

He scarcely heard the knock at the door for all of Madame Renard's shouting at Kate to move her foot thus, to put her hands up. He stalked to the door and yanked it open. He frowned. "I wondered when you'd come round," he said.

"I'm in no mood for your banter, Butler," Darlington said. "I want a word with Kate."

"You've had enough *words* with her, have you not?" Aldous sneered.

Darlington moved so quickly that Aldous scarcely had time to react. He shoved Aldous against the door, pinning him there, his arm across his gullet. "Don't presume to know me, Butler, for you don't know me at all. And in return, I will not presume to know anything about you. Now then, I would suggest you kindly heed me and take me to Kate if you value your neck."

Aldous smiled wryly. "That's more like it," he said, and shoved back at Darlington. "She's in there, learning to dance."

Grayson glanced at the open door of the drawing room. The music sounded like wailing cats to him. He let go of Aldous and strode through the door of the drawing room. His unexpected presence startled the young man with the violin; he abruptly stopped playing.

Kate faltered; the woman who was directing her stared wide-eyed at Grayson. He recognized her — she'd been a famous mistress among the *ton* for many years. He didn't want to know why she was here. "I need to speak to you," he said to Kate.

She blinked. "Now?"

"Yes, *now.*"

Digby suddenly appeared on Grayson's right. "Madame Renard, might I introduce you to the most delectable pastries in all of London?"

Grayson hadn't noticed Kate's rotund companion until that moment; his gaze was fixed on Kate, and the high color in her cheeks and the glitter of angry disappointment in her eyes.

Nor did he hear the others leave. He only knew when Kate moved across the room with such determination that the hem of her gown kicked up with her stride. She walked past him, brushing against his sleeve. She shut the door, turned around, and crossed her arms. "What do you want?"

"Why didn't you tell me?" he demanded.

"And when precisely might I have told you?" she asked, tossing her arms wide in a fit of pique. "At Marlborough House, when you were so clearly ashamed to have made my acquaintance? Or when you had me in a darkened room?"

"You might have sent a note along with the many I have written you that you returned, unopened!"

"And risked your ruin?"

This was an impossible situation. There was nothing Grayson could say to appease her or to help her understand the pressure he was under. He felt like a fool as it was — he'd always been so bloody careful about pregnancy, but with Kate, he'd been so caught up in the sensation of it that he'd been grievously careless. "Kate," he said, and ran both hands over his hair in frustration and looked at the floor. *"Kate."*

When he lifted his gaze to hers he saw green eyes full of sorrow. Something palpable moved between them; Grayson opened his arms at the same moment Kate ran to him. He caught her in his arms, lifted her off her feet in a tight embrace, and kissed her before putting her on her feet again.

"I have missed you so much!" she said desperately. "I have longed to see you, to hear your voice, to feel your touch."

"I know, I know — I have missed you, too," he said into her hair. "Are you all right? Are you well?"

"As well as could be expected."

He put her back and cupped her beautiful face. "Does he know?"

She pressed her lips together. "Not that I am aware. Digby says he certainly has heard."

"How . . . how was it discovered?" he asked, looking at her now.

"I don't know!" she said tearfully. "I had only just realized it myself! Digby says someone guessed, but I don't know how, I honestly don't know!"

Kate looked so lost, and Grayson would give everything he had to remove that look from her face. "Darling," he said, and dipped down to kiss her. "I will take care of you, you know that, don't you?" he asked, running a hand over her head.

"You will?" she asked, looking up at him hopefully.

"Yes, of course! Did you doubt it for a moment? I can provide you a country home, something quaint, like Kitridge Lodge if you like. Some place close to London so that I can come to you in two or three hours' time if necessary."

Kate's smile faltered.

"You and the baby will be quite comfortable. We'll make sure there is room for Digby and your butler."

"What do you mean?" she asked, frowning now. "Won't you be there as well?"

"I will visit you as often as I can, but I will be here, in London."

"Then I . . . I am to be your mistress?"

"The mother of my child. My lover . . ." He paused, struggling to find the right words. *Lover* and *mistress* sounded all wrong. "All your needs will be met." That sounded worse.

Kate dropped her hands from his arms and stepped back, staring at him.

"What is the matter?" Grayson asked.

"Your *mistress?*"

He didn't like the way she said it, as if she were displeased with what he thought was a very noble offer, especially given the circumstances. "Yes, my mistress. Were you expecting something more?"

"Yes! Yes, of course I was! Did you think I would be grateful to be your mistress?"

"Yes, madam," Grayson said crossly. "I should think any woman of your standing would be thrilled with such an offer."

"A woman of my *standing*," she repeated hotly.

Grayson instantly regretted those words. "I didn't mean —"

"I know *precisely* what you meant. God help me, I am so blind! You really are just like all of them, your protestations to the contrary notwithstanding! I would rather raise my child by myself than be treated like a poor relation raising your bastard child!"

He was stunned. He'd made her a generous offer and she responded as if he'd put her out like a dog. "What in bloody hell would you have me do, Kate?" he demanded angrily.

"I would have you love me as I love you!" she cried earnestly and beseechingly. "I would have you marry me, and be with me when we bring our children into the world, and live and love alongside us!"

"That's not possible," he said gruffly. "For either of us."

"Why not?"

"I am a *duke,* Kate! It is not in the realm of *any* possibility that I could marry you. But it is also out of the realm of possibility that you and *my* child might live apart from me —"

"Oh dear God," she said, whirling away from him. She rubbed her hands on her arms and paced restlessly before him. "Do you know what pains me most, Christie? It's that I've done the very thing I bloody well promised myself I would never do."

"What do you mean?"

"I fell in love!" she cried. "I have fallen so hopelessly in love with you that I cannot bear to hear the things you are saying to me now. But I am so angry with myself, for I have always known the rules of this wretched life I live! I knew what would happen if I allowed myself that one small hope, that secret desire . . ." Her voice broke and she pressed her hands to her abdomen, bending over.

"Kate!" Grayson said, alarmed.

"No," she said when he put his arms around her. "Please don't touch me, please don't make it worse. I love you, Grayson. You say those things and yet I love you. But I cannot bear to have you in my sight."

"God in heaven, don't you know that I love you, too?"

She tried to look away.

"I have been surprised and humbled by how much I do. I love you desperately and utterly, Kate, and I confess, I don't know what to do with it."

She sagged, sliding to the floor on her knees, Grayson with her.

"Look at me," he said, putting his hand beneath her chin, lifting her face so that she would look at him. "I had never considered the possibility of falling in love before I met you. I believed I would one day choose a suitable woman and marry her for the sake of producing an heir. I thought love was the game of very young men, not experienced men such as myself. But it happened to me, too, Kate — when I was least expecting it, with the one woman in all of London who is beyond my reach, it happened to me."

"I am not beyond your reach!" she exclaimed. "I am here, right here," she said, taking his hand and pressing it to her heart. "If I am beyond your reach it is only because you make it so."

There were so many things she didn't understand. He caressed her face, realizing, as he looked at her, that he'd perfected the art of being a lover, but he knew nothing of love. He felt awkward and ungainly trying to explain himself. He preferred to make love to her, to show her how he felt, but he couldn't do that to her, not when the ugly reality of their disparate lives would once again intrude into the one place they'd known perfect harmony. "Just know that I love you, Kate. More than life," he said simply.

"You do not know how I have longed to hear you say it these last many days," she said tearfully.

"Then I'll say it again. I love you, Kate. I love you as far and as deep as any ocean, as high and as vast as any sky. I love you."

"Then why is this so difficult? Why can you not love me and be with me?"

"Because, sweetheart, loving you does not change the responsibilities I bear. If it were only my happiness at stake, there would be no question of it. But I am the head of a large family, and my actions, my scandals, my disgrace, reverberates through all of them."

Another tear slid down her cheek. "And it would be a disgrace to marry me," she said flatly.

He didn't answer. If there was one thing he knew about Kate, it was that she understood her place in this world. She'd never been anything less than practical about it.

"I won't be your mistress," she said softly, and stood up. "I don't need you, Grayson. I have survived all my life without you, and I will survive without you now."

"You don't mean that."

"I do," she said resolutely.

"Then give me the child," he said quietly. "I will ensure our child is raised with all due privilege."

Kate's lashes fluttered with her wince of pain. "No . . . thank you, but no. It is good to know you would take my love and my child and discard me, but I will keep my baby."

"Christ in heaven, Kate, what would you have me do? I don't want to hurt you, I want to *help* you — but I cannot be what you want me to be!"

"I don't care any longer. I just want you to go."

He made no move to go. He couldn't bear to leave her like this.

But Kate was resolute. "I am begging you now," she said. "If you do indeed truly love me, if you ever loved me, please go and leave me be."

He was so foolish, so raw and inexperienced in the ways of the heart. Give him a tenant problem to solve, a social event to chair, and he could do it in a stupor. But *this?* He didn't know how to do this — he'd never done anything like this. He'd never felt such a painful vise about his heart, or such despair. "I am going," he said. "But only for now." He walked to the door, where he paused and looked back at Kate. "You should know that I will not, under any circumstance, turn my back on you, or our child." He opened the door then and walked out of her house, uncertain as to what he would do next.

Kate thought she cried for hours. Digby assured her it was no longer than an hour. After she had emptied herself of all her emotions, she began to wait for the prince to come and remove her from her house and replace her with another courtesan who wasn't foolish enough to have fallen in love with one of his friends, much less carry his child.

But the prince did not come.

In an effort to determine why he hadn't, Digby brought the *Morning Times* with him each day and pored over the news. The best Digby could determine was that the prince was engaged in a battle of wills with the king over the Delicate Investigation. According to Digby, public favor was firmly on the side of the princess, and the prince's demands for more investigation, particularly after the Lords Commissioners had found the princess guilty of nothing more than bad behavior, had many crying foul. "He'll not have his trial," Digby predicted. "The king cannot possibly go against public sentiment."

Whether the prince had heard the rumors of her pregnancy, Kate did not know. She knew only that as each day passed, she still had a roof over her head.

Three days had passed since the disastrous *on dits* had appeared in the paper, and still, the prince did not come.

In the course of keeping his finger on the pulse of high society, Digby also felt compelled to keep her abreast of the activities of the Duke of Darlington. He was involved in a scandal surrounding the Earl of Lambourne. The earl had been accused of adultery with the Princess of Wales, a charge of high treason, and the king's men were attempting to apprehend him. Digby said everyone knew Lambourne had fled to his native Scotland, but then he'd appeared and had asked Darlington to arrange a meeting with the king.

"What happened to him?" Aldous asked curiously.

"I wouldn't know what Lambourne discussed with the king," Digby said. "But I have heard he's been imprisoned in the Tower of London."

"Bloody hell," Aldous said.

Digby also noted that Darlington attended a charity event and a tea, wherein all the Season's debutantes were presented to him.

"'Miss Augusta F——was well received by the family,'" he read aloud.

Kate could picture the debutantes parading past Grayson, could imagine how he looked at them, assessing their worthiness to be his duchess. She wondered if he thought of her when he looked at them.

He'd sent a pair of letters to her, which she'd refused to read or allow anyone else to read. She couldn't bear to see or hear his words. She kept the letters tied with a ribbon in her jewelry box. To keep her mind from it all, Kate spent her days baking and carrying food to St. Katharine's.

The women were very excited to learn she was carrying a child. They asked after the father, of course they did, but when Kate demurely declined to answer, they did not press her. Such things were not uncommon to them. They planned to make some christening clothes for the infant and begged Digby to get them some fine linen cloth from Mr. Cousineau.

Kate did as Aldous suggested and began to sell some of the jewelry she'd collected from Benoit and the prince, building as much of a nest egg as she could possibly do before the prince dismissed her, which she anticipated with every day that dawned.

CHAPTER THIRTY-FOUR

"Word has reached me that Harry has gotten himself into a bit of a bind in Paris," Grayson's mother said. She glanced up from her plate. "*Gambling* debts. In all the years your father was duke, this family did not gamble."

The duchess was seated at his dining table, having imposed herself on Grayson's luncheon when he'd refused her invitation to dine. He was aware that the residents of Darlington House, as well as his family, were treading lightly around him and his foul mood, but he'd ceased to care. He resented the lot of them of late.

"Good for Harry," he muttered.

"*Really,* Your Grace," his mother said.

"Young men gamble, Mother. It is not the end of the world as we know it."

"I don't know why you are being so cross with me," she complained. "I think you should send him a letter and tell him he

443

must come home straightaway."

"If you think he should come home, why don't you send the letter?" Grayson asked wearily.

"You are the duke, Grayson. It is *your* responsibility to maintain the family honor."

Ah yes, the family honor, the thing that held him by the throat. The thing that kept him from openly courting Kate for fear of destroying it and bringing devastating scandal upon the golden heads of the celestial Christopher family.

He was so disgusted, he pushed his plate away. A footman immediately removed it.

"What is the matter?" his mother asked.

"Nothing. I am not hungry."

"I think Harry has been without proper supervision for far too long," his mother continued, in a not-so-veiled accusation. As she began to list the ways Harry needed supervision, Grayson's mind wandered.

He was sick unto death of hearing the lecture of how great and venerable was the Christopher name. He loved his mother, but there were days she wore on him. It didn't help that he hadn't eaten properly or slept in days. He could not seem to come to terms with his feelings for Kate. He wanted her, he wanted his child. When he saw his nephews, he thought of his child, growing inside the woman he loved and he, like Kate, wondered why they couldn't be together.

Would the scandal be so devastating? Would the moon cease to orbit the earth? Would the tide stop moving, the grass stop growing, the rains stop falling? Was his title so oppressive? If it was, then perhaps he ought to give it to Merrick. Merrick was much better suited for it than he.

"Are you listening, Darlington?"

"Pardon?" Grayson said absently, his gaze on Roarke, who had entered the dining room and was walking briskly to where Grayson sat.

"Impropriety makes it very difficult for your sisters."

"Your Grace," Roarke whispered, "His Highness, the Prince of Wales, has called."

"What — now?" Grayson asked curiously.

"Yes, Your Grace. He is in your study."

Grayson put aside his napkin. "Pardon, Mother, but the Prince of Wales has come calling."

"During luncheon?" she asked incredulously. "On my word, doesn't anyone call at proper hours any longer?" she complained as Grayson went out.

The prince's usual entourage was seated in chairs outside Grayson's study. George was standing behind Grayson's desk, openly perusing some of the papers there. "Your Highness," Grayson said curtly. "Are you looking for something in particular?"

"I will dispense with the usual greeting in favor of real news," George said and looked up. His eyes were as hard as ice. "It seems you were right, Darlington. The king has made it *quite* clear that he will not press for a parliamentary divorce with the nation's current mood so solidly against me. Therefore, as it seems my wretched fate has been sealed, I shall take solace in the arms of my beautiful mistress. I thought you should be among the first to know."

Grayson's heart stopped beating for a moment.

"I will trust her word that you haven't ruined her for me," the prince added coldly, watching Grayson closely.

It took a moment for Grayson to find his tongue. The thought of George's hands on Kate — a thought he'd worked hard to keep at a distance until now — caused a sudden swell of anger in him that felt as if it were choking him.

"I will take your silence as a sign of acquiescence," George said flippantly. "I intend to introduce her as mine at my annual fête on Friday evening."

Things were suddenly crystal clear to

Grayson. His love for Kate trumped everything else. He would not stand by and let this . . . this pig, this rooting, loathsome *pig,* take the woman he loved. Damn the consequences, he would fight. "You mistake me, Your Highness. I am not acquiescing at all," he said with great equanimity.

George snorted. "Pardon? I don't think I heard you clearly."

"I heard you just as clearly as you heard me — I will not step aside."

A loathsome smile curved George's lips. "I think you have no choice."

"The hell I haven't."

George walked out from behind Grayson's desk. "Do you think that because you have put a bastard child in *my* mistress, you are somehow *entitled* to her?"

"She is not a possession, she is a person of free will . . . unless the laws of Britain have changed."

"You forget, old friend," George said angrily, "that I bought her services from Cousineau. And I will one day be your king."

"You barter human flesh," Grayson said acidly. "You are no better than the slave traders. What you demanded of me was most reprehensible, but ironically, I must thank you for it. I love Kate and I will not allow you to use her ill."

The prince blinked with surprise, then laughed wildly. "Are you a bloody *fool?* Speak carefully — there are many who would suffer in the wake of your folly!"

"Your Grace?"

Grayson jerked an angry gaze to his butler's intrusion. "Not now."

"I beg your pardon, sir, but a messenger has arrived with imperative news."

"Imperative?" Grayson snapped, whirling around on him. "What is so damned imperative?"

"Lady Eustis has had an emergency and begs you attend her."

George laughed derisively. "She would have a true emergency if I were to invite her lord husband to dine," he said. "What do you think would become of your Lady Eustis then?"

"That is all, Roarke," Grayson said, and the moment the man left the room, he turned on the prince. "You are wrong to believe you will intimidate me. Do what you will, George, but don't dare threaten me."

"Do you ask for ruin?" George said incredulously. "Because that is precisely what you will receive!"

"You will threaten to ruin me no matter what I do or say. But I think you are bluffing, George. By your own admission public sentiment is widely against you. If you ever hope to be king, perhaps *you* ought to think twice about threatening me." With that, Grayson walked out of the room without further conversation. He had too much on his mind to waste another moment on George.

Chapter Thirty-five

Diana anxiously paced the floor of her suite, unable to sit still, unable to think. She glanced at the mantel clock over and over again, wondering if Grayson would come, fearful that Charles might have forgotten something and returned home. She had convinced him to pay a call to his gentlemen's club today since the weather was clear. She had a two-, perhaps a three-hour window of time.

She had to see Grayson today, for Charles had declared he and Diana would be returning to the country the day after the prince's fête, a decision for which Diana had had to barter heavily with Charles. He wanted her home, having been encouraged by her gift of a new hunting coat. But Diana had insisted she needed to be fitted for her Season's wardrobe and to help Prudence with some charitable endeavor. Fortunately, Charles never asked her which charitable endeavor, as there was none.

Charles did not want to attend the fête, and that was another battle. He said it was too extravagant and too indulgent when the Crown faced such controversy surrounding the Prince and Princess of Wales. "The prince has no conscience," Charles complained.

Diana didn't care about all that. "All my friends will attend," she'd said.

"Very well. You may go, Diana, but the following morning, we will depart for Shropshire. The air is too thick in London, and I do not believe it is conducive to conceiving a child."

Diana had wished he'd find the air so thick that he'd choke on it.

When she heard Millie's voice, she whirled toward the door. *Grayson had come.* She rushed to her mirror to check her appearance once more.

Millie knocked. "Come," Diana said and in the next moment, Grayson swept into the room, still holding his hat. Millie stood behind him at the threshold. "Thank you, Millie," Diana said.

Millie looked at Grayson's back and slowly backed out, pulling the door closed with her.

Diana smiled as brightly as she could,

given the circumstances. "I am so very happy to see you."

"What has happened?" Grayson asked, frowning with concern. "Are you all right? Have you come to harm?"

She shook her head. "No, I — I desperately needed to see you."

His face darkened. "There is no emergency?"

"The emergency is you and me."

Grayson pushed a hand through his hair and looked at the carpet a long moment. "Have you lost your mind?" he snapped. "I thought something had happened, that Eustis had discovered us and threatened you!"

Diana had foolishly imagined him rushing to take her into his arms, but as that was clearly a fantasy, Diana did the next best thing — she rushed into his. She ran to him, grabbed his head between her hands, and kissed him.

Grayson gripped her arms and tried to push her away, but she held tightly. He gave her a stronger push, setting her back on her heels. "Stop it, Diana."

But Diana couldn't stop. The moment he let her go, she reached for him again. Grayson put her back much more firmly. *"Stop."*

His rejection was so stinging that she reacted without thinking — she slapped him.

It stunned Grayson. He stared at her as he touched his fingers to his cheek where she'd struck him. "You have indeed lost your mind, madam."

"*Bastard!*"

"Did you summon me here and risk everything to seduce me? Or to call me a bastard?"

"How can you do this to me?" she cried. "How could you leave me so utterly alone?"

He sighed impatiently. "I haven't left you alone, Diana. I have said this to you the best way I know how — it's over between us. Our affair is over, just as we always knew it would be! I am not going to sweep in here like some chivalrous knight and take you from him!"

She had hoped he would do precisely that. "I hate him, Grayson," she said, suddenly tearful. "I hate him with all my being."

He at least had the decency to look as if that pained him. "Do you hate him so much that you might ask him to divorce you?"

"You know I can't do that!" she said angrily.

"Then what is it you want from me?" he demanded, his voice low and dangerous. "I cannot care for you as I once did. I no longer bear you in my heart, Diana, and frankly, I'm not certain I ever did."

She gasped.

"I do not want to be so blunt, but you have forced me to it."

"I *love* you, Grayson. Does that not mean anything to you?"

"Of course it does," he said. "But it doesn't change our situation. You have made it very clear from the beginning that divorce would never be an option for you. I did what I had to do to protect you from scandal. Yet it made me realize how fragile our affair is, Diana. It was built on risk and we cannot sustain it. We cannot nurture it. It is best we end it. Please try and accept that."

The sound Diana heard was her strangled cry; she turned around, fearful that she would be ill.

"Diana," Grayson said, and put his hand on her arm and forced her around. "I have admired you, cared for you, and I will be forever grateful for our time together. But I never gave you any reason to believe there would be more, or that it would go on forever. Nor did you expect it. You know you didn't — you have said as much to me. Now you must accept what is."

"What *is*?" she said hatefully. "That you have ended our affair for a merchant's whore?"

His expression turned hard. "I ended it because it was time. Don't send me more messages, Diana. I will not respond to them."

"You are a *bastard*."

He let go of her arm and walked out.

"Bastard!" she shouted after him. She hated him. She hated him with a white-hot fury, so hot that she crumbled, sliding down to her knees on the chaise, sucking in deep breaths.

"Are you all right, mu'um?"

It was Millie, conniving Millie. God, but Diana hated the world just now. "I am fine." She forced herself up and wiped her face. "Where is that blessed sailor?" she demanded, glaring at Millie.

"The ship will dock on the morrow."

"I want him here, just as soon as that ship docks, and by God, Millie, if he is not on the ship, you best not come home."

Millie's face darkened. "Very well, mu'um," she said. "But I'll need ten pounds."

"Whatever for?" Diana cried. "Have you not extorted enough from me?"

"He won't come along just for the asking, eh?" Millie said.

God in heaven, Diana had no idea how she would ever extract herself from this vicious cycle of extortion, but at the moment she hardly cared. She had one thought on her mind, and that was to destroy the Duke of Darlington in any way that she possibly could.

CHAPTER THIRTY-SIX

Kate knew the prince had come when she heard a ruckus on the street. She walked to the window of the drawing room and saw people gathering around his carriage, thrilled to see the Prince of Wales emerge and stride to her door.

Kate turned away from the window and swallowed. This was it, then. This was the moment she'd been dreading for almost a week now. She drew a deep breath.

A moment later, Aldous walked into the drawing room and bowed as the prince sailed in behind him. Kate instantly fell into a curtsy. "Your Highness, I am so very pleased to receive you."

His gaze flicked over her before he turned to Aldous and nodded toward the door. Aldous instantly went out, leaving them alone. Kate smiled at the prince. He did not smile back. He walked slowly to her, his gaze raking over her. He put his hand to her chin and held her head still while his eyes roamed her face.

Kate smiled, but inside, she was shaking.

"It's over," he said quietly, and Kate's shaking turned to panic. She felt short of breath and tried to lower her head, but the prince held her firmly. "The king refuses to allow me to seek a parliamentary divorce. That is unwelcome news for me," he said, his gaze drifting to her mouth. "But then again, it means that I am free to pursue what I think shall be a long and lusty association."

Kate gasped softly and instinctively tried to move away, but he captured her mouth with his, thrusting his tongue into her mouth. She cried out against his mouth and wrenched free of him. She pressed the back of her hand to her mouth as she thought desperately of what to do.

"What's wrong, *ma petite?*" he asked coldly. "Is my house not to your liking? Are the gowns I put on your back not of the finest quality? The jewels not shiny enough?"

"They are perfect," she said quickly. "You have been too generous."

"Perhaps I have, for I thought you understood clearly what accepting these gifts means you would give me in return." He reached for her again, gripping her arm tightly as he pulled her into an unyielding embrace. This time, she could not wrest herself free as he kissed her and roughly caressed her arm and hip with one hand.

Somehow, she managed to get her hands between them and pushed hard against him. The prince glared at her, his eyes ice cold. "Why are you behaving in such a displeasing manner?" he snapped.

"There is something I must say," she said.

"Save it. I'm in no mood for *talk*." He reached for her again.

Kate quickly moved out of his reach. "Your Highness . . . I cannot . . ." *God, what was she about to do?* "I cannot in good conscience provide you with what you need."

That admission seemed to startle him — into laughter. "I don't give a damn about your conscience. You are mine in fair agreement."

"But I am in love with someone else."

He surprised her with another awful laugh. "Darlington? You fancy yourself in love with the Duke of Darlington?"

"I do," she said, her voice shaking. "And I beg your pardon for it, for that is certainly not what I intended —"

"Don't be dull-witted, Kate," he said sharply. "You should know the truth about your bloody *duke*. I left Darlington House before coming here and your lover was on his way to pay a personal call to Lady Eustis."

Kate's stomach dropped. She gaped at the prince.

"Did you think he would risk all for you?" the prince scoffed. "That he would dare bring dishonor on his esteemed family by having some sort of open affair with a courtesan? You stupid girl."

His words devastated her, but Kate refused to believe him. She looked the prince square in the eye. "That may very well be true, but nevertheless, I have lied to you, Your Highness. I gave myself to him."

"I know you *lied* to me!" he exclaimed angrily. "All of bloody London knows you lied to me! Have I not suffered enough from the lies of women? Must I be made to suffer your perfidy as well? *You?* For whom I have provided dearly in the hope that you, at the very least, could be true?"

She flinched inwardly. "I never meant —"

"I don't care what you meant! I bought your services fairly and I will have them. Those services require your loyalty! Turn your heart and your mind from Darlington — he is in Lady Eustis's bed at this very moment, and if you don't believe me, you might send your man around to Eustis House on Park."

Kate felt sick. She took a shallow breath and felt her heart start to pound uncomfortably.

"I will present you at the fête as mine," the prince continued. "Buy whatever gown or jewelry you need and have the bills sent to me." He took her chin in his hand again and forced her head up to look at him. "I will have the entire guest list believing you are utterly devoted to your prince, do you understand?"

Yes, she understood. She understood that the prince's pride was at stake. She nodded.

He dropped his hand. His angry glare swept from the top of her head to the tips of her slippers, lingering on her abdomen. "There is one last thing. Get rid of that bastard in you."

Kate gasped, covering her mouth with her hand in horror.

"I don't care how," he said, entirely too easily. "Just rid yourself of it if you want to keep your house and your position of privilege. If you don't do as I say, you will have none of this, for I will see to it that *no* one will have you, especially not *Darlington*."

He ignored her soft cry of shock and strode out, leaving her gasping for breath.

Over supper that evening, Digby dragged the

details of the prince's visit out of Kate while Aldous listened silently. When she told them what he wanted of her, Digby was vociferous in his opinion that Kate do as the prince demanded. "He clearly intends to give you another chance, Kate, and thank God for that. You cannot afford to turn away from it, can you? You haven't enough to strike out on your own. Darlington is not coming for you. What else might you do?"

"Darlington came," Aldous said between bites of potatoes.

The news startled Digby. "He came *here*? When?"

"Around tea," Aldous said. "But Kate wouldn't see him."

Digby shifted his surprised look to Kate.

She shrugged and looked at her plate of untouched food. How could she have seen him, knowing he'd just come from Lady Eustis? How could she hear him offer her essentially the same arrangement the prince had offered her, save the demand of aborting her child? "I don't want to see him again. Ever," she said resolutely, and avoided Digby's gaze.

"Kate, love," Digby said, covering her hand with his. "At least consider what the prince requests. How will you ever raise a child?"

A tear slid from her cheek and onto her

plate. Kate didn't look up at either man.

Aldous and Digby accompanied Kate to St. Katharine's the following afternoon so that she might take some food and candles to the women. As they walked through the crowded streets of St. Katharine's, Aldous kept a close eye on Kate. She was even paler than she'd been, and she seemed to be fighting a constant flow of tears.

He didn't think Digby was helping in the least. "Won't you at least speak with Agnes Miller?" he'd urged Kate. "She'd at least know what to do."

But Kate shook her head. She couldn't seem to bring herself to speak, much less make such an extraordinary decision. Fannie Breen had died at the hands of the rat catcher's wife, and Aldous wasn't going to allow Kate to put herself in harm's way. Fortunately, Kate seemed to share his opinion of what Digby was suggesting — it went against nature and God.

When Digby seemed to finally accept that Kate wasn't going to pay a call on Agnes, he sighed, put his arm around her shoulders and hugged her fondly. "Buck up, love," he said. "You're going to need all your wits about you."

Aldous couldn't bear to watch her suffer.

Later that afternoon, he found her sitting in the drawing room, staring into space. He couldn't help himself. He'd put on his best suit of clothing and had tried to tame the unruly ginger curls on his head. He'd even practiced what he might say, as he was a wee bit anxious.

When he asked Kate, he did it properly, by going down on his good knee.

Kate's divine eyes widened with surprise.

"I know you don't love me," Aldous said quickly. "Or ever would. But I'd gladly give you and the bairn my name, Kate. Will you marry me?"

Her eyes filled with tears. She slowly stood and offered her hand to Aldous to help him to his feet. She didn't speak at first, but wrapped her arms around him and hugged him tightly to her. Aldous knew she'd not accept his offer, and closed his eyes and bent his head, touching it to hers, savoring the moment of feeling her body so close to his.

"Thank you for your offer," Kate said. "It means more to me than you will ever know." That was all she said, but it was enough for Aldous to know she had refused him. And while it pained him, he didn't feel awfully bad about it. He knew she loved the duke with all that she had.

It was the following afternoon at the St.

Katharine's quay that Aldous heard talk of *The Princess*. It had come into the West Indies dock. One chap told Aldous that there was quite a lot of commotion around it, as Wilberforce and his followers had staged a protest against the crippled slaver, trying to keep it from docking.

Aldous told Digby that while Kate napped he was going to the Isle of Dogs and the West Indies dock to find Jude.

"That's what our girl needs," Digby said, and reached into his pocket and withdrew several coins. "Here, take this. You'll need something to persuade him to come round to his sister. Look for a man who resembles Kate — fair hair, green eyes. Quite handsome, I've been told. He'll undoubtedly head for the nearest tavern."

Aldous took the coins and pocketed them, tipped his hat, and set off to find Kate's brother.

Kate awoke from her nap and sat before the hearth once more while Digby bustled about, fetching her water and food. She sullenly looked around her. The furnishings in the room were as fine as any she'd ever seen and the carpet had come all the way from Belgium.

But Kate hated this house. She hated that she had to live here. She put a protective hand on her abdomen; she couldn't bear to bring a child into this life. "I have to make my own way, Digby," she announced.

"Pardon?"

"I have to make my own way. I cannot be . . . *this*," she said, grimacing when she gestured to herself. "What sort of life is this for a child, with a whore for a mother?"

"Kate!" he exclaimed. "You are not a whore!"

"I am, Digby! A courtesan is exactly that. I trade my flesh for this house and a paltry little purse."

"What alternative do you have?" Digby asked. "This may not be the life you want for your child, but it's certainly better than toiling sunup to sundown in a cloth hall, is it not?"

"Yes," she sadly agreed. "It is infinitely better than that. But it is still horrible."

"Why won't you accept Darlington's offer?" Digby pleaded. "He adores you and I believe he'd provide handsomely for his child."

"No," she said, shaking her head. "How would it be for my child to be brought up knowing that his father has a better family elsewhere that he gives his name and his love to? I should think that would be worse than being abandoned."

Digby sighed and eased down on the settee next to her. "All right then. We must find your path, love. We're not entirely cleaned out, are we? Cousineau will be furious with us and dispense with my services if you run out on the prince, but I've a little put aside, and if I can maintain my toehold in the perfume trade, I can put aside a bit more. You've got some money . . . but you must stop giving it to the girls, Kate."

She groaned at that — she could hardly support herself and a child; how could she support them all?

"Now then, don't worry. We'll think of something to fly our kites again. But we must be diligent about selling the gifts the prince has given you. All of them. That ought to bring you a tidy little sum to keep you in fine fashion, eh? At least until you can open your bakery."

"When should I tell the prince?" Kate asked.

"Not until you absolutely must, and certainly not before the fête. That, you *must* attend, if for no other reason than to have the prince purchase the finest jewelry for you so we can sell it."

"Digby! That's stealing!" Kate said.

Digby made a face. "It seems fair game to me, but very well. You must go if for no other reason than it buys us a bit of time and you'll have a roof over your head until we've arranged for another one."

He was right, of course. There was no way she might avoid it until she'd arranged other accommodations. But the thought of attending that fête made her ill. She closed her eyes, leaned her head back against the settee.

"I know something that might cheer you," Digby said, nudging her in the side.

"Tell me. Anything. I desperately want to be cheered."

"*The Princess* has arrived at the West Indies dock."

Kate gasped and sat up.

"Aldous is there now, looking for one Jude Berger."

Her pulse quickened. *"Lud!"* Kate exclaimed and suddenly stood. "We've so much to do, Digby! Shall I make the plum pastries? You thought they were quite nice, did you not?" she asked, hurrying to the door.

She paused there and looked back at Digby, who was sipping from his tot of whiskey. "Digby! What are you doing there? Come along, we've much to do!"

But when Aldous arrived later that evening, and found them in the kitchen, Kate's exuberance faded. Aldous had not found Jude.

CHAPTER THIRTY-SEVEN

Grayson tried twice more to see Kate before the fête. The first time, he found no one at home. The second time, when he tried to get past Mr. Butler, Butler shoved him back with a force that surprised Grayson. "She don't want you," he said angrily. "She's with the prince now. Best you go to your lover and stay there." With that, he'd slammed the door in Grayson's face and turned the lock.

As angry as Grayson was, he didn't care to create a scene on a busy street, so he walked away.

But he was not giving up. If anything, he was more determined than he'd ever been about anything.

That evening, he'd invited his family for supper. The guests included his mother, his sister Prudence and her family, his sister Mary and her husband, his brother Merrick, four cousins, and his paternal uncle and his wife.

They dined in the formal dining hall at Darlington House. Grayson's cook had outdone himself, serving eight courses. It was a gay evening, with Uncle Richland regaling them all with a wild tale of a sledding trip gone terribly awry when Grayson, Merrick, and Harry were boys.

"It was Grayson's doing," Merrick said laughingly. "Harry was scarcely out of his Christening gown, and I was just a bit older. Grayson is the one who convinced us the hill was perfect for sledding."

Grayson recalled that day perfectly; they were supposed to be attending a secular celebration of the Epiphany. While the adults were preparing the church for the gathering, Grayson had convinced his younger brothers that the hill behind the church was a perfectly dangerous course for sledding. The danger was what convinced the boys to try.

"Never mind that there were trees and rocks beneath that snow, and no fool had ever sled down that hill," Richland said laughingly.

"In every generation, someone must set a course," Grayson reminded him.

"What happened?" Frederick asked eagerly.

"I shall tell you," Merrick said, settling back. "We tucked Harry securely between us. With Uncle Christie guiding the sled, we set off. But as we went down the hill, it got a bit bumpy, and we were going much too fast. I shouted at Grayson to bank the sled, but he refused to heed me —"

"I didn't *hear* you, Merrick —"

"— and by the time we reached the bottom of the hill, he'd lost control of the sled. So in order to avoid the stone fence we were headed for, he careened through the open door of the groundskeeper's shed, and we collided with various tools and hemp sacks and pots and whatnot."

Frederick gasped and looked at Radcliff.

"But it was the old turkey the groundskeeper could not bear to eat that did the most damage," Merrick laughingly continued as Uncle Richland howled at the memory. "That old bird was in the shed and flapped around, squawking and carrying on and bringing down more pails and garden implements and a host of things I can no longer recall."

"I have never in all my life heard such an awful racket!" the duchess said.

"Our father was so upset that he swore he'd send Grayson off to the Royal Navy."

"I am certain the Royal Navy would have rejoiced in an eight-year-old officer," Prudence said with a laugh.

"But what of the turkey?" Radcliff asked.

Grayson and Merrick looked at each other and burst into laughter. "The bird," Merrick said between gasps for breath, "was so excited that when the duke came to take a switch to our backsides, the turkey attacked him!"

"Oh, the duke was *very* angry with that wretched bird!" Grayson's mother said, laughing, too.

"And he made a fine Easter meal," Richland added, to which they all laughed uproariously.

As they continued to laugh and tell exaggerated tales from his youth, Grayson looked around his table. He'd lived a charmed life, that was true. He'd never wanted for anything — not food, not possessions, and certainly not love. He'd be damned if he'd allow a title to stand in the way of him giving that very thing to his own child. So it was with some consternation, but some relief, too, that he tapped his glass with his knife to gain everyone's attention.

The laughter and talking died down and everyone turned to him expectantly. "There is something I must tell you all," he said a little sheepishly. "I am to be a father."

That was met with a moment of hushed silence.

And then everyone was talking at once. Grayson explained to them that he had fallen in love with Katharine Bergeron — a statement that caused his mother to all but faint — and that he intended to marry her, to raise his family surrounded by love and devotion as he'd been raised.

Grayson surprised himself, really. The thought of marrying Kate, of risking his title and reputation and standing, had weighed so heavily on his mind, yet he hadn't realized he'd decided that he would actually do it until he said the words aloud to his family. And once he'd said it, he wondered why it had taken him so long to reach the only conclusion he could accept as far as Kate was concerned. He couldn't be without her or his child. Nothing could stand in his way.

He knew his family would come to accept that, too, for that was the sort of family they were. They had their own code — family first, duty second.

Grayson was the only one, initially, who believed that was true.

What followed was quite a lively and heated discussion. Prudence sent her sons from the room when Frederick began to ask what, exactly, did a courtesan do. The duchess declared they would be ruined, but Richland assured her that in the history of the

Darlingtons, there had been far, far, worse events, which prompted everyone to stop and lean forward attentively to hear what, precisely, could be worse.

When they moved from the dining room to the salon, there was more disagreement about the consequences to them all in the wake of Grayson's decision. "Merrick stands to lose the most," Grayson said solemnly, and fixed his gaze on his brother.

"God help me, but if the leaders of Britain will be swayed from doing what is right for this nation on the grounds of whom you've chosen to love, sir, then we are doomed to hell."

"Here, here," Robert Carlisle shouted.

But the duchess was unappeased. "You are mad, Grayson! You will do irreparable harm to this family and your father's good name. *Everyone* will talk. We will be shunned by the decent people of society — is that what you would ask of your family?"

"Mother," Grayson said patiently. "Would you ask that a child of our flesh, of our blood, live with less than the very best we could give it?"

"Of course not!" she said. "Why do you think I am saying this to you? You are *my* child, and I don't want you to suffer, Grayson. I am very disappointed that you would undo all your father and I sought to provide you, and worse, visit that on your brothers and sisters. What of Ginny? She's not even out yet — who do you think will have her if you go through with this?"

"But what of Grayson, Mamma?" Mary asked innocently. "Hasn't he as much right to happiness as Ginny?"

"Mary, you are young and naive," the duchess said. "Darlington is a man. He may do his duty and have his pleasure, whereas Ginny does not have that freedom."

"I understand," Grayson said, and while it might turn out to be one of the greatest regrets of his life, he felt emboldened to take charge of his own life for perhaps the first time, his mother's objections notwithstanding. She knew he would, too — from where he sat, he could see the tears in her eyes.

He wished he could do what she wanted, but for the first time in his life, following his heart was more important than his duty.

While Grayson was dining with his family, Diana was sitting in the shadows of a room in a public house, waiting. Her guest had been due to arrive at eight o'clock, but it was half past. When she at last heard the knock on the door, she stood up and calmly opened the door.

Millie walked in and looked over her shoulder. Behind her, two roughly dressed gentlemen entered, escorting a man between them who was even more crudely dressed. He was dirty, his clothes unkempt, and he had the growth of a beard that looked several days old. One of the men nudged him; he removed his cap to reveal matted blond hair. He looked around, absorbing his surroundings with eyes that were a remarkable shade of green.

He did indeed resemble Miss Bergeron. He was not a tall man, probably average in height, and if he were cleaned up, Diana thought he might be quite handsome. He was a young man, but he looked strangely old around his eyes.

"Good evening, Mr. Bergeron," Diana said.

The seaman eyed her suspiciously. "Berger."

"Mr. Berger, then. Thank you for coming."

"I weren't given a choice."

Diana ignored that and walked slowly toward him.

"Who are you?" he asked suspiciously.

"I am Lady Eustis."

"Who is that to me?" he demanded, his eyes taking her in.

Diana couldn't help but wonder if he liked what he saw. "Would you like a whiskey?" she asked.

He swallowed. The man liked his whiskey, she gathered, and nodded to Millie to fetch him one from the bottle she'd had sent up. "Please do come in and take a seat, Mr. Berger. I think I have some startling news for you."

"How could you have news for me, eh?" he asked. "I don't know you at all."

"But I know your sister."

That gave him pause. He peered curiously at her, then at Millie. "I ain't got no sister."

"I think you do, Mr. Berger. And she is the courtesan of the Prince of Wales."

"The what?" he asked, his brow furrowing.

"The prince's mistress," Diana clarified.

His frown of suspicion deepened.

"Oh yes, sir, your sister has made quite a good living." Diana paused to let that sink in as Millie handed him the tot of whiskey. But Mr. Berger did not drink it. He was staring at her.

"She is fairly flush in the pockets, to speak indelicately. But what I have found to be particularly reprehensible — in addition to the selling of her body, of course — is that she's known where you were all these years and did nothing to help you."

The man snorted. "You're cutting shams now, mu'um. Katie would've come round if she'd knowed where I was."

"I should like to think that she would have, sir, but the fact is, she was setting up a life of luxury and you didn't quite fit into it."

Berger blinked. He looked down at himself.

"If you don't believe me, I can prove it to you tomorrow evening," Diana said smoothly.

Mr. Berger brought his head up. "Who *are* you?" he asked coldly. "What's it to you who me sister is, then? What do you care?"

"Because I know her. I know the conniving, harmful woman she has become. She has stolen from me, and when I discovered that she had stolen a life from you — her own flesh and blood — I could not bear the injustice."

Still, Berger seemed skeptical. Diana smiled and gestured to the small table. "Are you hungry? I can have supper brought to you if you'd like."

He glanced at the whiskey in his hand and abruptly tossed it down his throat. "If you gots a stew, I'd eat it."

Diana smiled. "I will do better than that, sir. Millie, would you ask the proprietor to

bring a roast? And you may ask the gentlemen to wait outside."

Millie nodded at the two men and followed
them out. Diana gestured to a chair. "Please
do sit, Mr. Berger. There is quite a lot I'd like
to tell you."

CHAPTER THIRTY-EIGHT

Kate was certain there were more people at Carlton House tonight than there had been at the Twelfth Night Ball. It was so crowded it was impossible to move without brushing up against someone else.

Nevertheless, Madame Renard had a firm grip on Kate, dragging her through the throng toward the main ballroom, where banquet tables had been erected in a large U-shape around a raised platform that would serve as a stage. Beyond the ballroom, more rooms had been turned into dining halls for those who were not fortunate enough to dine with the prince and what looked like hundreds of his closest friends.

The décor for the night's fête was intended to provide the illusion of walking in a garden. The house had been filled with paper flowers, which were stuffed into vases and covered trellises erected around the interior walls. If one was still not persuaded that spring had sprung, incense pots exuded the scent of roses throughout the massive building.

Anyone who attended a ball at Carlton House wore their finest apparel, but tonight, the women's gowns and jewelry seemed to be more opulent than usual. Kate's gown of green and gold organdy, trimmed in elaborate beadwork, had cost a princely sum of one hundred pounds. The emeralds and amber she wore to complement the gown cost that, if not more.

There was also an energy Kate had not felt before — it seemed as if everyone was waiting for something spectacular to happen. She supposed it was excitement about the pageant, which Madame Renard said was a masterpiece of theater. Kate believed it must be true, for she had seen the mask she would wear during her portion of the performance, and it was quite elaborate.

Once she'd performed in the pageant, Kate intended to leave. Just this morning, Digby had found some rooms that she might let. They were quite small, and there were no furnishings, but they were above a cobbler's shop and the community water well was very close by so that Kate wouldn't have to go far in inclement weather.

Digby had paid a month's rent. Kate could

move tomorrow.

She hadn't told the prince of her decision as of yet. She was inclined to disappear into the streets of London, but Digby said the prince would look for her. So she'd decided that with Digby's help, she would write the prince a letter and then disappear into London. She could not be persuaded differently and, in fact, she'd already packed her things.

"I must see that everything is at the ready," Madame Renard said. "Please don't wander off, Miss Bergeron. The entire performance depends on your piece."

So Kate stood. She politely declined the offer of wine from a passing footman. She fanned herself as she waited, watching the crowd. She spoke to several gentlemen. Lord Bromley remarked on the festive evening. Lord Callendar tried to entice her to dance, but Kate politely refused with the excuse of a sore ankle. She didn't feel as if she could ever dance again, really.

She noticed Grayson's sister across the room — she was laughing at something her husband said.

"At whom are you peering so curiously?"

Kate turned to see who had spoken. She'd never met the woman who was speaking to her and squinting across the room. "You seemed so intent that I was very curious to know who had captured your attention so completely."

"Ah . . . just there," Kate said, said uncertainly. "Lady Beaumont."

"Aha," the woman said and nodded, and when she did, her feather headdress bounced over her eye. She looked at Kate. "You're very pretty, aren't you? What is your name?"

"Miss Katharine Bergeron."

"Miss Bergeron, you are speaking to Lady Hathcock," she said, inclining her head. "I should think with your exceptional looks, you will be in high demand this Season. Who is sponsoring you?"

"Sponsoring me?" Kate asked, confused.

"Your patron dear. Who intends to put you in society?"

Kate didn't know what to say to that. "The Prince of Wales?"

"The prince, indeed?" Lady Hathcock laughed, but then her eyes suddenly widened. "Oh my, you are *her*. I've heard all about you, yes I have!"

Kate winced.

But Lady Hathcock smiled. "Well *done*, Miss Bergeron!"

"Pardon?"

"Don't look so astonished," the woman chastised her. "Not everyone believes that this annual display of females is particularly civilized. At least *you* won't have to parade about and demonstrate your figure in order to entice a husband, will you? See that one?" she said, nodding to someone behind Kate.

Kate turned; there was a pretty young woman behind her.

"That's Miss Augusta Fellows. She's thought to be this Season's best catch. Don't know why that is — she looks like all the others if you ask me, and I see nothing to recommend her above Sarah Wilson or Susan Highcroft, yet everyone is all atwitter about Miss Fellows," she said, fluttering her fingers.

Kate looked at Miss Fellows again. She remembered that name from the newspaper.

"I shall tell you a secret," Lady Hathcock said, leaning into Kate. "Everyone expects that she will receive an offer from Lord Darlington. Yes, yes, I was rather shocked by that, too, as he's never shown any inclination of doing the right thing by his title and settling down and producing an heir. But I've heard very recently that he *will* make an offer of marriage this Season. I've had it on very high authority."

Kate's heart slipped to her toes. She stared at Augusta Fellows. She was talking with great animation.

"It's high time he did," Lady Hathcock said. "Miss Fellows is a perfect match for

Darlington. And she'll bring him an additional five thousand pounds a year. What do you think of that?"

That her heart was breaking. That she couldn't conceive of five thousand pounds in a lifetime, much less every year. "She's very pretty," she said.

"At the very least, you won't have to suffer through any of the matchmaking, will you? No, it's much easier to do what you are doing, Miss Bergeron, and you'll be happier in the long run, I should think. Oh dear, there is Lord Turlington. He's going to come over here and demand payment for that little bet we had. Do please have a pleasant evening! I hear the entertainment is divine!"

Lady Hathcock strode away. Kate glanced back to see Lord Turlington, but her gaze fell on Lady Eustis instead. She couldn't have missed her, really, for she was standing not more than ten feet away, staring so intently at Kate that Kate blushed all the way to her roots. God in heaven, she'd be happy to be away from this!

She turned away from Lady Eustis and moved deeper into the crowd. But luck was not on Kate's side this evening — as she sought to escape Lady Eustis, she came face to face with Grayson. He seemed as startled as she was when he glanced up and saw her making her way through the crowd.

Kate froze, her eyes locked with his. His dark gaze moved over her; she could see him swallow, could see him breathe deeply. "Kate —"

"Miss Bergeron! Please do come here!" Madame Renard cried. She put her hand on Kate's arm, drawing her attention from Grayson for a moment. "You gave me quite a start! I can't lose you in this crush — the entire pageant will be a disaster!" Madame Renard wrapped her hand around Kate's wrist and tugged lightly. "Come, dear."

Kate glanced back; Grayson was speaking with Miss Fellows and another woman. Miss Fellows was smiling so brightly, so hopefully. And Grayson was smiling at her.

Madame Renard tugged on her hand. "The performance shall begin in a half hour," she said, pulling Kate along.

Kate followed dumbly, but her thoughts were on Grayson, her heart on the verge of crumbling. She glanced back once more, but he'd been swallowed up in the enormous crowd. Her poor heart continued to labor under the strain of seeing him, of longing for him; she couldn't catch her breath as Madam Renard pulled her through the crowd.

It was an intolerably long evening, particularly after seeing Kate. Grayson had tried to find her after the surprise of seeing her in the crowd.

In that brief moment, he'd seen her eyes and he couldn't rid his thoughts of them. They were full of a darkness he'd never seen in her before, and the depth of the darkness alarmed him. Kate looked so forlorn. He had to find her, talk to her, but the place was too crowded, and moreover, it seemed like everywhere he turned, he saw Diana.

Diana's eyes were filled with contempt.

As Grayson searched for Kate, however, footmen began to filter through the crowd asking everyone to take their seats, as the pageant was about to begin. George was already seated at the head of the table in a thronelike chair with his inner circle around him. The sight of him disgusted Grayson.

He was moving away from the prince when he heard someone call his name. The voice was tinged with a slight accent. Grinning, Grayson turned to greet his old friend, Jack Haines, the Earl of Lambourne. Grayson had helped secure Jack's release from the Tower, where he'd awaited what he'd thought would be his hanging. Fortunately for Lambourne, his freedom had come with the end of the Delicate Investigation and the king's refusal to allow the prince to pursue a royal divorce.

Lambourne was smiling broadly, and on his arm, the pretty dark-haired Scottish lass Elizabeth Beal, who had captured the scoundrel's heart.

"You look decidedly more relaxed, Lambourne."

"It's a bit easier to breathe when one is no' concerned with the length of one's neck, aye?"

Grayson laughed. "Miss Beal, I was certain you'd return to Scotland the moment you could."

"I'd hoped for it, aye, Your Grace, but his lordship said I'd no' lived properly until I'd seen the prince's pageant."

"I would suggest the opposite, Miss Beal. Your life has been unscathed until now," Grayson said with a chuckle.

"Come sit with us, Christie," Lambourne said. "We'll need someone of your keen insight to explain it to us, aye?"

Grayson accepted their offer and the three of them found their seats very near the end of the U-shaped banquet table, and very close to the performance stage.

Grayson looked around for any sign of Kate but couldn't find her. He did see Prudence and Robert sitting only a few seats away from the prince. On Prudence's left was a sullen Diana. She was staring straight ahead, her mouth set in a thin line.

As for George, he was seated comfortably in his chair, laughing with one of his companions. A footman leaned over him to replenish his wineglass, and on his heels, another man leaned over and whispered in the prince's ear. George sat up, tapped his knife against his wineglass, as did his companions. The audience hushed and settled into their seats. With a lazy flick of his wrist, George signaled the show to begin.

The musicians began; the first performers to emerge from the curtains of the temporary stage were young women who carried out their own maypoles. They wore costumes of flowing gossamer silk and danced around their poles, singing about the start of spring. Into their midst walked a young man with a paper crown on his head. He dipped and swayed toward each girl, taking flowers from them all, but never favoring a girl. Grayson imagined that young man was supposed to be George.

Behind the young man came a very large woman with a mole on the tip of a hideous nose. She carried a baby in her arms and kicked the young man from behind as they moved down the stage. She was clearly meant to be the Princess of Wales, and the audience howled with laughter.

When the maypoles and the Princess of Wales had danced off the stage, several more performers entered, representing the king and queen. The prince was caught between them, pushed and pulled in a strange dance. The king would pause occasionally to run in little circles, which Grayson supposed was meant to convey his madness. The queen would pause to wag a grotesquely big finger at the young prince, much like a mother would scold a son.

The self-indulgent pageant continued on, and Grayson quickly lost interest — until the curtains opened and the music changed. It slowed in tempo, that much he knew; and the dancer who appeared was wearing an elaborate mask. He recognized Kate's shape and her gown instantly and sat up so quickly that he jostled Lambourne, who managed to catch his wineglass before it toppled.

Kate moved gracefully in her solitary dance, flitting through the sea of people in George's life, going behind the queen and king, weaving in and out of his companions, and slowly making her way down the makeshift stage to the head of the table where George was seated.

The prince, like everyone in the audience, was riveted on Kate. When she reached the end of the stage she went down on her knees, removed her mask and let it drop from her hand, and bowed low before the prince like a servant. George smiled and nodded at her, at which point Kate stood and turned slowly in a circle so that the entire audience might see who the mysterious woman was.

A gasp went up from the audience. George had made his statement, had introduced his mistress to one and all.

Impotent anger surged through Grayson. His hand curved around the knife at his plate as Kate began her slow dance back to the curtain. She was pale and the darkness in her eyes had seemed to go even deeper.

As she neared the curtain, three men appeared. They were dressed in plain clothes, made to look like thieves or beggars. Kate instantly stopped moving. Her mouth dropped open. Grayson looked at the three men and noticed that while two of the men looked about them in awe, the one in the middle was looking at Kate. He looked familiar; Grayson sat up, peering closely.

Jude.

There could be no mistaking the resemblance between them, and Grayson knew that these men were not an official part of the performance. He jerked his gaze to George; his heart lurched when he saw

Diana crouching beside the prince, whispering. He couldn't conceive of what was happening, what Diana had done, but he knew it was bad, and stood abruptly.

"Christie, what are you about?" Lambourne hissed.

"I may be about to take your place in the Tower," he said, and pushed back his chair and strode toward the end of the banquet table and the stage.

Kate was stunned to see Jude suddenly appear before her. Her heart climbed to her throat; she had to remind herself to breathe. *"Jude,"* she said, her voice full of wonder. "Dear God, it's *you!"*

Jude scowled as he looked at her from head to foot. The crowd shifted around them; people began to call out and whisper excitedly. The music stopped. Everything stopped. And still, Kate could not take her eyes from her brother.

"It's true, then," Jude said. His voice was low and rough, the voice of a man, and not the voice of the boy that lived in her memory.

Kate moved toward him, reached for his arm, intent on leading him off the stage, but he jerked his arm from her reach. "How did you find me? How are you here?" she asked, trying to touch him again, to get him off that stage.

"Why'd you not find *me?*" he demanded angrily, brushing her off again. He looked wildly about the crowd.

"Jude —"

"You left me there, Katie! You left me to rot whilst you found a way, aye?" he said, gesturing to the opulent surroundings.

"No, no, that is not true, Jude. I have been looking for you since I lost you —"

"You didn't lose me!" he scoffed. "You meant to leave me behind with Papa and Nellie! But you was all I had, Katie," he said angrily.

"Jude, listen to me." She was aware of the eyes on them, the movement around them. She could think of nothing but getting him off that stage. "Papa and Nellie moved," she said quietly. "Just like that, one day you were all gone, and I had no way to find you. No one knew where you'd all gone. But I looked and looked for you, and I have, all these years. I could have left St. Katharine's behind completely, but I didn't, I kept going back, because I believed that one day, you would come back. And here you are! You cannot imagine how hard my heart is beating now to see you alive and well," she said breathlessly, pressing her hand to her breast.

"Come, come, let's go outside."

Jude looked at her hand. He frowned uncertainly, and Kate saw in his weathered face the boy she'd once known. He looked so angry and so overwhelmed at once. Kate surged forward and threw her arms around him, holding him tightly.

The crowd broke into pandemonium.

"Who is this?" she heard the prince bellow. "How have these men come to be here? Put them out! Put them out at once!"

Jude grabbed Kate's arms and pulled them from his neck. "I want me compresation, Katie," he said.

"Pardon?"

"Me blunt!"

"I have more than that," she said frantically. "I have a place where we might live. We can be together again —"

"Get them out of here!" George bellowed. "Remove them at once!"

"One moment, Your Highness!"

Kate's knees went weak at the sound of Grayson's voice. He'd appeared on Kate's right, was standing on that stage with his legs braced apart, scowling at the crowd. The audience suddenly began to move like a living, breathing thing, whispering and whistling, and some, who apparently had not as yet understood this was not part of the pageant, were even applauding.

"Let's go from here, Jude!" Kate whispered pleadingly. "Come with me, and I will tell you everything you want to know. I've waited for you, I've searched for you, and there are people who will tell you this is true."

"It is true," Grayson said, and put his hand on Kate's arm at the same moment he threw up a hand to stop the four guards who were leaping up on the stage. *"Halt!"* he snapped to them.

"And who the bloody hell are you?" Jude demanded. "Are you the prince, then? Do you keep me sister in all this . . . this finery?" he asked, gesturing wildly to Kate.

"I am not the prince, sir, but I assure you that your sister is telling you the truth. And I know she will do as she promises you now, for I will personally honor them."

"Why would you do that, ye bloody scoundrel? So that you can use her ill?"

"No," Grayson said, and shifted his dark blue gaze to her. "Because I intend to marry her. And it would be my duty and my pleasure as her husband to honor any vow she makes to you."

Kate's love and gratitude soared within her at the same moment the crowd exploded into chaos. She unthinkingly grabbed Grayson's arm as people began to shout.

The prince bellowed that he would see to it Darlington's title was revoked, and Grayson loudly challenged him to do just that. He removed Kate's hand from his arm and strode a few steps toward the prince. "Who are *you* to judge *me?*" he roared.

It was such a remarkable outburst that Kate jumped a little. People started to hiss for others to quiet and leaned forward, watching Grayson closely.

"I ask you again, who are you to judge me? Or her? Or him?" he called out, gesturing to Kate and Jude.

Kate turned to Jude and put her hand out, palm up. Jude looked at her hand, then took it in his.

"We are an intolerant people," Grayson said to a stunned audience. "We would condemn this woman for her circumstances without regard for how she came to be there, or who she is. You will condemn me for standing up for her. Yet you will stand up for those who peddle human flesh in the slave trade! You will be indignant on behalf of those who would give a defenseless woman a roof over her head in exchange for pleasures of her flesh!"

The crowd gasped; a woman somewhere cried out.

"This is outrageous!" the prince cried angrily. "You will be ruined, Darlington!"

"I don't expect anyone to hear me, much less agree with me. But I will tell you all that I have come to respect and admire this woman," he said, pointing at Kate. "She has helped me to see past the prejudices of our class, and if I can bring one tenth of the happiness to her life that she has brought to mine, I will gladly forfeit all!"

Now the crowd went wild, with cheers and jeers alike.

Jude squeezed Kate's hand; she turned to look at her brother, but was suddenly jostled by Lady Beaumont, who threw her arms around Kate. "Welcome to the family. I hope you won't mind, but we might be sent from England after this."

Kate had no time to answer; a gentleman and woman suddenly crowded in next to her and Jude. "Take my coach," the man said to Grayson. "But were I you, I'd take it now, 'ere the prince calls you out, lad."

Several more people crowded in around them, forming a circle. Kate had no idea who they were, with the exception of Madame Renard and Lady Hathcock, who seemed to be enjoying the fracas.

The next thing she knew, they were moving. Grayson's hand was firmly and possessively on her back, ushering her through, and she clung tightly to Jude. They pushed through the crowd with the few people who had stood up with them, making their way to the door. They were ushered into a carriage and as soon as the door shut and they were moving, Kate glanced out the window. People were spilling out onto the street after them, watching them go, gaping at them, shouting things she couldn't understand.

"How do you do, sir? I am Grayson Christopher, possibly the former Duke of Darlington," Grayson said, and put out his hand to Jude.

"Jude Berger."

"I must be dreaming," Kate said softly.

CHAPTER THIRTY-NINE

"I ought not be here," Jude kept saying. "I ought not be here."

Kate knew precisely what he meant; she didn't feel as if she ought to be in the green salon of Darlington House either, surrounded by fine art and expensive furnishings and rich draperies. The whole night seemed a dream — how was it possible that a man like Darlington had stood up and spoken so eloquently for someone like her?

Kate gripped Jude's hand as hard as she had when they were children and she'd worried that he'd attempt to steal the oranges from the crate in front of the fruit stand if she let go. Tonight, she feared if she let go, the faeries would flit away and take Jude with them, and she would awaken from this dream.

Grayson had left her alone with Jude and had gone off to make arrangements for them to sleep.

At first, Kate and Jude looked at one another for several long moments.

She couldn't imagine what he must be thinking. He looked as if he'd had a hard life thus far, yet she could see the twinkling green eyes and slow smile of a brother she remembered clearly and loved dearly. "I missed you so," she said at last. "I looked for you, Jude, on my word, I looked for you, but you were always one step ahead of me."

"How'd you learn to talk like a lady?" he asked curiously.

Kate smiled. "It's a very long tale."

"Where'd you hie off to, Katie? I remember you came round a time or two after Nellie made you leave us, but then you disappeared. I figured you was dead."

"No, I never left St. Katharine's. My God, there is so much to tell you, Jude," she said, and gestured to a settee. "And there is so much I want to know. How is it you came to be at Carlton House? My friend looked for you when *The Princess* docked, but he said you weren't on board. And there you were, at Carlton House. How did you ever get past the guards?"

"I don't rightly know, in truth," he said. "Lady Eustis brung me."

Kate gasped. "Lady *Eustis?*" She sank onto the settee. "Tell me."

Jude looked uncertainly at the settee and sat carefully. " 'Twas the strangest thing, Katie. I come off the ship and wanted me pint, aye? A gent comes strolling along as if he's king and he says to me, 'Come on then, lad, come on, I've got a few pounds for a good hand . . .'"

They talked well into the night. Jude told her about Lady Eustis, and the things she'd said. That he didn't know what Carlton House was or what he'd be doing, but that Lady Eustis had arranged everything.

In turn, Kate recounted her life after she'd lost touch with Jude. She told him everything. All of it. The worst parts and the best. She told of how she'd become Cousineau's mistress, of how she'd been "given" to the Prince of Wales.

And then she told Jude about Grayson, feeling the irrepressible smile on her face.

Jude watched her shrewdly as she talked about the last few weeks of her life, and when she'd finished, he said, "You love the scoundrel, aye?"

She smiled self-consciously. "I do. More than anything."

Jude sighed and shook his head. "It's sure he loves you too, Katie, or he's a bloody fool. Never known a gent to do such a foolish thing as he done. He's brought ruin on him and his with this, I'd wager."

Kate couldn't help but agree with Jude.

"Do you know where Papa is?" Kate asked.

"Papa?" Jude snorted. "He died long ago, lass."

Jude told her that Nellie Hopkins had eventually cast him out of their father's house, just as she'd cast out Kate. He'd managed to keep up with their father for a year or two and saw him buried in a pauper's grave. That he'd been so ashamed of that he'd shortened his surname. After that, Jude said, he was lured to the sea by some friends, and had sailed to India twice. "I love the sea," he said. "I loved India. The people there are a bloody sight different than they are here, Katie."

"Is it true? Is *The Princess* a slaver?" Kate asked.

"Aye," Jude said, frowning darkly. "Wretched stuff, that." He explained that *The Princess* had only become a slaver recently, that the transport of humans was so lucrative the captain couldn't resist it. "I was right happy to see that mob in London, on me word I was," he said, and explained how *The Princess* had been met at port with angry protestors, led by the crusader William Wilberforce. "It's a nasty business, slaving.

I had in mind to take me pay and hire on a different ship."

"Are you happy?" Kate asked.

Jude smiled, revealing two missing teeth. "I'm happy enough, I reckon. I'm happier now, aye, that I've seen you. I've missed you, Katie, I'll not lie. You were the only thing I had in this world. I knowed what the Lady Eustis was speaking weren't true," he said. "But I'd always wondered why you stopped coming for me."

"I never stopped," Kate told him earnestly. "Even when you all vanished, I never stopped."

It was half past two in the morning when Grayson quietly interrupted them and told them rooms had been readied.

Jude stood up. "If by that you mean a right and proper bed, milord, I'm obliging."

"I do indeed, sir," Grayson said, and nodded at a footman, who indicated Jude should follow him.

Jude looked nervously at Kate. He put out his hand. Kate took it and squeezed it. "You'll be here on the morrow, aye?"

"Aye," she said and hugged him tightly before Jude went out.

When he was gone, Kate looked at Grayson. She opened her mouth to speak, but seeing him there before her, in the flesh, with love shining in his eyes, and knowing what he'd done for her tonight, all that he'd risked — she burst into tears.

"Kate!" he said, and enveloped her in his arms. "Kate, sweetheart . . . the worst is over. What are these tears?"

"You are so foolish!" she cried, pushing against him with her fists. "You risked too much!"

"No, Kate, I never risked enough. I love you — the only risk I cannot take is being without you."

"Grayson, did you see how angry the prince was?"

"His anger couldn't ignite a candle next to mine," Grayson bit out, and touched her face. "He's not important to me. *You* are important. Our baby is important. Jude is important. Obviously, I would have preferred to tell you in a manner much more civilized than what I did tonight, but you'd not see me —"

"Oh, I am such a fool at times!" she groaned, lowering her head.

Grayson slipped his fingers beneath her chin and lifted her face to his. "If you had seen me, I would have told you that I would give away everything that I have or that I am for you and our baby. *All* of it. I would give everything I have for you."

504

Those words left her too hopeful. And too overwhelmed. She'd lived a lifetime in poverty and peril, and this . . . being in his house, hearing those words, were too difficult to believe, not after all they'd been through. "You've changed your mind?" she asked skeptically.

"Completely."

She wanted desperately to believe him. "How? How can you risk so much?" she asked, looking around at the elaborately decorated room.

"The question is, how can I risk losing you?" he said. "I have never been in love before, Kate. I have never felt . . ." He sighed and pressed his hand against his heart. "I have never felt *this*. How can I risk losing that? I regret that it took me so very long to understand that I could not lose it, and for that, I am sorry. But I know without a doubt that I am doing the right thing for myself, for you, and our baby."

Her heart quickened. "But your family —"

"I come from a long line of inventive people. We will survive this and more."

His eyes were filled with such desperate hope that Kate couldn't hold back her own hope. She threw her arms around his neck and kissed him. "Grayson, oh Grayson . . .

what joy you have put in my heart!"

Grayson gently set her back. "There is one very important thing yet undone," he said solemnly.

"What is that?"

He looked at her, his blue eyes searching her face. "I never want to forget this moment or how beautiful you are. Kate . . . *Kate* . . . I have been lost without you these last weeks," he said, his eyes turning liquid. "I will consider it the greatest gift from above if I am never away from you again." He sank to one knee and extended his palm to her. "Katharine Bergeron, will you take pity on this lovesick soul? Will you do me the extraordinary honor of being my wife?"

Kate covered her mouth with one hand, unable to speak. The possibility of it was so unreal — even now, seeing him on his knee before her, his eyes awash in hope and adoration, she couldn't believe it. Was she walking about in some delirious dream? Had the faeries come at long last and spirited her away from a life of hardship? She was so stunned, so —

Grayson cleared his throat. "This is typically the moment in which a lady, who is inclined to say yes to the poor gent's offer, might put him out of his misery and actually *say* yes," he said, a little anxiously.

Kate gulped. She stepped around his hand and wrapped her arms around his head and bent over him. "Yes, Christie," she said, hugging him tightly. "Yes, dear God, *yes*."

Grayson rose up and gathered her in his arms as he did. "Thank you, God," he said, and kissed her mouth. "I love you, Kate. I love you with the parts of my heart that I think have never felt love. And I will always love you. I will honor you, protect you, defend you — but above all else, I will always love you."

"But you will never love me as much as I love you."

"That's a challenge I gladly accept," he returned, as he swept her up in his arms and carried her to the settee. He set her down, let his gaze run over her, and put his hand on her abdomen. "I have missed you," he said. "I have felt as if my life was quite empty without you."

"You have me now, Grayson," she whispered, and sighed as he kissed her neck and his hands began to move on her, riling her blood, arousing such indescribable pleasure in her, transporting her to that place of ecstasy that only Grayson could bring her to.

It was true, it was astoundingly true — the faeries really had come. The only thing missing was the forest.

■ ■ ■ ■

The duchess arrived quite early the following day — and well before a proper calling time, which she was usually so adamant about. Grayson groaned when Roarke informed him that she was in the family sitting room.

He hurried there, hoping against hope that he would reach her before she found anyone else.

He was too late.

When he strode into the sitting room, he found his mother standing almost toe-to-toe with Kate. A wide-eyed Jude was standing back, looking as if he needed an escape.

But Kate . . . God bless her, Kate was smiling with amusement.

"Your Grace," Grayson said to his mother. "I was not expecting you so early."

"Clearly you were not," she said haughtily. "Although one wonders how you could not expect *all* of London to be at your door given your ridiculously uncivilized behavior last night — that is, if I may believe the outrageous reports that have reached my ears with astonishing speed."

"I think you can," he said calmly.

"Dear *Lord,*" she exclaimed, and frowned at Kate. "You realize, do you not, son, that rumors and vicious lies are spreading as fast as the plague? There are things being said about you that are unkind and, I will continue to believe, *quite* untrue! But you must be forewarned — you have entered a storm that I fear you cannot weather."

"A man can ride any storm if he trims his sails properly," Jude offered.

Grayson suppressed a groan as the duchess slowly turned her head and peered at Jude. "Perhaps you are right, young man." She looked at Grayson. "You were certainly right about one thing — she is indeed beautiful."

Kate blushed.

"I'd say the same to her if you were to properly introduce the occupants of this room," the duchess sniffed.

"I beg your pardon, Your Grace," Grayson said, and with a grateful smile, he walked into the room to make the proper introductions.

CHAPTER FORTY

Everyone agreed that the wedding should happen with all deliberate speed, given the outlandish gossip about Darlington that was swirling around London. A ducal wedding was normally quite an event to behold, but this was one that would be held in the privacy of Darlington House with only family and close friends. Even if the family had been so inclined to invite others, they rather doubted that anyone in the *ton* would risk being seen celebrating the Duke of Darlington's spectacular fall from grace.

Fortunately, there were some stalwart friends and a very large family to attend the ceremony that would take place in the chapel later that afternoon.

The Earl of Lindsey, Nathan Grey, and his wife, Evelyn, had come. She was carrying a child, too, and Kate hoped that she looked as happy as Evelyn did. The Earl of Lambourne, and his fiancée, Elizabeth Beal

— Lizzie — were also in attendance, having decided to remain in London for the wedding before returning to Scotland, where Lizzie's sister, Charlotte, lived. Kate knew that Grayson was sad that another close friend, Declan O'Conner, Lord Donnelly of Ireland, would not be in attendance. "He's in Ireland just now. There is no way to reach him in time," he'd told her. "But he'll be shocked to find us all married when he returns," he'd said with a chuckle.

On Kate's side, there was Jude, of course, who had struck up a friendship with Aldous. As Kate walked through Darlington House to check on preparations for the wedding, she spotted the two men standing in the massive, two-story entry, talking about the sea. Jude — who looked so strikingly handsome in his new clothes — had told Kate they were thinking of hiring on with a new ship, *The Soaring Eagle,* which was set to sail to East India in pursuit of the perfume trade. *The Soaring Eagle* had a new investor: a Mr. Reginald Digby. Digby had made a tidy little sum from his first foray into the perfume trade.

Kate smiled at Jude and Aldous as she walked through the entry. "You are the most beautiful bride I ever laid eyes on, lass," Aldous said as she passed.

"I'd swear you never laid eyes on a bride,

511

Aldous," Kate said laughingly.

She continued on, past the formal green salon, where a champagne toast would be held when the vows had been made. The duchess and Digby were within, engaged in yet another argument. They'd discovered in these last few days that they both had very strong opinions about many things, including weddings. Kate paused just outside the door to look in.

"I realize that you fancy yourself something of a florist, Mr. Digby, but I assure you that in all the years I have been a duchess, I have never seen anything quite as ostentatious as what you are proposing," the duchess said, peering up at Digby.

"With all due respect, Your Grace, how many times will you insist on your preferences merely because you have been a duchess for many years?" Digby countered.

"I beg your pardon! And what, precisely, are *your* credentials?"

"I, madam, am a man about town," Digby responded, and bowed with a flourish.

"You are no such thing!" the duchess exclaimed, but Kate thought she was smiling a little. She lost what else the duchess might have said, opting to tiptoe past the open door in lieu of interrupting their debate.

She moved on, past the dining room,

where Esmeralda and Holly were carefully laying the china for the wedding supper. That had been the source of another argument between Digby and the duchess, as the duchess considered it the height of bad taste to have a supper as opposed to a traditional wedding breakfast.

Kate had offered all the women employment, but only Esmeralda and Holly would come to Darlington House. The others rather liked their lives, and now that Grayson had given her a wedding gift of the rooms Digby had found, as well as an empty shop below the rooms where Kate would have her bakery — she had a place for her wards that kept them safe from men like Fleming. Moreover, Digby had graciously accepted her offer to be the proprietor of her bakery and the landlord to the women. Together, they would see to the day-to-day business while Kate was free to perfect her muffins and petits fours and raise what she hoped would be a slew of children.

"Look at this, will ye?" Esmeralda whispered to Holly, and held up a knife. "It's as heavy as iron, but it's all silver!"

"Put it down, ye silly goose!" Holly exclaimed. "Anyone sees ye, they'll think ye meant to pilfer it!"

Esmeralda dropped it quickly. "I'd never!"

she said. "I'm not a goose, Holly — I'd not give up *this* livelihood!" she said, and both women paused to look around at the room again.

Kate certainly understood them for she was no goose, either.

She slipped by and walked on, rounding the corner of the hall and walking to the chapel.

She wanted to see it before she took her vows, to absorb the very real fact that she was about to be Grayson's wife. A duchess. A *mother*. She wished only that her mother could be here to see it. *Look at us, Mummy. Look at Jude and me.*

The chapel was quiet; hothouse flowers had been brought in and arranged, and the candles were lit. Kate walked to the front of the chapel, her fingers trailing along the arms of the pews as she went. She paused at the altar and looked up at the cross that hung behind it.

"Kate."

Startled, she whirled around. Grayson walked down the aisle toward her, smiling broadly, his gaze greedily taking her in. "Look at you," he said, gazing at the silver wedding gown she wore. "I don't think you could possibly be any more beautiful . . . except out of this lovely gown." He touched the pearl necklace he'd given her as a wedding gift. It wasn't the same necklace he'd sent her weeks ago, for he'd returned that one. He'd bought instead a much simpler, less lavish necklace. To Kate, it was much more beautiful.

"I have news," he said.

"Oh no. You haven't had to intervene with Digby and the duchess again, have you?"

"What? No," he said with a chuckle. "The news is that Merrick just arrived. The vote has happened. The slave trade has been officially abolished."

"That's wonderful!" Kate cried with delight.

"Interestingly, Lord Eustis was one of the votes that tipped it in Merrick's favor." Grayson glanced down at his feet. "He and his wife will be returning to the country and will not be in town for the Season. Merrick has heard she has amassed quite a lot of debt without the earl's knowledge and has had to reduce her expenditures and staff."

"Oh," Kate said.

"I suspect the earl knows everything," he said. Kate could hear the regret in his voice. "I rather imagine Diana will not be in London in the foreseeable future. There could not be a greater punishment for her."

"I'm so sorry," Kate said. "It must be difficult for you."

"She may have brought you and Jude together, but given the way in which she did it, I should hope I never lay eyes on her again." He smiled. "I have more news."

"Better news, I hope," she said with a smile.

Grayson kissed the tip of her nose. "I have heard from Declan. He has sent his felicitations on the occasion of our wedding as well as a gift for our unborn child."

"A rattle?"

He laughed. "A pony."

"No!"

"I asked Palmer to see to it that the pony is put at Kitridge Lodge because that, madam, is where our child shall be born. Is that acceptable to you?"

She gasped with delight. "Do you mean it, Grayson?"

"Absolutely."

"You don't fear you will starve?"

He laughed. "No. I have all the sustenance I need right here."

"That makes two of us."

Grayson kissed her, slowly and thoroughly. And as it was every time they were together these last two days, his hands caressed her, his mouth aroused her. Kate laughed against his mouth and pushed him a little. "No,

Christie, you mustn't. There's not much time . . ."

"My thoughts exactly, my love. We might sneak away for a few moments so that I can show you just how ardently I look forward to our life together," he said, and caressed her breast.

She smiled wantonly at him and took his hand, holding it firmly in her own. "But we have such little time to practice —"

"I didn't think we required much practice," he said, nipping at her lips. "It would seem to me we have perfected the art, but if you think we must, who am I to argue?"

"I meant to practice our wedding dance —"

His head came up. "Kate! You don't intend to make me go through with it!" he complained, but he willingly went along with her, holding her hand tightly as if he was afraid she might disappear if he let go.

ABOUT THE AUTHOR

Julia London is the *New York Times* and *USA Today* bestselling author of numerous romantic novels, including the Scandalous series: *The Book of Scandal, Highland Scandal,* and *A Courtesan's Scandal;* The Desperate Debutants trilogy: *The Dangers of Deceiving a Viscount, The Perils of Perusing a Prince, The Hazards of Hunting a Duke;* and the Lockhart family trilogy: *Highlander Unbound* (a finalist for the Romance Writers of America's RITA Award for Best Historical Romance), *Highlander in Disguise,* and *Highlander in Love* (also a finalist for the RITA award). She is also the author of *Guiding Light: Jonathan's Story,* the *New York Times* bestselling novel based on the Emmy Award–winning daytime drama *Guiding Light,* and the contemporary romantic novel *Summer of Two Wishes.* A native Texan, Julia lives in Austin. You can write to her at P.O. Box

228, Georgetown, TX 78627, or e-mail her at julia@julialondon.com.